Blood Influence
Apostasy

I C Lawrance

Chapter 1

Mortella looked out. The sun was below the Western Slopes, peaks silhouetted by golden rays that highlighted the white snow against a burnt orange sky. It was nature, inherently beautiful and awe inspiring. Its majesty was lost on her. She barely registered it even existed. She stared unseeing, confused, but more so irritated. She was yet to find out why she had been recalled. Escaping the Bowl had been an achievement she cherished. She had proven herself through the raw power she processed. Combining that with the skill with which she had weaved it. She had never expected to have to return. Her abilities had allowed her to progress far beyond the boundaries of the Bowl. Yet, to come back. That was a rebuke of everything she had created. What was it that she was to do here? There were so many more important things for her to do beyond the natural walls that surrounded this peasant land. The Code needed her. Yet here she was, brought back to this small and insignificant part of the world that she detested.

Angrily she turned away from the window. She was beholden to the pleasure of another. She felt the insult, but all she could do was wait. Halfway up the Tower she would wait in this room that had been prepared for her. Visitors were rarely entertained at the Tower. This chamber had been hastily readied once it was clear she was to stay. A place where she had to remain until summoned. To be summoned by the Abbatissa of the Tower. That in itself made her skin crawl. That one so lowly in the service of the Code should keep her waiting. It was a humiliation she would have to bear but not one that she would forget. She would make sure that the Abbatissa would regret the slight that had been delivered, however unintended.

She sat on the day bed and poured herself another glass of wine. At least the food and wine were decent. The Bowl was known for the best produce. All that thanks to the Tower and its permanent inhabitants. They never needed to eat. Never longed for a smooth, full-bodied wine. She swirled it about her mouth, allowing the flavour to linger. It was rich with a hint of blackcurrant.

Those who donated their Influences to the Tower were one with it. Never dying, forever remaining in servitude. Together they formed a composite whole that allowed the Tower to wield their powers, melding them together. Combining them to create the perfect incubator. A nursery for others to develop – others like her. She remembered the past. She, too, was a product of the Tower's work within the Bowl. But she had excelled and escaped it. Only now to be brought back. To be reminded of what she once had been. She had promised never, never would she return. She was much more than this place.

As the daylight faded, shrouding the chamber in darkness, Mortella remained seated. To the casual observer she appeared calm and relaxed. Reclining on the most comfortable piece of furniture available in the room, she waited patiently. To those who could read her, or for those with an Influence such as hers, it was a very different story. Beneath the facade of peaceful beauty and controlled calm whirled a tempest of fury tightly contained. The rage confined within her was barely detectable but for the eyes. Eyes that revealed that which the body did not.

The Influence of Perception was everything. It created a world in the image of the possessor. Born out of wedlock to a working woman of the night, Mortella had learnt early which impressions were best to leave. Endowed with natural beauty that was a gift not to be squandered. As a beautiful child with fiery, brushed-bronze hair, emerald-green eyes, and flawless complexion, Mortella was doted on by the harem that made up the knocking shop. When young she was protected from the worst of the punters. As she grew, however, their interests became more persistent and more intense. By the time she was twelve she had been given an ultimatum – either join the harem or face the streets. No mother or doting courtesan could now protect her. The choice was between the realities of life in the shop or hunger on the street. Town with its market and many high-bred folks was not a welcoming place for those such as she. Beauty without money or connection had limitations.

Lacking any skills apart from those that she had seen displayed about her since birth, Mortella decided to stay. She was quickly identified as a favourite among the patrons. Like so many that fall into such a profession she could have easily succumbed to its occupational predicament had it not been for one man. A high-born gentleman of advanced age took a particular liking to the now thirteen-year-old. He arranged to pay a premium. A sum to ensure his sole use of the product. To gain such a benefactor was considered a boon amongst the harem and, as he was advanced in years, attendance to him was irregular.

It was around this time that Mortella began to demonstrate her gift. It was not long before she had learnt how this could be of use with her benefactor.

Her sullen face and pent-up hatred of the man would be seen as sweetness and pliability. In order that she did not lose his patronage she made sure that on awakening he was well rested and relieved of any inherent tensions. Through her skill he thought that he was the object of the young girl's adoration and not her loathing. Her gift ensured that he eagerly maintained his exclusivity of her. This allowed respite, with her never having to further endure the corporeal activity from any man, including that of her patron.

It was not long after that the Tower collected her and removed her from the reaches of all such men. She had excelled. Much of her initial work had been channelling her Influence into creating a great deal of what was still all around her as she returned to the Tower. Her weaving and aptitude had formed the aesthetics of the Tower. Its starkness allowed for only the strongest to succeed. Isolation prevented outside help to the neophytes. For all are alone. One can rely on no-one apart from oneself. For Mortella, only those who succeeded on their own were truly worthy to progress.

Time dragged with no end to the wait.

The ferocity of her ire grew in proportion to the time wasted. Yet control was everything. Revenge was always best delivered with a clear head and when least expected. Only then could it be fully appreciated for what it was.

As the middle hour of the night waned a figure appeared at the door of the chamber – a Tower varlet. The people of the Bowl feared these insignificant servants of the Code. They called them the Dark Ones and considered them powerful. Oh, if they only knew. Such irony that the face of the Code was made up of such as these.

"My Lady, the Abbatissa will see you now," the form announced. Mortella scarcely turned to glance at the shadow. One such as that was beneath recognition. Not worth her acknowledgement. A member of the Code barely more than the mindless Tormentors that infested the Tower.

Without betraying her thoughts, Mortella rose and gracefully drifted towards the door. The figure fell back as she approached, allowing passage. Once on the landing outside the chamber Mortella turned. Seemingly without effort she appeared to float up the stairs towards the upper reaches of the Tower.

The Tower was large. The flight of stairs was long. It was surely made to invoke disadvantage for the suitor once they arrived at the Abbatissa. Perception was everything. She may well be feeling the strain from the climb, but she would make sure that none of that showed. There would be no advantage for that petty official once she arrived.

Eventually, Mortella reached a large landing near the top of the Tower. Here, at least, there was some opulence. The floor was a smooth, dark, mottled marble that reflected light from the numerous candelabras that were scattered around the space. Several plush velvet tête-à-tête chairs were visible. These were created solely for the purpose of private conversations prior to entry into the Abbastissa's rooms.

Mortella stood. To be lower than one's adversary was to be at a disadvantage. Never sit when another could stand above you. She waited. Summoned, and now waiting once again, did not improve her mood.

The great door to the adjoining chamber gradually opened. Into the light stepped the Abbatissa. A small woman, cloaked in the Black of the Code with the hood thrown back. She looked several decades older than Mortella. Seeing the Abbatissa look so old made her feel better. That after all those years, this was as far as she had advanced. What further punishment was necessary? In the few years Mortella had been with the Code she had greatly surpassed this lowly official. Revenge on her would be as pointless as taking revenge on a mosquito that bit you. No, one should just swat it out of the way and think no more of it. The Abbatissa nodded her welcome.

"My apologies, Mortella. This has all been very unusual. It was necessary for us to wait for the others to arrive before we could commence. I hope that your wait was at least somewhat pleasant. The chosen wine was believed to be one of your favourites."

"You are kind, Abbatissa. The wine was very good. My thanks. The wait was immaterial," Mortella responded sweetly.

"Please enter. You will find a seat awaiting you," directed the Abbatissa with a gesture towards the door.

Mortella moved forward and entered the chamber. It was a large oval space lit by numerous glowing orbs that hung in mid-air. The walls were smooth and black but reflected light back into the room unlike those in the lower reaches of the Tower. There were no windows. Instead, a large, draped curtain covered almost a third of the wall at the far end of the chamber. In the centre of the room was a long oval table. To her surprise, Mortella noted seven other figures already seated at the table. This left just the ornate carver of the Abbatissa's at the head of the table with another chair at the other end.

Of the seven, Mortella could not discern who any of them were. Each figure wore the Black and each had a face that was covered by the robe's hood. The air hung heavily about them. As she moved towards her chair, she could feel all eyes upon her. Once there, she was directed by the Abbatissa to sit whilst she herself remained standing in the place of authority.

Taking her time and with an air of dignity, the Abbatissa spoke.

"I welcome the Presence to the Tower." At the mention of that name Mortella took in a short gasp of air as she felt a chill permeate her. Bowing her head, she waited. The Presence was the highest order of the Code. Consisting of seven of the most powerful and influential of the Sisterhood. One representing each of the major Influences with the addition of the one unanimously exalted leader that was above them all. Breathing in short, sharp breaths she attempted to calm herself. What was the Presence doing here? Why was she their focus? Ambition demanded that she eventually would claim rightful membership within this arena. She was strong. She was powerful. Yet now was not her time. She knew that. There was still more that she had to prove. What did they need of her?

Finally able to achieve a level of calm, she managed to listen to the Abbatissa.

"… Much more still." Turning to the hooded figure on her right, the Abbatissa lowered her head with respect. "I ask the Supreme Potentate to give the honour of addressing us."

A figure rose and drew back her hood. The other six followed her example. There before her sat the Code's most powerful proponents. She surreptitiously examined each of them in turn. All were women who projected a kind of agelessness, younger in appearance but much older than the Abbatissa. Remaining silent they waited for their mistress to continue. As they did Mortella felt a confident but chilling authority emanating from each. She kept her head bowed in respect, only raising it when the Potentate began to speak.

"My Sisters, I add my welcome and give thanks for your timely arrival at this most unexpected location."

She looked at each of them in turn, her eyes lingering on Mortella significantly longer than on any of the others.

"This is unprecedented, but it would be best for you to witness it yourselves." Leaving her place she made her way around the table, past Mortella and directly toward the curtain. As she approached, it fell to the floor revealing what had been hidden behind. Mortella turned in her chair to look as the others arose and followed their sister. Remaining seated until they passed, Mortella also rose. She followed the others to the end of the chamber.

There in front of them was a cloud made out of a multitude of pinpoints of colour. Many more than could be counted. They hung in the air, swirling slowly and forming an ever-changing coloured mist. The Potentate put her hand toward the dots. As she did, their movement increased, the swirling hastened with the colours coalescing and then separating until they finally settled once more. Now hanging stationary in mid-air, the lights were not an incomprehensible mist of colour but formed a single word.

Mortella

Seeing this before her, Mortella was speechless. For one not used to being surprised it was even more unsettling. All eyes turned to her and waited. Eventually the Potentate spoke.

"Mortella, you now know why you are here. Never in the many centuries of history has the Tower attempted a communication like this." She waited, her gaze resting on Mortella. Now being the centre of attention but with no concept of the meaning of Tower's effort, Mortella steadied herself. Holding herself stiffly erect, she returned the gaze.

With a sense of panic, Mortella spoke. "Most esteemed Sisters, I regret that I also am at a loss as to the Tower's meaning." Breathing quickly, she looked around at the others in the room and continued

"My Influence has been deeply embedded in the Tower—" Before she was able to speak further, the Potentate cut her off.

"We are well aware of your work here at the Tower," she said coldly. "You have been greatly commended for the perceptions you have implanted within these walls. Now we have something else."

Dismissing Mortella with a look, she turned to the others in the room. "My Sisters, the Tower is semi-sentient. It contains the Influences of many thousands. With these, if I may also be allowed to surmise, it also retains what little is left of the remaining souls of those who did not progress. There is one other thing that we must also never forget. The Tower has also absorbed many of those who should never be tolerated. Those who possess the minor Influences."

The Potentate stopped speaking as a Tower varlet approached Mortella.

"You will be required to remain here until this is sorted," the Potentate said, directing the comment at Mortella. Then, turning her back, she moved toward the table as the varlet ushered a speechless Mortella out of the chamber. The door closed firmly behind her.

Left alone, Mortella slowed her breathing. She lingered only a little longer in the foyer of the Abbatissa's chamber. Turning her back on this, and those it contained, she descended the stairs. Passing by the door of her own temporary compartment she continued down. On reaching the base of the stairs she was able to enter the lower reaches of the Tower and its labyrinth of passages.

The Tower displayed her name. For hers it was. There was none other in the Code possessing it but her. She did not like the feeling of not being in control. She needed to discover what it meant. Another opportunity to display both her skills and her determination. To reveal the nature of the message to the Presence when they themselves were uninformed. This would place her in good stead for the future. It was also clear that she would not be leaving the Tower any time soon if the message was not fully revealed.

The key would lie in the Tower itself. After the many years she spent here drawing on the Tower's power as she wove her illusions, she had some insights as to where she may commence the search. Making her way unerringly through the darkened corridors, she stopped at a shallow alcove. There she turned to face the wall and concentrated. As she did the stone in front melted away, revealing rough-hewn stairs leading down. As she walked through the alcove the wall reformed behind her, once again as solid as it had seemed moments earlier.

She descended the stairs quickly. At the base she passed through a narrow and irregular opening into an expansive cavern of unfinished black rock. Without hesitation she strode directly into it. There she continued to walk until stopping abruptly. The space about her was empty. Due to the low light no wall of the cavern could be seen. The roof above was equally shrouded in darkness. Here she stood. Remaining still, she concentrated.

There were many things that she had discovered about her Influence. During her time in the Tower, apart from her, there had only been the Abbatissa, the Tower varlets and those of even lesser status. Spending a great deal of time alone was thus preferable. This had given her ample time to experiment. She discovered things. Things that were best not to share. If others were also able to achieve the same, then where would be the advantage? It was best to keep one's discoveries to oneself, for use later for one's own benefit.

The Tower had been established many centuries before. Its purpose was clear. It was to oversee all who fell within the confines of the Bowl. The goal of which was to create the most ideal breeding ground for Influence. Within a normal population the expression of an Influence occurred irregularly. Less than once in a million. Here those of families who had demonstrated such talents had been brought. Within this isolated and segregated population, the interbreeding over generations gradually enriched the genetic pool, resulting in a greater and greater chance of offspring with an Influence. From these the Tower could select, allowing the progression of those deemed worthy to join the Code and continue the fight.

What to do with those who were unsuitable? That had been achieved through the joining of Influences of the most talented. They created a means by which Influences of those deemed unworthy would not be lost. To this end, the Presence had created a way by which the Tower could absorb these talents. As Influences rested within the blood of individuals, those absorbed, by necessity, must remain alive. Their physical being would meld with and become part of the Tower. Yet their conscious selves would generally dissipate and fade. These Influences were then available for the use of more talented artisans of the Code. They could draw on its reserves of power without diminishing their own.

Over time, and through the acquisition of many thousands of individuals, the Tower had gradually evolved. No longer an inanimate structure, it developed a semi-conscious state, neither truly alive nor a non-living entity. It was a composite of the multitude of residual consciousnesses. Mortella had become aware of this as she worked her changes in perception on the Tower. In some ways it would assist her. In others it would hinder her work. Over time she had learnt how to interact with the Tower. Requesting its approval before attempting a change. Once received, the Tower would accept and then hold onto the changes. This made her work the most detailed and successful of any of her predecessors or successors. The work won her praise and had lifted her rapidly up the order of the Code. But this was a secret she would never share with another.

Eyes closed, she concentrated. In her mind she formed an image of the Tower. An image not of a towering black structure but of a lithe female form. She had found it far easier to interact with the Tower when it presented itself in such a way. Perception does help. Normally the wielding of her Influence did not affect her. She could picture what she wanted others to see, feel or hear, but she herself never experienced it firsthand. Just one drawback, that one's own Influence never altered one's own perception. Here, however, it was different. As she drew on the multitude of stored entities within the Tower, it was never just her own power but the joining of many. In this way all, including herself, could see and perceive the changes. It was the only thing she missed about the Tower.

Gradually a shape formed. A slender, willowy, partially transparent, blurred figure emerged from the space. It floated in front of her, seemingly made of shadows. Opening her eyes, Mortella looked upon the ever-shifting features of the Tower. The figure looked back at her and bowed its head in recognition.

Chapter 2

Felix looked at his brother. Looking back at him were the same brown eyes and unshaven chin that greeted him in the mirror each morning. The face before him also carried the same worried concern. Things were a lot more complicated than they had thought. They knew there were Influences and these were something that the Tower required. Yet it was much more than that. It should not have been a surprise. Whenever the Tower was involved, it was safe to bet that there were many more things to consider than at first sight.

He glanced about the kitchen where they sat. After so much work, over so many years, life had finally reached a level of stability. Things were going well. It was time, so Silas had gone out searching for some answers. They had put it off time and again, always finding an excuse, but they needed to know more about the Tower and what it wanted. There had to be others like them about, and they needed more than just rumour and vague warnings. Particularly if things were going to progress.

As children they had been considered special. Identical in all discernible ways. So identical that even their mother only told them apart by the clothes they wore. This lent them a form of immunity to inquiry. It was just accepted that two boys so alike would naturally share a link that defied logic. But things went a whole lot deeper than that. From as early as they could remember, they were in each other's head. A connection that allowed thoughts and images to pass freely.

As toddlers there had been little need for words. Existing securely in their own intertwining spheres their need to interact with the outside world was secondary. Speech languished. This caused much distress to their parents who feared the worst. Yet, over time the desire to engage with the world beyond themselves exerted itself and language developed.

The Tower, ever present and ever watchful, cast a shadow over the youngsters' existence. Unsure as to why, they both knew that the Tower was a threat. A threat not only to themselves but to all others like them. They felt muffled cries of misery that emanated from the structure. Cries of loss and longing, indistinct and ethereal but still very poignant and real. Under the cover of the shadow cast by the Tower they grew and matured, each year becoming more and more mindful of their differences. They also became aware of Influences. Aware and careful never to expose the connection they shared. But being careful did not prevent errors. Sharing experiences at times provided one with knowledge that the other should not have been privy to. However, no-one was ever sure as to which of the boys they were talking. Any unexplained understanding of one, could thus be easily rationalised away.

As adults, Felix and Silas learnt that they were able to communicate with each other over vast distances, although this took some effort. They shared their thoughts, together with the sights, smells, and sounds they experienced. When connected, even physical sensations were shared. This particular ability came both with benefits and difficulties. While children it had taken some time before they were able to differentiate between their own experience and that which was being transferred. In addition, although any physical damage would not transfer, the sensation of injury would. This became all too real when Silas had scalded himself with boiling water, causing Felix to cry out in pain, to the great surprise of all.

Once again together, without the barrier of distance, thoughts and images flowed effortlessly between them. Silas, more adventurous and foolhardier than the risk-averse Felix, had travelled to Town to further try and understand the Tower. As a precaution they had avoided forming any mind connection during the excursion. Now that he was back, Silas rapidly enlightened Felix of all that had transpired through the transmission of remembered images and experiences.

Town nestled itself securely at the base of the Eastern Slopes that culminated in high snow-capped mountains, daily silhouetted by the rising sun. It crept up the foothills, progressively narrowing, until finally ending at the base of the long, steep stairs that led to the great door of the Tower itself. Beyond Town was untamed, rocky ground. An uninhabited land strewn with large boulders and low scrub-like vegetation. Those from Town rarely had the need to venture beyond its borders and into this wilderness. But it was here that Silas had gone to observe the Tower.

On entering Town, he strolled through the markets. His destination was the rugged land to the north of the buildings. There he could leave the dwellings behind and enter the Eastern Slopes. Once outside of the Town limits he gradually made his way uphill. He might not be as young as he once was, but he was fit, and the slope was not that bad. As he approached the Tower, he felt its presence as cold and inhuman. Taking care to keep his movements as discreet as possible he kept close to the larger boulders as he climbed. This was the closest that either of the twins had ever been to the Tower. The despair that engulfed the Tower had always been palpable, but distant, from the relative safety of their home within the northern stretches of the Bowl. Now, as Silas reached Town, and slowly made his way towards the Tower, the wretchedness grew. Sorrow, loss, and an increasing sense of desolation, far worse than the barren landscape around, washed over him.

Having climbed almost to the base of the Tower itself, Silas prepared for a night in the stark landscape. He chose a spot that was almost on a level with the black stone landing that was before the great door. He made sure he was shielded from view. Now close to the Tower walls, he could feel the chill that emanated from them.

He waited and watched as the day began to wane. With the lessening light, the myriad of voices that arose from the Tower grew in force. Years of feeling these cries from a distance did nothing to prepare him for the mounting on-slaught. They were now less muffled and indistinct. The wails that formed a cacophony of sound were now accompanied by images that assaulted his senses. Unready for the attack, Silas locked down his ability, attempting to shield him-self from the pain that was being forced upon him. With effort he was able to deaden the voices in his head. Sleep, however, would not be possible this night. Now he would just have to wait. He would approach the Tower once day began, when the sun was over the mountains. By using the protection of daylight, he would place his hands on the Tower walls. He would try to connect with a single voice within. All in an attempt to understand what the Tower was and from where those cries had sprung.

The sun set and the moon illuminated the landscape in monochromatic tones. As evening progressed the pressure on Silas' defences increased. The voices, ever present, pounded on the barriers of his mind, demanding entry. To allow them in would be overwhelming. Such an assault of misery and loss would prompt a descent into madness. By force of will alone he had to hold firm. Yet with nothing to distract him he felt the incessant attacks gaining strength. His will gradually weakened. In the moonlight the voices gained further in intensity. In desperation he rose, determined to put some distance between himself and the Tower. Distance might lessen the onslaught. Struggling to stand, he started to descend the slope. Barely had he moved when he caught sight of something on the great stairs. Leaving his belongings, he made his way closer to the paved space before the great door. The distraction provided him some strength to re-inforce the barriers of his mind. Remaining hidden, he looked down the stairs at whatever was approaching.

A dark shadow ascended the stairs. Slowly, but smoothly, it climbed. It radi-ated silence. To Silas it was a pool of calm amongst the cries from the Tower that still rang in his head. Just above him the great door opened. It emitted a pale silver light that was barely stronger than the moon outside. A figure emerged from the space to stand on the landing. It, too, was dark, only able to be seen as a void silhouetted against the pale light of the opening. This one felt hollow. It waited. The shadow gained the top of the stairs and, without stopping, passed directly by the other to enter the Tower. As it did the void turned and followed it in as the great door silently closed behind them. Immediately there was a change. The cries from the Tower lessened. The pain, although still pre-sent, was less penetrating.

Silas stood and looked back at the Tower. The voices had lessened their at-tack on him. Whatever it was that had just happened was important. Now more able to cope, he decided to stay and watch further. Over the next few hours another two shadows climbed the stairs to the waiting void on the landing. On each occasion, as the great door closed, the wailings diminished further, their anguish less pronounced. Now, just before midnight, a fourth ascended the stairs. Just as for the others the great door opened. As previously, a dark form took its place at the opening. Instead of passing by, however, on this occasion the shadow stopped. The dark form appeared to diminish in size as if kneeling, or offering homage, before it regained its original height. In the still night Silas was able to discern voices although many of the words were lost.

"Greetings … if it please … Mortella … your pleasure."

"… Abbatissa … phenomenon … speak of … inform."

With that the shadow entered the Tower. This time, as the door once again closed, all the voices fell silent. Silas remained staring at the door. Something was afoot. Unsure if this was to his advantage or not, he decided to stay where he was and see.

The silence from the Tower persisted as Silas slowly began to relax his bar-riers. There was nothing. No voices. No cries. The silence, so strange. The constant hum that for many years had been the background for his every waking moment was silent. He found this even more confronting than the earlier at-tacks. He approached the Tower. The blackness of its walls was impenetrable. Pure blackness, lacking any light or sheen. Matt and opaque walls rose high above him. Tentatively he put one hand and then the other onto its cool smooth surface. He waited. Gradually he peeled back layer after layer of the protections he had created. He listened. Gently he started to probe the walls, searching for a voice. An entity to link with. They were there. He could feel them. A multitude. But they were silent. He waited, also silent. What were they? Were they individuals or part of a composite? He probed deeper, allowing himself to be open to any approach. Clearing his mind, he pushed his Influence further into the Tower. He felt fleeting pricks of consciousness and random images but mostly he felt emotion. Deep, heartbreaking feelings of loss. Tears came unexpectedly to his eyes. The hurt he had touched within the Tower was unfathomable. There were depths of sadness far greater than he would want to explore. Loss. There was such great loss. Of what, he didn't know, but it was everywhere. All around. Seeping through every part of the wall.

With both hands still resting against the Tower's walls he remained. They had been right to fear the Tower. A place so full of despair and pain could not be good. But he needed to know more. How was this happening? Who were those that were in pain? Why was there such despair? Waiting, he projected a calm and quiet compassion. He acknowledged the hurt. As he did, the entities within the walls, as one, seemed to shudder. There was building excitement as a thrill rippled through the Tower and into him. It continued to grow when suddenly it exploded with a force so powerful that it physically propelled him away from the wall. He landed heavily on the rough-hewn slope. A single word had screamed into his mind. He could see it in blazing letters as he slipped into unconsciousness – MORTELLA.

***

The sun was high in the sky by the time Silas once again regained consciousness. He ached all over having lain on the cold, rock-strewn ground for most of the night. Parched and hungry, he carefully climbed up from the ground and returned to his belongings. Taking the waterskin from his bag, he quenched his thirst. It took a moment for him to realise that the voices were back. Once again sorrowful but muted and without the intensity of the previous evening. He knew that he couldn't remain another night. But what of today? Should he try again now that the sun was up? Opening the bag once more he took out the bread and cold meat. Sitting on one of the smaller boulders, he considered his options.

They already knew that the Tower was a place to be feared. The rumours of disappearances were far too common and widespread not to be true. Everyone knew of some family that had lost someone to the Tower. Although very few would ever speak of it. Those who were Taken were never heard of again. Even whole families could vanish. Gone, leaving their landholdings to fall into ruin and decay with no explanation. Daughters would be Taken for their Influence. Sons gone without reason. The Tower wanted all.

The legends of the Dark Ones also seemed to be true if he could believe his own eyes. Spoken of as creatures cloaked in black that attended to the Tower. Servants of the Tower that were responsible for the disappearances. He had been witness to the attendance of five of these the previous night. Two of which may have been female, if their voices were anything to go by. Yet what happened to those Taken? Selected for Influence, but why? Why were they Taken? They needed to know more. He had to try again to connect with one of those within the Tower's walls.

Having broken his fast, Silas looked up at the Tower. In the midday light he could discern a window about halfway up. Apart from this, and the great door, there was nothing to break the continuity of the curved black walls. Homely was not a word that came to mind. Preparing himself, he closed down his ability and walked back towards the Tower. He approached it carefully, well aware of what had transpired on the last attempt. *Mortella.* Yes, now he remembered. That was what had been thrust at him. A single word that had exploded into his mind. Who was Mortella? What did this have to do with the arriving shadows? Mortella. One of those at the door had said that earlier. Nothing else he heard from that conversation lent any further light.

Reaching the wall, he stopped. He fortified his defences and, feeling the sun on his back, he placed the first and then the other hand flat against the wall. There was a slight tickling sensation. Shadows flicked across the periphery of his consciousness. He waited. Quietly he let those within the walls prod and probe the borders to his mind. He was careful to let none in. Gently he extended his consciousness to mingle with those already there. Catching flickering images, he continued to wait. None felt complete. Each small shadow was imbued with a sense of loss and isolation. Gradually more and more of the wraiths coalesced about him, drawn by the steady, unwavering proximity of a mind that was whole.

As the numbers increased, Silas began to feel a singularity develop among the fleeting shadows. A composite made up of each of the tiny shadow-like fragments. Focusing on each fragment revealed features of individuals that, when viewed as a mosaic of many thousands, formed the image of a waif-like child – a young girl. A slender form with features that constantly shifted as the shadows moved within it. He just knew that this must be the Tower.

He felt its desire. A need for the power to control. Even greater than this was a lust for the life that it knew was within him. It craved what he had with an eagerness that engulfed him. A yearning greed for what he had. It terrified him with its intensity. Silas held firm. He fortified his barriers further and stayed connected to the Tower. Images flitted past. Each were fleeting but infused with emotion; a girl huddled in the dark, a youth frozen with fear, a woman holding a child. Each unfulfilled and aching for something. There was no joy, just an unappeased craving. He watched as each faded and joined the multitude. Lost amongst the many. There it was again – Mortella. The letters wove themselves through the images. A voice, "not to be tolerated" echoed through his mind as a cascade of boys presented themselves while being broken apart with silent screams. Dark figures wandered at the periphery of the images. Quiet and menacing.

Silas held steady as the ethereal child wafted towards him, seeming to look directly at him as it presented one final image. This was one of pure darkness that contained a single, lingering cry of suffering, hopeless and destitute. Reacting instinctively he removed his hands, breaking contact with the Tower. Chilled to the bone, the intention was clear. The Tower knew him and had delivered a threat for he was *not to be tolerated*.

***

Felix wiped his eyes. Silas knew how deeply these sort things affected him. Breaking the link between them, he allowed his brother some privacy and time to collect his thoughts. Silas had experienced these things over a period of time. The additional few days that it had taken him to return home had further allowed him time to process the experiences. But Felix had to undergo them all within a few minutes. All the raw emotions of the Tower, and of those it contained. These had lost none of their potency through the transfer. They were as real as they had been the first time for Silas. Now Felix would need space. Space to think and time to try and understand what he had seen.

Silas relied on Felix's insights. Felix had a way of looking at things. A way that Silas could not. He needed his brother to take the time and unpick what it all meant. Felix got up and, pouring heated water into a pot, began to make some tea. Performing simple, everyday tasks allowed him time to think. The calming brew would also help. He threw a handful of dried apple peel and a pinch of spice into the pot and waited.

He let the images gently fade from his mind as he poured a cup for himself and his brother. Leaving the room, he went out into the sunshine. Dark thoughts were better to be had in the light – less overpowering. A myriad of souls all part of what formed the Tower. Souls that were crying from the loss they had suffered. Clearly there was no desire from the multitude to be part of the Tower. They were in pain. Lost and hopeless, but the Tower craved power – desiring control. A soulless thing, it coveted the life that was outside its walls. Taking it from those within the walls so as to live itself.

Felix walked to the stream taking time to admire their plot. He was proud of what they had achieved. They had started with nothing and now … it was something of beauty. A quiet and restful holding that was purposefully located well away from the others. They had learnt to live separated from others. It was safer that way.

He soon reached the upper dam that he and Silas had created. The replenishing waters from the stream above that circulated around the large, deep dam made the perfect environment for cultivating the golden perch. As he stood, he saw glints of silvery gold backs shimmering under the water. The larger ones were almost as long as his forearm. Things had been going well.

Well, the Dark Ones were real. Not the terrifying childhood story so many believed them to be. They came for those with Influence. "Not to be tolerated." Only the boys. Torn apart. Boys like they had been. But these ones were Taken, enclosed, and tormented within the black walls. Standing still, he calmed himself with the beauty that surrounded him. In truth, he had known it already. They both had. They had lived, made all their decisions inherently knowing that the Tower was a threat to them. The truth had been there, but he had never wanted to accept it. The Bowl was a prison. The high mountainous walls were keeping them in. Keeping all in view of the Tower and vulnerable to its appetites. They lived their lives at the whim of the Tower and its servants. There to feed it.

Sitting looking at the dam wall he sipped his tea. It would have been so much easier to have stayed hidden. Live a quiet life. That was what they had planned. So far it had worked. They paid the tithe and avoided the world beyond their plot. But the world had a way of invading. Now, Silas had exposed them. The Tower knew of them. Felix ran his fingers through his hair and scratched the back of his head. Silas had always been too foolhardy. Would always act before he thought it through. The Tower would not let them be. Eventually it would come. He could try to ignore this simple truth, but it would be of no benefit. No longer could they stay hidden.

Standing and facing the cottage, Felix sighed. No-one else should need to succumb to a fate like those he had just witnessed. It most likely would be a matter of time for them. Together they needed to resist. They would find others, others like themselves and would … and would … and would do what? Yes, and do what? What was it that they could do? Well, to start … they could find a way out of the Bowl. He would have to think – unlike his brother.

Chapter 3

The sun had risen. The air was warm. Mortella was now back in her makeshift chambers. The sunlight failed to light the room. It merely succeeded in emphasising the deep, dark shadows where she sat contemplating the events of the previous night. The Tower was rarely direct. Nothing was ever fully clear. Irritatingly, most communication with the Tower occurred through what appeared to be a random collection of images. Settling herself, she poured another goblet of wine and stood in front of the window. Staring off into the distance she neither saw nor registered the view. Motionless, she recalled the images the Tower had most recently presented.

During the time that she had spent creating her illusions within the Tower, a waif-like girl would occasionally present itself. As the representative of the Tower, and the souls it contained, it exerted a level of control. This was particularly obvious over any alterations to its form. Occasionally it would project a collection of what Mortella considered its wishes. These occurred through a mixture of both feelings and impressions. Following years of experience, Mortella found that most were simple and straightforward. These required little effort to understand. An image of a small, child-like figure linked with a feeling of calm would indicate acceptance of any proposed alterations. Agitation, and even aggression, however, were more frequent. These implied displeasure or distrust. It denoted that the Tower would resist the suggested embellishments. If Mortella was unwise enough to persist in their construction, then they would not take hold within the walls and would fade completely. Subsequently, and for quite some period of time after such an affront to the Tower, it would not allow any other alterations to take place. This irrespective of whether such changes had been previously acceptable to it or not.

This time, however, there were a multitude of images. Vastly more complex than she had previously experienced. They were also manifestly less obvious in their meaning. They appeared to have been presented in random order. Each one was intertwined with a series of strong raw emotions and desires. All, however, were linked together with a sense of urgency. It was almost as if the Tower was worried or distressed. Mortella had felt the immense importance it placed on what it wanted. This intensity was of a level she had never before encountered.

She needed time to think. She knew the Tower better than anyone. That was probably why it had spelled out her name. It knew that she was the best of the Code to understand. It would just take her time to figure it out. And figure it out she must. This would further cement her rise within the Code. If she was able to present the meaning directly to the Presence then … It was an opportunity that must not be squandered. An opportunity like this would never happen again. How long they would remain within the Tower she didn't know. It would not be long. Their attention was always needed elsewhere. Time was of the essence and every second counted.

She returned to the couch that had been placed to face the window and sat perched on the edge of the velvet cushions. A babe in arms. Mortella had only a little experience of infants. That was many years ago when she needed to supervise one or more of these creatures while their mothers worked. She never had had any real interest in them. Annoying and inarticulate in their needs. Repulsively helpless. They all looked the same at that age. Yet the child in the first vision felt like a girl. Well, naturally, she thought, the Tower would only be interested in girls. She also was quite sure that the Tower wanted to keep this one. It was something special, something that had some sort of immense significance to it. Throughout the entirety of the vision this desire was palpable. A feeling that was all-consuming. A yearning that could only be quenched by this one child.

As the image faded it was replaced with that of a woman. The figure felt youthful. She was standing and holding a small bundle. Her arms were outstretched as if trying to keep the bundle as far away from herself as possible. Emanating from the figure Mortella felt an intense craving. It engulfed the image, clouding its features and distorting the face with its ferocity. There was want, need and desire as well as fear and hatred. Mortella watched as it stood unmoving. Frozen in this position against its will. She could feel it trying to free itself but failing. Eventually it, too, faded.

Taking a sip of wine to clear her thoughts Mortella tried to remember more about the bundle. What was it that could have been able to generate such a mixture of emotions within the figure? It looked like a simple nondescript bundle of clothes. She had no clue as to what it contained. There had to be more to it. She had to think. Don't give up. She could do it.

The third instalment was that of a young woman not yet fully grown and standing with her back towards Mortella. She wore a garment of the most beautiful white translucent silk organza that covered the Black of the Code. Her hair was long and of a fiery gold that blazed in the light of a setting sun. The image slowly turned toward her. As it did, Mortella heard a piercing scream. It came from a face devoid of all features. Unlike the previous images, there were no feelings to accompany this. There was just a deadness, a coldness that penetrated deep inside her.

As the scream faded the final vision inserted itself. This was another of what felt akin to the woman with the bundle. Time had passed and she was no longer youthful. Still standing straight and proud the figure looked off into the distance. Mortella looked intently at the indistinct features of the face as they began to melt like a wax doll in the midday sun. The body too began to transform. No longer standing erect it began to slump to the left with the arm withering and the skin discolouring. Behind it all, however, Mortella could feel the same intense craving. If anything, it was now even more chilling in its ferocity.

Pleased that she was able to accurately recall the visions in all their detail, Mortella sat back against the cushions and took a deep breath. Sleep had been scarce over the last few days, and she was tired. This, however, was not something that could be contemplated. Not yet. Not until she had discovered the Tower's meaning. The sun was bright outside the Tower. Travel by the Code was undertaken during sunless hours. She hoped that this should give her enough time.

She was hungry, having not eaten for many hours. That she could use. The gnawing pain would keep her awake and allow her to think. Physical discomfort could be channelled and otherwise was of little importance. Breathing deeply several times to calm her nerves, she cleared her thoughts as she once again perched herself on the edge of the couch.

It made sense that the woman with the bundle and the other that melted could be the same. The hatred in the first would thus be justified if the bundle was the cause of the transformation in the second. Yet why the craving? Hatred, yes, that Mortella understood, but the longing? The two must be related. It was hard to fathom how both could be directed at the same thing. The result of one, however, might lead to the other. How? What could it be that would make the figure both desire and hate the bundle?

The infant and the girl may also be one and the same. The small child so desired by the Tower would eventually grow and take the Black. Why the organza? The Black was more than enough. None of the Code could want more. How could they?

Were all four visions the same person? The youthful woman, was she what became of the child? No longer taking the Black. Was that why there was such an intense longing? Was she trying to find her way back to the Code?

Mortella closed her eyes. Blocking out the sunlight helped. She needed to remove all distractions so she could think. The bundle, so small and unwanted, but also desired. Could this be a child? Did she leave the Code for a man? Mortella knew about men. Knew their needs and weaknesses. Yet for all their failings there were still women who wanted them. She had witnessed it time and again with her sisters in the knocking shop. How many times had she treated the blackened eyes and cut lips of her family following a beating? Yet, she had then watched perplexed as the perpetrator had been welcomed back. Time and time again they were greeted in the hope of something more. More than what? She had learnt to despise men. Within the shop they had allowed themselves to be playthings. Existing solely for the pleasure of men. It was the Code that had saved her from them. Never since then had she needed to hide her contempt in order to eat.

And then there was the almost inevitable consequence of their calling. She remembered looking on in disbelief. Those around her would oooh and ahhh while inspecting the growing belly of one of their sisters. They greeted the developing burden with anticipation. Not for her. The Code had also saved her from that.

Had the woman in the vision been tempted by wealth? The silk organza – was that what it symbolised? The desire for wealth that shrouded what should have been her destiny in the Black? Had she then defiled herself and carried a child? Was that to be the fate of this woman, to age and decay? Was this the destruction of the one so desired by the Tower? To be led away and to never return? Forever suffering for her choice. For suffer she must, having thrown away such a gift. Had this fool only realised after it was too late? She never would now fulfill her true desire. Was that the root of the unquenchable craving?

***

The sun was setting as Mortella smiled to herself. The day was gone, and the time had been well used. It fitted. It felt right. The Tower was right to spell out her name. The Tower wanted the Code to know that there was one of their own who would fall into great error. There was one who would be coming that the Tower deemed as special. It did not want to lose her. Now that they were warned they would be ready to act. Prevent the loss of this singular child from the Code. She was ready. She would now be able present this to the Presence. They would see that she was right. The Tower would confirm it. It wouldn't be too much longer.

Allowing herself to relax, she arched her back that was sore after such a long time sitting still. A bit of water should refresh her. Standing, she made her way to the side cabinet to fill her goblet with the liquid. No more wine now. Nothing to dampen the edge to her thinking. It helped when she needed her thoughts to wander, but not now. Draining one glass she poured another as she wondered how she could request an audience with the Presence. She would continue her rise. It had been far faster than any other. Eventually she would be one of the Presence. Only the strongest of each Influence must form the Presence. Eventually they would not be able to deny her her place.

Draining the goblet once more she turned back to the couch. As she did, she saw movement at the door of the chamber. A varlet emerged from the landing.

"The Presence have requested your attendance."

Without further thought Mortella glided past the messenger and re-ascended the stairs to the Abbatissa's chamber.

***

Standing once again outside the Abbatissa's chamber, Mortella waited. She felt calm and confident. This would be a stunning victory. She even felt slightly mollified towards the Abbatissa herself. It really was not that hard to be magnanimous to those so inferior to oneself. She had decided to ignore the slight she had endured. It was enough that she would be able to leave this place. She would return to her other duties knowing that once again she had excelled. Oh, to be stuck in this place. That was punishment enough.

Eventually the great door silently began to open. Mortella looked up as the Abbatissa appeared in the space that formed. She looked small and unimpressive.

"Again, thank you for your patience, Mortella. The Presence and the Supreme Potentate would speak with you now."

Oh, what a change, Mortella thought. Not summoned now but requested to be spoken with. She nodded to herself. That was much better. It must be very hard for them not knowing. Unable to see what the Tower wanted to convey. She did pity them … just a little. None of them would be used to being in such a situation as this. How fortunate that they had someone like her.

Holding her head high and being sure to hold Influence over her own person perfectly in check, Mortella passed by the Abbatissa and entered the room. It appeared as it had the previous night. Seven figures were seated at the table but now with the Abbatissa's chair also occupied. Only Mortella's chair remained empty. All sat motionless with their hoods raised. None acknowledged her arrival, but all waited with a composure that was threatening. Mortella held herself in check. Now was not the time to allow oneself to be intimidated. She must not doubt herself. Walking just a touch too quickly she made for the other end of the table. As she did, the Abbatissa silently left the room and closed the door behind her. Reaching the chair Mortella turned to face the Code's elite.

Remaining standing she centred herself and bowed her head towards the hooded figure in the Abbatissa's chair. Wetting her lips and controlling any tremor in her voice she spoke.

"Esteemed members of the Presence and to the most revered and venerated Supreme Potentate, may I request the honour to address you?" Stopping, she waited. After a pause that lingered well past what was comfortable, the figure at the head of the table responded.

"We will allow you that privilege, Mortella. This is a most unusual circumstance. We caution you to be brief."

Choosing her words carefully, Mortella began.

"My time at work here allowed me insights into the Tower. It called for me. A child will be born that is destined for the Code. This child is of great significance. The Tower fears that she shall be tempted away from her calling by material things and a man. If so, she will bear a child. This will be the destruction of her. She will be lost to the Code. The Tower is warning us of this." Happy with the clarity of her declaration, Mortella awaited their adulation.

"Mortella, you may sit," was the only response. Puzzled by this, Mortella sat while maintaining the mask of demure patience and respect. Her mind continued to whirl frantically beneath the surface. Had she got it wrong? It all fitted with the images. Was there something she forgot? Interpretations were only interpretations, but she was sure that the core of it was right.

The Supreme Potentate rose from her chair and made towards the wall behind her. Here hung a tapestry of demure hues and subtle imagery. As she approached, it fell to the floor. For a second time within this chamber a multitude of coloured pinpoints of light was revealed. As she watched, Mortella saw them move as the previous night to form a word.

Keep

Keep Mortella. She felt panic. Keep me? Did the Tower want to keep her? Why? How? Was she to be the Abbatissa? No. Surely not. She had already completed her time here. It couldn't want her to remain. No, not really. It just couldn't. Emotions, and a feeling of doubt that was unfamiliar, almost overwhelmed her. Yet, her face remained calm and placid thanks to the power of Influence.

"My Sisters, for reasons unknown the Tower desires this. Shall we endorse or risk potentially unseen consequences?" The Supreme Potentate paused as her gaze rested briefly on Mortella. Immobile, and hardly breathing, Mortella watched as each of the Presence stood. As one they raised both arms in front, hands cupped together and facing upwards, signifying the offering of their consent. The Supreme Potentate also nodded her approval of the decision. Immediately all the others turned from the table and exited through the now open door. The Supreme Potentate remained and gestured for Mortella to rise.

"You will stay here this night and then shall be taken to your new vocation."

Confused, Mortella was unable to contain herself.

"The Tower cannot want to keep me. What of the child? I am only here to decipher the meaning. It is done. There is no need for me to remain. I …"

It only took the raising of the Supreme Potentate's hood for Mortella to remember herself."

"Ahh, forgive me, I …" she mumbled, quickly lowering her head.

"Enough," the Supreme Potentate ordered. Her face was severe but also contained a tinge of regret. "The Tower does not want to *keep* you. You are to be Mortella Keep. Your fate is to bear the child foretold. That child so desired of the Tower. That child is yours to provide to the Code. It will destroy you but, if you provide the child, I will offer this one consolation. Remain near the Tower and it may be able to restore you to the Black. At least in part. Fail this and you will wither and fade as those beneath the Code."

Without further explanation, the Supreme Potentate turned and exited, leaving Mortella speechless. She was to leave the Code. No longer to wear the Black. To be given to a man solely for the purpose of procreation. Numb and unable to fathom the depths of the humiliation, she was led back to her chamber. Led back by a varlet. This most lowly servant of the Code whose sole task was to service the Tower now had power and authority over her.

***

Dawn came all too soon. The sky gently changed from black to grey and gradually gained the yellow and golden glow that heralded the start of another fine day. Mortella had not moved from where she sat on the couch after her return. Neither hungry, nor thirsty, she sat. Her mind was in a haze as she tried to discover a loophole. A way out. Looking for something that would change the Presence's mind. How could she have been wrong? What did it matter? She had no choice but to follow. There was then a chance she could be restored. Do not acquiesce and she would be fully lost. The Code did not allow its decisions to be thwarted. She remembered the shop. Detestable men. She loathed them.

Now this was to be her life. They would want to make her like one of their prized heifers. There to create a lineage. To be used as the owner desired and occasionally brought out for show. "Well, that will not happen," she declared to herself. She had no choice but to follow the directions of the Code but there was always room for interpretation. *Woe to any man who underestimates me.*

With the day fully begun, and all food left untouched, Mortella forced herself to change out of the Black and don the dress provided. A looking glass had been brought to the chamber. If she was going to have to do this, she was determined to make an impression. Looking at her reflection she needed very little Influence to perfect the look. Now in the full bloom of her life she was already strikingly beautiful. Her clear, smooth porcelain skin contrasted perfectly with the vivid green eyes and long bronze hair. The colour of the dress matched her eyes and fitted to perfection. Just the addition of a subtle glow to her skin and enhancing the sparkle of sunlight in her hair was enough. She was ready. Looking around the room she swore to herself that she would be back. No matter what it took, she would re-enter the Code. She would retake the Black. She had suffered much in the past. She would also be able to overcome this. At least now hunger and poverty would not be amongst the trials she needed to endure.

Chapter 4

Nestled in the gentle, undulating slopes of the northern reaches of the Bowl, Felix and Silas had created their oasis. By using the natural landscape to their advantage, over the years they had fashioned the perfect environment. Their farm was a delight with the golden perch growing well. They thrived in the sluggish flow of the upper dam. These fish had gained the farm a reputation for providing something fresh and tasty. They were in demand. As their popularity grew, the added coinage had provided the brothers a level of financial stability they never had thought attainable. It also made it possible for the more recent expansion. Construction of the lower dam.

The lower dam was now stocked with bluegill. These small fish had proven their ability to proliferate at an incredible rate. Small and fast growing, they were used to supplement the diet of the upstream yellowbellies. Felix was proud that they had created a self-perpetuating system. It freed them from reliance on any outside help to keep it all going.

He loved to come and just sit by the dams. Watching the shimmering forms that briefly caught the eye before they were gone was relaxing. It allowed for contemplation. It was time for himself. Unlike his brother, Felix thrived when allowed time in his own presence. Without the pressure of others being around he could think. He had made it his habit to treat himself to this luxury at least once a day. It may not be for long, but it was precious. He could allow his mind to wander. It was then that he came up with his best ideas. In so many ways he and Silas were identical, but in this they were poles apart. He craved the quiet, simple landscape while Silas loved people. He loved to be at the centre of, what appeared to Felix to be, chaos. He loved his brother dearly, but Silas could be incredibly frustrating. It was something he just couldn't understand. It didn't escape his thinking that to Silas, his way was just as incomprehensible.

He stood up and stretched. Their most recent venture needed attention. The bluegills had done so well that there was more than enough for the upper dam. Their numbers were now so great that he needed to find other uses for their numbers. For what use had been the question. Felix had thought long and hard. These were not good for the table. They would not sell. He had asked many people about it and had even travelled. Most recently he had gone to visit an elderly couple even further north than them and a way off to the west. For many years they had provided fish to the Bowl. Not only did they provide their fish fresh but also dried and preserved. They would preserve them in salt which allowed for long-term storage. These were particularly good in the making of fish stew. Delighted to speak of their trade with a like-minded person, they were generous in sharing their knowledge and even made him a stew from the salt-preserved fish. It was delicious.

Coming home he had tried to do the same with the bluegill. Following their advice, he salted several batches of fish. He covered them with a thick layer of coarse salt and left them a month before taking out one batch to make a stew. It had been less than successful. They were not made for the table. Discouraged, he resolved himself to the failed concept. It was only several months later that he got around to disposing of the other batches. Over time the fish had broken down into a grey sludge with a strong fish-smelling liquid floating on top. Curious, he tasted it. Strong and pungent. He collected what little there was. Through a bit of trial and error he found that its addition to certain foods would enhance the flavour. Even Silas agreed. So now he was trying again, but on a larger scale.

He walked over to the makeshift shelter the two of them had made down-wind of the house and dams. Here the fish and salt had been placed together in several larger tubs. On a daily basis he would collect the liquid that formed on top. He would then stir the remaining contents. Through evaporation, the collected liquid would concentrate and then be placed into sealed containers. He called it "fish essence". It was good. Now he had to think about how to get people to try it.

Stirring the tubs, Felix thought again about the Tower. It intruded itself into everything. After what Silas had done they would have to do something. Their curiosity about the Tower had backfired. It now knew of them. The Tower was evil. Holding the inhabitants of the Bowl in servitude. Taking what it wanted … or needed. The best that they could have expected was to be left alone. But that now seemed a lot less likely. For many others of the Bowl that would definitely not be their future. For some, they would be Taken and locked within the Tower. Felix and Silas had been careful not to reveal themselves. Had been until recently. Now it would just be a question of time before they too were targeted. What if they weren't? Did that really matter? Others would be, while they did nothing. If everyone did the same, then the Tower would continue unchallenged. Pressing his lips together he shook his head.

He looked about. The world they had created on their plot was as close to perfect as anyone could get. They could just stay here and hope they remained hidden. Let the Bowl outside take care of itself. As he looked and wished, he knew that that was not an option. The Tower would insert itself in their lives again. They could try and ignore it. Ignore it until it was too late. Or … or they could meet it head on.

∗∗∗

She graced herself with a moment to look back. The great door was closing as she watched. She remembered the first time she had approached that door. Scared, but also excited and curious. They had come for her at night when the rest of the shop was working. Her "john" was fast asleep on the bed. It had not been hard to get him to sleep following the significant quantities of alcohol he had consumed. She would be able to spin any story she liked after he woke. She found that he would believe anything.

They had come. Silent and strange. Not terrifying but awe inspiring. She had followed them willingly to a new life that valued her and what she could do. Now, turning her back on the closing door, she began the descent. Leaving the only life she ever wanted. It took every ounce of control for her not to fall to the ground and plead to be allowed back in. All that she had had now been taken away from her.

One might think that she was now to be tied to a man. To await his desires and play by his rules. No longer. She had been forced to do that in the past. She was very different to the child that first climbed these stairs. She would bear the child the Tower desired. Then she would return. That was what the One had offered. She would endure what was to come in order to return. Only for that would she submit.

They arrived at the high wall and impressive gate as the sun hung mid-cycle over Town. Passing through, they entered a fragrant manicured garden filled with flowers in full bloom. The marble path led past a cascading fountain toward an entrance door flung wide open. The varlets surrounded Mortella like an honour guard, which, from another perspective, might also be seen as a prison guard. Entering the vestibule, the varlets moved to the side allowing Mortella to advance on her own. There in front was her intended. Similar in age to me, she thought. At least he was handsome.

He was a slender man, youthful and trying his best to look in control of the situation despite manifestly being well out of his depth. Just a pawn in the process. He was scared. She could see it in the forced smile. Tension and anxiety screamed from every aspect of his posture. A forced bravado. She felt like she should pity him but couldn't bring herself to do so. Born into wealth and luxury he never had to want for anything. He was living his utopia. He neither knew, nor wanted for, anything more. Well, she thought, *I will let you maintain that illusion. Just don't try to impose your will upon me. It would not go well.*

Bowing his head, he greeted her.

"Mortella, welcome to your new home. You shall want for nothing here."

How little you understand, she decried. He smiled. It was pleasant. To many it would have been a charming and alluring smile. Mortella dismissed it. As she did, she returned the most radiant of smiles enhanced by Influence. She watched its enchantment on him. *They are so malleable.* Looking past him, she observed a maid emerging from the shadows.

"You may want to freshen up," he continued, "your chambers are prepared. Anything you desire, just ask, and it shall be done." He bowed, again gesturing to the maid. She tentatively approached Mortella and indicated one of the passages out of the vestibule. As Mortella left she could feel the youth's eyes still on her. He shall not be hard to control, she thought as she was led away.

***

His visit to the west provided more information than just about fish. The quiet nature of Felix allowed space for others to feel comfortable and talk more freely than perhaps they normally would. His gentle conversation style and genuine interest about fish seamlessly led into the discussion of other things. The good food, and the affable company, allowed conversation between Felix and the elderly couple to range far and wide.

Gossip is the staple of conversation in all small communities. The most insignificant of occurrences generates interest that lasts for weeks. More noteworthy events lasted a great deal longer. These never really went away. From time to time, when other news was scarce, they would raise their heads once again. There, ready and waiting for further conjecture and speculation. It was one such occurrence that was alluded to by the couple. It was only now, thinking back on it, that the details of this event sparked his interest.

At the time it had been easy to dismiss. Such stories gained numerous embellishments over time. The primary aim was to generate more interest. It gave more scope for outlandish theories and provided greater entertainment. Felix was well aware of that. In general, there was only a kernel of truth to any outlandish tale. The real story had been stretched and contorted in order to create the fable. In this one, a family known to those known to the elderly couple was the subject. It was said that they were in possession of a strange and inexplicable object. It was a thing that defied any explanation of what it was, what it was used for and where it had come from. Although neither the couple nor their acquaintances had ever actually seen the object, it was an absolute certainty that it existed. The holders of the plot abutting that of the family in question had seen it. They had told the sister of the friends of the elderly couple about it. It had terrified them. Although none knew what the object could be, the whole community had been unanimous in its agreement. The object was not of the Bowl.

The tale gained further momentum when one day the family mysteriously disappeared. One day they were there visiting the local store, waving to acquaintances on the road and then they were gone. No-one knew why. Opinions varied as to what had happened. They had always been diligent about paying the tithe and they had only sons. No daughters to attract unwanted attention from the east. But after one quarterly tithe they had never been seen again. It was as if they had never existed. Nobody remembered anything untoward happened during the collection. But now, their plot now lay empty and in ruin. The locals had since given it a wide berth. Even the neighbours had moved to a different holding further away.

Finishing stirring the vats, Felix went to get the lids to seal in the contents. They might not be back for a few days. He didn't want the fish essence to dry out completely. The salt would keep drawing out the fluid. Things might be a little slower but that was of little consequence. Hammering the wooden lids securely onto the vats, he made his way back to the house. Silas might be back from the markets by now. It all depended on how long it took him to sell all that he had taken with him. They were lucky. Although their plot was well out of the way of the normal travel routes, it was only a relatively short trip to quite a sizeable village. This one was big enough to have a market on most days of the week. The fresh, tasty fish on their stall was consistently in demand. Silas' outgoing personality was also a good selling point. He knew how to connect with people. He could laugh and joke with them. This in turn encouraged them to come back and buy more. They were a good team.

Entering the cottage, he stoked the fire to start on the main meal of the day. Not fish. Their product was excellent quality but being surrounded by it day after day did take a bit of the shine off it. There was a half leg of lamb in the cold box of the underground cellar. That, roasted with potatoes and some fresh garden vegetables, sounded perfect. He went back outside, making his way toward the stream. They had dug a small stone cellar beside it. The flowing water kept the stones cool. The careful laying of the stone blocks in turn kept most of the water out of the space. It was just big enough for a person to climb inside to retrieve whatever was wanted. Here they were able to keep many food stuffs.

Ones that would quickly spoil and others that would have otherwise needed to be salted. By the time he had retrieved the lamb, Silas was sitting at the table.

Silas looked up and smiled.

"It went well. All gone. Mrs Negee said that she might like to try some of your fish essence." Felix nodded. He knew that Silas would be able to convince their regulars to try it. "I got some dried fruits. Never know when we could possibly need more trail mix."

Felix busied himself with the preparation as he sighed to himself and shook his head.

"Okay, so what's going on?" It was virtually impossible for things to be hidden between the brothers.

"You're right. We have to do something," Felix began. "The Tower will continue otherwise. And eventually …"

"And?" Silas prompted. "You never start with something like that unless you have a plan."

Felix smiled. "Eventually it will find us as well." Turning back to season the lamb he continued, "Perhaps I have the beginnings of one." He shared his memories of the tale the couple had told him. "It's not a lot to go on. But it's a start. We will take the fish essence with us. That will give us a reason to go back."

Silas nodded. "There might be something there. There are enough of these stories floating about in the Bowl that there must be some truth to them." He patted his brother affectionately on the shoulder. "A bit of laughter and silly banter might also get us a bit more information. When should we go?"

"You have the dried fruit …" his bother responded.

"I knew it would come in handy," Silas laughed.

***

Her chamber was large and luxurious with an east-facing balcony. It was a mixed blessing as she would have to look at the Tower every morning. The pain of having to leave was real. It was difficult to have to confront it every morning as soon as she awoke.

Having dismissed the servant, Mortella looked around the space. It was a large, bright chamber. Definitely big enough for six, or even eight, workstations if this had been the knocking shop. Decorated in mainly pinks and purples, there were floral motifs strewn across the walls. *They will have to go*, she thought. Her attention was caught by a selection of foods that had been placed on the low table by the couches in the centre of the room. Inspecting them more closely she noted that these were exotic. Only a very few people in the Bowl were allowed access to items such as these. This household had been granted privileges.

As she sank into the down-filled cushions, she wondered what the family had done to gain such dispensations. Perhaps it was not what it has done ... but what it is going to do, she reasoned.

Placing the ripe fruit into her mouth, she remembered the first time she had experienced their flavour. Having left the Bowl for the first time, she had been welcomed into her new position. She had proven herself. The reward was advancement. She had been so happy. Now ... now ... well, now she would fortify herself. She would put up with the humiliation and do what she must. All this so she could return.

Unmoving on the couch, Mortella remained locked in her thoughts. It was only the light tap on the door that brought her back to the present. Rousing herself, she spoke.

"Enter."

"Milady, milord inquires if you will be joining him this evening?" was the timid question from a very nervous looking maid. Mortella looked at her. Yes, she thought you should be. Then speaking aloud, she responded, "I shall." Turning away from the door Mortella gazed out the window. *I need to do what I must. The faster it is done the better. It should not be hard to get him in the mood.* A tentative stutter drew her attention back to the door. "Would you like any assistance, milady?" Mortella looked confused.

"There are numerous gowns contained within the closet," the maid continued as she made her way to the side of the chamber. Opening one of the large doors to the closet she revealed a dazzling display of garments. "I am also very skilled with hair, milady."

Mortella looked at the array before her. Rising from the couch she approached the closet. Frills, lace, and gentle pastel colours confronted her. Dressed in these a woman was specifically designed to look soft, weak, and malleable. An overly sweet, sugary confection. A decoration. No more significant than the arrangements in the hallway. She flicked through them one by one, dismissing each in turn. Nearing the back of the closet she discovered another sort of garment. This one was near black and sheer. An off-the-shoulder bodice with a plunging neckline. There was a subtle shimmer to the material that was both sensuous and expensive.

Indicating the garment to the maid she stood back as it was removed from the closet for further inspection.

"This one will do," Mortella indicated as the maid gently laid it across the bed. "Prepare a bath. I will now wash and call you once I am done."

The maid nodded and left to get the hot water organised.

Staring at the gown before her, Mortella clenched her teeth. *Might as well be tonight.*

Dressed and ready, her hair woven into an intricate design about the face, Mortella looked into the mirror. She is skilled, she thought. There was almost nothing for her Influence to improve upon. Rising from the dressing table, she examined herself one last time in the full-length mirror. It fitted her perfectly. It accentuated her figure in all the right ways.

Evening had come. The sun had set. Supper would be soon. She felt more at ease in the dim light of evening. The play of shadows and not the glare of sunlight was her world. It was a game. She would win and get it over with. Leaving her chamber, she descended the grand stairway that led back into the entrance vestibule. The formal rooms extended off this. Tonight would be formal. The "lovers" were meeting properly for the first time.

She did not feel quite ready. Leaving the vestibule, she followed the sound of cascading water. This led her out into the immaculately manicured gardens. Jasmine and daphne blooms shimmered iridescent white. A gentle breeze spread their fragrance throughout the garden. Mortella looked up. There, silhouetted against the starlit sky, was the Tower. Strengthening herself with its presence she turned and re-entered the light. There she headed off to begin the campaign that had been set before her. Ready to submit in order to conquer.

Chapter 5

The trip was easy and took only a day. The sun was well past its zenith as they disembarked from the cart. All that greeted them were a few ramshackle buildings in what, euphemistically, could have been called the centre of the village. These overlooked a small, bare area of compacted soil that contained a few scattered stalls. A smattering of people were still making some final purchases before the most diligent of sellers would call it a day. Silas could see why the elderly couple had seen the need to dry their fish. There just wouldn't have been the demand here to keep them going. Expanding the reach of their product would have been a necessity. Essential to keep things above water, literally.

Felix gestured toward the building furthest to the left. Silas nodded and followed him. The elderly couple usually frequented the alehouse in the latter part of the day. It was there that Felix had first met them before being invited back to their plot for fish stew. Felix entered the establishment. Silas remained outside and had a quick look about. He saw an elderly couple slowly making their way along the lane behind the building. He informed Felix who emerged from the entrance just as the couple turned the corner, coming face to face with Silas.

Their faces lit up with delight at seeing Silas before settling into one of confusion as they looked rapidly from one to the other of the brothers.

"Well, you did say you were twins," the woman exclaimed.

"Joshua, Sarah, this is Silas … my brother," Felix began.

"Ain't that the truth!" Joshua replied. "Never seen two things look as much alike as you two."

"Lovely to meet you, Silas, I'm Sarah, and this craggy old codger is Joshua," the woman added.

"Come and have a drink," Joshua continued as he grabbed Silas' elbow and turned him towards the alehouse door. "It's the perfect way to end a day."

"Or spend an afternoon," Sarah chimed in.

"Can be just as good in the morning too," Joshua smirked as he winked at his wife.

"We'd never get you out if you 'ad your way," she chuckled in return. "And what are you doing back in these parts?" she continued, turning back to Felix.

"Coming back to see the two of you, actually. We have come up with something we'd like your opinion on," he responded as they all entered the building. "Something that I think you might like."

"Let's get a drink first. Talking is thirsty work," Joshua advised.

"You find everything thirsty work," Sarah admonished with a laugh.

"It's the golden lubricant of all social fabric. Such a thing as that is never out of place my dear … And it never has done us no 'arm," was the response. He coupled this with a soft pat to his wife's ample posterior. She giggled and blushed slightly.

"Four pints, George, if you please."

"Of course, Joshua. How are you, Sarah?"

"Bright and chipper as always, George, thank you."

"Who are your friends?"

"You remember Felix who has a fish farm to the east?" Sarah explained.

"Indeed. Welcome back, Felix. You enjoyed your stay enough to return!"

"Indeed, I did, George. Some of the best ale I've ever had," Felix replied.

"My own brewing. A secret recipe that is. And that's your brother?" George looked closely at Silas. "Like two peas in a pod … but more so. How'd your mother ever tell you apart?"

"She didn't. Well not unless we wore the different coloured belts she made for us. It made for a lot of fun as kids," Silas laughed. "The amount of mischief we could get into."

"I've no doubts," George said.

"We'll be at our usual spot."

"Of course, Joshua, where else would you be? Won't be long," George laughed as he made his way back to the bar.

Sitting next to Sarah in a wooden booth with well-worn leather benches, Joshua looked out the rather dusty window before gesturing for the brothers to sit opposite.

"How'd the salt'n go?" he asked as they took their places.

"Not as well as hoped, unfortunately," answered Felix, "but we may have stumbled onto something even better," he continued with a smile.

"You don't say." Joshua paused. "And you want a bit of advice?"

"You're the best!" Felix said with a grin.

Sarah smiled back at him. "You certainly know how to soften him up." Then looking at her husband she added with a wink, "But then, it's the truth."

Joshua winked back at her, "And well you know it."

"So, what is this better thing?" she asked as George arrived with the ale.

"Felix calls it fish essence," chimed in Silas as Felix explained the process to the others.

"We'll have to give it a go then and see if it's as good as you say," Joshua stated after Felix had finished.

"I think that that means dinner for us all at the plot tomorrow," added Sarah, downing the last of her pint.

Felix brought out one of the containers of the essence he had brought with him. Sarah took it with interest.

"I wouldn't open it in here," he warned, "it does contain a bit of a punch."

"If a fish man like you is saying that … well, then it must have some clout," she laughed as she put it away in her bag. "So tomorrow for dinner. That's set. What about another round?"

"I'll get that one," said Felix already getting up and making his way to the bar.

"That's the spirit," chimed in Joshua.

By the time Felix had returned carrying four more pints, a tray of bread and cheese had already made its way to the table. Silas was regaling the couple with some of the funnier and more bizarre tales of mishap and misadventure from their region.

"… And I'm sure that it's true. Even if I didn't see it happen myself. What else could be the explanation?"

"Oooh, so true, dear. There are so many things that are strange but true," agreed Sarah.

"What about here?" asked Silas. "There must be similar tales."

"Indeed, there are!" said Joshua. "We spoke about one such tale with your brother when he last was 'ere. Most strange it was."

"Really," encouraged Silas, "how so?"

"It was a few cycles ago. We had only just started having some success with the dried fish," began Joshua.

"It was now being sent to a number of places further away from our little village," added Sarah. "With just this tiny bit of success … it meant our tithe also increased." She looked at her husband who frowned back at her. "It made things quite difficult that quarter."

"It did," he nodded, "but we managed to get the tithe together … just in time."

"We wouldn't want to miss that. Particularly with what happened," Sarah added as she crunched down on the crusty bread with a healthy amount of cheese on top.

"What happened?" asked Silas.

"There had always been a few rumours. They had never been the most sociable sort of folk," explained Joshua, lowering his voice as he looked over his shoulder toward the bar.

"But the boys were lovely, very polite and always spotless," added Sarah.

"Boys ain't supposed to be spotless, Sarah!" responded Joshua as he pulled at his beard nervously.

"But they were very clever. They would use the largest words. They never were any sort of problem," Sarah objected, ignoring his discomfort.

"Mrrrrr, they were odd. Can't see how one can trust a man who doesn't like a pint or two. No-one ever saw him in 'ere."

"No, and their mother wasn't one to stay about for a chin wag," Sarah added, "but apart from that, no-one had a bad thing to say about them."

"No, no-one did," Joshua agreed, "but then no-one really had anything to say about them. Well not until they weren't about anymore to hear it."

"What did they say about them?" asked Silas.

Sarah looked at her husband. After receiving a nod she leant forward over the table before saying in a quiet voice, "They had books and could read! I'm sure that those boys could read too. It would explain why they were so ... so ... well ... so different."

"No-one around here wanted anything to do with ... books," Joshua explained in an equally quiet voice. "Not allowed. That's only for those fancy sort of people. Not for normal folks like us."

"They kept to themselves ... mostly. Polite. They were even generous when Tiberius' barn burnt down. There was no way that he could have afforded all that lumber without them."

"True, that's true, my dear. But where did they get the money? There's none of us here about, that has much more than what's needed to keep going."

"What did they grow on their plot?" interrupted Felix. "It must have been doing well."

Joshua looked at Sarah and she returned the look before facing the twins. "That's something that the rest of us would like to know," she said with a nod. "They were always there on tithe day. Never missed a quarter."

"What did they bring?"

"Never saw," Joshua sighed.

"It wasn't for lack of trying, mind you," Sarah added, looking at her husband. "Joshua wasn't the only one to try. I know of at least another half dozen who tried to see the tithe. Or take a quick peek at the ledger after."

"No success. Not once. George once had a look at the ledger. Don't help that none of us can read."

"Surely you could have just had a look at their plot to see what was growing," Silas said.

"Mavis said that her sister said that Tyler and his wife never saw anything," Sarah explained.

Silas looked confused. "Who are they?"

"Mavis, she crafts sweaters from the felt made from goat's hair. She collects all the hair that falls in the milking yards in the district …"

"And how does she know …"

"Oh … she has a sister who was friends with the Ponstans."

"And the Ponstans …"

"The Ponstans had the plot next to the plot of Fens."

"Who are the Fens?"

"The Fens are the family that disappeared," Sarah explained as if it were obvious.

"Oooh," exclaimed Silas.

"Nothing growing at all?" Felix sounded surprised. "How did they survive?"

"Indeed," Joshua muttered.

"Indeed, indeed!" Sarah exclaimed.

"So, what happened to them?" Silas asked.

"No-one knows. Soon after the quarterly tithe a few turns ago they just weren't there anymore." Sarah looked upset as Joshua looked incredibly nervous.

"Tyler went to have a look. No-one was home. Not that day nor any other day since. All gone … the boys as well. Wouldn't wish that on no-one. No matter how odd they are," Joshua added.

"I've always heard tales of families disappearing," said Felix, "but this is the first time that I have met someone who knew a family that did."

"Never seen again. It's all far too strange. Tyler was sure there was no-one left. Despite that he and his family would often hear things … odd things, coming from the direction of the house. Worse at night. Dreadful sounds. Like someone dying, over and over again, night after night."

"They're a fair bit further east now, the Ponstans," Sarah explained. "They gave up their plot and moved into a village. Couldn't face bringing up their girls next to a place like that."

"And now? What's the plot like now?" Silas probed.

"No sensible person goes near there now." Joshua gave Silas a dark look. "Sinister dealings. They were into things more than just books. Things no-one should be. Could only have one outcome." He looked over his wife and then back at Silas. "None of us wants the same, do they?" Joshua with furrowed brow had begun fidgeting with the near empty pint in front of him.

"Absolutely not," began Felix while letting his brother know not to ask any further questions. "Such places are best left to themselves. Very wise that the Ponstans decided to move." Turning to Silas he said, "I think our glasses are slightly dry, dear brother." As Silas rose, Felix turned back to the elderly couple and began a lively discussion into finer points of fish husbandry.

***

The morning broke clear and warm. Nothing unusual about that. Silas and Felix made their way downstairs to get some breakfast. Sleep had been deep and dreamless for both. Being a bit further away from the Tower helped, but it was more likely due to the copious amount of alcohol consumed over the previous evening. In this bright new day, the muffled voices that formed the background to both their lives were less penetrating. Talk had been free and easy between the four of them, but further discussion of the Fens and their plot had been avoided. There was no need to delve further. The anxiety that it provoked did not justify it. Rumour and hearsay were the only things more that their companions could contribute. Far better to investigate the plot themselves, and that better to be done in the light of day.

With breakfast done the brothers left their lodgings for a walk. What remained of the Fens' plot was north and several hours' walk away from the village. It was the last plot before the slopes of the Northern boundary of the Bowl made cultivation of the land difficult. Trying not to draw too much attention Felix led Silas eastwards away from the village.

"Why are we going this way?" asked Silas.

"So as not to draw any attention," replied Felix. "Don't want anyone to know that we're interested in the place." Silas looked about them. The stalls in the village square were yet to be set up. The two of them were the only ones out and about.

"The attention of whom?" he scoffed, waving his arms about him. "There's no-one here." Turning back to Felix, he added, "And anyway, didn't George say that visiting the Fens' place was the usual dare amongst the boys in these parts? It seems to be something of a local site of interest."

"Well, it's best to be safe than sorry," was the only response he received.

Once out of sight of the village Felix turned them northwest. Still being careful not to be seen, he led them across several well-cared-for plots to join the cart track that headed north. The walk was easy and pleasant. The land about them was lush and green with a smattering of clover across the paddocks. Here, well-fed, glossy black cattle meandered amongst the trees. Good natured and calm, they observed the travellers with minimal interest before concentrating their attention back on the task of grazing.

As the brothers drew closer to the lower parts of the Northern Slopes the land became overgrown and less well-kept. The homesteads were now further apart with non-arable rocky ground becoming more common. It all looked less hospitable and far less conducive to achieving a good living.

"Not somewhere I would look at staying," observed Silas.

"No," agreed Felix. "I can see why the Ponstans wanted to leave. Even without the problem of the Fens."

Unaware that they had been slowly climbing for some time, they crested a small rise. Here they were surprised to find themselves looking down over quite a different landscape. The ground fell away from them. About a league further on it began to rise and merge into the northern rim of the Bowl. The land here was once again lush and green without the rocky outcrops that had dominated the last hour of their journey.

Continuing on, they passed a track that led off to the right. The previously well-worn path was now partially obscured by grass. It made its way through a broken gate toward a cottage that had seen better days. Nature had started to reclaim the land and what had been built on it.

"The Ponstans' no doubt," Silas observed before directing his attention back to the overgrown track in front of them.

"It can't be much further then," added Felix. "Just as well, if we want to make it in time for fish stew."

"We better get on then," agreed Silas as he picked up the pace along the just-visible path amongst the greenery.

They were barely a quarter-hour further on when they heard a harsh, high-pitched squeal coming from in front of them and off to the left. They both stopped, hearts racing. The unpleasant sound caused a shiver to rise up their backs as they covered their ears in disgust.

A grima! thought Felix with revulsion.

Almost as bad as it was at the Tower. But only less so because it's further away, agreed Silas.

We've only ever heard them with our minds before!

What does it mean?

That we need to put up our barriers.

How will that work if we hear it with our ears?

Just do it! We will cover our ears if we need to. Don't let them in.

Breaking the connection, Felix concentrated on strengthening the protections about his mind, building one layer upon another and another to shield himself from whatever it was that might try to invade his mind. He felt Silas do the same. The grima, unpleasant and disgusting in its nature, was always there just on the boundary of their perception. Rarely did it intrude but when it did it hurt and made thinking difficult. Silas' recent experience with the Tower showed that when there were many of them, things could get much worse. This was hopefully only one. All caution needed to be taken.

They made their way along the track with care. A further five minutes brought them to a derelict wooden gate that had once blocked the track. Beyond, they could see the remains of the Fens' cottage. The roof had all but collapsed. Above what remained of the front wall could be seen the branches of a young tree growing within the deserted house. These began to sway as the breeze picked up a pace.

Without warning the sound hit them again. Tangible, almost like a physical insult. They blocked their ears. It was louder and more penetrating than previously. It came from just beyond the cottage. Unlike those at the Tower, it did not attempt to invade their minds. It seemed content merely to assault their senses. It ceased as abruptly as it started. Felix gestured for Silas to remain there while he would go forward to look. Despite the sun being high in the sky, he felt a cold chill as he crept towards the house.

Reaching the porch, he looked through one of the shattered windows. It was as he would have imagined. Remnants of wooden furniture were scattered across a floor that had been decimated by the weather and time. Bits of broken pottery and a few pieces of cloth could also be seen strewn amongst the decay.

The grima started again … but then stopped before the sound had barely registered.

Felix worked his way around to the side of the house as he waved Silas to make for the porch. Whatever was making the sound, it was different to what he was used to. Nothing was probing his barriers. Slowly and carefully, he removed some of them to allow his mind to search the space behind the house. He felt nothing. Being this close he should have been able to localise it. Know where it was. He replaced the barriers as the screech came again. Inhuman and jarring, it again stopped abruptly.

Finally reaching the back corner of the cottage, Felix glanced around the corner before standing up straight and calling out to Silas to come.

"It didn't feel the same!" he stated as Silas silently arrived by his brother's side.

"What is it?" Silas asked.

"See for yourself," Felix answered as he turned the corner and pointed.

There in front of them was a partially collapsed windvane. The blades intermittently connected with a sheet of iron that was resting on its side, having fallen from where it must have once been. As they watched the wind picked up again. They watched while the shrill sound emerged as the blades scraped the metal, causing them both to cringe at the sound.

"Well, that's easily fixed," cried Silas as he raced forward and dragged the metal away from the blade. "No more people dying night after night now."

"Look at this," indicated Felix. There was a tube connected to the base of the collapsed tower holding the windvane. Water was intermittently leaking out of it. "There was quite a stream when the blades were turning."

"Where's it coming from?"

Felix looked about. A bit further away from the cottage he noted that the ground had subsided, leaving a depression. He walked over to it. It appeared that there was something covering a hole or well of some type. Scraping away the topsoil revealed a rotting, broken wooden panel. A handle located towards one edge indicated that the panel was supposed to be lifted.

"It looks a bit like our cellar at home," commented Silas, looking over his brother's shoulder. "Give it a go."

Felix pulled the handle without moving the panel.

"I expect the hinges are rusted. Let's both give it a go," suggested Silas as he too bent over and took hold of the handle.

"On the count of three, one … two … three." Together they pulled, causing the panel to crack and break free of its surrounds. Regaining their balance, they looked down into the darkness with stone steps leading down into it.

"A lot larger than ours," said Felix, turning to his brother. "We're going to need some light."

"Might be something still in the cottage," suggested Silas, gesturing toward the crumbling building.

"It's worth a go," agreed Felix.

Leaving the opening they made their way past the slowly turning blades of the windvane. Both noted the water that came out of the tube at its base in spits and spurts.

After an extensive search of the cottage, they found an old oil lamp with some liquid inside. A rusted tinder box beside it still contained the iron and a piece of flint. Taking it back to the cellar, Silas was successful in getting a feeble flame.

"There's not much oil," he stated as he started down the stairs, holding the lamp low down and in front of him. As he descended, he lowered the barriers about his mind and reconnected with Felix.

Chapter 6

She craved solitude. With so many servants it was almost impossible to ever be fully alone. But this was what she needed. To be alone. She had never been one who depended on the presence of others. Her existence did not reside in their recognition of her. She knew her worth and that was all she needed. Sitting now within the garden listening to the cascading water was as close as she could get to being alone. She was fully aware, however, that she was being observed. Was this for her benefit? She was not sure. A simple flick of her hand would result in the attendance of a servant inquiring after her needs. Or was this a minder who was charged to report her activities to others?

The past few evenings had gone well. She had made sure that they would. The skill of Cook was extensive, and this helped. They had yet to endure a dish that had not been excellent. Being well aware of the effect that too much good food would have, Mortella, however, rationed her servings. Pride in her appearance was integral to her. She could use Influence for the benefit of others but that did not affect her. She would still see and know if she was losing her figure.

Charles was at least handsome. That helped. Ambitious to a fault but educated. He made interesting conversation yet was not nearly as worldly as he thought. He wanted power.

Mortella laughed to herself. Power, she thought, you have no idea. Your world, limited by the borders of the Bowl and you think that you have, or will get, power?

This in itself underlined the urgency that she felt. The need to get out of this confined space. Back to the real world beyond the mountains.

Thinking back over the last few nights, Mortella pondered how easy it had been to manipulate her betrothed. When a man feels so superior to everyone else, they tend not to notice when their ego is being caressed. Unaware that their opinions are being redirected elsewhere. And that is a word to the wise, she thought, I must never let myself get into a similar position. Always be aware of those around you. Never assume anything.

Glancing towards the house she observed the figure standing discreetly behind a pillar. Strategically placed with just enough view of her to be ready to attend yet partially hidden to give the illusion of privacy. She flicked a finger. Instantly the figure emerged and came straight forward.

"Milady?"

"A goblet of wine."

"Your usual?"

"Naturally."

At least this would give her a moment of pure solitude before his return with the aforementioned wine.

She liked to play little games with them. It kept her entertained and flexed her Influence muscles. Exactly how nimble were they when carrying the soup tureen over what now appeared to be shifting sand? Keeping her face a mask of sensual tranquillity as she ran a nail gently down the pewter, she was able to taunt them. She considered further. Did they keep their austere exterior when they could hear the sound of copulation in the room adjacent? It amused her. Tensing her lips as she closely watched the manservant by the door, she created the illusion. She was impressed. He had done well. Just the merest narrowing of the eyes and rise of the eyebrows in reaction to what he thought he heard.

How long would they remain at their station following the sight of billowing smoke engulfing them? It was all a matter of perception. Such thoughts and dalliances with their senses allowed her to pass the time. And there was so much time with so little to occupy her.

For as long as she could remember, she always had work to do. Some of this had been palatable, some odious, but it was work. It gave time structure. A meaning to existence. Now without any responsibility, time dragged. She was there to breed. Nothing more. If she wanted more, she would have to create it. This was what she intended to do. There was much that the Tower could still teach … if she were patient. It was a wealth of power. Very few attempted to tap this. Could its depth of Influence be manipulated when outside the Tower? To have this seemingly endless source of Influence at her disposal … well, that would ensure her rise to the Presence. While she waited in exile, she would devote herself to this.

The wine arrived. A silver tray carrying a decanter filled with the dark ruby liquid together with a long-stemmed pewter goblet. Sensuously she ran her finger around the lip of the goblet. It felt more like her. She was nothing like the fine crystal flutes that glinted in the candlelight at dinner. These had no strength to them. They were weak and insubstantial. Pewter had strength. It held a shadowy depth under its surface that captured and held onto the light. Far more in keeping with who she was.

It would soon be time to return upstairs to arrange herself for dinner. It had been essential to address the choice of clothes prepared for her. She needed to demonstrate who she was. A seamstress had been summoned early the first day following her arrival. Mortella knew what would draw a man's eye and where it would land. Simplicity demonstrated confidence. All those frills and frippery were distracting. These were removed. Colour was important. A powerful woman need not succumb to constructed norms of femininity. With her bronzed auburn hair and pale complexion, the darker hues were complementary. No pinks or pastels but deep olives, myrtle, cobalt, violet and black. The materials were to shimmer, to flow about her and hug her figure with carnality. Silks and satins that were luminous in the candlelight had been chosen. A new garment was commissioned to be ready each evening before supper. This had to be achieved. To this she added a bit of Fae glamour. The overall effect on Charles was as expected. He was entranced yet still he had not bedded her. His straitlaced propriety and upper-class formality appeared to hinder any advance. Her time was right. She did not want to wait for another cycle. She needed him to perform this night.

Draining her wine, Mortella stood.

"Ask the maid to attend me," she announced to the air as she left the garden. Out of the corner of her eye she saw her shadow leave his pillar and disappear. She knew that the maid would be waiting outside her chamber by the time she arrived.

The dress was perfect. It was black with long sleeves. The fitted bodice had a modest, yet plunging, neckline that allowed for titillating glimpses of her porcelain skin. This demure sexuality paired perfectly with the hobble skirt. It gave the impression of fragility coupled with a raw sensuality. Her hair she left free. No ornate styling tonight. She wanted to project the impression of being free – to be an enigma. She was a woman of decorum who was reckless. A dichotomy. One who displayed vulnerability that concealed ferocity.

Despite being ready on time, she waited in her chamber till well after the dinner bell had rung. He was not one used to waiting. It would do him good. He would pace a bit. He would snap at the servants. But he would notice her as she entered. He was so used to being deferred to. Her insolence would provoke a greater desire within him. That she could use.

***

She had returned to her chamber afterwards. She never slept in the same bed after the act had been done. Her sisters had been very clear on that fact. It was a contract. The contract did not extend to anything further than that which had been previously stipulated. That only included the physical. Nothing emotional and never let your guard down in front of the john. This included relaxing and most particularly sleep.

Sleep was not going to come easily. Well not easily for her. In his own chamber he would be already snoring. She felt betrayed. Betrayed by the Code. It had come and taken her away from the sort of life she detested, now only to put her straight back into it again. For how long? Only for as long as needed to get the child. And a child she must have. One to save her from this life. One that would allow her once again to return to who she was.

Staring blankly at the ceiling, Mortella wrapped her arms about herself, hugging herself tightly. Her dress had served its purpose. Now ripped, it hung on her body as a homage to her determination. It would be burned in the morning. She hoped that this had been enough.

***

Silas needed to duck his head as he entered the stairwell. It was just wide enough for him to progress without scraping his shoulders as he descended. The light from the lantern was poor but it illuminated the stone of the walls. Felix saw it just as if he was descending the stairs himself.

They went to a lot of effort constructing this, he projected to Silas, *all the dirt held back by stone blocks.*

It goes deep. This is a lot more than a cellar, Silas responded.

He took his time. The steps were covered with something soft and squelchy that made the surface slippery. Placing his feet carefully to avoid slipping, he slowly continued. Suddenly he stopped.

It's flooded. I just stepped in water, complained Silas. He lifted the lamp higher in front to reveal a tunnel that extended away from him. They could just make out the light's reflection on the rippling surface of inky black water.

Are you at the bottom?

Don't know.

Can you see how deep the water is?

No.

Are you going to find out?

It's cold?

And …

Oh, alright, whinged Silas as he placed one foot deeper into the water as he felt for the next step. This was repeated several more times before he was waist-deep in the water.

I think I'm on the bottom. It's a bit wider now and the tunnel keeps going.

I can't see anything in the dark.

Neither can I. I'm going in a bit further.

The lamp flickered and dimmed.

Better be quick, there's not a lot of oil.

Silas looked behind him.

I can still see the light coming down the stairs. There's only one way to go!

Silas started splashing his way into the darkness.

Be careful, you never know what's under— Felix warned as Silas suddenly slipped and disappeared under the surface of the water. It was freezing. On losing his balance, Silas had fallen face first and was engulfed by the water. He dropped the lamp as he hit his knee hard on the tunnel floor. He floundered about as he searched under the water.

No point going any further. Come back up.

I think that I kicked something with my foot.

What?

If I knew, I would tell you!

It was probably just the lamp.

No, it wasn't the lamp, Silas responded irritably. *It was something different.* He continued searching under the water. Eventually his hand landed on a hard, smooth object that he grabbed and pulled out of the water. Keeping hold of it, he turned and made his way back to the light that marked the way out.

Freezing, he emerged into the afternoon light, displaying a lidded metal box to Felix as he did.

"Definitely not the lamp!"

"No," was the simple, emotionless reply. "Let's look in the cottage and see if there's anything dry I can change into."

In one of the collapsed rooms there was a clothes chest still containing garments from the previous owners. In there they were able to find Silas at least something dry to change into. When he was once again warm and dry, they turned their attention to the metal box. It was smooth and unadorned with a firmly fitting hinged lid.

"It can't have been in the water long," observed Felix.

"Why do you say that?"

"Well, just look at it?"

"So!"

"It's still smooth. No corrosion. The hinges aren't rusted. If we left something metal in the water … it would only be a matter of weeks …"

"It doesn't look like our sort of metal," said Silas, turning it over in his hands. "I don't remember ever seeing something quite like this." He handed it to Felix to have a closer look.

The box fitted easily in his hand. It was about half a handspan long and about half that again wide. It was smooth and felt cool to the touch. Silas nodded as Felix attempted to prise the lid open. After some effort the lid opened, revealing a folded parchment inside that had been protected from the water. Taking it out, Felix unfolded it.

On the parchment was a diagram surrounded by writing. An arrow pointed to the top of the page. In the diagram there was a square with a cross next to it. Extending from the cross towards the top of the page was a snaking black line that ended at another cross. This was surrounded by several inverted Vs. On one side of the diagram were several columns of numbers with a sun and a moon above them. On the other side were several lines of writing that were indecipherable to Felix. After examining it he handed it to Silas. He looked at it closely before taking the box. After carefully folding the parchment, he placed it back inside and closed the lid.

"What do you think it means?" he asked his brother.

"It seems to be a map … most likely a map of the tunnel we just found," Felix replied. "Rumours normally have an element of truth to them. This one appears to have more than the average."

"Because?"

"Sarah and Joshua said the Fens were different. They told me that they were sure that they had something that was not of the Bowl, pointing at the box. Probably not this, but it suggests that there could be other things. They could read. No-one knew what they produced on their plot … but they always paid their tithe. All of a sudden, they disappeared. Right after the tithe when the Town guards were here for the Tower. And now it seems that they had a way out."

Silas looked at his brother as he repeated, "A way out …"

"We best be heading back. We will need to change." He gave Silas a once over and added, "Particularly you."

He turned to leave before looking back at his brother.

"No, no!" he continued forcefully as he shook his head. "We are not doing that ... not yet. There is a lot more we need to know. We need to prepare. We will be back. Now we need to have fish stew."

Silas reluctantly started to follow his brother. He knew that they had to head back. He also knew that, eventually, he would get to explore the tunnel.

***

It had been a fitful sleep. Against every urge to expunge his sweat and odour from her skin, she had not bathed when she had got back to her chambers. She needed to give it every chance to succeed. Now as the maid drew back the curtains allowing the morning light to enter, Mortella arose and demanded hot water be brought. Scrubbing herself in the fragrant water helped purge the previous night from her mind. She would focus on one thing. Getting the child and delivering it to the Tower. Everything else was merely in aid of that.

Had it happened? she thought to herself as she examined her naked belly after the bath. *How does one tell?* In the shop they were all supposed to be careful. None were supposed to work during the mid-cycle. But the lure of an extra dollar could lead to an extra mouth to feed. It was not only those who were careless that succumbed. There were those of her sisters who actively pursued a child. This in the hope that a child would attach the john to them. That they would be whisked away to another life. This didn't happen. The father could never be proved. Only the mother was certain and this so much more so in the shop than anywhere else.

She didn't feel any different. Should she? Was it too early to know?

Having dismissed the maid, Mortella slowly dressed in a plain, simple, dark green dress. Daytime attire that was comfortable without the need to be alluring. She never saw Charles except in the evening. So, the effort would be wasted.

She normally broke her fast on the terrace by the fountain. Here she could quietly sit and gaze at the Tower's dark silhouette that appeared to the east high above the garden. Despite her eagerness to leave the Tower and the Bowl, the Tower was the closest thing that she had ever had to a home. The one place where she had felt safe and protected.

Now dressed, she made her way to the terrace. Word to the servants would be racing through the house as she left her chamber. If she moved at an elegant pace, her tea would be there ready for her when she arrived. Shortly after, chilled fresh fruits would arrive, and any special request could be made for Cook. It was like a well-rehearsed dance with all the participants waiting in the wings to make their entrance at exactly the right time.

She was hungry. She had been careful in what she ate the previous evening. Nothing too strongly spiced so it wouldn't linger on the breath. Not too much so that his weight on her would be bearable. Pouring her tea sent a signal to her minder. When asked, she requested that Cook should surprise her with something both filling and delicious. It arrived hot and steaming before she had finished her second cup of tea. Once again, Cook did not disappoint.

Now comfortably full in the warm morning air after a restless night, Mortella gradually became drowsy. She lay back upon the day bed as visions began to skirt on the edge of her consciousness. She began to doze. She felt Charles' hand on her thigh as he smiled at her. To her confusion she smiled back as she rested her head upon his chest. She ruminated on her actions as she examined them from a point outside of herself. He had been a considerate lover. He had been active and looked to her enjoyment. But she was there against her will. There only to get a child.

Things faded and now she saw his face contorted with passion. There was a darkness to his eyes. They held a need so intense that it was vicious in its craving. This did not scare her. It caused her heart to race, her breathing to quicken. She saw herself return the stare with the same look in her eyes. As if frozen in time, she could see every detail of her own face as it too began to distort with yearning and desire. Opening her mouth, she felt a light brush upon her lips ...

She awoke with a start. There, framed by the blue sky, was Charles, looking down at her. He smiled but said nothing. He placed beside her a single long stem containing several dark purple flowers. Each flower was formed by a cylindrical helmet with two large upper petals. Leaving before she was able to say anything he made his way back into the house. She watched him leave, seeing him turn and wave a gloved hand at her before disappearing from view.

Looking beside her, she caught herself. Beauty and danger frequently go together. She looked towards the house. Charles was a lot more than he seemed. Taking the serviette that was left on the tray she picked up the flower. She was careful not to touch it or the sap oozing from it. She would keep it. One never knew when something like this would be needed.

Wolfsbane was not easy to find.

Chapter 7

There is a lot of essence, thought Felix as he ladled off the liquid that had formed on top. He looked at the grey sludge that had once been small energetic fish. It happens to us all, he mused. Pouring it carefully into another of the bottles, he smiled. Sarah had loved it. Joshua had also agreed that it was very good. Felix had been happy to share the process with them. He was happy that they could also benefit from his discovery. They had promised not to pass on the secret to anyone else. Not that he felt that it really mattered. There were not a lot of fish farmers in the Bowl.

Just now he needed a bit of time to himself. He was taking things slowly so he could enjoy the solitude. Silas had been hounding him nonstop about when they would return to the north.

"We need to look into it further," he stated over and over again. "What is there outside the mountains? Surely you must want to know."

Felix was not sure that he did want to know. The Tower was something that they had lived with. It had been there for much longer than either of them. It was at least a known threat even if he didn't quite understand why. Outside the Bowl … well that was something very different. They had no idea of what to expect. Within the mountains their life was good. There was nothing to suggest that what was outside would be better. The Tower could be protecting them from something worse. Anyway, they didn't even know if this was a map out of the Bowl.

He capped the latest bottle and placed it carefully into the crate. They had almost one hundred filled bottles now. It was time to start a concerted effort to get people to try it. A taste test would be best. Fish stews – one with and one without the essence for customers to try. He would talk to Fanny. She made some of the best stews. He was sure that she would like a bit of extra coinage. Especially with the twins growing so fast.

I've asked around. The magistrate will be coming through in a few days. Perhaps we can show it to him.

It could say anything. How can we risk it? What if it says something bad?

How else are we going to know what it says unless we ask someone who knows how to read?

We have to find someone we can trust. Or at least someone who doesn't know who we are.

That means that we will need to go to Town. There are people there who we can pay to read it.

At least we can be anonymous.

When will we go?

Let's talk when you get home, proposed Felix as he shut down the connection with his brother. His patience was wearing thin. Silas knew how to provoke him. And provoke him he would, until he got his way. Almost every fibre in him felt that this was a bad idea. That they should just leave it alone. But he knew himself and knew that he could be over-cautious. The Tower had taken, and was Taking, people. He thought back to the visions from the Tower. Such a deep sadness. Fear and loss, yearning and heartache made up the Tower. 'Not to be tolerated' meant that the stories were true. Doing nothing was not an option but doing something terrified him.

Finishing the last of the barrels, he put the lids back on and picked up the crate. With that much salt the essence wouldn't spoil so he was keeping the bottles undercover just outside the house. No need to take up space in the cellar. Before returning home, he stopped. Sitting down on the slope overlooking the lower dam he took a deep breath. He missed the calm of this place each time he went away. Silently he listened. He heard the sound of water and that of a gentle breeze in the trees. His eyes passed over the green grass that merged into the clay-rich soil that surrounded the lower dam. They then settled on the sparkling blue water that reflected the brilliant sky above. Occasionally its surface broke as an unsuspecting dragonfly filled the belly of a bluefin. He craved peace and quiet. He knew that Silas would keep at him. Resigning himself to the fact that the sooner they went the sooner they would be back, he picked up the crate and continued home.

∗∗∗

It surprised her. She enjoyed it … and him. He was able to do things that her john never had. It was something to look forward to after a day of boredom.

He wasn't exactly gentle, but his intensity and ferocity excited her. A primal physicality that was able to be aroused and enticed her. Over the last few weeks, they had indulged their passions, but she never stayed. Always making her way back to her own chambers to rest. Now in the midmorning sun she was again lounging on the terrace in front of the fountain.

She had forgotten to eat this morning. Just a cup of peppermint tea to settle the stomach. She had been eating more elaborately than she normally would. This was playing with her digestion. A day of simple fare should settle things down. Turning her head, she gazed up at the Tower. She had not forgotten the promise she had made to herself. She would make her way back into the Tower and learn from it. Learn how to use and manipulate the store of Influence it held. How was she to get back in? She was no longer one of the Code, but she knew the Tower. She would not demean herself and ask the Abbatissa for aid. No, she would ask the Tower itself. If the Tower granted her access, then the Abbatissa could not deny her. If the Tower had chosen her for this task that was outside of the Code … and the Presence bowed to that … then even the Presence would not oppose the Tower's will in letting her back in. She would go to the Tower and speak with it. Ask for its permission to re-enter. But she might just wait until she was feeling a bit better.

***

With the sun barely over the Eastern Slopes, the twins walked into the square through the main gate. Felix moved to the side to allow one of the carts full of produce for market to safely pass. He looked at Silas beside him who indicated that they should head further up into Town. The scribes and apothecaries were found a bit further up the slopes. It had been agreed that they would close down their connection whilst in Town. Being so close to the Tower increased the background voices. Those that had been so intrusive and distressing during Silas' last visit. They also did not want to draw any unwanted attention to themselves. Just two nondescript farmers requiring the services of a scribe to settle a business matter. Nothing unusual about that. That was until the scribe had read the text.

They were prepared. Felix would let drop that they were from the south of the Bowl. Silas would talk about farming and the price of feed for their livestock. Making sure that they were overheard, they would speak about staying a few days in Town to see family and deal with some business matters. Together they planned to leave a trail of false clues. Giving misdirection as to who they were and where they lived. All this just in case the text roused any unwanted interest.

Instead of staying, as soon as the text was read, they would be gone. Out of Town and away from the Tower. They would walk to the nearest village with a pickup point for the northern passenger cart. There they would take the afternoon cart north and back home.

Felix had meticulously copied the symbols from the parchment. They were not bringing the original. On one sheet he had copied the writing on the left of the snaking black line. On the second, columns of numbers with the sun and moon above. They would go to two separate scribes, showing only one of the sheets to each. They would say that they had found the sheet in their father's belongings after his death some years earlier. Now that they were in Town, they thought that they would see what it said.

Reaching the 'professional' section of Town they looked at the signs. The scribes could be identified by the tell-tale quill, or ink and parchment, on the plaques over their doors. They needed to choose which two scribes they would visit. Not too close so that the first could see them enter the second. Not too far apart that it would take more time than they wanted to stay. The one they chose to visit second would be closer to the Town gate. They saw one down a side ally off the main street. It had no direct view of any of the other ones on the main street. Noting its position, they walked further up the slope.

Choosing a second scribe at random, the twins entered through a brightly coloured door. As they did, they were greeted by a friendly young man.

"Good morning, gentlemen. How can I help you?"

"We are in Town for a few days, and we were wondering if you could tell us what this is?" said Felix.

"We found it in our father's things after he passed," added Silas. Felix handed over the first sheet to the young man who looked at it.

"Oh, that's a sort of calendar," he said. "It's rather old fashioned but it still can be seen in use from time to time."

"How can you tell what dates?" asked Silas

"That will be two copper coins," was the reply. Felix handed over the money. Taking it and placing it in a box on the desk, the young man sat down. He gestured to the twins to take the seats on the other side.

Looking at the brothers the young man began. "There are three columns. The numbers under the sun tell the time. The number of hours after sunrise.

The two columns under the moon tell the month and day." He smiled at Felix. "We know that there are thirteen lunar cycles each pass and in each lunar cycle there are twenty-eight days. The first number is the day in the cycle and the second is the lunar month." Felix nodded. Silas looked at his brother and then at the man across the desk. Noting his confusion, the young man continued.

"For example, this one." He pointed at the third row of numbers. "The first number is six. So, this is the sixth hour after sunrise. That is usually when the sun is at its zenith." Looking at Silas, he clarified further, "When the sun is at the highest point in the sky." Seeing that Silas understood he continued. "Then this number is the tenth day while this indicates that it is of the fourth lunar cycle," pointing to the two numbers under the symbol of the moon. He looked at Felix. "I hope that explains things."

"Very much so. Thank you. That was very helpful," replied Felix as he stood and gestured to Silas to do the same.

"Anything else that I can help you with?" the young man asked.

"No, that was everything," Felix replied as he opened the door. Following Silas out he closed it gently, giving a wave of thanks to the man as he did.

Leaving the establishment, they turned downslope towards the second scribe. As they turned into the alley, they got a better view of the shop. It had an air of decay about it. The paint was peeling off the walls and the windows were dirty. It sent the message that it was more accustomed to the shadier side of life.

The bell above the door tinkled as they entered. The light dimmed as it was filtered through the dirty panes, and it took a moment for them to adjust. A musty smell hung in the air. It matched the figure that was seated behind the desk that confronted them. Before them was a man extensive in years. With clear blue eyes he looked up over a leather-bound book. Grey hair escaped in all directions from under a green velvet smoking cap. Both it and he had seen better days. As they stood there the old man just looked up and said nothing.

"I'm sorry, we were hoping that you could help us," began Felix tentatively.

"Some things can never be helped," the man replied with a wry smile.

Silas looked at Felix confused. Giving a sigh the man held out his hand. "Show it to me," he demanded. Giving a quick glance at Felix, who nodded, Silas handed over the second sheet to the figure. He glanced at it and then back at them before raising an eyebrow.

"Mmm," was all he said.

"And?" asked Silas.

"And … I think it was fortunate that you chose me," was the answer.

Felix looked at Silas as he asked, "Why, what's the matter? It's just something we found in our father's things."

"Mmm, that so?"

"Of course."

"Not something that might have been recently copied, perhaps?" the old man inquired. Then looking directly at Felix, he asked, "Copied from something that might have had a bit more to it?"

Felix frowned as Silas responded crossly, "What are you saying? That we are trying to hide something?"

"Well, you said it," the old man responded as he looked again at the sheet in front of him. In a slow and patient voice, he spoke. "The hand on this sheet is untrained. The one who did this does not write. This was copied." He turned the sheet over. "The parchment is new. The ink unfaded. This was written recently. Unlikely to be done by a dead father." He looked at the twins. "So, which one of you copied this?"

Felix shifted uneasily. This did not go unnoticed.

"What is it copied from?" the old man directed his question at Felix. Felix didn't answer.

In an exasperated tone, the old man continued, "If I was going to do something, do you think that I would let you know that I know?" Looking from one brother to the other he added flippantly, "I would just report it to the Town guards and let the Tower do the rest." He waited for a response.

Before Felix could answer, Silas started speaking quickly. "We found it. In an old, abandoned farm. Down south. The parchment was damaged. Only some of it was still intact. We tried to copy everything that we could see on it. We have no idea of what it says."

"Abandoned plots are abandoned for a reason," the man commented, looking at Silas. "What business did you have for visiting one?"

"It was a dare. We lost a drinking bet. It was supposed to be haunted. There was nothing there. But we found this," Felix explained quickly.

"Mmm," the old man responded. "You seem a bit too old for that sort of thing." The twins couldn't tell if he believed them or not.

"This gives instructions. Ones that the Tower would like to know about. To know about this is to provoke the Tower." Stopping, the scribe looked at Felix. "Do you want to provoke the Tower?" He waited. Looking carefully at Silas and then again at Felix with his piercing blue eyes, he continued, "It appears that you do. Very well then. There are three instructions." He read them out slowly and clearly.

"At the times specified we will be at the entrance.

We will wait one hour.

Malintent will swiftly be known."

"Does that help?" he asked with a wave of his hand. Neither of the twins responded.

"Is there anything more that you would like me to read?" he asked, giving them a knowing and mocking look.

"No, that's all we have," replied Silas.

"Of course." After a long pause, the old man added, "Well, if that is all … I have a lot to do." Then, ignoring them, he picked up his book again and started to read.

"Ah, how much?" asked Felix cautiously.

"On the house," he replied without looking up. As the twins turned to leave, the old man raised his head and said, "There are many more than just the two of you, you know," before returning to his book.

Leaving the scribe and again outside in the alley, Felix nodded at Silas who responded in kind. Without further discussion they hastily made their way back to the gate and out of Town itself.

***

Food had lost its taste. Even the thought of food made her feel ill. She felt bloated and the nagging headache just would not go away. She had made excuses the last few evenings to avoid the after-dinner engagement with Charles. It seemed to be getting worse.

Today, Mortella had decided to stay a bit longer in bed. It all just seemed a bit too much of an effort to get up and make herself presentable. And not being presentable was not an option. So, with the curtains half-drawn she lay on her back staring at nothing. The sound of the chamber door opening caught her attention. Without ceremony Mrs Poole entered her room, followed by a severe, balding man. Even this audacious intrusion into her private sanctuary was insufficient for Mortella to want to exert herself.

Stopping at the side of the bed, Mrs Poole looked down at her.

"This is Monsieur Crab," she announced, indicating the stout man behind her. "He is here to confirm the pregnancy."

"The what?" cried out Mortella.

"The pregnancy," Mrs Poole repeated calmly. "Monsieur Crab has cared for all the women in the Keep family for some decades now. He will be taking care of you."

"No need to excite yourself. It is all very normal and natural to feel a bit disorientated," Monsieur Crab began as he approached the bed. "We will just check that things are all going well. That's what we all want, isn't it?" He gave a thin, humourless smile as he said this.

Shocked at the unfolding events, Mortella found herself unexpectedly answering questions about her private bodily functions as Mrs Poole looked on. Still in a state of horror and disbelief she then endured a physical examination that left little, if any, room for modesty.

Eventually the questioning and examination were done. It was then that Monsieur Crab, completely ignoring Mortella, turned to Mrs Poole. "I expect it is five or six weeks. I will go inform the master. Rest and nutritious fluids at present, I suggest. At least until the worst of the nausea settles … if it ever does settle." He shrugged. "If it does, it should do so in about seven or eight weeks' time. If not … Well, then we will do as we must to keep the child growing and remaining healthy." Then, without even acknowledging Mortella, he left the chamber, closing the door behind him.

After he was gone, Mrs Poole looked down at the dishevelled mess in the bed.

"I will send up something for you. You will need to drink it." She then looked directed into Mortella's eyes as she sternly repeated, "You will need to drink it … all of it. I am sending up your maid. You will need to bathe and sit out of bed."

"I will prefer to remain in bed this morning," Mortella haughtily replied.

"What you prefer … is of little consequence," was the response. "You *will* bathe and sit out of bed. Fresh air and sunshine will do you good." Without waiting for any further response, Mrs Poole turned and made for the door. As she opened it, she looked back at Mortella. Staring directly into her eyes, she continued coldly, "You are carrying the heir to the Keeps. Let things be very clear from the outset." Pointedly looking at Mortella's stomach, she added, "Your wants are secondary to his." With that, she was gone.

Chapter 8

It had taken them by surprise and Felix berated himself for not having foreseen it. Of course, it would be obvious to someone who could read and write. They would be able to see when something had been copied. But how else were they to find out what it said? He had been right. It had been a bad idea. Yet it was done now. Leaving Town immediately after the old man had seen through their ruse, they had made a fairly circuitous trip home. It had given them both a scare. Felix hoped that this would be a timely warning to his brother to leave well enough alone. On arriving home, they kept to their holding for a few weeks, neither going into the village nor contacting any of their friends.

Nothing happened. The fish essence continued to collect and be harvested. Those barrels that no longer yielded any more were replaced by freshly caught bluefin and the abundance of salt required. The sun continued to shine. The breeze blew and all appeared as it always had. Felix thought that if anything had caught the Tower's attention then at least they might get some sort of warning. At least a change in the hum of the voices that made up the background to their lives. Something along the lines that Silas had experienced at the Tower. But they just continued unabated and unchanged.

It also had not taken long for Silas to begin again.

Now we know. We should go and meet them.

We don't know who they are. They could be anyone.

Not anyone. Those that are against the Tower.

How can you be sure of that?

He said that to know about this would provoke the Tower!

Yes, but that could also mean that it is the Tower that wants it to be kept secret. We could be meeting someone from the Tower.

It didn't seem like that is what he meant.

Well, let's just assume that, shall we? That will protect us, won't it? Felix added sarcastically.

Felix felt Silas' frustration as he broke the connection.

Well, how on earth can we know? Felix thought to himself, feeling the same frustration as Silas. Why should we take the risk? We just don't know.

Silas looked directly at his brother as he entered the room.

"So?"

"And why are you so determined?"

"Why aren't you?"

"Because there is so much we don't know. There's more at stake than just satisfying your curiosity."

"Exactly. There is so much we don't know. But what we do know is that people are being Taken," Silas shot back. "People, both men and women, are being tormented, destroyed, lost, all because of the Tower. What about that?"

Felix dropped his gaze and in a small voice asked, "What can *we* do?"

Walking closer, Silas laid a hand on each of his brother's shoulders. "We can do what we think is right." Raising his head, Felix looked into his brother's eyes. Silas continued softly, "We can find out the truth." He paused. "I need you. Together we might be able to make a difference. I can't do this without you."

"When is the next date?" Felix resignedly asked, fully aware that what Silas said made sense. To do nothing, when something could make a difference, was not really an option. "We will need to prepare for the worst."

"That too, but let's hope for a lot better than that," replied Silas, giving his brother a hug. "So how do you think we should approach this?"

***

More than six months after visiting Town, the brothers were once again heading northwest. They were heading back to the village under the excuse to meet up with Sarah and Joshua. One of the meeting times listed by the parchment had already passed prior to their agreement to investigate further. This necessitated them to wait until the next meeting time approached. Waiting was not something that Silas dealt with well. He wanted to act, but there was nothing that Felix could do about that. The time had not yet come. Felix had thus decided to use Silas' nervous, pent-up energy by sending him out to the neighbouring villages and hamlets in order to promote their fish essence. The travel and social nature of the work suited his brother. It was also effective in reducing some of the constant discourse forced on him about the coming trip.

Fanny's help had been invaluable. Her stews were famous in their region, so it had not been hard to get people to try her fare. Having her endorsement of the new ingredient was equally as helpful. Sales of the essence were good, and Felix was kept busy maintaining the supply. But now, while still carrying many reservations, Felix and Silas boarded the early morning cart that would take them closer to the Bowl's rim.

Felix had given the trip a great deal of thought. He assumed that the entrance would refer to the other end of the tunnel and not the opening nearest the derelict farm. They would need light, dry clothes, food and some means of protecting themselves if things turned out for the worst. What that worst could be he didn't want to imagine, but if the Tower was involved then his imagination might not do it justice.

They would need to get to the entrance well ahead of those whom they might be meeting. As he didn't know how long it would take to get from one end to the other, they would go a day early. Hopefully they would be able to exit the tunnel unobserved and find a safe place in which to wait. There they would watch unnoticed and then decide if they would engage with those who were coming. If they did indeed decide to engage then only one of them would make themselves known. The second would hold back ready to rescue the other if needed. He didn't want another surprise like the one they had in Town.

Felix looked over at his brother. Silas, eyes closed and with his head hanging forward, swayed with the rhythm of the cart as it made its way along the well-worn track. His posture was in marked contrast to that of his doppelganger who sat straight and alert at the other end of the wooden seat.

That's just like him, Felix thought. *Nothing ever seems to worry him when there's something to do. But give him a bit of peace and quiet … Well, now that we are on the road … at least he might stop pestering me.*

The trip was uneventful as they once more disembarked in the village centre. Retrieving their bags from the back of the cart they made their way to the inn where they were greeted by George as they entered.

"Back again? The ale *is* good but if you like it that much, I could send you a barrel and save you the trip," he jibed.

"And deprive us of your company?" Silas retorted. George merely grimaced as he hid a smile. Travellers were not that common in these parts and ones who paid up front whilst being pleasant company were even rarer. He enjoyed the banter Silas provided. It was a welcome distraction to the routine.

"Up the stairs to the left, you know the way," he said over his shoulder as he made his way back to the galley. "There'll be a pint waiting for you when you make your way back down."

"You know us well," Silas responded.

Once in their room, Felix unpacked their things. He placed a couple of trousers together with the map in a waxed cloth bag. With this he placed an assortment of dried fruit and nuts. These were then put at the bottom of a rucksack with an old oil lamp, extra oil, a flask of water and a tinderbox.

"We can remove our shirts and place them with the trousers before we get wet. Our shoes, well they will just have to dry out after." He looked at Silas. "I'm not sure that this will be of much use," he said, picking up the machete he had hidden under the clothes in their travel bag. "But at least it is something. It might be of help if the tunnel is overgrown."

Silas had been looking out the window to the north. Turning to his brother he asked, "When will we set off?"

"We'll need to visit Sarah and Joshua first. Let George know that we are away for a couple of days."

"But they come to the inn every evening. It will be obvious that we aren't staying with them."

"No, we will tell them that we are heading to the next village to see what opportunities there are for the essence. That will give us a cover. We shouldn't be gone for longer than that. If we are … well, we might have bigger things to worry about than what they think."

***

Just because something is constantly there doesn't mean that you get used to it. Seven or eight weeks had passed. The nausea had not. It had been her relentless companion. It woke her in the morning and prevented her sleeping at night. Her other unvarying familiar was the chamber pot by her bedside. The periodic dry retching that punctuated her day had left her throat sore and her voice raspy and dry. This, coupled with periodic cramping, just added to her discomfort.

She couldn't remember the last time she enjoyed the taste of food. Nor even the last time she had eaten something solid. Mrs Poole would arrive punctually at least three times a day and feed her a thickened mush. Tasteless and textureless, she was forced to swallow. Protests were pointless. She didn't have the strength to resist anyway.

Headaches, backaches, sleep deprivation and the sensation of being on an ever undulating ocean were the essence of her life. The canvas on which she had gradually witnessed her ever enlarging stomach. It had been invisible for many months but now there was no mistaking the bulge. No longer could she lie on her back for long. The weight, the pressure of the thing inside her, forced the acid into her throat. It disfigured her body. And it was alive. It moved, it heaved, it kicked. Like a parasite it seemed to wiggle inside her.

Her hair, limp beside her on the pillow, was hardly ever brushed. Every few days a maid would come and wash her in bed where she lay. Lifting her head was inevitably greeted by rising bile within her stomach. So, this was better than being helped to the tub. A wet comb would then be run through the tangles. It was a far cry from the elegance and glamour of her arrival. She was merely the vessel to the heir of Keep. Nothing more. This was made all the more evident by the prodding and poking of Monsieur Crab. This monstrosity would visit weekly and subject her to more humiliation than she had ever experienced in the knocking shop. If she had the energy she would have fought back, used her Influence, or at least mustered the will to hate him. But as it was, she just lay there passively enduring the degradation with little more than resignation, and the wish for it all to be over.

"The heir is growing. He's a healthy size," said Monsieur Crab as he looked at Mortella. Satisfied, he turned to Mrs Poole. "The stomach is the same as it has been?" Mrs Poole nodded.

"She is confined to bed."

"She will need to eat more. The last two months need this. What is she eating now?"

"A mixture. We extract the uncooked bone marrow and blend it with boiled rice, milk and ginger."

"And how does she take it?"

"Without complaint."

"Good. Keep the windows open and the air coming through. It would be best to get her outside but if that's not possible then at least allow the air to flow."

"He will be a strong heir," said Mrs Poole.

"So it would seem if her bile were anything to go by," agreed the physician, heading toward the door as Mrs Poole opened it for him. "Same time next week," he concluded without looking back at Mortella as he vacated the room. Mrs Poole followed, leaving Mortella alone in her misery.

Turning her head she could just make out the Tower through the open window. Its presence strengthened her as nothing else could. She would deliver this burden and then return. Regain her position and claim her right to ascend. Clamping her teeth together against the periodic cramping, she winced. This time was worse than usual. But it would pass. She would pass through all of this. Fists clenched – pushing unkempt nails into her palms could distract her from the pain. It gradually subsided, being once again accompanied by the humiliating loss of bladder control. Exhausted, she turned her head away from the window, closing her eyes as a small red puddle formed between her legs.

***

They left early and headed to the old couple's plot. They wanted to have plenty of time to go there and then get to the Fens'. Once in the tunnel they had no idea how long it would take to get through and out the other side. There was no certainty that the tunnel was even passable.

Sarah was outside in the home garden when they arrived. She waved enthusiastically as they approached.

"Must 'ave been an early start for you boys," she commented as she eyed them up and down. "I doubt that you got much to break the morning's fast. George wouldn't 'ave been alive to the world when you left." She paused. "Would you like a bit to keep you going?" Silas grinned broadly.

"You read our minds, Sarah. We came early so we had time to make our way to the next village and arrive before sundown."

"Why go there?"

"We're here and close already. We'll make a round trip. Visit a number of villages and see what opportunities there are for the fish essence," answered Felix.

"Ahhh, the energy of the young."

"Not quite so young as we used to be," responded Felix.

"But not as ancient and we hope to get, either," chimed in Silas.

Waving towards the cottage, Sarah smiled. "It will take little convincing to get the 'master' to have a second portion. Come in, come in, we'll all enjoy the extra fare."

After eating and discussing how the elderly couple were progressing with their own essence production, the brothers said their goodbyes while promising to fill them in on any interest they found. Initially they left heading west toward the nearest village. They then doubled back and made their way north as soon as they were out of sight. Walking quickly, the distance melted away until they were once again overlooking the lush green landscape that merged into the Northern Slopes. The natural border to the Bowl.

Passing through the gate that marked the old boundary of the Fens' plot they quickly rounded the derelict porch and arrived at the windvane that marked the entrance to the tunnel. The blades were turning slowly in the breeze without the piercing squeal that accompanied their last visit. Felix noted a slow trickle of water coming out of the faucet at the base of the structure.

"It might make a difference," he said as he pointed it out to his brother.

"I'm not hoping for a lot," responded Silas. "There was a great deal of water down there. Such a stream as that won't make much of a difference."

"We'll hope for the best," answered Felix as he put down his knapsack and began to unpack.

The sun was now past its zenith, but the breeze was light, and the air felt warm.

"Put your shirt in here," he directed his brother as he placed his own in the waxed cloth bag. "I've already put some trousers in. You hungry?"

"After Sarah's cooking? You've got to be kidding. The amount that that man can eat!"

"Well, we'll want something later," said Felix, taking a drink and offering it to Silas as he put the trail mix back in the bag.

"How long do you think it'll take?"

"No idea. Hopefully not too long. We're very close to the slopes," he answered as he looked up at the rocky outcrops that loomed above them to the north. "I hope that it's not more than a league or two."

"Best to get going then. Sooner in, the sooner out."

Stripped to the waist, with Felix carrying the rucksack and Silas with the now-lit lamp in one hand and the machete in the other, they made their way to the entrance. Silas led the way down the stone steps, holding the lamp in front of him.

This is where the water started the last time. Looks like that windvane has been more effective than it looks.

Let's hope so.

Carefully descending a few more steps, Silas reached the tunnel floor which was now only calf deep in water.

Well, that's better. Still cold but …

A lot easier to pass through.

Silas held the lamp up high, looking around the tunnel as Felix joined him. Someone had gone to a lot of effort. The stone steps led to a passageway slightly taller than the twins and wide enough for them to move down it with ease. It was lined with stone blocks. A necessity to keep the soil from above filling the space. The ground also seemed hard and smooth, suggesting this too was lined with stone.

A bit further on, at the limit of the lamp's light, the tunnel walls become rougher as the space was hewn out of rock that formed the base of the northern rim of the Bowl. The removal of the trapdoor, at their last visit, had allowed sticks and brush to be washed into the tunnel by the regular rainfall. These were easily sidestepped as the brothers began to move forward. The air was musty and damp as they shuffled further into the tunnel. Gradually the light from the entrance faded completely, leaving the lamp as their only source of illumination.

The darkness of the tunnel continued uninterrupted. Without the sun to document the passing of time the trip seemed eternal. Gradually, almost without realising it, the brothers found that they were no longer having to walk through water. The rough-hewn floor was no longer covered. This didn't improve the discomfort of walking in waterlogged boots, but it was welcomed nonetheless.

Uphill.

Presumably.

Did you bring socks?

Of course.

Can we?

They will only get wet.

Less so than these.

Alright.

They stopped and removed their boots, pouring out the water. Wringing out the sodden socks, they put on the dry ones before replacing the boots.

Better?

Much.

Hungry?

Yes, but not here. It can't be too much further.

Faith may move mountains but the bread falls butter-side down.

Who knows, we'll just have to wait and see.

Stooping slightly to avoid any unwanted contact with the rough tunnel ceiling, they gradually made their way forward. No longer wading through water it was obvious that they were walking up an incline. The wet leather of their shoes chafed their feet despite the change of socks. Sweat dripped over their faces, contrary to the chill in the air. After an indeterminate amount of time the sides of the tunnel expanded about them as they entered a naturally formed cave. No longer needing to stoop they stretched their backs as they looked about. This was a sizeable cavern with the light of the lamp barely illuminating the dome above. Off in the distance was a glimmer of light.

Not far.

Still daylight.

Thankfully.

It's getting cold.

I'll get out our shirts.

Dressing again as protection against the chill, the brothers picked up the pace now that the end was in view. Emerging from the cave entrance into the light of late afternoon they stopped. For the first time they were looking at lands outside the Bowl.

They were in a valley running northeast, hedged in on both sides by steeply rising mountainous walls. The sun, already shielded from them, left them in chill shadows. An icy breeze quickly wiped the sweat from their faces. Standing on the valley floor wedged between the monumental fortifications, Felix approached a quickly flowing stream. Cupping his hands he bent down and took a drink.

"Freezing," he exclaimed. "It must be freshly melted."

"It's going to get colder."

"Sorry."

"What for?"

"I didn't think of that. No blankets. It's going to be an uncomfortable night."

"A fire will help."

"A fire will be essential."

"So, where to now?" asked Silas, looking up and down the valley.

"I expect that they will come from the north, so let's hold up on the other side of the cave's opening."

"When are they coming?"

"It said two hours after sunrise."

Having filled their flask from the stream, the twins walked down the rock-strewn valley, heading away from the expected approach of whoever it was they were going to meet the following day. Gnarled and wind-swept trees dotted the landscape, testament to the winds that must funnel down the narrow gorge. Dried and broken branches blocked their way. The stream was not always so gentle.

After putting a reasonable distance between themselves and the entrance, but still being able to see it, they stopped. Climbing the slope opposite, they took shelter in a shallow fissure-like fracture in the valley wall. It offered some protection with overhanging rock forming a roof. The stony walls also gave some relief from the strengthening breeze and declining temperatures that were already noticeable. Silas dropped the kindling he had collected as Felix took out the tinder box.

"We're going to need a lot more than this," he said.

"The light of a fire won't be seen if we place it here. We're also best protected from the wind," Silas observed.

"You get it started whilst I get more wood. The sun will be fully gone soon."

Felix left Silas expertly setting the fire and igniting the kindling. He gradually fed it slightly larger sticks until Felix arrived with more substantial fuel.

"Build it up. We'll need the coals to keep us warm overnight."

"I'm sorry. I didn't think."

"You did more than me," Silas said as he went to gather more wood. Over the next hour, as the sky got darker and the wind more penetrating, the brothers established the necessities that would get them through the night. Now with backs against the stone wall, and the fire finally drying their boots, they inspected the rations.

"What I would give for more of Sarah's cooking," grumbled Silas, looking at the trail mix before him. Ignoring his brother's complaint, Felix handed him a pair of trousers.

"You'll want to put these on. It's going to be cold and the more layers the better," he said as he pulled the second pair over his own breeches. "Double the socks as well once those lot are dry." Silas just grimaced as he followed his brother's example.

With nothing else to do the brothers tried to settle, but discomfort has many forms. The twins were able to experience most of them all in one night.

Half-empty stomachs were the least of the issue. Sleep would be difficult. A hard, cold rocky bed does little to entice it. Slightly damp clothes also contain their own unique sort of discomfort. These were then coupled with the dichotomy of being both too hot and too cold, depending on which part of you was facing the embers. But most of all sleep was not accessible as they pondered the day to come. Silas, once so eager for the adventure, now was plagued by memories of his time outside the Tower. *What if it was the Tower? Had they been too rash? Should they have waited and found out more?* Questions that only the day to come could answer spiralled in his head, robbing him of any hope of slumber.

Felix, curled quietly on his side, suffered the same physical discomforts as his brother, but he was vigilant. They had arrived a day early. *What if the others had as well?* Their fire, although now just embers, still gave out the tell-tale glow that would be seen for a fair distance. *They would know where we are.* He kept his ears alert to any sound of an approach. *Should we move and reposition before sunrise? Silas will go but we need to be close or how can I protect?* Almost unaware of the hard cold rock beneath him he worried. *We have no idea what we are going to meet.*

Chapter 9

The sun, low in the western sky, created long shadows that stretched from the Western Slopes. From halfway up the Tower, the fading light highlighted the natural beauty of the land. Sheer, snow-capped mountains encircled the fertile fields and rich pastures. If one had been watching carefully, it may have been possible to see a figure illuminated through the Tower's only window. If they were particularly vigilant, and watched for long enough, they may have seen a bundle fall from this window. Small and black it dropped from the window – gathering speed.

Just on the verge of dozing, Felix awoke with a start. He saw his brother sitting bolt upright staring back at him. They both had felt it. A cry that cut through the hum, clear and piercing. Something had broken. The Tower was awake. Alert in a way they had never experienced. Terrified, they looked at the glowing embers. In unison they rose, stamping them out. Speechless, they shivered in the darkness. A cold, friendless darkness. Far from familiar comforts. If the Tower knew … would it be coming? Neither voiced the obvious. They waited, huddling together against the cold, Silas clasping the machete.

***

The pain was getting worse. It was nothing like anything she had ever experienced. Wave upon wave of nauseating cramps. Shaking uncontrollably, Mortella cried out. A maid entered, moving quickly toward the bed. The single bed sheet had been kicked to the side. Getting closer, the maid gasped before running from the room. Within moments she returned with Mrs Poole in tow. Seeing the blood-stained bedclothes Mrs Poole cried, "Call the midwife." Lifting Mortella's sodden nightgown she yelled after the rapidly departing servant, "And alert the Tower."

Gently separating Mortella's legs, she let out a sigh of relief. "There's nothing there yet ... but it won't be long." Two more servants arrived in the chamber. To the first Mrs Poole barked, "We need linen and warm towels. Lots of them. Start a fire, keep them near ... and boil the water." To the second she directed, "Stay here, any change and inform me at once." Racing from the room she muttered to herself, "I suppose the master should be told."

***

The great door opened silently, allowing pale, unnatural light to escape. Three shadows appeared, silhouetted within the space that formed. In unison they emerged. Dark forms, almost invisible, as they began the descent to Town below. Behind them the cold light was cut off by the closing door.

***

A youth returning home from his last delivery stopped. He knew not to ignore the feeling. It had never been wrong before. Something was happening and it could be exciting. He was not disappointed. Within moments he heard a thundering crash followed by an eerie silence as if the world stood in anticipation.

***

Wave after wave of contractions came. Barely was there time for her to catch her breath before they would start again. If she thought the last few months had been bad, then this was worse. It felt like her body was trying to expel her organs by the brutal convulsions. She was barely aware of what was happening about her. People had arrived. First a few and then others. Someone was yelling at her. They wanted her to do something. But the meaning of the words were lost in the pain. She felt a slap on her face as her head was pulled to face another's.

"Breathe, pant!" it yelled.

Through the fog Mortella remembered something. *Pant.* They had told her about this. *But it was too early. It shouldn't be yet. No not yet. It was too soon. It won't work. It won't survive. I can't go through this again.* The pain subsided for a moment before abruptly beginning again. *Pant.* Pulling in short sharp puffs of air and then pushing them out through pursed lips, Mortella concentrated. It gave her something to focus on. Something other than the pain.

Through the haze she was aware that more had arrived. The commotion settled as several dark forms approached the bed. A silence descended as the contraction abated.

71

"The child will survive," came a calm, melodic voice that contrasted sharply with the shrill, impassioned voices that had been silenced by the figures' arrival. Quiet filled the room. "You are fulfilling your task. The Tower awaits this child."

Mortella looked up at the hooded figure. There was nothing suggesting anything like compassion in the stance. Her body convulsed involuntarily. It took a moment for her to realise that she was once more in the throes of a full-blown contraction. But this time without her feeling the agony. It was then that she recognised the Abbatissa standing beside her. Choking down the shame she felt having been forced into this subordinate position, Mortella brushed back the sodden locks from her face.

"Of course it will." Being careful to match the tone of the Dark One before her she continued, "My honour it is to serve the Code and the Tower. It shall be good to return to the Black."

With a movement that suggested a laugh, the Abbatissa responded. "Return you may … once the task is done. Once the child is of age to take the Black for herself." After a pause, the figure added, "If she *can* take the Black."

In that one simple phrase Mortella felt her hopes being crushed under the weight of the years before her. What if the child could not take the Black? Then her task was not completed. She would remain as she was. A mere vessel for a man. Without the Black she could not be herself. Yet in that moment, Mortella was able to fortify herself. She was so much more than this petty Abbatissa could ever realise. She would not submit to one such as her.

Seeing the change on her face, the Abbatissa turned her back. Approaching the Dark Ones, she allowed Mortella to again feel the full strength of the contraction. The sudden intensity of the pain almost caused her to cry in agony. But her steely resolve was once more in place. She gritted her teeth, suppressed the desire, and allowed her body to convulse in silence, vaguely aware of a change as the room started to empty.

***

Having climbed through the rugged landscape to the base of the Tower, the youth found a figure clothed in black, small, and lithe. Picking it up, he carried it away from the destruction that marked its impact. Careful to avoid it any further injury, he headed back to Town. With no-one on the streets, home was the only logical choice.

Arriving there, the youth placed his charge on the bed and waited. Waited for his mother to return. She would know what to do.

***

Sleep was not something either of them were chasing. Not that it would have been possible even without the Tower. The stone was cold and Felix's back hurt. But vigilance was now also needed. The Tower could be close. How were they to know? If it was, what could they do? Fearful that they had made a terrible mistake following the map, they waited. Not knowing what they would do but hoping that which was coming would not find them.

***

The midwife arrived and made straight for her patient. Exhausted after just having left a difficult birth, she fortified herself. Finishing the examination of her patient she stood up. Now, with time to assess those about her she saw the three figures standing silently off to the side. She paused. A chill shot up her back and a cold, clammy sweat coated her face – the Tower. How she detested them. So much suffering, not only hers but for so many others. What were they doing here?

But she was here for the mother-to-be. She had pledged herself to help those who needed it. She had to ignore the hatred she felt. Refocusing her attention back on the matter at hand, she considered. It would still be some time yet. Things often progressed slowly the first time. Mortella was not more than halfway dilated. How much longer it would take was always a guess, but her experience suggested that the child would not be born till the morning.

She crossed over to Mrs Poole who looked at her expectantly.

"It will be some time yet," she said. Looking at the Dark Ones she sneered, "And them?"

Mrs Poole turned her back on the figures and spoke low and quiet. "The Tower has an interest in the child." Taking a breath she continued, "Sybil, there is so much more here than you know. The mother is one of *them*." Looking back in shock at the woman in the bed Sybil remained silent. All knew that once Taken by the Tower, none had ever left. Nothing good ever came out from the Tower. That was one thing she knew. Knew this to be true with all that she was. The Tower only destroyed.

Feeling sick to her stomach she pondered her position. She didn't trust herself anywhere near the Dark Ones. She didn't feel safe. How could she

73

use her skills to help such as these? She knew she would have to get out. She also couldn't do what she normally would. Far too risky. She couldn't expose herself. Her pledge couldn't include them. Not even to prevent suffering.

"I have to go and check on another patient," she lied. "I won't be long. I'll be back long before I am needed."

Without waiting for a response she headed for the door. Once outside the room she quickly made her way along the corridor, raced down the stairs and away.

***

He watched carefully for signs of life. The pale skin that was icy to the touch. It did not give him confidence. Placing yet another blanket on the small frame he paced the room, willing for his mother to return.

***

She headed home. Never before had she left a patient. Never had she turned her back. But how could she stay? She couldn't support the Tower. Never would she aid it. If it had an interest in the child then she must oppose it. But her actions went against everything she had pledged herself to. Her life was dedicated to relieving suffering in every way she could. She had read and learned from any source she could find. Experimented and innovated, always trying to find ways to help those who needed it. And then there was her curse, the Influence that both tormented her and gave her hope that there was another way. The child was innocent. The sins of the mother could not be the child's. But the Tower had an interest.

She was not of the Tower. She rejected everything that it stood for. The abomination of the Tower disgusted her. Her Influence did not mean that she was anything like them. She was different. She had given her life in service. She had left her former life once she knew what the Tower was. How could she now have anything to do with it? How could she help its plans?

Wrapped up in these thoughts she arrived home. On opening the door she was greeted by her son. Agitated, he grabbed her arm and pulled her into his bedroom. Uttering a single word in desperation, "Maima?" as he pointed towards his bed.

Surprised and alarmed she approached the bed. There, enveloped by the bedclothes, was a small, pale girl clothed in black. Suppressing her initial response to recoil she held her ground. She looked back at her son. His worried expression tore at her heart. She had promised herself to help all in need.

Regardless of their means or their position. She had never turned anyone away. Now, before her was another in need. This child before her, cloaked in the Tower's garb. Would she be any better than the Tower if she turned her back? Torn, she didn't know if she should or should not help. Quickly she inspected the child. The girl was alive. She smiled weakly at her son before sending him out to boil water. It wasn't something she needed but it would keep him occupied. She had become well versed in the ways to manage people. Small tasks, no matter how menial, could relieve all sorts of mental turmoil. It also allowed her time to examine her charge more fully.

Her son's compassion touched her. She had taught him well. He rejected no-one. All were worthy of care. Chastised, she completed her examination. Satisfied that time and warmth was what was required, she got up and left her son to watch their new charge while she made them some supper. It gave her time to think.

***

Cold, uncomfortable and sleepless they passed the night. Aware that something had provoked the Tower but not able to determine who or what. The multitude of voices that lived on the margins of their minds rose and fell like waves. Sometimes there was a hum of anticipation while at others the voices penetrated their senses with piercing aggression.

In the freezing cool light of dawn nothing had changed. Huddled together in their draughty, rocky chamber they watched as the sky gradually changed from a steely grey into the pale blue of another fine day. Felix looked at the worn, worried face of his twin.

"Two hours," he said.

"Should we?"

"I don't know."

Silas looked toward the entrance on the other side of the valley.

"We'll wait. I don't want to get caught in *that* tunnel."

Felix nodded. At least here they would be able to see what hunted them.

"No connection. Words only." Silas nodded as he rubbed his thighs vigorously to restore some sense of warmth to his body.

***

She had retired to bed and attempted to sleep. But sleep was something not to be found this night. There was a Dark One in her house. Her son had brought it here. But she was only a child. A small, fragile child who needed help. She had brought her son up well. She was proud of him. He did not care who it was. It was someone who needed help. He had not refused. How could she?

After tossing and turning for hours she got up. Dressing, she checked on the other room. There was her son, sound asleep, slouched in a chair facing the bed where the girl also slept. She was now warm to the touch and her breathing deep and even.

Having made up her mind, she quietly left the cottage to make her way back up to where she should have been all this while. Back to care, to relieve suffering and be the woman she was, regardless of for whom and heedless of those around her.

***

The Dark Ones could have made things easier. Of that Mortella was sure. But she was not going to let the Abbatissa see any further weakness in her. She was determined not to allow *that* thing any form of satisfaction in seeing her suffer. The pain seemed interminable. Barely had one contraction finished before the next commenced.

In all that is sacred in the Code, why is it taking so long?

She felt a hand on her shoulder as a soft voice spoke. "I'm going to have to have another look. See how things are going. I'll be as quick and gentle as I can."

Her face ruddy and hair plastered to her forehead, Mortella steadied her breathing as she looked into the midwife's face. Giving her a smile, Sybil moved quickly down to the other end of the bed and lifted the bed sheet. After yet another uncomfortable and intimate examination, Mortella finally heard the long-awaited words.

"Fully dilated." Looking directly at Mortella, Sybil added, "Now, dear, now is the time to push … Push like you've wanted to all this time." Then, taking Mortella's hand she said, "Squeeze this and push hard … as soon as the contraction starts. Continue, don't stop. Keep on pushing until the end. The more you do, the faster it'll be." Then with the side of her hand she gently brushed back the greasy locks from her patient's forehead. Giving Mortella another encouraging smile she continued, "It'll all be over before you know."

With that the next contraction hit. Now without restraint, Mortella held her breath and bore down. The pain tore at her. She felt her insides forcing their way out of her. But she wouldn't stop. She couldn't stop. Face purple with the effort, she held. Not a sound escaped her lips as she pushed. Not willing to waste any effort in order to get this finished. At the peak of the contraction she felt something give. A jolt that tore but relieved some of the terrible pressure.

"It's crowned," was the cry. "Well done, dear. Almost there."

Behind the midwife stood the three clothed in black, unmoving with faces hooded. Further back, keeping quiet in the presence of the Dark Ones, stood Mrs Poole, surrounded by her staff. The insult of relinquishing control etched across her face. Mortella didn't care. Her task would soon be done and then never again would she suffer this. The mother of one the Tower wanted. She would then be able to reinsert herself. What were a few more years. For when she returned she would be a force with which to be reckoned. The Abbatissa would no longer matter – an insignificant …

The pain began again. But this time it was different. She was more in control. Following the instructions of the midwife she pushed, held, and pushed again. Exhausted, she waited for the next contraction. When it came it lasted only a moment before she heard, "It's a girl."

***

The sun crept its way down the valley walls. It did little yet to warm them, but it would eventually. They listened. It had changed again. There was now a calm. No longer were the voices rising and falling in waves of emotion. The Tower seemed peaceful. More peaceful than it ever had. Whatever seemed to have provoked it was now passed. This in itself brought relief to the brothers who now sat glassy-eyed while watching the day begin.

"Perhaps it's not us."

"We can hope so."

"And now?"

"Now, I supposed that we do what we came for."

"I'll go."

"We'll both get closer. I'll stay hidden. See that rock above the entrance. I'll be there." Felix got up. "We have about an hour. Best to get in place."

Together they left their night's refuge and made their way back to the tunnel's entrance. Climbing the slope above the cave they found a space behind a boulder that allowed a view of the approach to the entrance while providing protection from unwanted eyes. It gave a vantage point that was directly above the entrance. Quickly they collected a series of rocks and boulders that could be used to throw down on anyone as the need required.

Leaving Felix hidden above the cave, Silas climbed down the slope to the opening. He carefully hid the machete behind his back whilst making sure that it was still readily accessible. Waving back up to his brother he entered the opening and was lost from view. It wouldn't be long now.

Chapter 10

Barely the size of a large rodent, its skin translucent in the room's flickering light, the infant emerged into the world. Taking up the tiny bundle, Sybil placed it onto Mortella's chest, who felt its warmth on her exposed skin. A small alien creature, but perfectly formed with tiny hands, and fingers that even had nails. At total odds with her revulsion towards the parasite that had infected her body over the last eight months, Mortella cradled it gently. Opening its eyes it looked directly into those of her mother's. For the first time in her life Mortella felt a connection with another person. One that demanded her attention.

Oblivious to all, she immersed herself in the moment. Calm and centred, she dwelt until she felt another's hands seize the infant from her grasp. Shocked, she looked up into the hooded face of the Abbatissa.

"The child will survive," she stated as she lifted the child away. "The Tower will attend to that." Mortella watched helplessly as the Dark Ones converged on the child, hiding it from view.

"And how do you expect to do that?" sneered a voice that cut through the air.

The Abbatissa turned to face the one who dared to challenge. Defiant under the gaze, Sybil continued, "What is it that you know about infants? Have any of you ever had a child?" Looking back at Mortella she added, "The child needs to suckle." Again facing the Abbatissa, she continued sarcastically, "And how do you think you will manage that?!" Shaking as she stood her ground, the midwife awaited her punishment. None who faced the Dark Ones would expect anything less. But stand her ground she must. A child this young seldom survived, but without its mother it had no chance.

As she waited the child twitched, giving a weak cry before going limp in the Dark One's hands. Without waiting, the midwife leapt forward, snatching the child. Wrapping it in towels warmed by the fire she rubbed it gently.

Rousing, the child gave another whimper. Without regard to those about, she took the infant back to her mother.

"She must feed." Showing Mortella what to do, Sybil placed the babe on the breast where it latched. Suckling slowly for several minutes she gradually succumbed to a peaceful sleep, safely cradled in the warm embrace of her mother.

Feeling gratitude for the strength of another, Mortella roused herself. Rising slightly off the bed, eyes clear and face determined she declared, "Clara will stay here … with me. The Tower may visit … but this child is *my* responsibility and mine alone."

The Abbatissa pulled back her hood, revealing her grey hair and age-worn face. She glared at the defiant tableau before her. The midwife hovering protectively over the semi-recumbent form of Mortella who gently rocked the sleeping infant.

"The Tower chose me to have this child. To go against me is to go against the Tower."

"Be it on you," the Abbatissa spat. "Responsibility to deliver the one foretold by the Tower shall be yours and yours alone." Pausing, she added, "One hopes that she shall be all that she should … for your sake." Pulling up her hood, she turned to vacate the room, followed by the two silent black shadows that had accompanied her. The room remained silent as Sybil placed a reassuring hand on the shoulder of her patient.

"She needs to keep warm. It will be hard. There is no guarantee." Looking towards the rest of the room her eyes landed on Mrs Poole. In a loud voice she proclaimed, "These first few days are critical. The child's best chance is to stay with her mother. Bring food and drink so that she may regain her strength and can provide for the child. Warm blankets must always be nearby." Turning back to Mortella she crouched down, coming face to face with her charge. "You are in control. Remember that. It is now all up to you. She will need to suckle every two hours. For now, at least. It will get easier … but for now everything must focus on her."

Rising again she walked directly over to Mrs Poole. "I will come back later in the day." Moving closer to her ear she then added poignantly in a clear, harsh tone, "And no more of this spiteful treatment. Do you think I could miss the lack of care and attention that has been given to this woman? The odour of dirty linen and an unwashed body is not hard to detect." Turning to the rest of the room she declared in a loud voice, "Whatever the mother wants, the mother gets. A maid shall always be near, ready both day and night."

Before exiting the chamber, Sybil once again come close to Mrs Poole and added in a soft voice, "If anything does happen to the child, be assured that I myself will inform the Tower that it was due to *your* neglect." On that she smiled back at Mortella before exiting to make her way back home and to her next charge.

∗∗∗

At least the air was starting to warm up as the sun crept down the slopes. Silas wandered about the cave's opening, no longer able to maintain the level of anxiety that had compelled him to stay awake throughout the uncomfortable night. Some things were better just to get over with. Like pulling off a plaster. He just wanted it to happen. It couldn't be that much longer now … could it?

Felix was sitting in the morning sun behind the boulder above the entrance. He thought of things differently. For him, some things should just never be examined. At this time, he was not too sure if this was one of those things or not. Whatever it was that had provoked the Tower overnight, that at least had gone. Well, had settled – for the moment. But vigilance was needed. He was not convinced that all was well.

He peered over the boulder to the north. That would be the direction *they* would come. At least that was the direction that made the most sense. It couldn't be much longer now, he hoped. He tried to make out any movement in the valley amongst the vegetation. He thought that he saw something. As he peered forward he suddenly cried out. A searing pain had begun behind his eyes. Everything began to blur as it rapidly spread over his scalp. Burning, scalding, it filled his mind as the intensity increased. Clenching his eyes and stifling further cries, he was only dimly aware that someone had grabbed his arms and pinned them painfully behind. Unable to move, barely able to think, he was forced to the ground. In a last desperate act, as the agony intensified, he attempted to throw a warning to his brother. One last thought before he succumbed and was lost to a merciful blackness.

∗∗∗

He woke. Tight bonds immobilised his hands by painfully pulling his shoulders back, numbing his fingers. He was lying on his side on a cold, hard surface. How long he had been out he had no idea. Thinking took a bit of effort. It was like trying to move through treacle, slow and laborious. He had no idea what had

81

happened. He had seen no-one, but that pain. That pain, he had never felt anything like it before. Nor did he want to feel anything like it again. Where was Silas? What had happened to him? Was he here? Did he get away?

Felix opened his eyes only to see little more than he had when closed. The pain, what had it done. He needed to see. Panicked, he rapidly blinked his eyes, trying to clear his vision, willing himself to see. It was only then that he became aware that there was something covering his head. Musty and damp, it blocked his vision. Settling his panic, he breathed. He wasn't blind. It was the bag. Slowly the fog over his mind began to lift. He listened. It was quiet, but there was someone there. He was sure of it. He could hear soft sounds of movement. What now? He had to know. Where was his brother?

Without lifting his head Felix gently opened his mind. The familiar hum of the Tower was there, unchanged from the morning. It was almost mellow. Whatever had occurred overnight appeared to have passed. Gently he searched for his brother. Aware to try and hide himself as much as possible from any other. Relief flooded him. He could feel Silas. He was alive at least.

Gradually he prodded the closed mind of Silas, suggesting they engage. There was no response. He was there but either unwilling or incapable of engaging. Perhaps he was being wary. He shut down his mind. He would just have to wait.

The hard ground caused his hip to hurt. Rolling onto his other side he flexed his knees causing them to come in contact with something. It wasn't that hard, and it moved. He gave it another prod with his knee. It moved away with the force and then returned to the same spot. Unable to see and unable to use his arms, Felix stopped. He wasn't going to be able to work out what it was the way things were. It was also unlikely that he had just been left here. Wherever here was. Whoever had done this obviously wanted him alive. So something must happen eventually. He would just have to wait. And do nothing that might provoke another episode like the one that brought him here.

Opening his mind again he felt for his brother. Something was odd. He couldn't quite put his finger on it. He focused on the voices, feeling, and weighing the sounds of the Tower. No words were discernible, they rarely were, but there was a peace about them. There was a type of unity amid the chaos that he had never before felt. They had come here to find others. Others who thought as they did. What did the old man say – there are more than just the two of you – and the parchment – malintent will swiftly be known.

The Tower wasn't provoked. Whatever they were doing now had not provoked it. Surely this meant … Silas responded and opened the connection.

I'm sorry. I should have listened. You were right. We shouldn't have.

Silas, it's okay.

No, it isn't. We wouldn't have …

It's okay.

It's all my fault … if I didn't—

Where are you? Felix interjected, cutting off his brother.

I don't know. Somewhere cold and dark.

What happened?

I was out of sight sitting near the cave entrance. Nothing unusual. Just waiting. Then this pain. That's all I remember. Until just now. When I felt you.

Felix could feel Silas' agitation and regret.

Silas, we're okay.

How on earth can you say that?. I'm tied up with a bag over my head and …

But we're alive.

We're not okay.

We're going to be. Where are you?

I don't know. It's cold and the ground is hard.

Can you see anything?

No. Where are you?

Silas, can you move?

My legs are free. My arms are tied.

Felix felt something hit him on the shin.

Oww. Did you just kick something?

How did you know?

I think it was me … Stretch out your legs again. But this time be a bit more careful.

Again Felix felt something hit him.

Was that you?

Yes.

What are we going to do?

I think that it's going to be fine.

What?

Listen. Silas, Listen.

I am listening. What?

Not to me … Listen.

Felix waited. Silas was silent.

I don't hear anything.

Exactly.

Stop being so bloody frustrating. Just say it. Explain it to your dumb brother.

You're not dumb. You just need to calm down and listen.

Taking a few slow, deep breaths, Silas concentrated. Like Felix, the backing to his life was as familiar as his own reflection. Any subtle difference was immediately obvious. And there it was. The Tower was not agitated. No piercing, aggressive tone but instead a fluid tranquillity that flowed about him. Calmer and gentler than he could ever remember. Since the early morning there had been no aggression, no cadence of thwarted desires, just a soothing croon.

It's calm.

It's not us.

What?

We didn't provoke the Tower. It's not just us, "there are more than just the two of you", and the parchment, remember "malintent will swiftly be known".

So?

So these cannot be from the Tower.

Why?

Because it's not just us. If the Tower was aware do you think it would feel like that? And from what we have heard, do you really think the Tower would put a bag over our heads? We don't have bad intentions. They will know.

How can you be sure?

It isn't the Tower. It's as you thought. These are just not anyone. These must be those that are against the Tower.

***

Exhausted, but elated, Sybil arrived home. Any chance to stand up to the evil that beset this place was a thrill. But then to have a win, to triumph so wholly over a Dark One, now that was something to celebrate. Pondering this turn of events, and the inevitable consequences, she quietly entered her cottage. She quickly checked in on her son. She found him as she left him, slumped in a chair facing the small, sleeping frame that occupied his bed. Leaving him as he was, she reached her own room. There she wearily undressed and climbed into bed, thankful for a bit of peace after all the excitement.

Almost asleep she was jolted awake by frantic cries.

"Maima, Maima. Come quickly."

The urgency in her son's voice compelled her out of bed before she was even aware that she was standing. Arriving moments later in his room, she saw the figure on the bed flinging itself about uncontrollably before bursting forth with a terrified scream.

It hit her like wall of sound as she saw her son flung across the room by its force. Without thinking she raced toward the bed. Placing both hands on the child's head she began. Using her gift she began to pull the terror from the girl. Absorbing the fear, making it her own and then allowing it to dissipate through her. Accepting and controlling the terror that she now felt while pushing through a wave of peace and calm into the girl. The child quietened, closed her eyes, and once again fell asleep.

Checking that her son was unhurt, she took him from the room. This child changed things. Until now she had kept the Tower at bay. But now it had entered their home. It was now time, she thought. He needed to know. The Tower and its evil, they were part of this world and more part of his than he knew. Then there were the Influences. Her particular one was both a gift and a curse. She would never call it her Influence. That name belonged to those from the Tower. Hers was a gift. One that she chose to give to others. She could use it as a physician to aid many who were sick or in pain.

She could modify her patient's body, their physical presence. But it cost her. Each time, it cost. Over time it would gradually cost her more and more. She knew this. She could feel it. Simple things like fear were easy. She could absorb and control them by the force of her will alone. Allowing them to fade till they had no lasting consequences but to make her stronger, more resilient to their effects. Pain was more difficult, but mostly she could bear it. Taking it into herself, knowing that it too would dwindle and fade. The rest had their dangers. The careful extraction of small amounts of disease. Small bits at a time would work as long as she didn't take too much too often. She could rely on her own body's ability to deal with that.

Making the tea, Sybil considered what to say. She had always hidden her past from him. His father had died, and she earned their keep by caring for others. That is what he knew. But the way his father died and the Tower's role, those she had never discussed. Nor had she spoken of the Influences that haunted the land. He was old enough. Now that the Tower had entered their home he needed to know.

***

She licked the knife. A guilty pleasure she could rarely indulge since her first admittance to the Tower. Such things as forks were not needed during her time at the knocking shop. Something was needed to cut the meat, when available, but a knife was just as effective in piercing the food as any fork. Then there was the delight in licking all of the juices off the blade. A pleasure not matched by the use of any gilt silvered fork.

Placing the knife down again, Mortella stroked the fine hair that covered the infant's head. A dark black like her father's. He had made only a brief appearance exuding a facade of happiness over the child. She wasn't a boy and thus it didn't really interest him. Not the son he so desired. His sentiments didn't interest Mortella. The requirement for a man was only needed to begin. After that he was as redundant as a third nipple. A girl, this girl, was what the Tower desired and she brought with her the reinstatement of Mortella as a Dark One. A Dark One with ambitions to the Presence.

Clara roused slightly, opening her eyes, looking directly into the face above. Blue eyes, but these may change, thought Mortella. Turning the child slightly, Mortella allowed her to find the nipple and latch. So very small, but pink and warm, Clara suckled for several minutes before once again falling asleep. Every two hours the midwife had said and, thus far, that was exactly what was happening.

With the child asleep, Mortella rang the silver bell beside her. Immediately a maid appeared.

"More wine."

"Milady," was the response as the maid brought a fresh decanter. Such a change in so short a time. Food had regained its flavour. It was now a pleasure. And wine, how she had missed that. Fear was also a wonderful thing. Despite detesting the Abbatissa, her arrival that previous evening had had its benefits. It reminded all about her who she was and from where she had come. Now she was no longer at their mercy, as she had regained her strength. The nausea had gone. The pain had all but settled and she was again in control. Mrs Poole would have to watch herself.

Remembering the previous night, she thought back to the midwife. There was a woman that even she was able to give some grudging respect. For Mortella, standing up to the Abbatissa was a mere trifle, but for one not of the Code, that showed some strength. And the threat delivered to Mrs Poole. The memory caused Mortella to smile. The look on the housekeeper's face! Now that was something to increase the appetite.

Ringing the bell again Mortella ordered for a bath to be drawn. She had been able to wash earlier, but now she had the desire to soak. She had enough time. Perfumed, steaming hot water to invigorate her. She needed to do something about her hair. It had been far too long. A little bit of tweaking by her Influence to enhance the glamour and all would be back in order. She would make sure that they would never again forget who she was. No-one should try to take advantage of her again. It wouldn't go well for them. No-one would ever take advantage of Clara either. She would see to that. For this child was going to be so much more. More than anyone could imagine. And there beside her, all the way, would be her mother. Looking down at the bundle she held, Mortella smiled. It will be worth it. Of that she would make sure.

***

It had been hours. They lay uncomfortably on the hard stone in the dark and cold. Unsure of what was around them and how any sort of movement would be considered, they moved rarely. Neither wanted a repeat of what had brought them here.

Is someone even there? Silas asked.

There was, was the response.

Yes, but now, is there anyone still here? They could've gone. Left us alone.

And why would they do that?

Well, can you hear anyone?

No, but that doesn't mean anything.

But what if they have? Are we just going to stay here and starve because we didn't try?

What do you suggest?

Can you move closer to me? If we can try and undo these bonds …

If no-one is here, let's get these things off our heads first. At least then we can see where we are.

Agreed.

Felix shuffled sideways until he felt Silas next to him.

That was my shoulder. Move down further. I can still move my fingers. I should be able to grab a hold of whatever it is that is on your head. You might then be able to pull it off by moving backwards.

Pushing his head against this brother's shoulder, Felix manoeuvred his head further down his brother's back until he felt Silas' fingers grappling with the cover.

Got it. Move away from me.

As Felix did, Silas lost his grip.

Try again.

This time was slightly more successful but again Silas was unable to get a good enough hold with his cold and numb fingers.

We'll get there, his brother encouraged as eventually the material started to move over his head uncovering his mouth, then nose, and finally allowing him limited vision from under the edge. They were in the darkness of the cave. He could make out some light in the distance. He shared the images with his brother.

Daylight?

Most likely. Just a bit more. If you can grab the edge it might be easier. Now able to see a bit, Felix wiggled closer to Silas' fingers, pushing the material edge into them with his nose.

Got it.

Awkwardly, Felix squirmed and twisted his head and body, trying to rid himself of the bag that hindered him. Finally, success as the covering dropped away.

"Now that was painful to watch," came a voice out of the darkness. "I was wondering how long it would take you. You certainly are two of the most patient people I've ever come across. I'm not sure that I could've persisted quite that long."

Looking behind him, Felix could just make out the form of the man sitting above them on a rock ledge, feet dangling over the edge.

"This has been one of the more boring things I've had to do. I had hoped you might try something. It would have made it a lot more interesting." He paused as if waiting for a reply. "At least the last half hour was fun. Watching you try to get that bag off. Very impressive. I haven't seen a body move about in such a strange way before … that was well done. But, in the whole time, you didn't even ask for water. Didn't say a single thing, not one question. You have no idea how bored I've been."

Felix just looked at him.

"Not that I would've answered of course. But it would've been nice to have been asked," he said with a laugh. "So now, what? You have legs and can see, but no hands that are of much use."

"What do you want with us?" yelled Silas.

Laughing, the figure replied, "More to the point, what do you want with us?" There was silence. "Never mind," he laughed again. "We'll know soon enough. Won't be long now."

Chapter 11

It had been a long and tiring journey, although how far they actually travelled was hard to say. The uneven ground caused them to frequently stumble. It didn't help that they were being led blindly along unknown paths, head coverings back in place and secured tightly. Specks of light filtered unevenly through the material, but this didn't result in any meaningful sight. They were only aware that they were passing under trees, or perhaps it was a rocky outcrop, solely by the dimming of the light.

Things had not gone well after Felix had removed the bag. All questions had gone unanswered to the increasing delight of their captor. At least he now seemed a lot less bored. Yet the consequences of any dissent had been readily demonstrated. The slightest misstep and they would know it.

It was getting colder by the time they were finally told to sit. Having neither eaten, nor drunk, a thing since the night before, Silas felt lightheaded as he carefully lowered himself to the ground. He heard quiet voices off in the background.

You still okay? he queried his brother.

Been better.

It can't be too much more, he paused. *You hear the others?*

Seems like at least a couple have joined. Could be more. Felix stopped as they heard footsteps coming towards them.

"It isn't often that we get visitors," came a deep, dry voice. "How did you find us?" he waited for an answer.

"We found it," began Silas. "In an old, abandoned farm. We lost a drinking bet. It was a dare. It was supposed to be haunted—"

Felix cut off his brother. "We went looking. We heard of the Fens … and the rumours …"

What are you doing? Silas was clearly agitated.

Trust me.

"That they had something from outside the Bowl … that they disappeared suddenly."

As he spoke, Felix felt a wave of cold wash over him. His skin prickled as the hairs on the back of his neck rose.

"And why's that of interest to you?" was the curt response.

"Because we are no friends of the Tower."

"Why is that?"

"The Tower wants us, and those like us … to be gone." He paused. "Because some of us are not to be …"

No, stop, snapped Silas sharply. *Don't give them too much.* Felix stopped.

"… Not to be how they want us to be," he finished lamely.

The brothers waited in silence as the footsteps retreated, followed by low, unintelligible voices. Soon another voice spoke to them.

"Interesting. Not a lie but not fully the truth." Felix felt the cold dissipate and the tingling cease. "There's a lot more unsaid. Speak true. We have ways of knowing." Felix felt someone untying the bag that blocked his vision. Once removed he saw an elderly man stooped over him with another five figures arranged about them.

"Words are just words. The Tower, like any other, can use them just as convincingly." Crouching down and looking directly into Felix's eyes he continued. "We need more than just words. What else can you offer us?"

Tell them.

Tell them what?

About your visit to the Tower.

Felix sat there silently as Silas reluctantly told a little of his visit to the Tower. As he did he felt the same cold encase him. Wary, he glossed over his need to understand the Tower and the voices that accompanied them day in and day out. He decided not to tell of the Tower's yearning, downplaying its lust for life. The lust for something that it didn't have nor fully understand. He told them that there had been visions but didn't describe the waif-like child created from thousands of fragments. He ended suddenly, without mention of the word that had flooded his mind and held such significance for the Tower – Mortella.

While he had been speaking, the second man stood silently behind him, listening attentively. Once finished, Silas felt the cold evaporate from around him as the man nodded to the older one.

"He's not saying everything. There's more. But he believes what he says … or he's good at lying to himself."

Directing for Silas' head covering to be removed, the older man introduced himself. "I'm the leader here, and these brave souls do whatever I say … whenever I say it. We're choosing to make a difference. We'll see what sort of difference you're going for." Glancing back at the youngest of the group he added. "About time you undid those bindings of yours, don't you think?" The young man approached and began to untie Felix's bonds. After making very little headway, he removed a knife and gradually cut through them.

"I'm a lot better at knots than I thought."

His arms now free, Felix tried to move them. As the numbness from shoulder to fingers went, it was replaced with throbbing. The slightest rotation of this shoulder resulted in a shooting pain down his arm. This caused him to wince. The old man noticed.

"It will go, but be warned, there's potentially much worse in store."

Facing his brother, Felix saw a similar look in his face.

"Oh, and just one thing more, consider this a period of grace." Looking from one to the other he continued. "You're a long way from earning any sort of trust. So remember, the young'un here can knock you out with a thought. And that's only the start of your miseries if you give us any cause. So I suggest you don't get any ideas. We're a great deal more than we appear."

"He's not kidding," said the young man as he helped Felix to his feet. "I'm Pick. It hurt a bit, I'm sure. I'm told that I can be a bit overzealous. But we didn't know you … and … well … I might have gone just a bit too hard on the mind thing." Looking back at the others he straightened up in attempt to display an air of authority before saying in a slightly over-loud voice, "I'll do it again, no hesitation, if I have to." He then added in a quieter voice, "You hungry? They've brought some food."

Nodding while turning to Silas and helping him up he added "I'm Felix, and this is Silas …"

"Your identical twin. Yeah, pretty obvious. Come on, I haven't eaten since this morning. I'm starving."

***

Sybil sat cradling a cup of tea. So it appeared Angus could see the Influences. It shouldn't surprise her. But it was the first she had heard of it. To him, hers were like colourful fireflies, or in the case of the girl, shooting stars that had hit him with the force of a brick wall. It was something to ponder.

She was a healer. She tried to be the best healer she could. Everyone came to her looking for relief. She never turned anyone away. From those who lived in the upper part of Town where servants and high walls protected them, down to the most lowly without anything but good will and gratitude to pay for treatment. All sought her out.

She saw how he looked at the girl. So delicate, so pale and beautiful. He would have been only vaguely aware of her disdain of the Tower. She had never before spoken of it, as she busied herself in making tinctures and pastes to aid those who needed them he would watch in silence.

She was from the upper parts of Town. Well placed in birth meant that she could read. Because of this she could make a difference. That was why she was so insistent that her son needed to learn to read as well. The Tower had Taken his father. She was not sure how he felt about that. He had never known one. She had always been there. He knew no different. There really had been nothing for him to miss. But he would never be able to understand what it was like for her to have lost him.

The girl was from the Tower. Yet despite how she felt about that place, she would accept her care for Angus' sake. She looked at her son. He made her feel anxious. She had tried and tried to get him to read but he had always found excuses to do other things. He was not a good student. He wanted to be like his friends. They couldn't read. She worried what would become of him. And now with this child of the Tower? What would it mean for him, for them? From now she would have to be even more wary. Be alert to any new threat to them.

Rising, she looked at Angus standing in the bedroom. The small figure still lay quietly on the pallet. Sounds of gentle breathing with no signs of distress reached her at the door. Looking at his mother Angus saw her smiling at him.

"She'll be fine. Don't worry. I won't leave her alone. Now off you go. There are deliveries to make. There are others who also need our help. The sooner you go the sooner you will finish."

Taking one last look, Angus started to collect all the items ready for delivery and placed them in his sack before kissing his mother goodbye as he went out the door.

***

It had been a marvellous day. She felt amazing. Despite only catching small amounts of sleep between feeds, these had been deep and refreshing. No back aches. No nausea. Excellent food and wine with a content, quiet baby wrapped up and kept warm by the open fire. At present she stood on the balcony looking up at the dark silhouette against the Eastern Mountains. How attitudes change. One day ago she had been enclosed by her own filth, at the mercy of those so wholly inferior to her and now … now she had returned to herself.

Looking up at the Tower, she was also aware of the irony. Once she had had access to so much more than the Tower could offer. She had surpassed its occupants such that they were no longer worth her consideration. Now, however, she craved that very place. Ached to be once again enclosed within its walls. To be bathed in its darkness, immersed in those windless halls. How things had changed. Such a lowering of her expectations. Yet this would not be forever. She would return, return stronger and with more than she had before. Being the mother of *she that the Tower desired*, she would be a force that could not be denied.

She gave a dry chuckle. The Abbatissa. Poor thing, she had no idea with whom she was dealing. To threaten her! To think that one such as she could challenge her. Such insufferable petulance. It really was quite funny. The Abbatissa, that lowly servant of the Tower, thought that she was a match for her. One who had already surpassed her and now was fulfilling the Tower's wish. Mortella would give it time. It was always better never to rush but savour one's victory. To watch one's opponent wither to suffer increasingly more over time. Now that was so much more satisfying.

Hearing a small cry, Mortella hastened to the cradle. Clara's eyes were open and looked straight at her mother. Unconsciously smiling, Mortella gently lifted up the small bundle, cradling it to her breast. Clara's eyes closed once more as she slept. Keeping the child warm, Mortella returned to the window and gazed to the east. She would need to talk with the Tower and regain entrance. She had no doubt that the Tower would wish her presence and that of her child. It would be at least another 11 or 12 years yet before her Influence would manifest. Yet in the scheme of things that was not long and there was much that Mortella could learn and accomplish. Fortunately the wine was good, and she had comforts of sorts. It could be fun. Being back in the Bowl would have its share of entertainment. Not least of which would be meddling in the affairs of these mere mortals. She would be able to show Clara how it should be done.

The fire was warm. Felix and Silas sat close together relishing the hot food. Nothing special but it was hot … and it was food. Apart from Pick they had been given a wide berth. The others all kept their distance and eyed them with suspicion.

"Don't worry," said Pick when he saw Felix lower his head toward the plate while watching the others warily out the corner of his eye. "They're a good bunch. But we are a suspicious lot. We've all lost someone." Silas looked at the young man. He was less than half their age. How had he come to be here?

"How long have you been with them?" he asked.

"Must be coming on to four years. They found me. Just in time, really."

Felix looked up. "Why do you say that?"

"Because it's true." He looked over his shoulder at Henry. "He found me just after."

Pausing he took another mouthful while the brothers waited for him to continue. When he didn't, Felix gently asked, "After what?" Ignoring the question, Pick rose and returned to the others.

Left alone, they finished their food in silence.

Pick looked back at the brothers. He didn't like thinking about it. Why on earth did he even mention it? He had to learn to control himself better. Stop talking so much. Keep things together. He sure as hell had enough reason to. If it hadn't been for him … It was something he relived again and again.

Just like any other day he and his father had finished work. Still early they arrived home after having wet their whistle at the pub for an hour or so beforehand. It was the first time his pa had allowed him to partake with the others. Until now, he had not been considered old enough. Not that that had stopped him from having an ale, or two, with friends without his father knowing. But this was the first time he had shared one with his pa. He was now sixteen and considered old enough to be a man. It was a special occasion and they had gone through quite a few more pints than would have been normal. Many more than Pick had ever been able to sneak past his pa. Feeling relaxed and happy they had wandered home in the twilight of early evening. The sky was red with the sun now below the Western Mountains.

Once home there were still chores to do. It was just the two of them. Ever since his mother left. It was never spoken of. One day she was there, and then, when he had returned home after work a bit later than usual, she wasn't. A few things were missing but not a lot. Nothing was ever heard from her, and no-one knew where she had gone. That was a few years ago now and Pick and his pa continued on. It worried Pick that his father might be alone. Fortunately they both enjoyed working with wood. They made the barrels needed to transport a multitude of things about the Bowl. He planned on staying. He and his pa, they would be there for each other.

As his father entered the cottage to prepare the evening meal, Pick made his was around the back to feed the chickens. Fresh eggs and every so often a roast hen were always welcome. These, together with the couple of goats and the house garden, provided many of the staples in their diet. They weren't a lot of work.

Through his slightly dulled senses Pick heard a commotion coming from around the back of the cottage. Squawking from overexcited hens got louder as he rounded the corner. In front of him was the hens' enclosure. The creatures were notoriously stupid. If they got out they would wander anywhere and get lost. Not infrequently they would end up stuck in some awkward to access alcove. This normally would require Pick to squeeze through narrow openings in order to rescue the offending bird while being viciously pecked for his efforts. Expecting that one of them was in some such position he looked about. At the other end of the chicken run he spotted a large black dog. Its snout was at the base of the run's fence where it had been digging. The hens were clustered at the other end. As he watched, the dog squeezed under the fence and bounded towards the hens. Pick raced forward yelling loudly, trying to distract the dog.

Without stopping the dog lunged for the nearest hen, too stupid to get away. It jaws clamped down on the feathered body with an audible crunch as blood sprayed across the ground. Reaching the run, Pick started to unlatch the gate as the beast macerated a second. He was finally able to get it open as a third met its fate. His eyes met those of the dog's. Savage eyes full of pain and danger. Barely was the gate open before the dog lunged forward. Pick stepped to the side of the opening a moment before the dog charged through. Pivoting, the animal turned to face him. Steadying itself before the next assault, it snarled. Baring its teeth with nostrils flared, the growl was deep and threatening. Taking the opportunity, Pick sprang through the open gate. Landing on the ground he closed it behind him holding it shut with his foot. The beast crouched back readying to jump. The gate was made of wire. It wasn't made to resist a full-bodied attack.

Bounding forward, the animal launched itself at the gate. Forcing it open, it tumbled past. Pick had no time to rise before he saw it turn again and prowl towards him. Slowing, purposefully it approached. Nothing was now between it and its prey. Pick could feel it's cold hard focus. He felt the hot, metallic breath from the drool-coated snout as it neared. Immobilised by fear, he saw his world held by those powerful jaws. Now only inches away, he saw finality in eyes that held no mercy.

A cry from his father cut through the fog of Pick's mind. The animal turned momentarily before refocusing on the object before it. It raised its head as jaws widened. Pick watched helplessly as his fate began to unfold when suddenly the world inhaled and stopped. Before him were the blood-smeared gums and glistening teeth. Immobile, they were held there. Confused, he looked at the tableau frozen before him. Gradually the head started to move. Slowly it began to descend upon him.

Without warning his mind exploded outwards, flooding everything about. He watched as the dog's eyes widened. Its jaws opened further as time sped up. He then saw the head snap away from him with the eyes rolled back in its head. No longer focusing on him, it convulsed violently before falling heavily on him, pinning him to the ground. Out of the corner of his eye he also saw his father collapse facedown on the grass as he, too, lost consciousness.

***

The sky was dark as he looked up at the worried expression of his father. He was aware that he was on his back, still in the run and things were quiet. His head hurt. And his back. But nothing else. He moved his arms and legs … still there.

"You're okay. Just stay still. Take a bit of time. You've been out for a bit."

Turning his head, Pick was aware of a large black shape beside him. It gave him a start, causing him to push himself up from the ground.

"It's okay. It's dead," he heard his father say.

"How? I don't remember. What happened?"

"Let's get you inside. Hold onto my arm. Here you go." Still supporting Pick, he asked, "Does anything hurt?"

"No, nothing much. I just landed heavily. I'm okay."

Slowly they made their way back to the cottage. Looking behind him, Pick was able to make out the lifeless form of the animal that attacked him. Scattered about the run were other smaller shapes. There was no sound. No movement. Only he had made it out of the run.

"It was attacking our hens. It then attacked me …" he tried to explain.

"I saw," his father cut him off. "I was only able to get out the door." Clearly agitated he paused, wondering what to say next. "You remember the stories?"

Yes, Pick knew the stories. He used to play games about them with his friends. Stories to be told about the fire, in the dark. No-one thought they were real. Just stories used to scare, nothing more.

"The stories are not just stories. They do exist." Red-faced and breathing heavily, his father stood up and looked out the window. "Your mother knew." Under his breath he swore to himself. "From the seven layers of hell, how did this happen … again." Pausing, he turned back to Pick, "You did it," he said accusingly as he sat down again. "You did that," he continued angrily while pointing to the hen run. "After all we've been through."

Pick watched his father, feeling ashamed but not sure what he was ashamed of. Trying to defend himself, he began, "It was going to kill me …"

Seeing the distress on his son's face, his father stopped. Tears in his eyes he said in a sad voice, "I know …"

"Whatever it was, saved me. That's a good thing." Pick looked at his father, "Isn't it?"

"Your mother knew. She knew the Tower didn't like it. They would come. They did come." He bowed his head. "I can't go through it again."

"What?"

"We must prepare." He looked about as if there was someone already there. "They might not have seen."

"How can they see? No-one was here," Pick pleaded, unsure of what was happening. His father's words scared him, "go through it again". His mother?

"Yes, how can they know?" his father agreed, nodding vigorously, but his words didn't match the look in his eyes.

***

Pick slept badly that night and the next, worried about what his father had said. How could anyone know? He didn't understand what was going on and his father remained silent and tense. But maintaining this level of anxiety was not in his nature and, as nothing had happened by the third day, he thought that they were safe. It was only on the fourth evening, when day had passed into a moonless night, that he saw the light. It was red, like an eye, far in the distance, searching. Moving this way and that. Never staying still. He told his father, who clenched his teeth and said nothing. The light appeared over the following two nights and then stopped.

From the day of the incident, Pick's father forbade him from being outside after dark. He would nervously keep an eye on his son. He made sure that the day's work finished early, and then they would come straight home. There he watched as Pick completed all the chores before the sun reached the Western Mountains. Each night at sunset he would then lock them inside the cottage and keep the fires burning bright throughout the night.

Pick was forced to sleep under his bed pallet instead of on top. "Just for the moment, until we are sure," his pa said. "Best that we are not too easy to find." But his words seemed to be more an attempt to reassure himself than being true.

It was just one week after the incident, as the light of day descended into night, that it happened. Pick was bored. Being locked up for the last week was getting to him. To waste time he had started whittling another wooden figurine to add to his collection when he saw his father stand and go to the window. Without looking at his son he called out, "Pick, can you go down to the cellar and get a piece of goat's cheese? I'm feeling a bit hungry." Pick sighed. It was dark and stuffy in the cellar. It wasn't big, with only a small opening in the upper wall that barely let in any light at the best of times. Reluctantly he got up and lifted the trap door. He opened it fully to allow as much light as possible to flood the space. Carefully he climbed down the ladder. Once at the bottom he looked for the wax-coated cheese when the trap door closed heavily above him. Startled, he heard his father threaten him. "You stay there. You hear me. Do not move, or else …"

Cross and confused, he yelled out, "What the hell, Pa …"

To which his father replied sternly, "Silence. You hear me. Not a sound." The extreme anger and fear in the voice forced Pick into silence. Confused, he made it to the opening and looked out.

He heard the door unlock and then open. Peering through the small window, he could make out three shadowy figures standing in the kitchen garden. Careful not to be seen, he watched. He saw his father outlined by the light from the door take a few steps into the yard before stopping.

Facing the figures, Pick heard him say, "That didn't take long." Looking at all three in turn he then added, "Just like last time."

The three appeared to turn to face him as he spoke and silently moved forward.

"Not going to say anything?" Pick heard his father sneer. "Manners not your thing?"

Pick could just make out the shadows as they slowly raised their arms. His father reacted as a chair on the porch suddenly flew toward the beings, only to be deflected and land harmless away to the side. The arms of the figures were now fully raised. His father turned his head and looked directly at him. Locking eyes with his father, he saw the sadness and love in his eyes. Before he could react his father began to dissolve, into broken fragments, like the ash that flies from a campfire only to linger briefly before disappearing. Shocked, he watched as the figures turned and began to melt back into the shadows. Realising what had happened he let forth a gut-wrenching cry of loss that shattered the air and froze his heart.

And now he was here. No longer alone. He looked at the men about him. They were getting stronger. Every day there were more of them. The crones from the Tower would answer for what they had done. He would make sure of that.

Chapter 12

The cascading sound of water provided a gentle background to the idyllic scene. A small child gurgled with delight as she was tipped over onto her stomach by her mother, only for her to immediately roll again onto her back. This had been the source of great amusement for both over the last half hour. Sitting next to the child on several large silk cushions, Mortella's smile shone with a radiant beauty that required no Influence to augment. What a joy it was to know that she and her daughter would share the Code together. None there had ever been gifted with such a treasure as she for, prior to her, none of the Code had borne a child. She looked up at the Tower. Time had sped. The last few months were a bit of a blur. Sleep had been claimed in the moments when Clara allowed it. It had been hard, but dealing with difficulties and challenges had never daunted her before. Feed, sleep, wash, cuddle, feed, sleep, and repeat. There were the maids that waited to be called, but Mortella preferred to do it herself. She knew that none but she could ever do it as well, and … Clara needed her to do it.

The child giggled as once again she rolled unceremoniously onto her back with arms and legs wriggling in the air like an upended turtle. Looking at her mother, she blew a bubble as she waited to be flipped again so the game could continue. Instead of turning her, however, Mortella picked up the precious bundle and faced the black oblique that dominated the eastern sky. Lifting the infant high into the air, Mortella pointed her toward the Tower before once again clasping the child tightly to her breast.

"You see that?" she whispered into the infant's ear. "That is our destiny. Through those doors we shall walk and then out into the world beyond to be all we can be." Clara gurgled as she blew more small bubbles out of her nose. "You don't have to worry. You are expected. You will have nothing to fear there, and I will be with you. You will never have to be alone, for we can be together forever."

Mortella continued to gaze at the Tower. It made her think. It would soon be time. Time to address the Tower and regain access to its walls. She would need to make sure that things would be ready for Clara when it was time for her to be presented to the Code. There were those who didn't make it through the Tower. Lowly ones not even worthy of being one of the Tower varlets, or as those of the Bowl knew them, a Dark One. That would never be the case for Clara. She was foretold. Together they would join those outside the confines of the Bowl. Clara would rise to power, and, with her mother's help, they both would ascend to the Presence. Mortella smiled to herself as she thought, beware to those who have disregarded me.

Turning from the view of their future, Mortella took Clara inside. She had avoided much of the finery offered to her since Clara's birth. But now, she had a craving for something a bit special. Clara was doing well and tonight she wanted to spoil herself. Beckoning one of the maids that was busy cleaning the drawing room, she handed Clara over to her care.

"Call the nursemaid. She will care for Clara for the rest of today." Mortella walked past the servant as she called over her shoulder, "Oh, and call the seamstress. I will need something special. Let the master know that we shall dine together this evening." Leaving the room Mortella made for her chambers where she planned to luxuriate in a bath.

Undressing, she sat looking at herself in the dressing table mirror. She commenced brushing her luxurious auburn hair when her eyes landed on the small but exquisitely crafted gift that Charles had sent to celebrate the birth of his first child. A broach consisting of two midnight onyx berries, each mounted on a five-pointed star enamelled in lustrous dark green. With them was a small five-petaled flower crafted out of amethyst of the deepest purple. Captivated, she ran a finger lightly across each before sucking the tip. He did know how to entice her. Belladonna. Fathomless and dark it drew her into its possibilities. She felt ready to engage with him again. Ready to engage, but only after a long, luxurious soak in a deep tub of rose-scented water.

***

Back at their plot, Felix and Silas worked hard to try and get some sense of normality back. They needed to be wary. Ready to protect themselves from the Tower. Felix knew that they had to be ready to disappear if threatened. Things were no longer the same and they knew that they had to do something. But what, was the question and, even more importantly, how?

Their time outside the Bowl had been confusing. After a few days camping out in the weather, they had once again been blindfolded and led to what appeared to be a more permanent encampment. Even so, it was just a collection of roughly hewn buildings made up of wooden frames and canvas coverings. Hardly a comfortable place to stay for any length of time. Here, there were others that also looked on the brothers with suspicion.

It was in this place that they were to be questioned further, but until then, they would have to wait. Once the blindfolds had been removed Henry warned them to keep to themselves. Never to wander far from the encampment and speak to no-one unless first approached. He indicated that things may be revealed in time and as appropriate.

They were allocated a small sleeping tent that at least had a thick layer of dried rushes to insulate them from the cold that had permeated deep into their bones from the ground beneath during the previous nights. A blanket of sorts was provided to each, and they were to be allowed to eat with the others, if somewhat separated. As the sun set on that first night, the brothers looked back at the mountains that formed the northern-most border of their home. The sky above them was already dark, covered with ominous thick black clouds. To their surprise, the setting sun could still be seen lighting up the sky above the Bowl. They looked at one another with confusion.

"Odd, isn't it? came a voice behind them. Recognising Pick's voice they turned and smiled. They had taken a liking to the young man, brash and confident with the enthusiasm of youth. "It's always like that. It's rarely the same out here."

"Why's that?" asked Felix.

"They say that it's the Tower," Pick replied, looking grim. "It gathers all those who can do that sort of thing and locks them inside. Takes and uses what it wants to make that place … different." Flexing his fingers, he continued. "Out here it gets cold. In there, it never seems to."

"Why?" Felix repeated.

"I'm not supposed to know … but there's more to it than just that." He looked behind him. As no-one was near he continued. "That place," he said pointing to the Bowl, "is just the start. There's a lot more that the crones want than just that place." Pausing, he looked at Felix. "I don't know much but I know that it's a lot bigger." He stopped again and then smiled. "Supper's ready. Come on, you want to get there early in case there are seconds."

It was cold that night and the blankets weren't thick. Fortunately the brothers had also been provided with thick jackets to protect against the chill. These, together with the blankets, and each other's body warmth, were barely sufficient to allow a passable sleep. At the break of day they arose tired and stiff from the uncomfortable night.

"Breakfast won't be for some time," grumbled Silas, "and no-one seems to want to talk to us."

"It takes time," was all the response his brother provided.

"Well, don't you want more?"

"Of course, but it all takes time," he repeated. Seeing Silas' face looking grim, Felix continued, "What if we were in their shoes? What do you think we would do? Hmm?"

"Well, *you* would wait …"

"And you?"

Reluctantly Silas conceded. "I suppose I would want to know more about them."

"Exactly! So we will have to wait until they are ready." As he was speaking, Pick arrived at the tent.

"I've got oranges," he called. "I traded them for a bit of information and … also what I heard whilst I was helping clean up last night," he added in a smaller voice as he got closer.

Felix smiled at him. It was like seeing a younger version of his brother. A bit dishevelled and overconfident but gregariously engaging and immediately likable.

"I would be more interested in the information than the orange," he said as he started peeling the fruit handed him. Silas nodded in agreement to encourage Pick further. Giving them both a conspiratorial smile, Pick sat down with his back to the tent.

"Well … I heard that they will arrive today. Seems like they're interested in you." He looked at Silas and then at Felix.

"Arrive from where?" Felix asked.

"They're Outlanders. They come from somewhere outside the Bowl.

"But we're outside the Bowl now," said Felix, looking toward the boundary of the Northern Slopes.

"Yes, but they … well they never were from the Bowl. Not like the rest of us." He paused. He continued in a whisper, "They're called the Apostasy.

They come here sometimes, bringing supplies. At other times we go a couple of days' travel east and meet them. Things aren't going too good out there."

"Have you been further out?' asked Felix.

"Only once. My job is to find others, others like us. I do that in there," Pick answered, pointing to the mountains. "Supposedly there's not a lot like us further out."

"Why not?"

"Something to do with the Tower. Those crones have spread everywhere."

"Do you know who's coming?"

"Didn't get any names but they're supposedly some of the boss ones, those supposedly most in charge."

"And what was the other information?" Silas prodded.

"Oh … well … that's about you two. As I said, there's lots of interest." Pick looked at the ground as he blushed a little. "I may have exaggerated … just a bit. It makes for a better story. And now," he paused as he looked up, "they will be less likely to, well, less likely to … cause you any problems."

Silas chuckled. "We hardly look dangerous, and our Influence can't hurt anyone."

"But *they* don't know that," replied Pick with a grin.

***

As the morning waned the brothers remained sitting by themselves. There was very little for them to do but wait. Apart from Pick no-one had approached or even acknowledged them.

How much longer do you think?

…

You don't have to roll your mind's eye at me!!!

We both have to wait. How should I know? complained Felix. Sullenly Silas looked back toward the camp. Someone was coming. He stood, grabbing Felix's arm to warn him. Felix also rose, awaiting the approaching figure.

"They want to talk with you," was the less than friendly greeting. "Follow me." The man immediately turned and walked back to the camp. Looking at Felix, Silas smiled.

Now we're in for it.

Felix was asked to sit. Silas had been taken elsewhere but was being asked to do the same. In front of him were two figures, cloaked and hooded. It

105

reminded him of the stories of the Dark Ones. In all other ways, however, they were nothing like the Tower. There was no grima, nothing about them that tried to invade, trying to cross the boundaries of his mind.

Their cloaks were rough-hewn, and travel worn. Confidence and authority emanated from the one on the left. The other exuded an inner calm.

Will we keep things open?

I expect that is what they will be wanting.

Will do.

Once seated, the figures then sat facing them from the other side of the room.

"We have heard what happened and what you have told the others. Can you add to this?" Felix could hear Silas being asked the same.

Start with your visit to the Tower.

Can do.

Together they spoke of the Tower and how it had always been the background noise to their lives, about their need to understand more about it and of their first close-up encounter with the Tower. Felix was surprised at the emotion in his voice as they tried to explain. The Tower was a multitude. A thing of innumerable tormented individuals. A thing of unquenchable desire, encasing a yearning, a lust for life. A thing it didn't possess.

Felix stopped, as did Silas, and gazed at those before him. Looking from one to the other he signalled Silas. Together they described the waif and the voice and words that had flowed through their minds, "not to be tolerated", as a myriad of youths were torn apart amid silent screams.

There was a change in the one on the left. The shoulders, no longer straight, had drooped as the hood fell even lower over the face. The calm it exuded had gone. Knowing what they said held truth and significance for their interrogators, Felix signalled Silas.

Now?

Agreed.

"It knows of us now, and we know it will come. We know that we can't stay hidden. But it gave us a word. Stitched through everything was a single word." Felix watched as both figures straightened. "It was a word it wanted us to know. As a warning, taunt, or perhaps just to gloat. We don't know. But it was a word that had great meaning for the Tower." He waited, breathing slowly. Simultaneously with Silas he whispered, "Mortella."

***

Whether the revelations convinced their interrogators, or not, neither knew. Now having been left alone, each remained where they were. Each waiting while watched over by a silent guard.

They left rather quickly.

They've heard it before. Did you see how one responded when we spoke of the boys?

Personal experience, I expect.

It hit them hard.

So what now?

We wait.

And then?

Let's see.

It was not too long before the cloaked figures returned. Once again seated, proof of the brothers' story was to be assessed further. Silas was told to inform Felix what was happening and that he was to report this to those in his room. He was then shown various items. Once done he was blindfolded, and several phrases were whispered into his ear. Finally earmuffs were also placed over their ears, and he was handed various items to feel and given several things to taste. The process was then reversed with Felix to inform Silas. The figures again left the room before Silas was requested to join them with Felix.

Back together again the brothers sat facing the four figures, now uncloaked. They were haggard. Three men and one woman made up the group. Felix noted that it was the woman who had reacted most to the youths being Taken.

"What do you know of the Code?" asked the eldest of the group. Silas looked at his brother.

"Nothing," he shrugged.

"The region called the Bowl is under the 'protection' of the Code." He looked closely at the brothers as he added, "The Bowl is not their goal but a means to achieve their goal." he waited. As there was no response, he continued. "There is far more going on outside of your insular land."

"But what's the Code?" asked Silas.

The man looked at Silas. "The Code wants control. It insinuates itself into everything. Insidiously it manipulates events, people, the world, so that the Code are the masters of all without almost anyone realising."

The woman continued. "The Bowl extends their control through the ones it breeds. It collects those with the power, or as you call it, Influence.

They warp the users to their will. Gradually the Code extends its power over all by subverting them." She paused. "They only accept women. But they do not waste the men. From these they strip what is human from the power. They take the essence of who they once were. Imprisoned, they keep what is left of them with their power intact within what is called the Tower. There they linger, without thought or individuality. They are held and are used." Taking in a slow breath, she added, "The Code uses and controls."

The elder man placed a reassuring hand on the woman's arm.

"What's outside the Bowl?" interrupted Silas.

"Something that you're not prepared for," was all the reply they received.

"If this Code is so strong, what can be done?" Felix asked.

The woman looked at him. "To reduce the impact of the Code we first must cut its supply. To this the Tower is central. If the Tower can be reduced, then much more may be done." She looked at her colleagues, who nodded. "We have heard of Mortella. She is a practitioner wholly committed to the Code. Why the Tower gave her name …"

"We need to know her role and what it means. To know this, to be fore-warned, may allow intervention." Standing, the elder man nodded to the others. "We will talk further. Until then, have the freedom of the camp."

Outside, Pick was waiting for the brothers, holding two cups of steaming hot soup.

"How'd it go?" he asked cheerfully, handing a cup to each of the grateful brothers who had missed the midday fare. "Talk in the kitchen has been all about you and little else. We haven't seen four of them all at once before. Rarely any more than one. No-one can ever remember seeing a woman among them. We thought that they were all part of the Tower."

"They called them the Code," said Felix.

"And they're everywhere. What's further outside? They wouldn't tell us," asked Silas.

"I've never seen. Few from the Bowl ever do. We're told that it isn't safe. That we're not ready. Those who have, come back changed. They won't talk of it," Pick responded. "But if it's a choice between these here and them … I choose these guys."

***

Now back in the Bowl, enjoying the last of the warmth of the setting sun, it surprised Felix how much hadn't been told them. He pondered what little they did know as he worked. Stirring the barrel of pungent rotting fish in front of him was relaxing. They still needed to tend to the fish and collect the essence. Life at least had regained a semblance of normality to it while they continued to decide how to proceed. They knew of the Tower and now that there were others outside the borders of the Bowl. From what he gathered from the Outlanders, out there were many more people than inside the Bowl. There were great cities the size of which he couldn't comprehend. He looked over at the waters of the lower dam. Few there had plots like he and his brother. Most lived in what were these ever-expanding cities. There, life was controlled, regulated, restricted, with each citizen maintaining their place. He paused and tried to relax. He loved watching the sun flicker on the rippling surface of the dam. He concentrated on the moment, felt the breeze, and heard a dove cooing. How much they were risking. How much had they had jeopardised of their idyllic world solely out of curiosity. The Tower knew of them. Their actions had exposed them. Had they only kept quiet and hidden. He sighed as he shook his head. Now, now, they *could* choose to keep their head down and hope to remain as they once had been. But the memory of that single, lingering, hopeless cry still chilled him. The Tower had seen them, and it would only be a matter of time before it acted. Keeping their head down and doing nothing was no longer an option. They needed to do something. And that something needed to happen before the Tower got to them first.

Chapter 13

Once again in her chamber, Mortella began cleaning herself after the evening's activities. She prided herself that she had never looked better. And that was without the use of Influence. Supper had not disappointed. Cook consistently surprised her, rarely failing to delight her senses of taste, sight and smell with every dish presented – a real craftswoman and one worth remembering once Clara and she would leave this place.

She washed carefully. Charles had been ferocious. Well, she thought as she admired her reflection, it had been a while. Clara was over four months old, and this was the first time they shared themselves since she had found out that she was pregnant. She had worn the broach at the centre of her dress, just below the plunging neckline of her tightly fitted bodice. Shamelessly drawing attention to the creaming smoothness of her voluptuous figure. Not that Charles had needed any other incentive to look. But it delighted her to see the unsettling affect her beauty had on him.

Another bath was in order. Beside the tub she had placed a bowl of lemons. It was routine practice in the knocking shop. Never pleasant, but necessary. One and one only, that was all. She never wanted to go through that again. Clara, wonderful little Clara fulfilled everything. Just watch them rise. But never again would she allow herself to be subjected to the control of Mrs Poole and that magot of a man who abused her in the name of caring for the heir.

She felt just an ounce of pity for Charles. He wanted a son. But then we all want things that we never get, she thought. And there is nothing stopping him getting one later on. Just not from me. He will have ample opportunity to get an heir once Clara and I are past the Tower and into the world beyond.

However, in the meantime she would indulge him, and they would be able to enjoy all the physical pleasures. She smiled to herself. Another thing that those who took the Black would never experience. It may not have been her wish to be so unceremoniously ousted from the Code, but there were at least some benefits. And time was something that she would have more than enough of once she regained her status and continued to rise.

Cutting the lemons she squeezed their juice into a bowl and soaked a soft woollen sponge in the clear golden liquid. Undressing, she immersed herself in the fragrant water. First a thorough cleanse, and then she would leave the sponge in place as she slept.

***

They needed to be prepared and the cellar seemed the perfect place. It was separate from the house with an entrance that could be easily hidden. It would become their safe place if, or more realistically when, the Dark Ones made their visit. Silas had been working on it since first light. To begin he had removed everything that had been stored there. He even found a few treasured items that had been totally forgotten. Then he started making it bigger. It was slow, cramped, and backbreaking work but it made him feel good to be doing something and not just waiting. As always, he was once again expecting his overly cautious brother to decide what to do next. This at least was something that he had control over.

The roof needed added support. The ground above was not particularly solid and as the space was enlarged, collapse became more likely. It was also near the stream. They had placed it there by design as it helped keep the area cool, but it also kept the soil moist and even more likely to move.

Without discussing it with Felix, he made his way to the lower dam. Near the lower shore they had stacked stone blocks, kept in advance of creating a small holding pond for breeding fish. Fish when big enough could be seeded back to the dams. The space underground needed to be watertight. Well, at least as watertight as he could make it. So now these blocks were needed for something else. The breeding pond would just have to wait.

It took time and a lot of effort, but he had finally enlarged the space to at least twice its original size. Looking about, he admired his efforts. The fresh walls were now lined with the stone blocks. The mortar between would aid in the waterproofing so needed to keep the space dry. Topping the walls were beams that spanned the open space providing support to the ground above. In the furthest corner from the entrance was one remaining gap in the stone wall. Through it he saw the rich dark soil. That, he thought, could be made into another exit. A *just-in-case* exit. Just in case the main entrance was compromised. In case they needed another way out.

111

Satisfied with what he had achieved, he climbed out of the cellar into the diminishing light. It had been a successful day. Wiping his face he felt both tired and fulfilled. He stood relishing the breeze as he watched Felix make his way back to the cottage from the upper dam. Then unexpectedly something caught his eye – off in the distance. Something was moving, a figure, barely made out, was making its way towards their cottage.

You expecting anyone?

No. Why?

Well, there's someone coming this way. They should be here in about fifteen.

Seldom were the visitors that made their way out to their holding. The brothers had carefully chosen a plot a bit further away from the village. Their peculiarities were best kept from others. Meeting friends would normally occur within the local tavern. Unexpected visitors were even less likely. Those that made their way out here all came with a purpose. Others never made the journey.

Go around the back and keep out of sight until we know what's going on.

I'll keep close. Close enough to bring them down from behind if needed.

Hopefully that won't be necessary.

You never know!

Silas quickly made his way to the back of the cottage and picked up the axe they used for chopping wood. Looking at it, he reconsidered. Prising off the metal head he kept the solid handle, giving it a few good swings. *I don't think I would be able to … even if needed. But this should be enough.* Now armed, he remained out of sight whilst maintaining as much of a view of the path as possible. The approaching figure continued making its way to the cottage. He saw Felix emerge from the front door and look towards the approaching figure. They had never been this anxious about visitors before. But things had changed.

You okay?

Yes. You feel anything?

Nothing out of the ordinary.

Silas could feel Felix opening up his mind, probing the area about them while gradually extending the range. He did the same. The rumble of the Tower with its inhabitants was there like static, nothing new, nothing different.

All seems quiet.

They waited, listening with their minds to any change, any discord, any grima. The figure was lost to Silas' view as it passed the grove of trees about six minutes' brisk walk from the cottage. He wiped his face again on his sleeve. Not that it made much difference. It only smeared the dirt across it instead of removing any. How he hated waiting. What would they do if it was from the Tower? They would come again and there would be more of them. They would have to leave. He hadn't considered that before. He didn't want to leave. But they would have no choice. This was the first time he considered that perhaps his journey to the Tower all those months ago had not been the best of ideas. *Felix will know want to do. He always knows what to do.*

Feeling uncharacteristically nervous, Silas carefully made his way around the other side of the cottage. This would allow him to sneak up on the figure from behind – if necessary. Why was it taking so long? Couldn't they walk faster? He felt the tension rise within him as he raised the axe handle high above his right shoulder, ready to strike. Slowly he crept around the corner. He saw no-one. They must surely be on the last stretch. On the path just before it turned directly toward the cottage. So stupid of us to have so much of the path unseen when it was so close to the cottage, he thought. That will change.

He listened. Nothing. Nothing but the wind and occasional bird call. He felt uneasy, unsure. Feelings foreign to him. He stretched out his mind. Nothing new. Then he saw the back of the figure as it finally came into view. Steadying himself, watching, hidden, ready to pounce forward and bring them down. Dirt laden sweat stung his eyes, causing him to try to wipe his vision clean. Held tight like a loaded spring, he was ready. Almost time.

Silas saw the figure raise its arm. Threat or greeting? He couldn't tell. A yell to distract them. Then one firm hit to the head. They'd have no time to react. The figure moved out of his vision again. Wait, almost, not just yet. They needed to get a bit closer.

Silence, he felt and heard nothing. The world around him was frozen in anticipation. No breeze, no sound as he held himself ready.

It's Pick. It's only Pick. The relief in Felix's mental tone was physically palpable to his brother.

Without lowering the handle Silas quickly turned around the corner. Now he was now able to make out the features of the young man as he walked quickly toward the cottage.

Was it always going to be like this now?

***

Felix and Silas shared a wry smile with each other as the three of them sat at the kitchen table clasping their ales. Something stronger might have been better in order to calm their nerves, but this would have to do.

"We get word almost every week of another one. That's where I come in," said Pick.

"Nobody's safe."

"Not if they have an Influence." Pick paused. "And it's getting worse. Most of the time I don't get to them before …"

"Before?"

"You know … before they come." Grabbing his tankard, Pick took a nervous sip. "Usually there's not a single person that'll say anything. Like they never were there, never existed."

"They're scared," said Felix softy.

"So? Why's that an excuse?" interrupted Silas, standing up abruptly while glaring at the walls about them. "Doing nothing just lets them get away with more. And … and we're not going to do nothing!" He looked down at his brother, almost pleading for him to say something, to tell him anything that they could do. Felix looked back at his twin and gestured for him to sit and calmly added.

"No … we're not going to do nothing."

Sitting down, Silas watched Felix.

You have a plan?

Naturally.

You're not just saying that?

Ignoring his brother, Felix looked at Pick. "I think it's about time for supper. I've got out the salted pork. Was going to make a pork and legume soup. It shouldn't take too long." Looking at Silas, he added, "And we have the bread you got a couple of days ago. Better if it gets toasted."

We'll talk about it later.

Getting up from the table, Felix went over to the kitchen fire and stoked the coals.

"Pick, there's a trough of cleanish water near the lower dam if you want to wash off some of the travel dirt."

"Out the door and head up the slope," added Silas.

"Food should be ready when you return."

"You best be quick then, I'm not one to take washing all that seriously," quipped Pick as he left the cottage.

"So?" said Silas, turning back to face his brother.

"We are going to do something," was the reply he received.

"No, you're not getting away with that. What are we going to do?"

Felix busied himself with preparing supper. But he understood his brother all too well. He knew that he was not going to be given any peace until he relented and said something. Eventually he added, "You remember when we were in Town … the old scribe."

"And?"

"You remember what he said?"

"That we copied the parchment and were provoking the Tower."

"No … well yes, but he also said, just as we were leaving, 'there are more than just the two of you', remember? It's a starting point. He must know about the Apostasy … and the Code. I'm sure he knows a lot more than he was willing to say."

"We must get as much information as we can. The Tower and those … *things* it holds … can't continue."

The brothers looked at each other. A cheery voice broke the silence as Pick entered the cottage. "As clean as I'll ever get. So … food ready?"

We will find out about this Mortella.

Nodding, Silas continued to toast the bread as Felix began to serve the soup, giving the bowls to Pick who put them on the table.

"Wasn't too hard to find you," started Pick as he took a spoonful of soup. "Everyone in the village knows who you are. The best fish anywhere, they say." He lowered his head and studiously examined the table while he continued in low voice, "Things aren't going too well out there, supposedly. They really need your help … more than any of us can really know." He looked up briefly without catching the eye of either brother. "They want you to go back." When neither brother said anything, Pick sheepishly added, "I know … I remember what you told me. About the last time. But … they're picking us off. One by one. Every day there's less of us and they get stronger."

Felix nodded. "No, we know, they can't be left. Something has to be done to stop them."

"We were planning to head back to Town anyway," added Silas.

Pick immediately brightened, "I'm coming too. I was heading near there anyway," he added with enthusiasm.

***

Early the next morning the three left the dams. Travelling light they headed toward the village to catch the eastbound cart to Town. The expectation of an uncomfortable journey fulfilled, they arrived at the Town gates with the business of day in full swing. At least the trip had been uneventful. Grabbing their packs they entered the gates to join the mallee that comprised Town, dodging the heavy-laden carts bound for market as the tide of people ebbed and flowed along the buildings surrounding the square.

"We'll need lodgings." Turning to Silas, his brother added, "You know this place better than I do. Where should we go? We may need to be able to get out quickly. Any problems and we go."

"I know a place," interrupted Pick. The brothers looked at him in surprise. "It's not my first time! Follow me," he added as he led the brothers out of the square. For half an hour they weaved in and out of the narrow streets and back alleys. Occasionally they doubled back on themselves before eventually emerging at the northern edge of Town that bordered the rugged, untamed terrain. There, dominating the slopes above them was the Tower, a black velvet shadow despite the bright light of day.

"It's quiet during daylight. But we will need to strengthen our barriers," warned Silas.

"We need to rest," added Felix.

"Wait here," said Pick. "They know me. I'll get things organised. Won't be long." Pick bounded off with the energy of the young, leaving the brothers to contemplate the evening before them.

Placing his belongings on the ground Felix looked at the Tower and shuddered from the memory of the last visit. "We're so close. It wouldn't take much for them to feel us."

"Keep things shut down. Only use them if we have to. I understand … but," continued Silas, placing a hand on his brother's shoulder, "it's going to be a lot better with you here. We'll keep ourselves hidden and find out everything we need." Looking back at the Tower he added grimly, "Don't think we're going to sleep much tonight."

***

Sybil continued grinding the herbs as she looked at Jess, for that was the name they had all agreed upon. For the girl her son had brought to them had no memory of any other. The gentle, pretty girl eagerly watched every step of the process. Sybil was teaching her the making of basic tinctures and tonics she used on a daily basis. Jess had demonstrated a natural talent for the work and a desire to excel. To those who visited their cottage, Jess was the apprentice. There was more than enough work for another healer and Sybil enjoyed both the company and interest of another.

The last few months had passed quickly. With it, so had the hypervigilance that had accompanied Jess' arrival. The constant watch for anything that suggested an interest from the Tower. But as time progressed it seemed that the Tower and those within didn't care, or had failed to notice, that the child had left its walls.

Angus doted on her. That much the most casual observer could not doubt. She in turn returned to him admiration in equal measure. Acknowledging her enthusiasm to learn, Angus offered to teach her to read. Each evening they sat, heads close together, talking quietly as Sybil watched a bond of compassion and understanding gradually develop between the two. Jess' enthusiasm had also prompted Angus to apply himself to the books in a way he never previously had.

Yet all was not calm. The nightly terrors that tore at the sleep of their adoptee continued. And for every one of them Angus was there. Ready to comfort and reassure. To Jess, Angus and his mother were everything. She remembered virtually nothing before the time the great door of the Tower blocked out the light and world beyond. Inside the Tower, alone and tormented, she had wandered until chance had let her leave. Of her time there she spoke little, and she never spoke of, or used, her Influence.

Sybil in turn used her gift with caution and only when needed to heal. She always had. The Tower had never shown any interest in her. But still, she was wary. Stopping, she handed the mixture to Jess.

"Now you know what to do. Gradually add the oil while you mix. We want a smooth paste."

Jess took the mortar and slowly added the oil, stirring as she did. Exactly as she had been shown. Sybil smiled. It wouldn't be long before Jess could do this unaided. This would allow for more time to search for other remedies to aid her patients. It would be a benefit, but for how long was unclear. One thing Sybil had learnt, over her many years was that the Tower was never safe. Although things may be calm now, eventually …

"I think it's done," said Jess, showing her mentor the paste.

"That's good. We'll be needing that for Mrs Fith this afternoon." Jess smiled broadly at the acknowledgement of a job well done.

Sybil returned the smile but this time it was mixed with a sadness. Things would change. She could never know when, but she was sure they would and not for the better. They would have to be ready.

Chapter 14

As the sun dropped below the Western Slopes there was a palpable change. No longer was the hum merely in the background. It had begun to assert itself further. Trying to intrude into the brothers' consciousness. Locking down the prickly sensations that tirelessly prodded their thoughts, they waited. Eventually Pick returned.

"More than enough room for us." He grinned at them and then grimaced, "If you don't mind that we all share the same room." He glanced briefly up at the Tower. "It should be fine to take you there now. The streets are mostly empty. We don't really want anyone to see where we go." Turning, he led the brothers back into one of the allies, now even more shrouded in shadow than when they came.

He was taking them to what he called a "burrow". "It's somewhere that vermin like us can feel safe," he joked. A shadow crossed his face as his voice dropped, "But, in truth, we need them. None of us are safe. Not really. Not with that," he said, finishing with a flick of the head towards the east.

They arrived at a nondescript door located in an unremarkable alley with a pile of garbage as a welcoming mat. Felix looked sideways at his brother who just smiled. "Well, what did you expect?" He responded.

"It's better inside … well, just a bit," Pick added. Knocking on the door provoked movement inside. Eventually the door was partially opened allowing a weak light to escape into the alley.

"And?" came a gruff male voice.

"It's time for all good boys to be home," Pick responded, causing the door to open wide, revealing a stooped, dishevelled, frail looking elderly man accompanied by a large hound.

"Far too late for that, young Pick," retorted the man with a crooked smile. "Good was never a word that was used for you." Seeing Pick looking uneasily at the dog, the old man nodded. "Forgot," was all he said as he turned and put the animal safely behind a door off to the side. Pick nodded his thanks as the man ushered the travellers inside and closed the door.

"These are the ones I told you about … those outside need their help." The old man looked the brothers up and down with renewed interest.

"I won't ask, so don't tell," he said as he turned and started to walk away. "Follow, I'll show you where you can sleep. If sleep is something you'll be wanting," he added looking over his shoulder. "I expect you might be wanting a bit of added freedom in the night. Pick can show you another way in. I'll leave that unbolted a bit later if you need it."

He led them through a surprising labyrinth of small, winding corridors. The outside of the burrow gave no suggestion as to the extent of the building inside. The room he deposited them in was windowless, containing two wooden slabs for beds. A couple of chairs were against the wall. Sitting on a bed, Pick looked at Felix.

"What's the plan?"

Watching Silas, Felix also sat and said slowly, "We're going to the Tower."

"We need to see if we can talk to the Tower," added Silas grimacing. "I've done it once before."

"We'll be stronger … the two of us," added Felix in a voice that was less than reassuring.

"Great, when are we going?" chimed in Pick, a little too cheerfully.

"We're going … not you," said Felix firmly. "Don't you see how serious this is? It's the Tower."

"We're going up to the Tower," added Silas, exasperated.

"Yeah sure, I know you are." Pick looked grim then added with a laugh, "I suppose you might be able to stop me." Becoming serious again he looked Felix straight in the eyes. Speaking in a sombre tone, "You're not leaving me out. No chance."

Silas looked at his brother. "Told you."

"Anyway, who's going to show you the way back once you're done?" Pick smiled again. "I'm also pretty damn good in a scrape. Didn't take much for me to put you two out."

Silas scowled at the memory of the hours of discomfort. Pick noticed, looking rather sheepish. "You can't blame me. We had no idea of who you were."

"No Influence," said Felix firmly. "Not that close to the Tower. It can sense it." Looking directly at Pick, his face serious. "No Influence. Agreed?"

"No Influence," Pick nodded. "Anyway, from what you've told me about last time, it mightn't be too bad to have someone not able to hear the Tower. Just in case."

"Agreed," said Felix.

"So when are we going?"

Nodding slowly, Silas explained, "The Tower's more active at night. Always has been. Better chance of getting it to talk to us."

"We'll go soon. As soon as we can, but also when we'll be least likely to be seen."

"Well, in this place, everyone's tucked up at home as soon as the sun sets. Never anyone on the streets after sundown." The real reason for this was left unspoken. Pick looked about the room. "Anyone hungry?"

***

It was when evening came that she felt more herself than at any other time of the day. As a child she had her chores at night. That's when the johns came. That's when things needed cleaning. Daytime was for rest. To recover from the night before. Now, standing at the balcony overlooking her favourite garden, she gazed at the Tower, dark and majestic. She had, in truth, enjoyed her time with the Tower. Better to have surpassed it, but still! It had given her time to be her own mistress. Time did soften memories … but now that she was outside the Code, the Tower looked that much more inviting.

She turned back to the room behind. Its lush extravagance, so starkly obvious in contrast to the tower that loomed beyond. She felt it. It was time. She had waited long enough. She had been away too long. Tonight, she thought. Yes, tonight. No longer would she wait. Tonight she would.

***

Finally able to straighten up, Silas emerged from the narrow opening that led him into one of the more unsavoury allies he had ever experienced. Felix noticed the look on his face.

"Well, it makes it less likely to be found."

"We purposely put all this stuff here," added Pick whilst holding his nose. "One whiff of that and no-one's gonna come down."

"What is it?" asked Silas, grimacing, trying to breathe as little as possible.

"Oh, anything that's gone off. The more pungent the better." He paused, "I thought that you of all people would cope. You make rotten fish!"

"And that smells a thousand times better than this," chimed in Felix.

121

"Can we just get out of here? I can feel my nose hairs burning."

"It's not far," Pick stated as he led them between the piles of rubbish that hid the opening. "At least you can follow your nose to get home," he sniggered.

Enjoying the fresh air as they left the alley behind, Pick weaved them through the shadowed streets to the northern side of Town. The moon was yet to rise but the sky was clear, allowing starlight to illuminate the untamed land that existed outside the borders of Town. They looked up the slope to the Tower. It could only be distinguished as a void. A void outlined by stars. Silas glanced knowingly at his brother. Felix looked back. They would need to work hard at their defences. At least being forewarned allowed them to be more prepared.

"It's already started. So much louder," Silas complained.

"So many voices …"

"But no real individuals."

"No, more like just traces of someone … echoes of who they used to be."

"Not fully there"

"No. We'll have to keep them fully blanketed. There's no benefit from listening to it now."

Silas nodded.

"Only when we try to engage … and then only one of us."

"The other will keep watch. Ready to raise the barriers if needed."

"Agreed."

Pick looked at the men slightly bemused. "You don't really need that mind reading stuff, do you?" He scoffed. "You already know what the other's gonna say."

Felix smiled, "We've been together for a very long time." He turned to face the Tower and asked, "Which way?"

***

Donning the Black felt good. She may have been ousted from the Code, but that was only for a time. Soon she would be wearing it, and it only. She glanced at the elegant gown that was draped on the day bed. Not much of a loss. Not when compared to what she would gain. She raised the hood over her head as she silently left her chamber. Clara would be with the nursemaid. She was weaning now. Anyway, she wouldn't be too long. Only long enough for a chat.

Making her way through the brightly lit passages of her gilded prison, Mortella passed unseen by the servants and a number of late supplicants there to see her husband. A simple use of the Influence was all that was required. No-one perceived her, so no questions would be asked. Leaving the overly bright interior she emerged into the welcoming night. It would take a little more Influence to get the gates unlocked but nothing that was too challenging. Scanning the sky to the east, the Tower's velvet blackness soothed her mind as she glided through the scented garden.

Alone in the shadowed street she turned and began the gentle climb. It would get steeper and then there were the stairs. Those long, beautiful, graceful stairs that led to a destiny that enticed and thrilled. Wrapping the cloak about her she began to walk. With a light and graceful step, she began her reacquaintance with her future and her way back to the Tower

***

The climb was slow as the ground was rough and uneven. Boulders littered the way and coarse scrub caught at their feet, threatening a fall. As the land became wilder, the cacophony of voices increasingly cried for entrance. An onslaught of desperate and frenetic cries crashed upon the barricades of the brothers' minds. Each felt the other's barrier. Each provided further support to strength and buttress the other against the relentless assault. But such effort took concentration, giving little reserve for anything else. Their focus was already taken. It was thus Pick who led them. Guiding them towards the Tower and the black stone landing that lay before the great door.

Now off to the side of the stairs and hidden from the great door, the brothers sat facing each other, heads down and eyes closed. Felix rubbed his eyes.

"We need to focus. It's more than expected."

"It's … worse than before," Silas grumbled. "So much … desire."

"Ignore. Don't listen. Let nothing through."

With one clasping the hands of the other they wove together walls to block out the cries. Strand by strand they meshed together barriers that muffled and softened the voices.

Pick watched in impotent distress, not knowing how to help or what to do. Their faces were strained and pale in the starlight. He could see the concentration and discomfort in their postures. He offered them water, giving what comfort he could. Time passed slowly as the twins worked together to protect themselves. Finally, after an indeterminable length of time, he was able to see a slight, but visible, relaxation in their bodies. Their faces were not as contorted as previously. Felix looked up and gave a thin smile.

"Is a bit worse than we thought," he understated.

"Well, now you can see why I wanted you to experience it firsthand," snickered Silas.

"What can I do?" asked Pick, looking from one to the other, anxious to help in any way.

"We're doing okay," Felix said as he closed his eyes again. "We'll rest a bit. Then we'll get it over and leave. Just need to recover a bit before ...."

Pick nodded and turned back to face the Tower, allowing the brothers the time they needed. Gradually he made his way toward the stairs and the landing before the great doors. Despite the many times he had been in Town, this was the closest he had ever been to the Tower. He didn't have the Influence of the twins, but he could still feel it. It felt empty. Like a void. A hole in space that you could fall into and drown forever. He felt its need. Under the cover of the boulders he moved forward. Drawn towards the place almost against his will. Rash he might be and at times even rather foolhardy, but this ... this was not one of those times. This time he approached with caution, with alarm, if against his better judgement. But he wanted to know. What was it? Why was it? Why was it doing the things it did? Now almost to the edge of the landing, he stopped. If he took another step he would be revealed to the Tower. Once on the landing there was nothing between him and the impenetrable black of that door. Did it know he was there? Could it feel him? Did it want him to fill that void? He waited. Wanting to step forward and sure that he should not. He looked behind him, just able to make out the motionless forms of the others in the dim light. Looking back at the door he thought, it wouldn't be long. They need time to rest. I'll be back very soon.

Just as he was to break from the cover of the boulders he caught sight of movement out of the corner of his eye. Down on the long stairs, something was moving. It was coming this way.

***

It was not as easy as it had been the first time, but she was still enjoying the climb. She had thrown back the hood and was relishing the still, fresh air. She felt the Tower embrace her as she climbed. Welcoming her home, back to where she should be. Now she could make out the landing exposed above her. Just beyond her vision was the great door. A fine sheen had formed on her forehead from the effort. The effort had also enhanced her natural beauty had anyone been there to see it. But all her attention was focused on the Tower. Soon, very soon she would meet it once again. Call to her, and she would appear. Mortella had no doubt that she would appear. She allowed no doubt. The Tower would manifest. For her not to … that was not even a consideration.

In the shadows, Pick had returned to the brothers. "There's someone coming. On the stairs." Helping them to their feet, he guided them to where he had been. It allowed a full view of the door and landing while providing protection from sight as needed. There they waited until they saw a figure lightly attain the top of the stairs.

Catching her breath, she took the final step onto the black stone landing before the door. That door that had opened to her such a life. She stood drinking in the sight before her. Silently she glided forward to the Tower. Reaching the door, she lightly placed her right hand upon it. Resting it there. Feeling the cold hard stone under her fingers. She caressed it gently before stepping back.

Mortella closed her eyes and bowed her head. In her mind she formed the waif-like image of the Tower. Calling out to the Tower. She greeted it with respect and admiration. Placing her supplication at the forefront of her mind. She waited. Careful to appear calm and humble in the presence of the Tower. She would not come if she was not honoured and respected. Nothing happened. This was not unexpected. It had been a while. Mortella reintroduced herself. Extended her respect and gratitude for all the Tower had done for her. She waited, careful not to displace any level of frustration.

Felix watched as the air in front of the door began to shimmer. Gradually a shape formed before the red-haired figure. It radiated a cool grey light as a sinuous, wispy image of a girl formed from the air. As it formed he felt the wails fade. No longer were they breaking like waves against their barriers. Silas looked at him and nodded. As before, the approach of a figure clothed in black caused the cries to calm. They watched intently as the figures acknowledged one another.

Felix watched. The Tower was before them. Physically manifest and not just a series of images. This was the entity, the soul of the Tower. He needed to understand. They all needed to know. What was it it wanted? Slowly, carefully he started to deconstruct the walls that protected his mind. Silas grabbed him, spinning him around to face him, shaking his head. Felix looked calmly at his brother who gradually regained some composure. Silas nodded ever so slightly, his face grim. Felix turned back to the door. Little by little he began to extend his Influence. Out into the air, testing, probing, seeking hints of what it was that was before them.

Mortella smiled. The Tower knew and the Tower remembered. It felt right. It had chosen her, and she had fulfilled its desires. Now it was only a matter of time. She presented her petition. Her desire was to again receive unlimited entrance and freedom to the Tower. To be allowed to come and go as she pleased. As once had been her right. She waited. She knew it could be petulant, so she stood waiting, head bowed and submissive before the entity.

After a while the waif nodded as it began to raise translucent arms in a gesture of welcome. But as it did its attention towards Mortella waivered. Mortella could feel its waning interest. She looked up to see the ever-changing features of the figure became even less distinct as its inherent luminescence faded slightly.

***

Jess awoke with a start. This wasn't one of her usual night-time terrors. She looked over to see the sleeping figure of Angus in his usual place in the chair by the door. She sighed. How many times had she begged him to get a good night's rest in his own bed. But just having his presence, so close, made all the difference. She smiled at him before she remembered.

This was the same but different. This time the figure was clearer. A child-like image, indistinct and silent, had been looking for her. A yearning, a need emanated from it that only she could fill. Yet what this need was had never been clear. She couldn't remember, but she was sure. Her time in the Tower was clouded, but she was sure. Sure that this was what had helped her. When she needed it most. Left there in the Tower in that dark and lonely place, trying to find a way to endure but failing. When the only thing that she knew was the darkness of the Tower it was this that had been there.

She climbed out of bed and went to the window. The dark lane outside was empty and quiet. But beyond, off to the east she could feel it. The Tower was awake. She could feel it. She may no longer be within the Tower, but she had never really left it. She took it with her wherever she went. Hugging herself as she wrapped her arms around her, she shivered. Not from cold but from the certainty that it would never let her go.

***

Felix was careful. Hiding his mind while undoing the protection. He allowed his Influence to extend beyond himself through a small hole he had created in his mind's barriers. He projected it toward the great door and that which was before it. Slowly, carefully, he felt for what was there, without probing or prodding, but just gently sensing what filled the space. He felt the control of the red-haired figure. Within her the pent-up force like waters held back by a dam. Potential power, that if left unchecked could release destruction on all those around. Closing his eyes to the mirage in front of the black-clad figure, he paused. Thousands of fragments flicked past his mind. Broken images, splinters of thoughts and feelings not able to be fully realised. There was craving, longing that gored straight through him. He felt the incompleteness that defined the child-like waif that his eyes had seen. He experienced its feeling of loss, the agony that defined its existence.

Unnoticed by the figures before the door, Felix put forth a tentative tendril of his mind to caress the wraith. He felt a connection between it and the cloaked figure. There was an unmistakable sense of calm that imbued this connection. It stood in stark contrast to the turmoil that dominated the apparition. Suddenly an image flicked across his mind of a red-haired woman holding a small babe. In an instant the babe was a small child with glorious auburn hair cascading down her shoulders. Again this child changed, now older and wearing a hooded black cloak and smiling gleefully. As he watched he felt a rapid build of tension. Involuntarily opening his eyes, he saw the shade turn to face him as a scream began to build in his mind. Shards of the icy cry began to pierce his consciousness, ripping through him. He felt pain and could not control the fear and suffering that flowed directly into him. He was losing control, he knew it, he was powerless before such destruction. Defenceless before the devastation, he resigned himself to the oblivion that was being thrust upon him. With screams of thousands flowing into his mind, he felt the opening in his mind's protection gradually close. Silas was raising the barriers. But not before he heard the name Mortella shrieked across every conscious thought. As the shards dulled by the renewed protection he saw the red-haired figure turn to face him with a look of disgust.

***

Mortella felt the connection. The Tower knew her. It would give her what she desired. She smiled to herself. Let the Abbatissa beware. Never think that it will be forgotten. Her memory was long and the patience immeasurable. Acknowledging with gratitude the grace of the Tower, Mortella was ready to withdraw when she felt the Tower's screech in her mind.

Not to be tolerated.

Confused as to the source of such a change in the Tower's attitude she looked up to see the waif looking off to the right. Following its gaze her eyes fell on a figure shrouded in shadow amongst the boulder of the slopes. Furious that she was being observed, she flung out her Influence. She immersed the figure in the perception of inky blackness. Cloaking it in the impression of glacial ice as she withdrew any idea of breathable air. She watched dispassionately as the figure began to slump forward onto the stone landing.

***

Pick had watched all as the brothers engaged with the Tower. He could feel the tension but was protected from the onslaught of the multitudes that harassed the others. He saw the red-headed figure lock eyes with Felix. He watched as his friend went rigid and began to fall. Without thought he jumped forward and caught Felix before he hit the hard stone. Looking up he saw both figures before the door start to react. Instinctively he withdrew into himself. Feeling the power of his Influence flow through him, his focus was on the figure in black. He wove together threads of his Influence. Gathering and organising, pulling all into what felt like a single ball of molten metal ready to explode. Fixing his gaze on the woman, he let his power rage forth, pushing the shaft of Influence as hard as he could toward his target. He felt it hit the cloaked figure, causing her to lift from the ground and to be thrown backwards. The force appeared to hold her frozen for a moment in mid-air before she fell into a crumpled heap of black barely distinguishable from the black stone landing.

Unconcerned by any damage that he might have inflicted, Pick looked to Felix who took a single shaky breath before opening his eyes.

Silas pushed past Pick to cradle his brother's head, fear and concern etched on his face.

"It's okay. I'm okay," reassured Felix weakly. "Not as bad as it could be."

Pick indicated the wraith in front. "We've got to go. And quickly."

"Are you able to stand?" Silas asked as Felix attempted to struggle to his feet.

"No choice. I'm better. Pick's right, we've got to go now."

Helping Felix up, and with Pick on one side and Silas on the other, they made for the black stairs. No point hiding now. They needed to get away. Away from the Tower and the Dark Ones. They had been exposed and now the Tower would hunt them. With more haste than caution they descended the stairs, too terrified to look behind.

Chapter 15

Felix recovered quickly as they descended the stairs. Partially from the support he received from the others but mostly because he had no other choice. Things couldn't have been worse. Not only had they been attacked but they had also been identified. Not just noted but actually seen by the Tower itself.

Reaching the bottom of the stairs the brothers followed Pick as he ran into the nearest alley. From there he weaved a path this way and that until they were totally lost and exhausted.

"Hold up a bit," panted Silas. "We're not at young as you." Pick turned back to look at them. Felix had stopped. He had propped himself up against a convenient doorframe, gasping for air.

"The gates are shut till sunrise. We can't leave Town. We're stuck here." wheezed Felix. "We'll just have to hide."

Pick was about to speak when Silas stated the obvious.

"We can't go back to the burrow."

Felix nodded. "Not with the Tower on our tail."

They all stood silent.

Pick closed his mouth and looked back down the alley.

"No where's going to be safe now," he said under his breath. Looking to the ground he spoke softly, more to himself than the others. "But better to be indoors than out." He paused before continuing in a louder voice. "I might know a place. He's dealt with other things like this before."

Turning he started walking back the way they were going. He turned around and called over his shoulder, "You coming?"

***

Angus was holding her tight. His warmth comforted her, but it didn't stop the feeling. She had screamed. She hadn't meant to. It had just come out. She had felt it, the fear. A distress so intense that it cut straight through her. That was what had caused her to scream. One moment she was calmly looking into the street and then she was hit with a feeling of pure panic and dread. The feeling had waned, but its effects still lingered.

He felt her shaking uncontrollably. This was more than her usual night terror. Something had happened but he knew better than to ask. That only made things worse. He wouldn't force Jess to relive whatever it was that she remembered.

Jess knew that this wasn't a memory. This was not one of those twisted tricks that the Tower usually played on her. Of that she was sure. This was something that had just happened. This was really not in her imagination. Whatever it was, it had shaken the foundation of the Tower, and she had been forced to experience it.

***

Mortella gradually opened her eyes. The pounding in her skull was almost unbearable. She lay on something soft with her head propped up. It took a moment for her eyes to adjust before she was able to see a Tower varlet standing over her. She pulled off the cold compress that was laid across her forehead and tried to sit. This simple small movement caused the pain to intensify. It caused her to fall back again, clenching her eyes shut.

What the … she thought to herself. *Who the* … *How the* … She was one of the most proficient. How had he been able to resist her Influence? She remembered him falling forward. And that … that was the last thing she remembered until now. She had hit him hard. No-one had ever been able to resist. She clenched her teeth. She wasn't going to show weakness to the lowly varlet before her … but the pain. *How long have I been here?*

Breathing slowly, Mortella tried to relax. She remembered one of the tricks she had learnt from the knocking shop. Gently she began to separate herself from what was happening physically. Gradually she was able to put some distance between herself and at least some component of the pain.

"Welcome back," came a familiar voice which seemed to echo around the chamber and clang on her skull like a mallet. "We were expecting you … at some stage … but this was a little … unexpected!" continued the voice in a honey-sweet tone with an extra helping of disdain. Mortella forced her eyes open and attempted one of her most gracious smiles. The Abbatissa stood looking down at her from the end of the couch.

"As always, your hospitality is perfection," was all that Mortella was able to force between her clenched teeth before she was obliged to abstain from further banter.

"You should have let us know you were coming. We would have opened the door for you," sneered the Abbatissa. "It would have been a lot easier than finding you slumped on the threshold … with the Tower in a frenzied state." The Abbatissa waited for a response. When none came she added, "Anything that you would like to tell us?" She paused for a reply. In feigned interest she continued, "The child is thriving, I hope?"

Mortella ignored the question. The Tower had already granted her access. There was nothing she required from the … individual that stood before her. And she would never reveal what had really happened. Never, and certainly not to her.

"A glass of wine would be nice," was all that she would say. "I shall not stay long."

***

Pick knew his way around, even in the dark. It didn't take long for them to get to where he wanted. He stopped before an old and decaying door. Silas gave a surprised look at Felix.

"You remember?"

"Of course. How could I not."

Pick looked confused.

"We've been here before," said Felix. Looking back at Pick he explained, "The scribe in there was the one who told us how to find you." As he was speaking the door opened, notable for the lack of the customary tinkling bell. A dishevelled, grey-haired figure wearing the same gown and velvet green smoking hat as previously waved them inside.

"In here before you cause more commotion," he hissed as the three quickly entered. Once inside he closed the door and locked it before raising a lit candle to look at them. "Whatever you did, the Tower is not pleased," he said, looking directly at Felix. Glancing at Silas he continued, "So I see you followed through on the information you asked for." Turning, he led them through the cluttered room, past the desk and further into the dwelling. Felix followed, confused.

"He was rather quick in opening the door," he whispered to his brother.

"And how does he know about the Tower," Silas muttered back.

After working their way through a variety of small and dingy rooms they reached a locked door. The old man took out some keys and unlocked it. Opening the door he ushered them inside before locking it again behind them. In the feeble light of the candle the brothers could see that they were on a landing at the top of a flight of stairs. Holding the small candle high above him the old man began treading carefully down the stairs. The meagre light hardly penetrated the darkness. The brothers followed, more having to feel, than see, their way down the stairs. Once at the bottom the man lit a few other candles and handed one to each of his companions.

"Hello, Pick. It's not your usual way of coming to Town." Eyeing him up and down he added, "You're not normally so noisy."

Looking about Felix saw a small square room. Against one wall was a narrow sleeping bench. Shelves on the opposite wall contained various items such as cups and bowls. Beside him was a small table with a couple of chairs. The rest of the available space was almost completely taken up by the four men.

The elderly man watched Felix with curiosity. "There's not a lot of choice you have at the moment," he said dryly. "This may not be much, but at least the Tower cannot feel you here." He continued, "In this small space your Influences are invisible. There's no way they can follow them to find you here. I think that that would be best for you at present."

Seating himself on the closest chair he fixed his eyes on Silas before returning his gaze to Felix. "Not the most sensible thing you have done, I'll wager. And, if my mind's eye is anything to go by, you've caused quite a fracas." Seeing them all still standing he testily gestured for them to sit. "You're not going anywhere anytime soon." Looking at all of them he added, "I think you should tell me what happened."

Silas pulled the second chair a bit further away from the table and sat down, watching their host warily. Felix sat on the edge of the bench with Pick beside him. Silas remained silent and looked at his brother. Pick followed this example and looked at Felix.

"I suppose it's up to me then," Felix said irritably, aware that the others had already elected him to admit their errors. Looking at the man he cleared his throat and began. "Well you know about the instructions. It wasn't long after—"

"Oh don't bother me with that," their host cut him off irritably. "Pick here has been a semi-regular visitor here on business for the Apostasy for some time. You're not going to tell me anything I don't already know." He chuckled to himself. "Always liked that name. Never been one to join the crowd." He then became serious. "The Tower and its ilk should be renounced." He said with emphasis. Looking back at Felix he said again dismissively "No need to tell me all that. I knew when I met you that you had Influence. I can see it … in my mind's eye. I can feel it when it's used and may see what it does." He paused. "Tonight, however …" pointing his finger at Felix, "that was a bit too much for me to decipher. What did you do?"

"We were charged to find why the Tower's interested in a woman called Mortella." No response followed his statement as the man just kept watching him, waiting for him to continue. Felix took a deep breath and told them all about the image he saw. "It was just after that when the shade turned to face me as did the black-cloaked redhead. I don't remember much after, until Pick was looking down at me."

"The black-clad bitch attacked," said Pick. "But I got her good. She won't be feeling the best for a few days, I reckon," he added sardonically.

"Mmm," was the response. "That would explain what I felt." After a moment of silence the scribe looked up and gave a thin smile. "Wasn't a complete waste of an evening then, I should think." Looking at Pick he said, "And you, young master, will be needing to take this information straight back to the elders so they can decide what to do." Pick looked confused.

Standing and rubbing his back, their host asked, "Anyone for a cup of tea?"

***

She had stayed far longer than she had wanted. Not that she had not tried to leave earlier, but she had had no choice. She had stayed until now only out of necessity. It was only now that she was able to stand without the blinding pain forcing her down again. Finally forcing herself upright, she gestured to the door of the chamber.

"I shall leave now."

The varlet, who had watched, unhelping, as Mortella had struggled to her feet, now opened the door. She waited for Mortella to pass through before closing it again. The cool of the air in the darkened corridor helped but Mortella still felt that her mind was clouded, fogged in, making both thoughts painful and decisions difficult.

"Lead me to the great door," she commanded with as much dignity and authority she could muster. The varlet paused. Noting the hesitation, Mortella scoffed, "The Abbatissa will know I have gone soon enough." Then, after adding in just a little Influence to lend more power and authority to her voice, she again commanded, "Now." Yet even that little use of her Influence almost brought her to her knees as a wave of nauseating pain crashed against the back of the skull.

No longer hesitating, the varlet proceeded down the corridor. Mortella battled to keep up, despite the pace being orderly and even paced. She found it hard to recognise where she was in the Tower. She knew this place so perfectly. How could she not know where she was now? But each time that she tried to focus the pain worsened. She thus continued to follow the varlet, feeling lost in the labyrinth of the once so familiar confines of the Tower.

Reaching the antechamber before the great door the varlet stopped. Gradually the door inched open. Just enough to let in the cool light of morning and barely enough for Mortella to squeeze out. Squinting against the pale light after the cool shadows of the Tower, Mortella stood on the stone landing at the head of the long, steep stairs before her. She felt, but did not hear, the door close behind her. She would wait until none would be able to see her descend. She would take it slow, knowing that she would need to rest often, seating herself unceremoniously on the stairs. As undignified as that would be, it was vastly preferable than retching forth whatever contents might remain in her stomach by provoking further pain from any unchecked effort.

***

Sleep had not come easily for most of them. Two could squeeze uncomfortably onto the narrow bench against the wall. A head at either end that resulted in the feet of one remaining in close proximity to the nose of the other. Rolling over on such a narrow space was also out of the question. Pick had opted for the chair. But this was hard and uncomfortable, yet the floor was worse, being both hard and cold. The only one of them who appeared to sleep was their host who, wrapped in his gown and wearing his velvet green cap, slouched in the chair as if it was an overstuffed lounger, and snored to his heart's content.

Once tea had been made using a small burner that had been retrieved from under the bench, their host finally introduced himself. Ambrose had been scribing in Town before the twins were born. He had the ability to feel Influences. At times he could see them at work in his mind's eye when a

135

significant amount of Influence had been used. Rarely, he was able to see what their effects had been. To him the brothers were surrounded by their Influence. There had been no mistaking it the first time they had met.

Despite being questioned, he refused to explain the comment he made after Felix's explanation of what he saw. He would only smile and tap a finger to his nose before sipping slowly on his mug of tea. The others had little choice but to do the same. Sitting in silence, cradling the hot mugs, awaiting any further words that Ambrose would offer.

Finally, after placing the now empty mug on the table beside him, he spoke. "There's always time to enjoy the little things," he started. "Without the little things, what else do we have?" Looking at Felix he nodded, "Remember the little things. They are what we are fighting for." Felix thought of their plot. The upper dam with sunlight dancing on its surface. The gentle sound of rustling leaves from the trees above. He nodded back as he clasped his hands together in a silent plea for them never to lose their place.

"The big things will take care of themselves if we remember the little ones," Ambrose continued. He smiled sadly as he lowered his head. "There will always be trials, and we are measured, not only by the outcomes, but more importantly by the ways in which we respond." Looking up, lips together, he took a deep breath.

"A redhead cloaked in black at the door to the Tower." Glancing between each of the three before him he added, "There is one who fits this description." Silas gave a quick look at Felix whose eyes were riveted on Ambrose.

"Mortella is known to me. She wore the Black until only a shortish time ago. Discarded from the Tower in order to become the first lady of society. The man who yields more control than most became her husband and, more recently, she bore a child … a female child." He paused dramatically as he looked longingly as his empty mug. Ignoring the looks of supplication he poured what remained in the tin kettle into his mug and took a sip. Grimacing slightly, he took another sip. "Never as good when it cools."

"And?" interrupted Silas, causing Ambrose to look up at him. "And so?"

In a voice soft but chastising Ambrose responded, "The little things." He then remained totally silent as he slowly slipped the remainder of the cooled tea.

Felix looked at his brother, frustrated.

Really, don't you ever listen?

But—

We'll just have to wait till he's ready.

But—

No.

Eventually Ambrose placed the empty mug once again on the table and glanced longingly at the kettle. Clearing his throat he began again. "A babe cradled by a red-haired woman who grew to a child who took the Black." He paused. "Those of the Code forsake many earthly pleasures. Most particularly that of male company. Never has a child been born to one who has taken the Black. And this one had power. I have heard her Influence many a time."

"The Tower desires this child?" asked Felix.

"It would seem that this Mortella is not fully beyond the Code if she meets with the Tower. And ... the noise you created when you engaged ... well that was excessive."

"What does it mean for a member of the Code to have a child?" asked Pick.

"Who can say? But power is inherited. Further concentrated in the offspring. This could enhance the Tower's control."

"So it is the child the Tower wants," added Silas.

"So it would seem," concluded Ambrose. Then, looking directly at Pick, "So this is something that I would think the elders of the Apostasy might take some interest in. When morning comes and those of the Tower are less active, it would be best for you all to go. And ... for you, young Pick, to make your haste to those who need to know."

Chapter 16

She walked slowly through the streets in the early morning light. For many, the day had already begun with tradespeople and market stall holders making their way to work before the real rush of the day began. Hood lowered against any unwelcome looks, Mortella once again appreciated the great blessing of wearing the Black. To those around she didn't exist. No-one dared look in her direction. None found themselves in her way. Through the streets in which she walked, the Black made her all but invisible.

Reaching the entrance gate to the estate she merely raised her hood. It was opened immediately by an attendant who was almost successful in masking their surprise. No words were exchanged.

The rest of the estate was quiet. Servants went about their duties silently and efficiently. All were more than aware never to provoke anything that might disturb the still recumbent family on the floor above. Pausing at the base of the stairs Mortella rested, supporting herself on the balustrade. Slowly she began the ascent, having to pause every few steps. With great relief she arrived at her chamber. She entered, ready to fall into bed, only to find her maid efficiently preparing for the day ahead. Irritably Mortella forced out a single word, "Go," as she fell, more than climbed, onto the downturned, yet unslept in, bed. Clasping her hands against the back of her head she squeezed, trying to do anything to distract herself from the pounding within her skull. *When would this end?*

Now that she was once again recumbent and unmoving the pain gradually lessened. Sleep, however, was not to be found as she lay unmoving, afraid even to roll in case the pounding would be roused once again.

***

With the door unlocked the four men exited their sanctuary, that had also been their prison throughout the previous night. Light filtered through the dirt-covered windows as Ambrose began making tea with the delight of a child ready to receive a treat.

"The gates will open soon … and then off you all go." He looked pointedly and Felix and Silas. "The Tower perceived you. It knows the pattern of your being. Do not give it a trail by which to follow you," he warned in a low voice. "Nothing ever good comes from the Tower." The kettle now boiled, he smiled broadly as he added a broad-leafed tea to the water. "Tea anyone?" he asked as he expertly swirled the water around the container before pouring the now amber fluid into four mugs.

Making his way to a cluttered sitting room he sat on an old, threadbare sofa cradling his mug, relishing the fragrance of the liquid within. Silas followed behind, carrying a mug and looking serious.

"Will the Tower come for us?"

Ambrose looked at him. "Its actions are its alone to know," was all he said.

"So what can we do to hide our trail?" asked Felix who had followed his brother into the room. Pick had also entered, looking worried.

"The owner of each Influence has a fingerprint. Something unique and distinct only to them," Ambrose explained while sipping his tea. "Its use leaves a trace, a snail-trail if you will, that can lead to the one who used it. It fades over time but … for those who can see this aura, it can lead them to the one who has the power." Fixing his clear blue eyes on Felix he added, "Don't leave any more traces by which they can find you." Felix looked at Silas.

"A snail-trail?" Silas sounded confused. Ambrose looked at him and shook his head slowly. Speaking slowly as if to a small child, he explained.

"Your Influence is uniquely yours. Like a face it can be recognised. When used, each Influence leaves a district mark that can lead those who can see the traces back to the one who used the Influence." He paused. Seeing Silas nod he continued. "Over time these traces fade but once their signature is learnt, it can be detected again and again. For some it can be used to locate the user. This Mortella, I can feel and locate by her Influence's fingerprint. It surrounds and encompasses her … like many others. If the Influence is strong enough." He looked at Pick as he smiled and winked. "Others may be able to do the same." Turning to Felix he said, "The trace of your Influence remains on you. This aura of Influence … it is your personal perfume. Use it sparingly."

Felix nodded, his face unmoving. "We should go," he said.

"The passenger cart will leave soon." Silas nodded. Turning to Ambrose he said, "Thank you."

"Without your help …" added Felix.

"United we thrive, divided we fall," Ambrose responded with a nod. "You know where to find me," he added as he indicated the way to the front door. "Leave it unlocked. Unexpected visitors are always the most interesting." Felix turned to Pick.

"You coming?"

Pick shook his head. "There's something else I need to do before I go."

"You'll be okay?" asked Silas.

"Me? I've been through worse," smirked Pick. "It takes a lot more than that to rattle me." His bravado, however, sounded a little hollow. Felix stepped forward and wrapped Pick tightly in a bear hug.

"Come back and stay with us as soon as you can. You're always welcome."

"Even if you did scare the pants off of us the last time you arrived," added Silas, smiling as he clasped the youth to himself before turning to go.

"I'll be there," promised Pick as the twins made for the door. "Just as soon as I get this done."

As the door closed Ambrose looked at the young man and sighed.

"I know," said Pick. "I've seen it before," he added as tears began to collect in his eyes.

"Nothing is certain," added Ambrose, "there is always hope. That is what sustains us." Pick nodded slowly.

"Did it perceive you?" the scribe asked with concern.

"It was so fast," replied Pick, looking scared. "Up till then it hadn't. I can't be sure, but I don't think so."

"So then go. Leave today and tell the ones who need to know all about this." Ambrose placed his now empty mug on his lap. "And this time stay for a bit of time outside the Bowl. You'll be safe there."

Pick nodded again as he bent down to give the old man a hug. The scribe held him close as he stroked his hair. "Your father would have been so proud of you."

Pick stood up as he wiped his eyes clear. "Thanks, Grandad."

***

It was late afternoon with lengthening shadows testament to the setting sun when the twins disembarked from the cart. The last of the stalls were packed away as many of the local inhabitants had already sequestered themselves into their favourite booths of the most substantial building around … the inn. Silas stood forlornly in the middle of the dirt road watching the cart recommence its journey. Felix watched his twin, feeling just as lost as his brother. This homecoming had none of the normal joy. No anticipation of the comforts of their own little cottage.

"It's going to be dark soon," sighed Silas, unsure what else he could add. Felix remained silent. Silas looked at him, his eyes pleading for something … for anything that Felix might say to reassure him. Getting nothing he tried again. "Only a couple of hours before we're home." Attempting to sound upbeat he added, "Might even be faster than that seeing as we don't have any bags." Felix nodded but still said nothing. After a long pause he took a deep sigh.

"No snail-trail, he said." Silas nodded. "It fades with time." Again, Silas nodded. "So now is the greatest danger." Looking at the inn in front of them he added, "I would rather be taken where there are others who will remember, rather than disappear with no-one the wiser." He looked at Silas. "Wouldn't you?" Before his brother had a chance to answer, Felix had started walking to the open door of the inn. Silas turned and followed.

***

Pick raced back to the burrow. He would have to warn them about the Tower and what happened the previous night. Staying as short a time as possible he grabbed his shoulder pack and left for the Town gate. He would take the northern coach. He had contacts. They would be able to pass the information onto the ones who needed to know. He could then make his way further north and then out of the Bowl. He had been made to promise to do as much before his grandfather would let him leave.

"I lost a son to them. I'm not going to lose my grandson." It had not been a discussion but a heart-felt plea that Pick could not refuse.

"For a couple of months. I promise." He then smirked. "The aura, remember. I'll just wait for my particular perfume to fade."

"The aura of Influence," his grandfather repeated. "Remember I can find your particular note. I'll know."

"I already promised, Grandad," grumbled Pick. He then added in a more serious tone, "I remember, Grandad. I was there. I saw it. I'm not going to let them take me, not without a fight." Seeing his grandfather's look of despair he then added softly, "But I promise, solemnly swear, I will leave the Bowl and let any aura fade." With that, he again hugged his grandfather. He turned. Over his shoulder as he left, he added with fake assurance, "I'm sure it didn't perceive me."

The journey for Pick had been no less tense than for the twins. Daylight afforded some protection, but the Tower came at night. His journey would take two days. That meant at least one night within the Bowl before he was safely beyond its borders. The carriage was faster than the passenger carts and Ambrose had made sure his grandson had enough coinage for the trip and board at the tavern located at the evening stop. This, however, would not stop the Tower if its sights had been set on the young man.

The first day's travel over, the last remaining travellers alighted from the carriage. Pick finally climbed down from his place on the top of the coach. These seats might be the cheaper ones, but he preferred to be outside. Far better to feel the air and see the land passing by than be compressed within the airless box. He looked to the west. He estimated that there was at least half an hour before twilight. Full night would then fall about an hour after that. Turning, he began to follow the other journey folk towards the tavern. Smiling to himself as he did. His contact would arrive sometime later in the evening.

Inside was already fairly full as patrons congregated in groups enjoying good company and ale. This village was the routine stopover for carriages heading both north and south as well as ones coming from the north-west. A substantial trade had thus developed for the servicing of such travellers. Pick was fortunate enough to find a small table in a dark corner on his own. Located well away from the rest he was able to survey the situation mostly unseen. He knew that there were rooms for hire on the floor above. Prices were steep as the demand was high. For those not fortunate enough to secure a room, or as was the case for Pick, unable to afford the price, they were allowed, for a small fee, to sleep in the bar room on whatever was vacant.

Not counting the tea, he had had nothing to eat since the night before. Primarily he had had no stomach for it when the opportunity had arisen.

When the churning of the stomach had finally settled, and it had been re-placed with the gnawing pains of hunger, there had not been the opportunity. He caught the eye of one of the young serving girls who smiled and made her way directly over. Placing a hand on her hip and she looked at him and winked.

"What be your liking?"

Blushing slightly, Pick rallied himself and ordered a pint and whatever was the stew of the day. She smiled again as she turned and left, accentuating the sway of her hips as she walked away. It was not long before she returned. Onto the table before him she placed a bowl of steaming beef stew with still warm bread and the pint of ale.

"You be staying here?" she asked, indicating the corner he already occu-pied as she eyed him up and down.

"No real option," responded Pick. "It's all I can afford."

"You picked a goodun place. Out of the way … almost private," she said as she bent over to give the table a cursory wipe. Pick quickly sat back in his chair to make room for the ample bosom that was now only inches away. Standing back up, the wench looked down at him expectantly. Dropping his eyes Pick felt the sudden need to get something from his pack. Bending down he retrieved the first thing he found. Looking back up he saw the maid still watching. "If you see anything you like, let me know," she said with a smile as she wetted her lips. Turning, she then looked back at him over her shoulder and added, "Here's almost as personal as a place upstairs." Seeing Pick's look of discomfort she giggled. "Just holler if you need something. I'm never far away and am always ready to please." With that she left, swing-ing her ample hips as she went.

***

Twilight was over and night had begun. Seated in their usual place the brothers held tightly onto their ales. The room about them was brightly lit and full of the sound of comradery. The workday was over, and the village folk had come to-gether to mingle before heading home and another day began. For them it was a time for friendship and relaxation. For the twins the night brought uncertainty and fear.

On arriving at the inn, they had been greeted by various friends and ac-quaintances. Engaging in only the minimum of exchange required to avoid being rude, they had made their excuses and went to sit alone. The tension between them was palpable.

"Keep it all locked down," said Felix for the umpteenth time.

"No need to say it again," responded Silas irritably.

"I'm sorry," replied Felix. "It's all I can think about."

"I know, me too. But what really is the use? Either they know and come or not."

"I know. And it's all my fault."

"No … it's not. You didn't go the first time. I did. We did this together." Silas fell silent. After a long pause he asked, "What are we going to do if they do come?"

"What can we do?" answered Felix defeatedly. Silas remained silent. "Exactly," said Felix, "what can we do?"

"Are we staying here tonight?"

"I would like to."

"I'll get the room … say we're too tired to walk back to the plot tonight." Silas stood and made his way to the bar. Felix watched despondently. He then dropped his head and listened. Not with his ears but with his mind. With all the barriers up the Tower was faint but just audible. He could feel nothing different, nothing out of the ordinary. He wondered if this was a good thing or not. When something big occurred they would hear it. When the Tower was in one of its moods they would know. *But now, would they know? The Tower had identified them … well him. Would it now know not to let them feel anything different? Hide its moves from them? Were they even something important enough to cause a change?*

Silas returned. "The room's ours whenever we want it." Felix looked up.

"Let's stay here until closing. I want to be where there are people about." He paused. "It might make a difference," he added without conviction. Silas nodded in agreement although his face told another story. The Dark Ones had never before been thwarted by the presence of others when pursuing their designs.

***

Eating and drinking nothing Mortella had lain unmoving in bed throughout the day. As night fell she started to stir. Risking the return of the crushing pain, she lifted her head. She waited, but nothing happened. It just remained stable as the silent pounding within her skull. Gradually she raised herself to a sitting position. She surveyed the chamber. Her personal maid had been attentive enough but had been sent away with strict instructions not to return until summoned.

She, however, had continued her duty by making sure that there was wine, and sustenance prepared and present within the room for whenever it was desired.

Mortella observed the platter left on a side table accompanied by a goblet of wine. She had started to feel hunger. A good sign. The worst would now seem to be over. She swivelled her legs over the edge of the bed and sat there. She still wore the Black but did not yet want to take it off. It was who she was. Part of her. Again she waited. Nothing.

Her mind went to Clara. She needed her near her but knew that she was not yet ready. She could never let herself become that incapacitated again. Reaching up she grabbed the bell pull and gave it a tug. She heard nothing, but within moments the chamber door opened, and her maid silently entered. She waited in the middle of the room for her instructions.

"Help me up," Mortella commanded as she held out her hands. The maid approached and placed her hands below Mortella's elbows and braced herself to take the weight. Leaning heavily on the support, Mortella rose and slowly walked toward the side table to sit in the easy chair beside it. The maid then stood back to await further instructions.

"Inform the master that I am indisposed and shall not make supper." She gently lifted the goblet and took a sip. She allowed the full red liquid to trickle down her throat. Looking at the rich food that made up the platter she felt her stomach heave. Settling herself she looked back at the maid.

"Take this away." She took another sip. It was good. She needed this. But she also needed to eat. Thinking back to times in the shop when comfort was needed she said, "Get Cook to make some pottage. Simple and plain. The way she would have had it as a child." Dismissing the maid with a flick of the hand, she looked out the window to the Tower beyond. *What had happened there*, she thought. *How was that possible?* She would need to look into this. He was not to be tolerated and she would make sure that he would never do what he had done ever again.

***

Ambrose sat with his eyes closed. He listened, working his way around Town. Listening for any changes. The Dark Ones on a search would be heard scanning far and wide for the distinct vibrations that each Influence produced. He heard the Tower unchanged in its cacophonous commotion. Rarely the sounds would coalesce into a more unified cadence. But, as usual, it was a mess of discordant notes clashing and grating upon one another. He could hear the note of Mortella within the upper reaches of Town. None were pushing forth. As far as he could tell, none were searching. Not yet.

The old man sighed. He hoped, and felt, that Pick had not been perceived. Anyway, he would be safe in another day or so. Out of the Bowl and away from the Tower. The others, for them things were much more uncertain. One had definitely been perceived. Once identified, the vibration that defined them would never be forgotten. The trail may fade but any use of the Influence would readily be observed by any who knew it and were looking.

***

She did her best to hide it, but the feeling had still not gone. Jess sat at the table doing her best to concentrate. Angus was teaching her to read. She wanted to, so much. She wanted to impress him and show them both how much she thought of them. She saw Maima look across and smile at them. She tried, but tonight she just couldn't concentrate.

Her mind kept telling her that the Tower wanted her. It needed her and was never going to let her go. She knew it. The Tower wanted it and there was nothing she could do. Nothing but to wait for the inevitable.

Angus laid his hand lightly on hers.

"You're tired. Perhaps this is enough for tonight."

Jess began to protest as he gave her hand a squeeze. "It's hard. I know. I had to learn it as well. It took me ages," he said gently. "How about some tea?"

"I'll make it," said Jess, jumping quickly to her feet, happy to do something that might be of help. "Maima, tea?" she asked quickly.

"Why, thank you, Jess, yes. Why don't we all have lavender and sage? It might help us all get a good night's sleep," Maima suggested, giving Jess a quick smile. Jess smiled back before turning to put some of the leaves into the pot. She would try but doubted it would make any difference.

Chapter 17

He knew that she would be here at some time. When that would be … he'd just have to wait and see. Sitting in his corner Pick watched various different gatherings within the tavern. He watched as some of his fellow travellers rose and slowly began to make their way upstairs. Some of the ones from inside the carriage, he thought. A room upstairs was not for the likes of him. Anyway, he felt safer being in the midst of many others. Better to be one among many than one alone.

Supper had hit the spot and he was feeling sleepy after the long day's journey coupled with the lack of any sleep the previous night. Having already paid his fee to remain inside, he started looking to see how he could make the best use of his space. He could place his back to the wall using his pack as a pillow. By moving the table and chair a little to the left he would still be able to see the whole room while obscuring most of himself from it.

Looking up, he saw the same young serving girl watching him from the bar. She winked at him in an exaggerated manner. He returned her an awkward smile as she grinned back at him, giving a flick of her hair. He dropped his eyes sheepishly which only caused her to laugh. The sound carried across the hall and made him blush. Trying to ignore his discomfort, he looked around the room. Things were unlikely to quieten down any time soon. Any thought about settling down for the night was, therefore, a bit premature.

Placing his pack on the table as a mark of ownership he left his corner. A long day secured on top of the coach together with a pint, well a couple of pints, of ale were having their effect. He needed to relieve himself. He made his way through the various throngs in the still-busy hall. He was aiming for the door that led out the back while trying to avoid heading anywhere near the bar. Once outside it took a moment for his eyes to adjust to the darkness. The moon was yet to rise. In the field beside the tavern, and set at a significant distance from it, he saw a darker patch of black outlined against the starlit sky. The latrine was simple but effective. There were enough holes dug in the rich earth to service a full contingent of drinkers. These were deep enough and far enough away for any noxious fumes to dissipate, at least somewhat, before reaching the revellers. Seeing the proximity of the latrines suddenly exaggerated the urgency of his need for them. Without hesitating, Pick made his way quickly toward them.

On entering the wooden, roofless structure he stopped and assessed what was before him. A series of partitions separated the open space within. Not that familiar with its layout, and with shadows confusing what was solid ground or not, he chose his path carefully. Any misstep and he would not be the first to become intimately associated with some of the contents the holes contained.

Having made his way judiciously, Pick secured a safe position and relieved himself with gratitude. It was then in a much more relaxed state that he turned to make his way out when he heard something move on the other side of the wooden partitions. Stopping, he listened. Hearing nothing more he ignored it as a trick of the imagination. The night was still and warm and he was feeling the most relaxed he had since leaving Town.

Exiting the confines of the latrine he began to make way back towards the festivities. Almost halfway to the tavern he felt something light touch his shoulder. Turning in fright he saw the outline of a hooded figure against the sky. His mind raced to his greatest fear. He tried to yell, but the sound stuck in his throat. Petrified, his mind went blank. Unable to move or cry out, he could only watch as the figure stood silently, menacingly before him.

Time appeared to stop. Pick froze, unable to breathe, move or scream. His mind then started to race. *How had they found him? So soon. It had perceived him. What would his grandfather say? Was this what his father felt? What would it be like?* The worst was now to happen. He was powerless to stop it. He saw himself. Felt his individuality. Clutched onto that which was the very essence of who he was. He was determined to remain himself until the final moment. He closed his eyes and waited …

"You alright?" came a concerned voice. "Looks like you've seen a ghost." Pick opened his eyes, taking the first breath in what seemed like forever. The figure turned him fully around by placing both hands on his arms and then gently guided him as he crumpled weakly to the ground.

"What happened in there?" asked the figure, indicating the latrine. "Not another one of those creeps again."

Pick remained silent, still unable to respond, breathing deeply and quickly. Eventually he regained enough control to look up at the figure. "Feeling better?" it asked as it raised the hood of the cloak. There, to his surprise, now kneeling beside him was the one he had been waiting for.

"I saw you go outside," she explained. "Came to see if there was anything new."

"Ah."

"Take it easy. What happened? You need a drink?" Looking alarmed she indicated the door of the tavern. "Can you get up?" she asked. Pick nodded as he attempted to rise. The figure grabbed his elbows, preventing him from falling again as he gradually stumbled to his feet. Giving her the briefest of thin smiles he started to walk back. Regaining his strength quickly now that the shock was over he tried another smile. Opening the door, they re-entered the tavern together. Pick's companion waved to the serving maid behind the bar, calling for two ales as Pick led the way back to his corner.

***

The inn was almost empty by the time Felix and Silas climbed the narrow stairs to the only room for hire. Having only managed enough to eat to curb their hunger they had avoided any liquor that might dull the senses. Opening the door they entered the room with the lit lamp and looked about. The silence of the room was unsettling. Silas sat on the chair as Felix washed his face and hands with the water and bowl provided on the dresser.

"You rest. I'll keep watch," he said. "I wouldn't be able to sleep anyway." Silas nodded.

"Doubt I'll be able to either." He paused, weighing his words carefully. "You hear anything?" he asked eventually, clearly not wanting to know the answer.

"With everything shut down … it's hard," replied Felix looking up. "But," he paused, "nothing seems to have changed. Not yet anyway."

"How would it happen?" asked Silas. "How would we even know?"

Felix shook his head and shrugged. "Would it even matter if we did?"

"Are we going to live like this forever?" Silas asked the air. "Never knowing if they're just outside."

"Aura of Influence," was the only response he got.

"The trail will fade with time. And then what? Don't we ever use the Influence again?" Felix looked at him, face solemn, saying nothing. Going to the window he looked out.

"Turn off the lamp. Lie down. Try and get some sleep." Silas nodded and started taking off his boots. Placing them at the side of the bed he lay down. Felix took the chair and placed it by the window. Sharing a final grim smile with his brother he took his place upon it and began his vigil gazing through the glass.

"Don't let the bedbugs bite," he added as an attempt at levity.

"They better bloody not. Not with the price we paid," retorted Silas. Both fell silent again, locking themselves fully alone within their own thoughts for one of the very first times in their lives.

***

Julia studied Pick over the tankard.

"Do you want to tell me what's going on?" she asked gently. Pick looked up, still a bit shaky but mostly recovered. Julia was pretty. Just a bit older than him with luscious auburn hair that framed her oval face with chestnut eyes. He smiled a cheeky smile at her.

"Did you see her face?"

"The barmaid?"

"Yes, that one."

"What was going on there?" asked Julia with a smirk. "She almost covered me with my ale the way she thumped it on the table. She was scowling at me like a banshee." Pick shrugged nonchalantly.

"Haven't the faintest idea," replied Pick smugly.

"Well," responded Julia with a giggle as she eyed Pick, "it looked to me like a case of lost income."

"There was no chance of that," answered Pick with mock offence going a little red. "Not my type."

"And what is your type then?" Julia needled.

"Someone a bit more adventurous," Pick responded with a wink. It was now her turn to turn a slightly darker shade of red as she tried to ignore the inference. Pick smiled. He always made sure that he caught up with this particular contact whenever he was able. Never hurt to keep up good relations.

"It's not like you to be so jumpy," she said, changing the subject.

"I know … been a hard couple of days."

"So?"

"Well, if you must know …" he said with feigned vexation. Julia smiled her winning smile at him. Her even white teeth glistened despite the dimness of the room. His voice dropped, "Not good. They need to know … all of it … and know it now!" Her face instantly became serious. Her eyes focused on him, giving him her full attention as she hung on his every word. Taking in a deep breath, Pick held tightly onto his mug to steady his nerves and began to explain.

***

Everything was quiet. Felix sat in the dark facing the window. There was nothing to see. Despite his fears and the warnings, he had to keep reminding himself not to drop the barriers. Not to listen more closely to the Tower and hear its voices. Not to do what he had been doing his whole life.

He looked over at Silas. He was asleep. At least one of them was. Turning his attention once more to the empty lane outside, he signed. His eyes felt gritty. He rubbed them with the back of his hands and stood. He was getting sleepy, but he mustn't sleep. What good would that do? He didn't know, but someone should keep watch. Tomorrow they would be back at their plot. Nothing there would have changed, yet for them, everything had. What were they going to do? He walked over to the dresser and poured himself a glass of water. Standing, he drank. He then splashed some more of the cold water from the bowl over his face. He would stay awake. Sighing he ran wet fingers through his ruffled hair. What did he hope to achieve by staying awake? If they did come, he would know. He was sure of that. Even with the barricades fully up he would be able to hear them. Sighing again, he sat. Leaning back against the chair he stretched his legs out in front while staring off into space.

***

He had slept. Despite everything, he had actually slept. With the sounds of numerous others still asleep filling the hall he sat up. Julia had stayed, keeping him company, and preventing any further advances from the barmaid. Pick looked across at the sleeping figure. Her hair was tousled, framing her face as she slept. Her cloak was wrapped tightly about her. He had insisted that she use his pack as a pillow. Getting up as quietly as possible, he weaved his way through the recumbent bodies scattered about the floor. Outside, the morning light made everything seem different. The night was over, and a new day had begun. With that there was always hope. He had survived this night and the trace of his Influence would be fading. Now with the information passed on, he could make his way out of the Bowl as promised.

151

Having relieved himself, he returned to the tavern. Many of the others were now stirring, and the smell of breakfast was seeping through the air. Seeing that Julia was awake he walked towards her. She smiled as she attempted to tame her hair by tugging it back and fixing it securely into a ponytail.

"How'd you sleep?" he asked, approaching their corner.

"Well enough," was the reply.

"Breakfast?"

"Naturally. We've both got a big day ahead." Pick looked concerned. "Don't worry, they'll hear it soon enough." She looked at him with concern, "And you'll be outside before night falls a second time."

"Will you visit me?" he asked imploringly.

Looking at him shyly she responded, "I might."

Happy with even the slightest potential of the prospect, Pick went off and ordered their food. Using the last of his money he chose the best he could afford. It left him nothing for him to spend on food later in the day, but he didn't care. Not when his aim was to impress.

The food placed before them induced a far better mood in both. They chatted easily about many things, never once mentioning the Tower and its happenings. Having finished everything and searching for anything they may have missed, the time was approaching for Pick's carriage to depart. Standing opposite each other they made their goodbyes. Julia suddenly stepped forward and embraced him. Before letting go, Pick quickly dipped his head and gave her a quick peck on the cheek, causing them both to break apart and look at the floor. Smiling broadly, Pick looked at the silent girl and waved.

"Make sure you come. I'll look for you every day." Without waiting for a reply he turned and raced out into the street. Seeing that his coach had been made ready, he went straight towards it and climbed into his perch on top. Once settled, he looked down and saw Julia watching. She smiled and waved before heading off to progress the information further.

***

Felix woke with a start, blinded by the sun in his face. He didn't know how, or when, but he had fallen asleep. Behind him Silas was still sprawled across the bed snoring softly. Outside, things were quiet. Life in the village did not start quite as early as that within Town. He stretched. His neck felt tight, and twisting caused a pain to shoot across his lower back. It had not been one of the most comfortable of places to sleep. Not being used to it and getting older would mean that he would suffer the consequences for the next few days.

Getting to his feet he walked quietly to the door. Opening it, he was about to head downstairs.

"Did you stay up all night? You should have woken me," came a voice from the bed.

"No. I fell asleep as well," Felix responded, rubbing his neck. Silas climbed out of bed.

"Do you want to go?"

"Where?"

"Home."

Felix nodded, imagining the sparkling waters and gentle breezes as he sat by the upper dam just watching and being. He had never felt the longing to be home so acutely before. It was theirs and no matter what, that was where they belonged.

"Come on. It's only a couple of hours," added Silas. "We'll be home to have breakfast in our own little cottage." He placed a hand on Felix's shoulder and gave him a little push out the door. He could see how much this was affecting his brother. He didn't need to have the barriers down to feel it. Knowing what his brother was thinking he added, "It's that much further away, and that makes it much more difficult to find us."

Felix remained silent as Silas followed him out the door.

Without speaking further the brothers left the village and began the journey home. The day was glorious. The sun was warm but not hot. Birds filled the air with song and the fertile land was tilled and well cared for. With everything about them so perfect it was impossible for them not to feel it. Gradually their moods began to lift. It was now over a day, and nothing had happened. They were a long way from the Tower and the trail left by their Influence was fading. The worst was over. It had to be.

They stopped and listened. Making sure to keep the barriers up, they closed their eyes and felt for the Tower. It was calm, quiet.

"We're never doing that again," said Felix finally. Silas agreed without even a single attempt at a "but". Felix continued, "They now know what they need to know and we're going to stay out of it." Looking at his brother he added firmly, "And we're never going to mention that name again or talk about what happened."

Walking on, each of them quietly enjoyed the country and its beauty in their own way. Faster than either of them expected they found themselves turning onto the last stretch of path before they would gaze upon their cottage once more. It seemed an age since they had left, but it had only been a few days. How much had changed in such a short time and not for the better. Now home, Felix knew that he would not be leaving again any time soon. Looking across at his brother he hoped that he felt the same way. Reaching the cottage they opened the door and entered. The familiarity of the place comforted them even more as they set about making a welcome home breakfast.

***

Cradling Clara, Mortella strolled about her chamber. The sun streamed in the windows and a scented breeze wafted through the open balcony doors. Clara smiled up at her mother. Mortella stoked her hair absentmindedly. She was getting heavy but they both enjoyed these times alone together.

Seeing the stark outline of the Tower, Mortella thought again back to that evening. *How had that happened? Why had the Tower allowed that to happen?* Such questions had circled around and around her mind every waking moment since that evening. This was something that she would not let lie.

Putting Clara down, she sat. She would give it a few days and then send a formal message to the Abbatissa informing her that she would be coming to visit. Too soon to take Clara with her. There was more than enough time to introduce her to the Tower later.

One with such Influence could not be let be. They could not be tolerated, and she would make sure that they got what they deserved. The Tower would know more. She would have to approach this delicately, but she was sure the Tower would help. And once she knew, then she would take steps.

Chapter 18

As Mortella waited and looked about the cavern, the space seemed eternal with darkness expanding in all directions. She had been back many times since that evening. Always there for the same reason. There to find the aura of the one that had resisted her and, though she would rarely allow herself to admit it, bettered her.

Having silenced her mind, with eyes closed, she opened herself to the ebb and flow of the Tower. She felt the potency contained within the black walls, tangible and wild. She sensed the vibration that melded the multitude into a singularity that was the Tower. But this was frenzied and chaotic. There was no peace among its inhabitants.

With patience and supplication she waited for the Tower to acknowledge her. To grant her audience. Responding to the stillness she brought, the Tower once again bowed to her appeal and manifested itself before her. Maintaining the feeling of calm and tranquillity she opened her eyes and peered into the ever-changing features of the slender, child-like urchin that hovered before her. A sense of turmoil permeated the cavern. Mortella could feel its longings and desires. She understood that its only focus was to have these needs satisfied. So like Clara. A being solely defined by its needs. And as for Clara, its needs were paramount. Everything else would be measured through this lens. It was oblivious to all others.

Bowing her head in respect, Mortella again asked permission to search the collective of the Tower. To once again search for a way to avenge the events of that night. By couching her request as a need, as the way to protect Clara, she had been able to win the Tower's approval. Again she waited. Forever careful never to demand and never to display her irritation, frustration, at the need to do so. Eventually the Tower embraced the request, delivering its acceptance of her entreaty. As it did, there appeared about her a multitude of images. Auras filled the massive chamber. Each a colour, but ever moving, ever changing. Each a part of the mosaic. The collective that created the Tower. Each piece a remnant of one of the many living, mindless souls that formed the essence of the thing she petitioned.

She was now free to walk around the space, choosing an aura at random and seeing what it contained. The Tower had innumerable. Countless were of those who had been chosen to enter the Tower. And many had been deemed inferior. Never able to rise even to the level of a mindless Tormentor. Yet Influence was never wasted. Such Influence was to be kept and could be utilised by those who had the skill. These remnants still possessed scattered memories, fragments of who they once had been, and together they formed the whirling chaos she now experienced.

Then there were the others. Those never meant for the Black. Abominations in their existence. Yet Influence still of value when suitably controlled. None of these atrocities possessed a major Influence, but the lesser ones could still be of use. It was for one of these that she was now searching. She knew that it existed yet had yet to find one of sufficient potency.

There were some among the abominations who possessed the Sight. The ability to see Influence and identify its source. For those with power, the aura of Influence glowed. The one who had confronted her would shine bright. How could they not? Once identified they would no longer be able to hide. Her need was to identify the signature and then search the Bowl for where it now hid.

Through much trial and error she had learnt what shimmering shades of colour were of no interest. The subtle nuances of colour matched the Influence. Strong colours were major Influences. It was the minor hues that now interested her. She stretched out her hand and touched one of the floating images. There was a faint tingle in her finger. A vibration akin to excitement as the remnant of the soul recognised contact with one of independent life. It clung to her hand. Within it showed a splash of green that entwined itself with earth and vegetation. Ignoring it further she shook it away. She touched another. A spark of light appeared in the dark then vanished. She moved on.

Hour after hour she continued as she had previously, day after day. Searching for the elusive, yet still determined to find it. The Tower could show her the event of that night. Once she had found the one with Sight she would then be able to implore the Tower to match the two. With use of the Sight, the aura's signature could be found and then … well, then the real search would begin.

Frustrated, she rested on the stairs that led back up into the halls of the Tower. Reclining uncomfortably on her elbows, Mortella considered the situation. Once again she had rifled and searched through many of the vestiges of souls that continued to swirl slowly about the cavern. Time and again she found traces of power that could see an Influence. While here in the Tower, with its permission, she could also appreciate the hues and colours of each. Outside the Tower, however, she could only feel their effects. For one with the gift of Sight, they could identify an Influence by its colour, a rudimentary aura, when in play before it. But she was yet to discover one that could feel the aura of an Influence at a distance.

Looking about the many and varied tints of colour that floated before her, Mortella wondered, not for the first time, about the Tower's lack of action. Why had the Tower not pursued the abomination? There was a legion of others that had been considered not to be tolerated and were now circling above her head. Why was this different? She understood that some of those with talent must remain in order to sire offspring. To breed those who would be acceptable to take the Black. The breeding pool must not be detrimentally starved of Influence. But why this one? How was he different?

Irritated, but determined, Mortella rose once again to continue the work. She wandered about the cavern. Scanning, but largely ignoring, the pieces of the mosaic passing by. She had searched for many days and found nothing. She had not even yet scratched the surface of those Taken. Doing more of the same would simply achieve just as much unless she had great luck. She must consider a different approach.

One advantage she had was her Influence. Thinking back to the thousands of interactions she had had with the inhabitants of the Tower, there was one thing that was almost universally consistent. Each and every aura appeared to tremble with delight at her touch. They would cling to her, seemingly reluctant to be let go. Perhaps she could use this. What was it that these once human shades desired? If she knew and created the perception that she could fulfill the desire of the one she desired, then it may come to her. She would need to think. Looking back to the stairs that led to the ordered corridors above, she paused. That would be best done over good food and wine. Turning her back on the expanse she returned to the stairs in anticipation of enjoying the begrudgingly given hospitality of the Abbatissa.

****

The rain poured down, soaking everything. Although he had been granted lodgings in one of the rough-hewn buildings, it was barely any better than sheltering under the canvas outside. He wasn't enjoying it and that was rare. He could normally find some sort of pleasure in almost anything. Moving the chair a little further away from the leak in the roof, Pick sat down again, determined to practise. He had promised Ambrose that he would leave the Bowl and remain outside, at least for a few months. He was determined to keep that promise. If he didn't then his grandfather would know anyway, and that was not something he wanted to have to explain.

Now outside the Bowl and alone in his shack it was safe to experiment with his Influence. Beyond the sight of the Tower he would not be detected. He needed to hone his ability. Give it more focus. Control it better. Well, controlling it at all would be good. So often it just came out, without him even thinking, uncontrolled and unfocused. He would then confidently strut around and brag about the effects … but he knew better.

Over the last month he had been practising whenever he had the opportunity. Making sure that he was away from others in case his lack of control caused collateral damage. He was attempting to govern the amount of Influence he let forth. Felix and Silas had experienced the effects of his lack of control, as had others. His Influence would just erupt in full force. There was no modulation. It just exploded. He would then be drained, unable to use it again, until recovered. He looked at the cup resting on the table. Concentrating hard on the small vessel he focused his mind. He imagined that there was a stream of light connecting him to the cup. Gradually opening his mind he let the Influence trickle out down the light and into the cup. Nothing happened. Resting, he tried again. The result was the same. Looking with disappointment at the table, he sighed.

Clamping his eyes shut and clenching his fists he concentrated on creating a link between himself and the vessel. This time he created a wider opening to allow the Influence to flow more freely while still regulating the amount that left. All was going well until, unexpectedly, the stream turned to a torrent and was followed by sound of cracking of wood and rain hitting the floor. Opening his eyes, the cup was no longer on the table in front, but there was now a sizeable new hole in the roof.

Frustrated yet again, he calmed himself by remembering what his grandfather constantly said, "there will be trials, and we are measured, not by the outcomes, but by the ways in which we respond". Grabbing another cup, he placed it on the table with a groan and was ready to begin again.

***

Mortella congratulated herself on avoiding the Abbatissa. Had she not, there would have been the usual play of snide comments couched in polite concern and interest. Such verbal combat did not concern her, as she gave better than she received, but she just wasn't in the mood. Instead she enjoyed good food and excellent wine in her own company. In the relaxed state this induced, she had allowed her mind to wander and look at the problem from a different angle.

Having broken her fast, she wandered through the dark and silent corridors of the Tower. She found the cold that emanated from the black walls refreshing. Up here she could not see the auras. Perhaps they were not here, but she felt sure that they were. They were everywhere.

The mindless, disembodied fragments that inhabited the Tower were what created the Tower. It was the sum of their longings and desires that fed those of the spectre with which she interacted. They clung to her when touched. It would be reasonable to assume they searched for that which was lost – their humanness. Arriving at the stairs that led to the cavern below, she stopped. She could draw on the Influence of the Tower to enhance her own. This would then not drain her and allow for the perception to remain.

Slowly descending the stairs she clasped her hands together in anticipation. To create a perception of life. Of life that could be regained. It would take time and finesse, but she had each of these. Patience may not be one of her strengths, but she knew how to persevere. Reaching the cavern, she saw the swirling vortex of colours that stretched far beyond her sight. She would make it come to her.

Gracefully she returned to her place within the cavern, more confident and determined than she had been in days. Closing her eyes she stood with hands held open in front as she slowed her breathing and started to fall into herself. Her mind withdrew from the outside world and focused inwards. No longer perceiving anything about her, she began to weave. Calling on all those within the Tower with the Influence of Perception. She felt them respond. Each little turquoise fragment of Influence she borrowed. Stitching each one together with the others. Piece by piece she melded them. Together they formed an ebbing, flowing wave of colour. A turquoise lake that surged around a nidus of black.

Having gleaned enough power, Mortella now started to create. She tapped into her desires. Never to be ignored. Never to be demeaned or decried. Never to be used. Her craving to know who he was. She wanted this more than anything. Channelling these longings through the Influence, she began to craft her lure.

Carefully she formed a vessel. This one would need to look male. It would need to feel more realistic than look that way. She fashioned a face and limbs, constructed rudimentary clothes. Into this vessel she would create a sense of life, of vitality. A being of independence and self-determination. That was what must fill the vessel. That was when the real work was to begin. Having completed the shell and solidified its permanence, she took a breath.

Opening her eyes, she saw the Tower watching her. She felt no malice from it, only curiosity. Bowing her head to the waif, she gestured to the construction beside her. The benefit of using the Tower's Influence also meant that she could see the figure. It was static. As unlifelike as a wooden doll. Yet it would do. It would feel alive. It would welcome those that could identify an aura. For those, it would appear to offer them rebirth. If only they would come to it.

It would be a long night. Fortunately, Clara was now weaned, and the nurse maid would see to her needs. Calming herself once more, now that the Tower had accepted the use of its Influence, Mortella once more fell into herself ready to infuse her perception with the allure it needed to snare the ones she required.

Having made her way back through the streets as the sky just started to turn steely grey, Mortella sat exhausted but content with her efforts. Clara would wake soon and require attention. The maids were sufficient but Clara was special and needed more than what they provided. She would bathe and then get Clara brought to her. Placing the now empty goblet back on the table, she leant back into the overstuffed chair. Her creation now stood within the cavern, exuding vitality. Immobile, yet it still called out to the darkness, offering rebirth, newness and most importantly, life to any that could fulfill its request. Proffering to satisfy one desire if its could be met. It could take some time. How long she could not know … but work it must.

Pushing herself up from the chair, she stretched. Her back was sore from standing still for so long. The warm water would help. Letting her black robe fall from her she made her way to the steaming tub to soak and recover.

Once done, she and Clara would speak about what was to come and the heights to which they would ascend.

***

Felix scooped off the fluid that had formed on top the salted fish. He force himself to go through the motions of daily life. Maintaining the dams and collecting the essence. He hadn't sat by the upper dam since they had returned. He glanced up in the direction of the upper dam. The sun still glinted off the water's surface. The flashes of silvery gold still flicked beneath the water's surface and the breeze still rustled gently through the leaves. But Felix no longer saw it.

They had continued to shut down their Influence. His world was now silent. He felt isolated, alone. Silas was no longer there with him. There was a distance between them he had never experienced. No longer did they share a view, a passing thought, a comment. When once he would share everything with his brother, now he was lost to him. He turned and looked at the filled bottles. They seemed to be multiplying. Silas hadn't been to the market in a while so none were selling. They were also running out of empty containers. They would have to do something, or perhaps they could just put the essence on hold for a bit.

Putting the lid back on the barrel he turned to head back to the cottage. They should have something for supper, though neither of them had displayed much of an appetite recently. But still it was important to eat something. He sighed for the umpteenth time and started to walk slowly away from the dams.

Silas was still covered in dirt as he emerged. He had to get this done. Make it safe, make it undetectable. His focus was on getting their cellar ready. If they needed it then it would be ready. He had expanded it further. Running water was now accessible from the stream through a pipe that ran into the cellar. There were stores of food, a place to sleep.

The second exit was now also complete. Its entrance had been reinforced and was bolted from the inside. This would not be able to be entered easily. He had then worked hard to conceal the opening with rocks and vegetation. Any casual observer would fail to discern it. The main entrance he had also reinforced and worked hard to conceal. He looked up at their cottage. It was only a short run from there, and then they would both be safe within less than a minute.

Looking up again he saw Felix making his way home. His face dropped, seeing his brother. Watching him stooped over, shoulders hunched, slowly making his way down the slope. Like an old man. He also felt the separation, but it affected Felix more. Composing his face he raised his arms and waved enthusiastically at his brother, who failed to notice. Shaking off the worst of the dirt, he too started to make his way back to the cottage. He was determined, fortifying himself again, he was now that much more determined to break his twin out of this state of utter dejection.

Chapter 19

Progress was slow but at least there was some. The constant practise was starting to pay off. He could now focus his Influence and not use it all up in a single burst of power. Pick knew that his ability was of use to the Apostasy and that gaining control of it would only make him of greater use. And more importantly, it made him an even greater threat against the Tower. He was looking forward to showing off his newly developed control to Julia when she arrived.

Sitting in the communal dining area of their ramshackle little village, he watched as dinner was being prepared. Supplies were low again, but the hope was that more would arrive in the next week or so. It did mean, however, that the fare was a bit limited. Yet as his father had always said, as long as there are potatoes, no-one is going to starve. Sissy smiled at him as she worked at the fire. He was always the first to arrive. There was always the prospect that there might be seconds, though this had not been the case for quite some time now. But his optimism was real and engaging. Pick smiled back, feeling his stomach grumble in expectation. Sissy knew how to make the most out of the little they had. Incorporating herbs that grew about to add just a little more interest to what could often become a tedious repetition of many of the meals before.

"We've got something a bit special tonight," she stated softly to the expectant Pick. "I discovered a bit of dried beef jerky that had been wrapped up and forgotten about. It will make a tasty sauce to pour on the spuds." He smiled back at her, noting the tinge of sadness that crossed her face at all that could be offered.

"It'll be better," he responded with confidence. "Supplies will come and …" he paused. "We will take down the Tower."

***

Sybil watched from her favourite chair as Angus and Jess sat at the kitchen table, heads close together, engaged in quiet talk. The pretty, slender girl was nothing like the Tower. Gentle and sweet without demands or expectations. They had spoken about trying to find her real family. To let them know that she was free from the Tower. Yet without any memories of her life prior to the closing of the great black door that blocked the light from the outside world, there was no place that they could start. For as long as the oldest alive could remember, fear and intimidation had forced families who had lost a child to never speak of them again. And there had been so many.

Yet again Sybil considered what they should do. Were they safe here in Town? Her work among the sick and needy was important. But did this put her son at risk? She had had to leave Town once before. Travelling as far as she could to avoid the Tower and her family. Angus and she had been safe there, but she had needed to return. That was years ago, but things had changed once again. Should they make that journey another time? Remove themselves from Town and its proximity to the Tower?

Rising from her chair she made her way past the two most important people in her life. Angus, her pride, and Jess, the one he had obviously chosen. She would have to stay vigilant. Watch for signs of any interest in them. Any move from the Tower and she knew what they would have to do.

***

She had now been back several times and the result had always been the same. Once again standing in the expanse beneath the Tower, Mortella looked at the vessel she had created. As previously it was awash with colour. Every shade and hue covered all aspects of its surface. Thousands of auras pressed themselves tightly against the effigy. All drawn to the perception of life as moths were to a flame. Impatiently she started brushing them away. With each pass of her hand she experienced a multitude of different feelings and images as she swept away the swarm. None possessed the Sight she sought, yet all yearned for the gift she offered.

Frustrated, Mortella sat on the stairs that led to the Tower above. What had seemed to her an excellent idea was failing. She would not concede but what else could she do? The concept was sound, but the unifying desire of the Tower's inhabitants drew all to the hope her creation projected. She gazed into the void that was filled with swirling pinpoints of colour. Suppressing her vexation, she rose and walked calmly into the vastness of the cavern. After several minutes she paused and lowered her head. Standing still, she centred herself. Placing her mind into a pool of calm as she formed an image of the Tower. She waited. She started to feel the flickering of the Tower's presence at the peripherals of her consciousness. This then faded. Again she waited in supplication. The Tower probed her consciousness but again it dwindled away.

Pushing down the irritation she felt, Mortella remained still and compliant. The Tower was testing her. Playing with her as it provoked her. Now was not the time to display emotion. Continuing to wait, she cleared her mind, not allowing herself to feel anything.

Patience was everything. Time meant nothing to the eternal Tower. She would have to wait, eyes closed and mind submissive until it deemed her worthy of its presence. Eventually she felt it come. Raising her head she opened her eyes to see the familiar form looking down at her. Within the centre of the ever-changing mosaic that created its form was a vivid red core, held in place, rigid and unmoving. An image gradually formed in her mind's eye of a belligerent child crying out as it demanded its desires. Chastised, Mortella lowered her head in acknowledgement of the Tower's rebuke. Nothing in this place was of her making. Here was only the Tower and its will. Remaining contrite, she pleaded her need and that of Clara's. She requested the acceptance and aid of the Tower in recognition of her own inadequacies. Mortella humbled herself to the will of the waif that confronted her. She conceded her weakness and dependence on it, the Tower. With penitent acceptance of the Tower's will, whatever that would be, she felt its approval.

***

The afternoon was clear and warm as Silas forced his brother out of the house. They had been isolated for far too long and even for his introverted twin, that was not good. They were going into the village for a drink. To catch up with friends and perhaps even drink too much. There had been nothing for months now. Not that they were able to discern too much of the Tower's voices as their barriers remained permanently up. But this was not life. They were barely existing. They were doing to themselves what they feared the Tower would do. Diminishing themselves until they were nothing more than a shell of who they once had been. No more. He would make sure that that would not continue. Whatever it was that was to come they would face it together. But they would no longer cower from what was yet to be.

"Oh, come on," called Silas irritably. "We can get there just as everyone arrives if we leave now."

"Do you really …"

"Yes, I do. And so do you," answered Silas as he laid a reassuring hand on Felix's shoulder. "We can take a couple of bottles of fish essence. You know how much Fanny uses it. She's always happy for more. And …" Silas continued, "we've got more than enough stocked up." He looked at his brother with concern. Then he added gently, "We can't go on like this … you can't go on like this. We've got to move past it." Felix nodded slowly.

"You're right. I know. But …"

"But nothing, we're going and … we're going to get drunk."

***

Ambrose was listening. He heard the call. He knew that sound. The Tower was looking. Who it was searching for he didn't know but he dreaded it every time he heard it. Frozen in his chair, he focused. Turning his attention outside of himself he searched. He knew this aura as well as he knew his own. He searched but heard nothing. Extending the reach of his Influence, he systematically searched all the lands that lay within the mountains. He heard nothing.

Clasping the mug to his chest he sighed deeply. He wasn't within the Bowl. If it had perceived him on that night, then it would not be able to find him.

***

She was tingling with excitement. Cloaked once again in the Black, she stood on the landing before the great door looking toward the west. The Western Slopes continued both to the north and south until the natural barriers reached the Tower itself. Natural walls that enclosed within them all that was the Bowl. The Tower had allowed her to lead the Taking. Beside her stood two of the mindless Tormentors. These vestiges of what had once been human resided in the Tower. There to be used as vessels of the Tower's Influence. A portable source of its power. Influence to be used by her both to resist and then to contain he who must not be tolerated.

It would not be long now. The red light lit the sky as it searched for the aura of the one she desired. Having been directly perceived by the Tower on that night, its note could never be hidden. There was no need for there to be any trail for her to follow. These traces of Influence once used faded over time. There would be no trail now. But the unique signature of an Influence

166

once learnt … could be found anywhere in the Bowl. He would be hers. She would revel in the collection of another soul to inhabit the Tower as she delighted in asserting her worth.

***

They were greeted with enthusiasm as soon as they arrived at the inn. No-one had seen them since that first night when they had returned home several months previously. At that stage the brothers had been given their space as they looked so tired and worn-out from the journey. Very few travelled more than a day's walk from the village. Almost none had strayed as far as Town itself. That was one of the very reasons that Felix and Silas had found their home within this mix of people. Things were quiet and communal, allowing them to be themselves, left to their own devices.

Tonight, however, was different. Much had been happening in their hamlet, and there was a lot to discuss. A small village thrived on small details. Who had done what and when had such a thing occurred were things to be mulled over and rehashed whenever several of the inhabitants got together. Now that Felix and Silas had arrived back into the fold there was renewed focus on such events as neither of them were aware of the specifics of the goings on. The excitement at getting another opinion of the facts and speculations became palpable as soon as the twins walked through the door.

Waving at the figure behind the counter, Silas directed Felix to one of the more public tables instead of their usual one which was hidden away in the corner. Tonight he was going to talk with people and not shrink back. It would be good for him. Good for both of them. By the time they sat down at the table two tankards of ale had been placed in front of them as Fanny made her presence known.

"You 'aven't heard, 'ave you?" she started as she sat down in one of the vacant chairs. "I couldn't believe it myself when I 'eard. But then you know me … always thinking the best of people. Never one to talk badly of anyone. But still, who would've thought. John Milligan of all people, he just …"

"Hello, Fanny," interrupted Silas. "No, indeed, we have not heard. And you are just the one to tell us all about it." Silas looked quickly over at his brother as he smiled. "There's no-one who would be able to work this through better than you." Fanny smiled and was about to restart when Felix opened his bag and brought out the two bottles.

"We thought that you might be liking these," he said.

"Oooh, what sweethearts you are. I'd almost run out. Didn't know what I was going to do," she began as she leant over and kissed each of them on the cheek. "The best I've ever had. It's what I tell everyone. Can't get none better than this 'ere fish stuff. Just gives the stew that bit of extra. And never need to use much."

Felix picked up his tankard and took a long draw, looking back at his brother as he half listened to the continuous flood of words that poured forth from Fanny's mouth.

It was going to be a good night.

***

That hadn't taken long, Ambrose thought to himself. The aura's trail must have been strong for the Tower to find its source that quickly. He felt the note dwindle but it was still there. There to be used to follow the trail. All he could do now was hope that the one that had used the Influence had had the sense to move on. The trail led to the place the Influence had been discharged. If the practitioner was no longer there and, he hoped and against hope that this would be the case, was no longer using the Influence anywhere nearby. Then they had a chance of escape. Otherwise there would be another life removed. The Tower would strengthen itself as another family grieved.

***

Mortella sat in one of the black carriages drawn by two black steeds. Sitting opposite her were the two Tormentors. There for her use as protection and the Taking of the perpetrator. The Tower's coaches were silent and quick. They would be there before the peak of night had passed. She would then be back home and rested before Clara would need her in the morning. The itch that had been annoying her these last few months would soon be scratched.

***

Having consumed well and truly more ale then either had in many years, the brothers were enjoying the walk back to their plot in the mild, moonlit evening.

"Now that was worth it," slurred Silas as he held onto Felix for support. "We've not done that in ages."

Felix steadied his brother over some of the rough ground. He had revelled in watching his brother enjoy the evening so much. And Silas was right. It had done him good as well. There was only so much isolation that was good for anyone. They all needed others around them. Particularly when things were hard.

"Yes. You're right. We should've done that long ago," he responded as he looked up at the full moon. It lit the way home, highlighting the landscape in a cascade of monochromatic tones. They would soon be there. And then off to bed. A little worse off in the morning but much better for the engagement. Steering Silas around one of the many potholes, Felix caught the first glimpse of their cottage through the trees. He smiled to himself. What better place could there be than being together on their own little plot.

Arriving at the door Felix put down the bundle that had been forced upon him. Fanny would not take no for an answer. And when Fanny took something into her mind, it stayed there, and nothing was able to crowbar it out. They didn't need any more, but there was no telling her.

The walk home had already had a sobering effect on Silas.

"I'll take it to the cellar," he offered, looking rather uncomfortable. The dual alcohol effect of dehydration and increased urination were having their toll. Without waiting for a response he raced away from the cottage to where he could relieve himself. Felix opened the door and went inside to place his bag on the kitchen table. He too would need to drink more water to mitigate the worst of any hangover in the morning. He knew that Silas was probably already lying facedown on the grass, drinking his fill from the stream by the cellar. He took a mug and scooped up water from the bucket before downing the lot.

The carriage stopped as Mortella alighted, followed by two dark shapes barely visible despite the moon's light. A short way from them was a simple rustic dwelling, the likes of which caused Mortella's skin to crawl. He was there. Gliding silently they moved up the path towards the structure.

The air had changed. Felix felt it. Cautiously he listened. The normal sounds of night were gone. The loved-crazed calls from amorous crickets could no longer be heard. Putting down the mug he walked outside onto the cottage's porch. He looked over to the cellar and then down the path. He could not see Silas.

The haze of alcohol left as the chill hit him. The hairs on the back of his neck tingled. Silas placed Fanny's gift on the cellar floor as he carefully raised himself out of the entrance and looked towards the cottage. He saw Felix standing on the porch facing the path that led up to them. Looking down the path he could barely make out something moving. Its outline was vague and difficult to discern.

Through the "eyes" of the Tormentors Mortella could see a figure outside the shack. Looking at it closely she saw the aura's signature within it. There was a second one further off to the right but less distinct. Ignoring what appeared to be the residual of used Influence, Mortella prepared herself. She drew around her the shields provided by the two accompanying vessels, enclosing herself within the protection. Any attack would be absorbed by these, leaving her free to complete the Taking.

Through the trees Felix could now make out figures. Black as the abyss. He opened his mind to them. They were devoid of anything. Voids that moved within the world about. He looked back to the cellar, just making out Silas at its entrance. Silas waved at his brother to make for the entrance. Moving off the balcony toward the cellar he stopped. The voids had moved far faster than expected and were now facing him down the path. He looked back at his brother before giving a short shake of his head.

Silas waved and willed his brother to run. Within the cellar they may not be found. He must hurry. He watched uncomprehendingly as Felix shook his head. What was he doing? Together they would have a chance. Climbing out of the entrance he would make him come. As he started a shattering, *NO* cut through his barriers as Felix shot his Influence directly at his brother.

STAY … Hide. Frozen in shock Silas couldn't respond. He wanted to scream, cry out "no, you can't".

For me … please. He heard the pleading in Felix's thoughts. *Not both of us.*

Standing firm, Felix faced the threat before him. From the first time they had visited the Tower, he knew that this was inevitable, but not for both of them. No, Silas would be safe. Identical they were, so only one of them would be known.

Silas opened his mind to his brother. Connecting with him with all the fullness of his being. He poured forth all his love, his trust and admiration toward his brother. Crouching in the entrance of the cellar he felt his love returned with all the pride that Felix had for his twin. Tears falling uncontrollably down his face, Silas curled into a ball and waited helplessly.

Mortella smiled to herself. She could now see the abomination clearly before her. That face she remembered. It haunted her dreams, but now it would be erased. She awaited its attack, confident in the protections about her. None came. Intrigued, she waited. Still nothing as it held its ground facing her. She lifted the hood of her robe. Let him see. Let him know that she would never be defeated. She watched as recognition washed across his face.

"Mortella."

Suppressing her surprise that he knew her. She responded, "All abominations will be dealt with." And then she added sneeringly, "But be not distressed, the Tower will make use of you."

Feeling bolder than he ever had before Felix answered her. "Nothing lasts forever. The Tower will fall. Others will see to that."

Regaining some composure, Silas raised his head above the entrance. He watched as the three figures in black raised their arms in unison. Fully linked with Felix he experienced everything. He felt a sucking as tendrils emerged from the voids to begin latching onto every facet of who he was. Each one began to pull bits of who he was away from every other part of him. Tearing and ripping at him, they gradually fragmented and dissipated his essence. He felt Felix diminish bit by bit as one after another the connections between them were lost. Memories were shattered into pieces. Feelings began to twist and fall into themselves before vanishing into the void. In one last extreme implosion he felt his brother torn from his mind with a groan of immeasurable loss. And then … he knew he was truly alone.

Chapter 20

Harvests were collected. New seeds were sown. The weather in the Bowl was perfect for both. Wagons took produce to Town. The Tower took its tithe. Families celebrated new births while mourning the passing of the old. Yet for those that were Taken, they had never existed. Gone, erased from history, community and recall but still held secret and tight within the memories of those who had loved them.

Outside the Bowl the directive had been disseminated. The Apostasy had decided. The offspring of the Tower was too dangerous to leave. Too much of a threat to allow it to take the Black. Steps were now in motion to modify the situation.

Pick had returned to the Bowl, more sure and determined than ever. He had not wasted his time. His control had improved and with the constant practise, so had his endurance. He had kept his promise to his grandfather and had stayed away. But he needed to return. He had to play his part. The Apostasy must prevail. He would make sure that it did.

On returning his first desire was to see his friends. Those diametrically opposite identical brothers who had become more like family than anything else. He caught the passenger cart and alighted from it in front of the only inn in the village. It was, as usual, a beautiful mild sunny day. It had rained the night before, filling the air with the rich smell of fertile soil as they passed by the lovingly cultivated fields that surrounded the hamlet.

It would take him no time at all if he walked quickly. This time he would yell out, identifying his presence well and truly before he reached the cottage. As fun as it would be to scare them both again, he didn't have the heart to provoke it. It must not have been an easy time for them since that last incident at the Tower. Striding confidently along the grass-strewn trail the young man enjoyed the pleasant, peaceful day that surrounded him. Yet he was still aware how much the Tower was controlling all of this that he was now enjoying with the use of stolen Influence.

***

Clara fell over again with a laugh. Her steps were getting more confident, but more often than not she would end up crawling the rest of the way. Mortella laughed with her daughter, encouraging her to try again. The little smiling face that looked up at hers filled her heart more than she had ever thought possible. She now understood some of her knocking shop sisters' attitudes to carrying a child. But never again. In time Clara, her darling little Clara, and she would arrive at the Black to take what was theirs. Until then, however, life was pleasant enough and she would have more than enough time to reassert herself before rising to the Presence.

Reclining on the day bed that had been brought out to the terrace, Mortella listened to the tinkling sound of the fountain as Clara pulled herself up on the table to giggle at her mother. Despite the Abbatissa's disdain, she had been attending to the Tower several times a week. The cool darkness of its walls were a refreshing reminder of who she was and a welcome break from the formalities that encased her life as the first lady of Town. Charles' position, though always highly considered, had now been cemented as the first above all. She was now, by position and authority, the first lady of Town. It was no secret that she had returned from the Tower to marry Charles. She had also encouraged the rumours to flow that she still wore the Black. Fear and admiration were a powerful cocktail to promote control. And she did like control.

It took little to no Influence to control these politically, and socially, ambitious sycophants. They were more than happy to do that all by themselves. Yet she always made sure that there would be nothing that they could criticise. She would only ever appear as perfection in their eyes.

Tonight would be a ball. Many of the elite were already vying for a betrothal with their daughter. Carnivores surrounding their prey, little knowing the depth of their self-delusion. For them this would be another occasion to flaunt their position and wealth. None of this mattered, but still Mortella enjoyed seeing these sops fall over each other in their race to ingratiate themselves. To her, the daughter of a purveyor of sex at a knocking shop. There was now such joy in making them pay for their disdain of her sisters in the so many and varied ways she devised. Slights and takedowns, which none of them felt at liberty to combat.

Signalling her ever-present silent watcher, Mortella ordered a bath be prepared. A luxurious soaking in the warm, scented waters was in order while she planned her attack for the evening. Clara would be kept well out of the way. Let them scheme and vie with each other for her amusement, as she watched them fawn and grovel their way through the evening. Charles enjoyed that even more than she did. But it made no difference. Clara and she were of the Code and Charles would have to find another to wife who would furnish him with the bargaining chips required to cement such alliances through marriage.

***

Ambrose was aware as soon as Pick arrived back in the Bowl. So attuned was he to that aura that he felt it even before he was aware that he was looking for it. Seated in his tatty but comfortable easy chair he cradled the empty mug as he stared into space. Things felt a little different. There was the same ring to the Influence but there was something more. More potency. There was a clarity to the note that was clearer, a purer sound. As he rose to make another cup, he pondered. Something had changed. Pick sounded more like himself than he ever had before. He smiled gently to himself as he poured the heated water into the pot. He gave a contented sigh. His grandson had grown up.

***

Turning the final corner in the path just beyond the grove of trees, Pick looked up at the cottage. Smiling broadly, he waved enthusiastically as he yelled out, "Silas, Felix … Hey, it's me. No need for that axe handle!" He waited for a reply before moving forward. Not hearing anything he yelled again as he started walking closer to the cottage. There was an air of hollowness that was unsettling.

Feeling disturbed he moved slowly, cautiously. Getting closer to the building he saw leaves and debris scattered upon the porch. Confused he yelled again, but much louder, his voice cracking with the effort. "Felix … Silas … It's Pick. You at the dam?" Again there was no response. Climbing onto the porch he stopped in front of the cottage door. Gently placing a hand on it he waited, unwilling to push it open to see what he feared would be behind. Slowly turning the handle, he pushed. The door creaked open as the smell of stale air wafted towards him through the opening.

Inside mirrored the porch. On the kitchen table were fragments of food surrounded by the tiny footprints of numerous scavengers. The air was heavy. Its weight appeared to muffle sound. He walked silently through the

174

kitchen to look into the bedrooms. There was little relief in seeing no-one … no remains, but only unslept in beds. There were, however, some things that were preferable to what he feared would have happened.

Quickly leaving the cottage, Pick began frantically searching the plot, calling out as he did. He looked to the cellar. The door was open and much of the stores had been spoiled by the subsequent rodent invasion. Racing up to the dams he was confronted by the pungent smell of rotten fish. Arriving at the barrels he saw that the lids were still securely in place but several of the bottles of the distilled essence had shattered, allowing the thick, heady liquid to soak into the crates and the ground beneath. He looked to the upper dam. On seeing no-one he collapsed to the ground, head held in his hands as he fought with the reality forced upon him.

When he finally roused himself, the sun was low in the west with shadows stretched out as if held in tension by what had occurred in this once idyllic place. Unable to remain, he rose, wiping his eyes as he raced down the slope. Turning his back on a place he had so longed to see, he lowered his head and ran.

***

The inn was bright and noisy when he arrived. Entering the fray, Pick chose an isolated corner well out of the way of any festivity. He had not been seated long before a voice roused him.

"Som'in to eat?" Looking up he saw the smiling face of the barmaid. He just nodded. "Drink?" she asked. Again he nodded, unable to bring himself to answer in any other way. She left, looking back at him over her shoulder as she did. Caught up in his thoughts he stared at the wall. Eventually he shook his head and looked about. Without him noticing a tankard of ale and a bowl of stew had been placed on the table in front of him. Not hungry, he prodded the stew listlessly with a fork as he tore off a bit bread and took a bite.

Out of the corner of his eye he saw a woman looking at him. She gave him a small smile when he looked over. He just looked back without recognition as she stood and made her way over to him.

"You're Pick, ain't you?" she asked. "I'm Fanny," she paused and then tentatively restarted. "I'm a friend of Silas'."

"And Felix," said Pick without thinking. Fanny looked at the floor before looking back up.

Glancing over her shoulder at the room behind she added quietly, "I was." The word hit Pick like being immersed in iced water. He started to shiver uncontrollably. Fanny placed a soothing hand on his shoulder as she sat in the only other chair at the table.

"He'd said you'd come. That I was to look out for you." She waited patiently, watching him with sad eyes as he gradually regained control.

"They came," she said. "No-one else knows," she added, placing her hand on top of his. "At night." Tears filled her eyes as she fought to find the next thing to say.

"The Tower," Pick said. It was not a question but a statement. Fanny flinched at the words, again looking about to see if anyone could hear. But the noise of frivolity surrounded them. People totally oblivious to the horror that had occurred. She nodded. Pick remained silent as Fanny waited, willing that her presence would provide some comfort when so little could be offered.

"He wanted you to know … to say … that they knew … they chose to do it." Pick looked up at her, his eyes glistening. "For you not to blame yourself … for anything." She grasped his hand and squeezed it. Again she waited.

"Where is he?" he asked.

"He couldn't stay. He said he had to go. Away. Anywhere … but nowhere that they had been together," she responded. "I don't know where." Seeing the despair in his face she leant over and held him as buried his head in her shoulder. Stroking his hair softly she said, "Tonight you come home with me. As soon as you're ready, we'll go."

***

A glamorous affair with all the ostentatiousness overtly displayed. People had hovered about her, her brilliant flame lighting the room such that all else was eclipsed by the light. It provided amusement. She had played with others' perceptions of some of her self-professed rivals. Malodorous emissions from these personages at the most inopportune times. It was petty and beneath her, but it did lighten her mood, however immature.

Now that it was over she had retired to her room. Undressed and cloaked in a silken gown she stood on the balcony overlooking the terrace. In the garden she saw an indistinct movement within the darkness. A disconnect within the familiar outlines of the shadows beneath her. Her suspicion roused, she began to watch attentively. She saw nothing more, but still felt unsettled. A mother's intuition. She went to find Clara.

***

The Apostasy was clear. The Tower must be resisted and if that meant this, then so be it. If a single soul could be saved then no matter. Her innocence would be lost eventually. Now was the time to prevent worse to come.

Careful not to use any Influence until absolutely necessary, he moved through the estate. Attention would be drawn elsewhere with all the clean-up and excitement from the evening. He could slip through the gaps and make his way into her chamber. There, he would steel himself for what must be done. For the greater good. To stop the Tower.

The halls were now in half shadow as the servants busied themselves clearing away the mess. Waiting for one to descend into the servant's area, he then made for the stairs. Climbing them quickly he disappeared by melting into a darkened doorway. The family would have already retired to their rooms while the child lay sleeping in its cot.

The third door on the left of the landing and he would be there. Silently he reached for the handle. Opening it slightly he slipped inside before closing it behind him. There against the wall was the cot. An unnatural silence encased the room as he approached the sleeping child. Reaching the bed he looked inside to find it empty.

***

Standing in the corner of the room, cradling her sleeping child, Mortella waited. Paranoid she may be, but her instincts told her otherwise. Encasing the room in a perception of silence she hid the gurgling sounds of the sleeping Clara. It was not long until she heard the door open and watched as a figure quickly entered. It made for the cot before stopping, appearing confused.

She was not going to let him see her. There would be no repeat of that night in front of the Tower. Focusing her Influence she directed it at the figure. She withdrew any perception of air, or warmth, from it. As it turned toward her she watched it start to collapse, when suddenly it was no longer there. No longer having something on which to focus her Influence, she faltered. As she did, she heard a gasp and then moments later the sound of something falling into the bushes under the balcony outside of Clara's room. Racing outside she looked down, searching the shadows beneath without success.

Leaving the room still holding her daughter, Mortella returned to her chamber shaken, but more so enraged at the affront to her and her child.

***

Pick arrived back in Town and made directly for his grandfather's. Ambrose greeted him at the door, unprepared for the appearance of the severe-looking man that stared back at him. The face was familiar, but the demeanour was so different. Forcing a thin smile, Pick gave his grandfather a hug before striding through the rooms to the kitchen. There he started boiling the water as his grandfather looked on in astonishment.

"You'll need a cup," was all he said as he washed out the pot and filled it with fresh leaves. Looking up and seeing concern etched across the old man's face, his features softened a little before giving a genuine smile. "Go sit. I'll bring it through," he added softly. Looking back at the simmering water he said coldly, "We need to talk."

***

Mortella had not waited. Clara was safest with her, and she had to go to the Tower. There had been no argument. Not that she would have entertained any. Any dissent to her will and she would have gone straight to the Presence. Even the most obstinate streak in the Abbatissa knew that that was best to be avoided. By morning it was settled. Within the estate, permanently embedded within the house, were two Tower Tormentors. These unsleeping products of the Tower were there to watch and warn of anything that the Apostasy may present. Reservoirs of Influence, there for her use and hers alone. There to protect Clara, with their vigilance never faltering. Woe to any that attempted such a thing again. For them there would be no mercy. For them the Tower had provided her the means to safeguard her heritage while providing sustenance from the Tower's power.

***

Pick paced restlessly as he spoke. Ambrose listened quietly, observing the barely contained frantic energy manifest before him. Finally Pick fell silent. Ambrose rose, putting down his cold and unsampled tea. Walking slowly to his grandson he grabbed him in two forceful arms. Pulling the young man forwards he held him, squeezing tight. Not lessening the grip, he waited. Gradually the tension started to release. A head buried itself deep into his shoulder. Shaking uncontrollably, Pick clung to the old man. Long-awaited tears wet his cheeks as he sobbed. Encased in the safety of family, Pick finally allowed himself to feel the grief. The loss of his friends that he had denied himself to feel until now as it again invoked the memory of the day his father was Taken.

Cleansed by the release of emotion, they sat unspeaking, side by side, content just to know that the other was there. Finally turning to his grandfather, Pick asked, "Can you find him? I can't … can't just let him … you know … Felix was … was… it'll be like losing himself."

"I'll look. I know the ring of his aura. If he's in the Bowl I'll find him." Looking at Pick he nodded. "You need to go to him." Standing up, Ambrose walked back into the dusty storefront and sat down at his desk. Rustling through the paper that covered it he pulled out a scrap of paper. "I'd already made a list for you of others I'd found. Ones that are in need of advice … to defend against … them," he concluded with a jerk of his head to the left. Looking back at his grandson he added, "Go, rest, I'll have it by morning." Sitting upright in the chair he closed his eyes before opening them again. "Oh, if you wouldn't mind, a mug of tea would help greatly."

***

On his way again, Pick sat atop the carriage. Ambrose, as always, was true to his word and had located Silas. He was far to the southwest. Far from the Tower and greatly removed from the plot that he had once shared with his brother. Looking again at the last name newly inscribed on the parchment, Pick wiped his eyes with the back of his hand. In a clear, confident hand was written the name Silas. What followed was where he was to be found and then the urgency for the need of intervention – a ten, imminent need.

It was long and tiring, but Pick didn't mind that. It was the time that it was taking. *Were they unable to move faster?* The evening stop was unbearable. He ate, for he must, and lay down as he counted the minutes till the carriage could leave again. Sleep was not something sought, nor found, that night. How could he sleep when Silas was there, alone? Up again and outside before anyone else, Pick watched as the carriage was prepared. *How long?*

Having grabbed a loaf of bread and a block of cheese to see him through the day, he finally was able to climb back to this place on the carriage. Looking to the west he willed himself to Silas. Eventually Pick was disembarking at a small village. Immediately he started the walk to the hamlet his grandfather had identified. He walked quickly. The closer he got the more urgency he felt. It was only a few hours away. Once there he could ask. All would know of the new arrival and where he was to be found. By tonight, there would be Silas and then … then … he had no idea.

Mortella watched the shadows that lurked in the corner of the room. Sufficient but not enough. What if she was occupied. There was need of three. The Tower slaves were unable to respond on their own. They were there to be used. It was her oversight. One she put down to her anxiety for Clara. It had never occurred to her that she would not be there to protect her daughter. But reality was that she could not always be there. She would have to swallow her pride and admit that she was not enough. Not sufficient to protect the one desired by the Tower. She needed the services of the Tower varlets. She loathed the need to approach the Abbatissa, but for this she must.

Clara was not yet of the Black. But had she not resisted, her child would have been Taken from her. Encased in those cool black walls, she would be safe but removed from her. The defiance of the Abbatissa at Clara's birth had cemented their animosity.

Prepared, she had already approached the Tower. She had its consent that Clara would stay with her. Having the Tower's support she would now attend the Abbatissa. Lay her supplication before that vile pedant as the remembered words would circulate between them that responsibility to deliver the one foretold was to be hers and hers alone.

Chapter 21

Arriving at a small, nondescript cottage at the edge of the hamlet, Pick stopped, wary of the stray dogs that seemed to be congregating. They considered him. He watched them back, ready if need be. Taking a slow and cautious step toward them they scattered, leaving him alone, much to his relief.

It was the last of the buildings that marked the settlement before the road ran freely further westward, unfettered by the need to stay within the lines. He looked. It was nothing like their plot. There was nothing that spoke of the person who resided there. There was no lightness to the building. As if no-one cared. Nothing, no brightness, no life. It was dingy and dull. Walking toward the door he felt a heaviness settle on him. The weight of the air dragged him down. How could this be Silas, lively and gregarious Silas? Always ready for a laugh, a person who thrived around people. This was not him. This was isolated, desolate.

Unsure now what to do, Pick stopped. The barmaid had been certain. There had only been one who had joined their community and that only a few months ago. But who it was she was unclear. She had never seen them. They kept to themselves, never coming into the inn. Never taking an ale. Never had she known anyone who had spoken to them. Pick looked at the parchment. Ambrose had marked it, highlighted this hamlet, he was sure of it. He had followed the directions. Right down to the last. Surely he must be in the right spot. There wasn't another settlement closer than a day's walk. He must be in the right place.

Perhaps Silas was not in the hamlet but in a plot close by. They had been doing well so there was coinage to settle on another small plot. Pick looked down the road wondering if he should walk further out. But his grandfather was never wrong. He knew the sound of the brothers' aura. He had heard it before. He could follow it and find it. The unique hum that identified both Felix and Silas. He wouldn't have been mistaken.

Turning back to face the dismal, grey structure he moved closer until his hand was resting on the door. Forcing himself to knock, he waited. He heard nothing. No movement within. He knocked again. This time louder. Again he waited. Again he heard nothing. Moving to the one window beside the door he tried to look inside. The room was in shadows. The panes were filthy, allowing little light to penetrate the gloom. He saw no movement. There was no-one there.

He had not come so far to not know the truth. So, turning, he followed the outline of the structure to the back. All the windows were equally as informative as the first with grime obscuring, and curtains concealing, the rooms within. At the back was another door as decrepit as the structure itself. Again he knocked. Again there was nothing. Trying the handle, it turned, allowing the door to open inwards. Warily he stepped inside, unsure quite why he was doing so. Shouldn't he call out? Let whoever was inside know he was there? But he didn't. It didn't feel right to do so, to intrude into the desolation in such a way. This must be done gently, without imposing himself on what was happening within.

Stopping, Pick looked about the small, enclosed kitchen. Grey light filtered through the murky panes, exposing a mess and clutter that indicated that someone was living there. Moving between a chair and the wall he looked into the narrow corridor that led to the front room. To the right of the corridor was an opening, presumably leading to the bed chamber. He heard a rustle and sigh as he waited. Quietly stepping into the corridor, so as not to disturb the sombreness of the place, he went to the opening and looked in.

A small wooden bed occupied most of the space within the poorly lit room. Most noticeable was the stale still air with a coating of old sweat. Upon the cot was a figure that panted and wheezed as it tossed in the throes of a fitful sleep. Pick watched it as it gasped and then sat up in a state of fright. Seeing the shape in the opening it cried out in what was a mixture of both hope and despair.

Shocked, Pick spoke out of necessity, confusion, trying to explain his presence as he attempted to calm the figure.

"Sorry … I'm not a thief … Didn't come to hurt you … Was just looking … There's someone …"

"Pick?" came a quiet voice from the bed. "Pick is that you?"

"Silas?"

"I thought you might find me."

"I wouldn't let … I'm sorry. Felix … I'm sorry," Pick blurted out, his voice cracking as his vision blurred. Silas rose from the bed and grabbed the youth, clutching him tight as the young man trembled and his body convulsed. "I didn't know … I'm so sorry …"

"Shhh. Let it go … I know," whispered Silas into Pick's ear. "We knew," as he too was forced into silence, unable to say more.

Together they stood, holding onto each other. A physical support for the unfathomable emotions that gripped them. Eventually Pick raised his head to look at the man before him. He looked exhausted. Drained. In the dim light Pick saw the shell of a man he had loved as a friend. Drawn and dishevelled, deprived of sleep by his ability to feel pain. Silas looked back as Pick gave an exaggerated grimace of discomfort.

"You're a bit over ripe," he said in an attempt at lightening the mood.

Silas forced a smile. "Supposed to help keep people like you away." Then looking at the filthy bed clothes he added, "But that doesn't seem to work as well as I expected."

Pick had started the stove and heated some water before getting Silas up and out of the squalid bed chamber, forcing him outside to wash and shave. In the remnants of the kitchen he found some stale bread and a few eggs. At least there were some dry tea leaves in a tin. Moving two of the most serviceable chairs out onto the porch, he made Silas sit down in the sun as he prepared something for them to share. He hadn't eaten that day and had barely stomached anything the night before. Now they both needed to eat.

Bringing out the toasted bread with fried eggs on top he placed them on a small, rickety table he had found within the mess inside. Going back in he brought out two steaming mugs of tea. He felt better having had something to do. Finally he sat down and looked at Silas. Now in the light of day he was able to have a better look. Still, it was a shock. He tried to hide his surprise but knew that he had been less than successful. It was Silas but … he was so much older. The wet, slicked-down hair was now fully grey, scattered with white. His face was pale, thinner, and marked with deep lines. It was him but not as Pick remembered him.

"It's not your fault," Silas said abruptly before even tasting the tea. "You've nothing to blame yourself for."

Pick's face crumbled as he shook his head. Lips pressed tightly together he held onto his emotions. Willing himself to speak but unable to do so. Silas put his hand lightly over Pick's.

"Neither of us blamed you," he said gently. "You saved Felix that night. You're not to blame."

Pick dropped his head, unable to look at the man beside him.

"I could have …"

"No, you couldn't. There was nothing you could have done." Silas looked down at the mug beside him with trepidation. Tentatively he picked it up and gave it a sip. Remaining lost in his thoughts he gradually took a few more sips. "It had been months," he started. "Months with nothing. The trail must have gone. But then …" he fell silent again. Looking back up at Pick he continued as he blinked away the tears. "He saved me." Abruptly he became angry. "Not that this is bloody saved," he yelled out, crying. "They should have Taken us both," he whispered as he began sobbing into his tea. "At least we'd be together."

Pick knelt beside the weeping man and clasped him tight in his arms. Together they wept united in a loss so unwarranted.

***

May stood at the door waiting for it to open. She didn't have to wait long before her Noona opened it with a smile.

"May, what a surprise. Come in, come in," she said as she opened the door wider and ushered her granddaughter inside. "How's Joseph?" she asked as she went into the kitchen to put on the kettle.

"He's good. We're good," came the less than convincing reply. Noona looked back at the young woman with concern.

"Mmm," was all she said before filling the pot with the hot water. "Herbal?" she asked. May just nodded. Noona threw a handful of dried herbs into the pot and swirled the water around as she looked back at May. "Go sit," she yelled from the kitchen, "I'll bring it out."

When she returned to the sitting room May was perched on the edge of her chair, clasping her hands tightly in front of her. Noona set the tray down on the table beside her and took her seat. She then asked simply, "And?" May looked up from the floor, her face telling everything a book able to be read by the most illiterate.

"No luck?" Noona asked. May shook her head.

"It's been almost two years." She paused. "Joy was within 6 months."

"Yes, dear, but everyone's different," Noona replied gently.

"I've seen the midwife. She can't find anything wrong," May said despairingly. "We've saved almost enough to see Monsieur Crab."

"Oh, dear, no. You don't do that,' said Noona quickly. "What did Sybil say?"

"That these things can take time."

"She's right, you know."

"But ..."

"But nothing. Drink your tea. Let me have a chat with her and see what we can come up with." Looking at May with clear, certain eyes she added, "I promise you, my dear, you will have a child. Just you wait and believe."

***

Ambrose sat across from the lanky figure reclining on his couch. It had not gone well and now it would be far harder. Fortunately the man had not been perceived and was still free of the Tower's interest.

"There will be other opportunities," he said slowly, his tone expressing his utter distaste for the Apostasy's directive. "Peace and security over time breeds complacency, but ..." He looked at the man closely. "There are other ways." He looked down at the empty mug he cradled in his hands. "We will be remembered by the way in which we respond, not only by the outcomes." Looking back up at the figure on the couch he added, "Let us be better than those we resist."

***

The Abbatissa had relented. How could she not, yet Mortella fumed at the need that forced her to present the petition in the first place. Clara, and she, were paramount. The Tower had declared its need and only they could fulfill it. Still she must bide her time. She was not yet back in the Black, but once she was ...

Putting Clara down, she looked over to the shades lurking in the shadows of the building. They were outside on the terrace. Clara at once made for the tinkling fountain, plunging both arms into the water as she giggled with delight. The mottled sunshine filtering through the cherry blossom sparkled on the water as Clara splashed enthusiastically.

There would be a varlet present every evening, remaining throughout the night. There to watch, ready to counteract any threat that presented itself. During the day, Clara would be Mortella's responsibility. One she embraced

185

wholeheartedly. She was ready to use whatever means necessary to protect her legacy and future. The Tormentors would always be close. Always there ready to provide Influence from their store … and to absorb any that should not be tolerated.

***

Most of the time they just sat, saying nothing as they stared at naught in particular. Eventually Pick stood up.

"We're going to the inn," he stated emphatically. Silas didn't respond. "No arguments. We're going." Silas just shrugged. His face was distant and tense, as if straining to hear something but unable. "Come on," said Pick. "It's not far."

Again Silas didn't respond, remaining locked in a silent, isolated world. His whole life he had always been with someone. Every waking moment of every day he and Felix were together. Sharing thoughts, feelings, sights, and sounds. Ready to argue and irritate but always care. Never had one not been there for the other. Even when barriers were locked in tight, they could still feel each other. Know that the other was there … if just a bit distant. But now … now there was nothing. Silence filled his mind where Felix once had been. He didn't know how to feel … what to think without Felix there. Desolate and alone, he wished he had also been Taken. Nothing could be worse than this desolation.

Roused out of his stupor but the touch of Pick's hand on his shoulder, he looked up.

"Get up, we're going to the inn," Pick repeated softly. Helping his friend out of the chair, Pick led him inside to find something a bit cleaner to wear.

It was a quiet evening, but the inn was warm and well lit. Much better than the hovel that Silas had barely left since he arrived in the hamlet. The barmaid greeted them warmly as they entered.

"You found 'im, I see" she said cheerily.

"Yes, thanks to you," responded Pick. "This is Silas … and I'm Pick," he added. She nodded and smiled.

"A round of ales and whatever is hot and ready to eat."

"Right you are. Won't be long," she responded with a flick of the hand to a young boy, who ran off to the kitchen with the order. Leading Silas to one of the tables they sat as the tankards arrived. Looking directly at Silas,

Pick raised the ale in front of him. "To Felix," he said. Silas did the same and they drank.

***

Pick had been there a week when Silas gave some appearance of starting to improve. He would now get himself out of bed instead of remaining in a foetal position for most of the day. He would wash and shave before sitting on the porch. Yet still he just stared out into the landscape. He said little. He always looked ashen and drawn. Pick was certain that he hardly slept despite the hours upon hours he lay in bed.

The kitchen was now clean and ordered. The windows had been cleared of the grime and everything had been dusted and swept. Sunlight now fell unhindered into the dwelling which now was only slightly better than a hovel. Pick couldn't stay there forever, but he felt an obligation to Silas.

No matter what Silas said, he knew that without him this wouldn't have happened. Without the Tower and without Mortella, Felix would still be with them making his fish essence and enjoying the sun-speckled waters topping the dams he so loved. He was part of the cause and it plagued him. His lack of control. His impetuousness. Had he just pulled Felix away, none of this would have happened. But no, he just let loose with everything. Causing the Tower to perceive his friend. He could have taken them out of the Bowl with him. Why didn't he? He didn't think. He never did. And now the Apostasy had failed to remove the cause of everything. A bastard born of the witch that attacked his friend. Their loss of Felix now meant nothing. There had been no point for them going to the Tower that day if the child one day took the Black. Silas deserved better. Felix deserved better.

He would have to go back soon. He had work to do. There were others who were at risk. The Tower cared not who it took or when. There were others he could help … save. Taking some of the coinage he found while cleaning, he made for the inn. Silas and Felix had indeed been doing well and Silas had at least brought their savings with him. It would be enough for a long time with careful monitoring.

Arriving at the inn, he spoke at length with the innkeeper and his daughter. He explained as much as he thought was needed and handed over the coinage. Returning to Silas, he sat down next to him on the porch.

"I'm going to have to go," he said, while avoiding looking at Silas. He just stared straight ahead. Looking over to see if Silas heard him, he said it again.

Getting some sort of response he added, "They'll bring you a hot meal every evening. Promise me you'll eat it. Not just leave it for the rats."

Silas grunted.

"Silas, promise me," Pick demanded sternly.

Roused from his lethargy, Silas looked back and nodded. "I'll eat it … I promise."

"I'll leave tomorrow. There are some things I have to do," Pick stated matter-of-factly as he looked off into the distance. "You'll be okay. They'll check on you. Make sure you're okay." Silas just nodded. Shaking his head, Pick got up to make them some supper. He dreaded leaving Silas like this, but it would be a relief not to have to face it day after day.

***

Jess watched him. She was as happy as she ever had been. Not that she had any memories with which to compare. She loved making the tonics for Maima. Helping the one who had helped her so much. She looked out the window. The Tower had been quiet now for some time. Her days were serene and her nights less disturbed than ever. She didn't expect it to last, yet while it did she revelled in it.

Angus sat at the table designing something new. Something to help one of Maima's patients. He revelled as much in this as she did in aiding Maima. Looking up and seeing her watching him again, he smiled. His find in the wastelands of the Eastern Slopes had brought completeness to their little family. Focusing back on his work, he again vowed to himself that he would do everything to protect her.

***

Pick walked through the gates and made his way straight up to his grandfather's store. The trip had gone quickly with him trapped within his thoughts. He had practised and practised honing his Influence. Gaining control, improving his endurance. Just wandering the Bowl warning others of the dangers of the Tower and the Dark Ones was not enough. Not when he could do more. He had the Influence to do more. The Apostasy must not let the Tower be strengthened. The Tower must be stopped and those that supported it must give way. Silas was broken. Felix was gone. He had to do more. More, so that others would not suffer the Tower.

The child … if he did it, it would hurt the Tower. That witch would suffer. Take the child. Keep it safe but removed it. Take it away from the Bowl.

188

Let the Apostasy claim one of theirs. Let her grow to fight for them not the Code. She was young, she wouldn't remember.

Almost to the store he stopped. He knew where this Mortella lived. He had spoken with his grandfather about it. Her aura was strong and Ambrose, if he looked, could place her easily wherever she was. He would need to know the layout. Know where the child was kept in order to find a way to take it. He could take a look. See where there was a way. Nodding to himself he hitched his bag higher on his shoulder and strode further up into Town where the roads were wider and paved with cobblestones.

Chapter 22

Angus waved goodbye to Jess as he left. He was taking his latest design to one of Maima's patients. Well, he thought, she was now his, and Maima's, patient. He smiled to himself as he started up the slope. It would make a difference and that was everything. Being able to make life just that little bit easier for just one person. Just one person. One at a time. That was enough for him.

It was late in the day when he left but the sky was clear and the air warm. It would be a clear night with the stars lighting his way home. It wouldn't take long. He would then head back to his own snug little family.

***

It hadn't taken Pick long to get up into the posh part of Town. He didn't come up here all that often. There wasn't the need. The ones the Tower Took were from the Town poor and the country folk. Those in exalted positions within Town, those with wealth and power, never seemed to be on his list. They required no warnings. He often wondered about that. Did the men just not get an Influence, or was there something more? He looked up at the Tower now looming menacingly over him. He made his way further up the slope. There was bound to be something more. The Tower controlled everything that happened in their Bowl. It wouldn't be by chance that some were Taken and others not. There would be an explanation for it.

Pick stopped and looked about. High walls lined the wide, cobbled street. Above the walls he could see the canopy of trees and, here and there, the roofs of mansions that sat well back from public gaze. Those who lived there had no desire to see, or be seen by, the likes of him, nor the others who delivered their food and took care of their welfare. Unsure of where he was he looked about, trying to get his bearings. She was higher up, nearer the Tower. He was sure. The first among the social structure, and so she would be found in the most palatial of the estates. He would climb further up the slope. He was sure that he would eventually remember where he was, and which one was the object of his search. Failing that, he would just look for the biggest, grandest, and most ostentatious of buildings and head there.

***

Ambrose felt it in the back of his mind. He was reading a wonderful treaty on how the government should work when the niggle started. Distracted by the dissertation in front of him he ignored it. Now that he had finished, it was clear. Pick was back in Town after his visit to Silas. Walking into the kitchen, Ambrose looked about. He would be hungry. He always was. Picking up an onion he started to dice it. Something hot with some nice fresh bread would do them both good.

***

Noona expected her that evening. Of course, she no longer existed. Not once the Tower invited them in. No-one in the Black ever did. No-one spoke of them. Their names were removed from the family tree. They had never been born. Noona smiled. That was the way it was supposed to be. But not for her. Tilly had not disappeared that day. She had been gone for a while, but Noona knew that she would not be gone forever. They had a bond that could never be broken. They were incapable of forgetting each other. It just would never be. And she was right. Tilly had returned to her. Different but the same. They spoke of many things but never of the Tower. Never about what it was or did.

Her room became a little darker as the light from the hall was blocked by a figure in black. It entered silently as Noona stood.

"Tilly," she said warmly, "a tea … or something a bit stronger?"

The figure raised the black hood to reveal a round face with a bright smile. Giving a tinkling little laugh she replied mockingly, "Oh, Nara, need you ask?" Walking over, Tilly hugged her sister before flopping onto the sofa with a sigh.

"Whisky it is then," Noona responded as she unstopped the bottle and poured two generous portions in the glasses already waiting on the table.

***

It was fortunate that there were not many cobbled streets that led to the wealthy. Town was a pyramid. The masses were at the bottom with only a few at the top. It hadn't taken long for him to find the place that held Mortella and the child. It was surrounded by a wall just that much higher than the others. Its gate was just slightly more imposing. It was as he expected. What was the point of having

191

all that wealth and power if nobody noticed any difference, Pick thought with a shrug. Still, here he was, and now he would have to find a way in. Steering clear of the east facing entrance gate and noting where the servant's entrance was, he walked along the length of the wall. It was one of the last buildings before Town ended, only then to be crowned by the Tower further up the slope. He was alone on the street. All the townsfolk were indoors at the setting of the sun so there were none to observe his movements. He would just have to deal with those within the estate itself.

Finding a mature fig tree well established on the other side of the road, Pick began to climb. The long, sturdy branches were easy to scale. Climbing as high as he could, he looked over the wall and into the estate beyond. He saw light flickering through the leaves of the garden near the house, if that was not too lowly a word to describe the massive building. The lights were being lit as the sun set and sky began to darken. There was a courtyard and what he thought was a fountain. These were just off a large, lit door that led into the building. As far as he could see it had two stories, although he was sure that there would be another below. A level below ground for the multitude of servants that such an estate would require. The family suites would be upstairs. Yet which would be the child's? On this he could only speculate. It would be unlikely that the suites with the best views would be the babe's. Yet which had the best views was something he was yet to determine.

The wall that surrounded the estate was high and wide. A very study looking construction. That gave him an idea. Gaining access to the wall would allow him easy access to circumnavigate the house. Its height and closeness to the building might even provide views inside allowing him to decide which of the rooms was whose. As night fell and with the lights from the house blinding people's eyes to the darkness outside, he could move with caution and not be seen. Anyway he thought, it's not as if I'm not entering the place. I'm not trespassing. Climbing down the tree he crossed back over the road and made his way to the southernmost corner of the wall where it turned west. Here the roughness of the corner allowed him, with some difficulty, to climb up onto the wall. Hoisting himself up he got a face full of leaves from the shrub that grew next to, and then over, the wall. At least he was hidden from any casual observers from the house. Finding his feet on the wall, Pick started carefully making his way westward. He stopped frequently, remaining hidden behind any convenient cover, before quickly making his way to the next hiding place.

***

"It's been too long," said Tilly as she sipped on her second whisky.

"Well, you know you're always welcome. Don't have to wait for an invitation," chided her sister.

"Yes, I know," was the response. "But remember I don't exist anymore …" she smiled, "and it's going to be of some interest if someone wearing what I wear is seen walking into your cottage."

Nara laughed. "They already think I'm a bit mad. That would just confirm it."

"But seriously, Nara," Tilly said as she took another sip, "we have to be careful. I can hide my presence from most, but not all. They wouldn't want me to be here. You know that." She looked at her sister. "They would come for you. They don't care. They would do it without a thought … if they had any inkling." She paused. "I couldn't bear that. I know what happens."

Nara nodded. "I know." She smiled sadly. "I do miss you."

"And I you, but I would not lose you." Putting down her glass, Tilly looked over at her sister and asked, "So?"

"It's May. Almost two years and nothing. She's always wanted it. Ever since she was little." Nara looked at the face of her sister imploringly. "Is there anything you can do?"

"I've asked some of the others. I've been able to call in a favour or two." Lifting her empty glass she gave a little sigh. "We don't get this." Nara smiled again as she got up and refilled both their glasses. Nodding her thanks, Tilly continued, "I can only alter perception. There are those who, as you know, can alter things in a physical way. She has agreed … but she must not be implicated." Nara nodded. "May must be unaware it has ever happened." Again Nara nodded. "I will arrange it."

Finishing the whisky in a single gulp, Tilly put down the glass. Standing, she went to her sister and embraced her. "I'll let you know when and where. But now I am best to be gone. I am supposedly needed elsewhere."

***

He faced yet another balcony that led off a brightly lit room. This one, however, caught his attention. Unlike the others this balcony had no settee, no sitting nook for its occupant to enjoy the outdoors and the view while being separated from the world below. The glass door was shut, and the height of the wall was not sufficient for him to see more than the ornate ceiling and sumptuous chandelier. He needed to get higher to be able to see in. Further down the wall there was a large tree that may allow him to see in. The angle would not be ideal, but he could get an idea. The only problem was that it was too far from the wall for him to reach it without entering the estate. He didn't like the idea. He had heard of places such as these allowing vicious dogs to roam the grounds after dark. One of those bitches in black he could handle but ... he knew he would freeze if confronted by the other. The memories were still too fresh and the loss so great.

Reaching the spot nearest the tree he looked down. Vines had grown up the wall allowing for greater ease in scaling its height. It was only a short distance then to the tree. He scanned the tree. It didn't look too hard. He should be able to get up into its branches. Safe in just a few moments after leaving the wall.

Taking in a deep breath, he pushed down his anxieties. He started down the wall. Stopping halfway to listen. He only heard the sound of wind in the leaves. No barking, no sounds of footsteps, or paw steps, could be heard. Not that he expected to hear them even if they were there. Yet he needed the time to fortify his courage.

Suddenly he jumped to the ground and ran for the tree. Reaching it, he grabbed wildly at the lower branches. Pulling himself up frantically, he was insensible to the sounds he might be making. Once he was as high as the wall, he stopped. He panted, only now aware that he had been holding his breath. He looked down at his grazed and bleeding forearms. Sitting on the branch, back against the trunk, he closed his eyes.

Nothing happened. He heard nothing. Eventually he opened his eyes. Looking toward the building, he saw the balcony and the room beyond. A shadow was moving within. Looking up he assessed the branches above. He should be able to see in. Climbing around the trunk to be furthest away and hidden from the balcony he started to climb. Peering around its bulk he could see more, yet not quite enough. He climbed higher.

***

It was almost time for Clara to sleep. Mortella would then be able to pass her protection onto the varlet. Behind her in the nursery the two Tormentors, silent and as unmoving as statues, had been placed at either side of the door. Shades that only animated at the desire of one of the Code.

Tonight Clara was unsettled. This was unusual for her. Normally a bottle, a cuddle, and she was off … fast asleep. But not tonight. Tonight she fretted. Wanted to be held and would not lie down. Wearied by the day and now the trials of a demanding child, Mortella paced the room, holding her precious daughter as she wriggled and squirmed. She was getting so heavy.

She remembered back to her days with the sisters at the knocking shop. It was at times like this that a bit of gin would be mixed with warm milk. That would settle the child. She had it there already prepared. Sitting on the table. But Clara had refused it. Her temper frayed and her patience at its end, Mortella continued to walk to and fro, trying to soothe the infant. She looked out to the balcony. The darkness called to her, inviting her to enter its presence. It was a friend and companion that soothed and comforted her.

Reaching the lights she turned down the gas, allowing the room to descend into twilight. Turning her back on the room she opened the door and, taking Clara with her, she went out onto the balcony. A warm breeze caressed her cheek as her eyes grew accustomed to the starlit sky. She looked east but the Tower could barely be seen. Noted. She would have to decide which chamber Clara would be moved to when she was a little older. It would not do to have her separated from her destiny like that.

The night was calm and quiet, peaceful, and rejuvenating. Mortella revelled in the feeling, scarcely aware that Clara had settled and was now breathing slowly and deeply as she slept. Relieved and delighted that her daughter had found solace in the night, Mortella returned inside, leaving the door open to allow the night to enter.

***

He had seen the child and its mother. It was unmistakable even in the dim light that exuded from the room. That long red hair he would never forget. He had found the room.

Once they returned inside he quietly climbed down from the tree without fear. Making for the vines he easily scaled the wall and was once more on top and ready to leave. He would be back again at a later time. Armed with a better plan. One that would allow him to take the child, keep it safe and deliver it to the Apostasy. The Tower would not have what it so desired. She would grow to fight for them.

Looking down the wall he considered which way to go. The land sloped steeply away on the other side of the wall, making the drop excessive and dangerous. He could continue west and then around the other two walls to reach the road on the eastern side. Perhaps he could enter the next estate just north of this one. Or he could return the way he came. He looked down the wall. He knew that way was manageable and mostly likely shorter. Now was not the time to stick around. Quick in and then quick out. Always the safest way.

Starting to move back along the wall, he froze. A figure had reappeared on the balcony. It stood still, looking out. Remaining motionless, Pick was unsure whether he should crouch and reveal his position by movement or remain as he was, unmoving but potentially silhouetted against the sky behind. He slowly, very slowly lowered himself onto the wall. The figure didn't move. Pick remained still, barely breathing. Eventually the figure turned and went inside. Taking in a long, slow breath Pick remained where he was, waiting for any return of the figure. It didn't appear. Tentatively he began to crawl, slowly, keeping very low, hugging the top of the wall and forever watching the balcony. Eventually he reached some level of cover. Hidden behind the foliage he climbed to his feet as he prepared to cross the next section of wall, unprotected from the sight of the balcony. Taking one last look at the balcony, and seeing nothing, he ran along the narrow base to the next hiding place.

***

Placing Clara in her cot, Mortella sat down as the door opened. The Tower varlet entered. Her time was done. She would be able to rest. Clara's safety would now be in the hands of another who dared not fail. The consequences of such would be dire. Looking wearily at the youthful face of her sister in Black she nodded. It pleased her that Clara had been settled by the night. Going over to the sleeping infant she kissed her daughter lightly on the forehead before once again facing the balcony and the darkness that beckoned to her.

Crossing the room, Mortella emerged onto the balcony to enjoy the evening's delights. Breathing in the night air she looked off into the distance, remembering other such times in so many and varied locations. Out of the corner of her eye she caught something there. Without moving, she directed her eyes to the place. She saw nothing unusual. Yet her mother senses were troubled. She waited and watched but saw nothing more. Turning, she went inside. The lights were now off, allowing the night to enter with her. Waiting at the window she continued to watch. Wary of any danger to her precious child.

196

Eventually she noted a subtle movement along the wall. An animal of some sort? There was no sound and the movement was barely perceptible. It had now reached the cover of the bushes. Moving to the opening to the balcony she remained vigilant, already drawing on the Influence contained in the Tormentors at her disposal. She was wound and ready. She waited.

A figure sprang forth from behind the foliage. Now outlined by the stars behind, its movement clearly identified its form. This was no animal. Racing onto the balcony, Mortella focused her mind. Drawing her Influence and that from the Tormentors into herself, she focused it and hurled it forth. Withdrawing all warmth, all sight, all sound, and all feeling from the intruder. There would be no air, nothing but an emptiness to surround this invader. Let it suffer and then be joined to the Tower. There to be subjugated, ready to serve her forever. Just like those that had previously gifted their Influence and now aided her in securing his gift as well.

***

The air grew unbearably cold as the wind was knocked from his lungs. All about was darkness. All sound disappeared into the inky darkness as he lost the sensation of the wall beneath him. Panicked but determined he turned and focused as much of his mind as he could. He let loose one might blow to where he hoped was the balcony.

***

She watched as the figure stumbled and fell to the wall. She smiled. Let them come. Each shall strengthen the Code with their gifts. She watched as it turned, struggling.

An explosive thud violently shook the balcony. Cracks appeared beneath her. Blocks of the solid structure began to fall away. Rotating quickly she took a step to the door as the floor crumbled, leaving her foot hanging in mid-air. In slow motion she began falling backwards. She saw the varlet looking down at her from the entrance. Clara gave a cry. The air was thickly silent as the chamber gradually withdrew itself from her. Rotating to the left she watched as the ground grew closer and closer until ... there was blackness.

***

The air warmed. He was able to take a breath. His sight cleared. Lying on top of the wall, Pick pushed himself up. Glancing to the side he saw the destruction. Where the balcony once had been was emptiness. Rubble cascaded over the ground beneath. Without waiting further, he rose and ran as fast as he felt safe to do so along the wall away from the ruin. Turning along the final side he raced to the road that fronted the estate as cries erupted from inside the building. As he climbed down the wall he saw figures rushing out into the garden and around to the destruction. Gaining the road he started to race down the sloping cobbled road, away from the turmoil, forever glancing behind in fear of a chase.

Chapter 23

Ambrose stood unmoving, the frypan hovering in mid-air. His eyes were blank, staring off into the distance. The sound of boiling water broke the silence. His face was grim, lips pressed tightly together as he held his breath, searching. Even the least talented with his Influence would have felt the seismic shock that had just occurred. He knew those notes. He had heard them in concert before. And he had hoped never to hear them joined together ever again. What was he doing? Why was he there? What on earth had possessed him to go to her place?

Ambrose put the pan down slowly and turned away from the fire. He had felt Pick. He was leaving the spot. Now racing down from the upper reaches of Town. She was harder to discern. She was there, where she should be, but something was different. There was a haze, a blurring of her aura's note.

Leaving the kitchen he slowly made his way to the store front. His knee was hurting today. It made the distance seem much longer as he shuffled forward. Collapsing into the chair at his desk he waited. Clenching his hands then wringing them together, Ambrose fidgeted, trying to control his anxieties so as to be better able to continue to monitor Pick's progress through the streets by the ring of his aura.

***

Accepting their thanks with gratitude, Angus left. It was now so clear to him why his mother did what she did. He knew now that he too had found his calling. For such a simple thing, that he had created, to make such a difference. To be able to have an effect that was real and tangible. Now that was what he wanted to do. Smiling to himself and fuelled with the fire to find more and better ways to help, he started making his way home. Reading had many advantages. And he would remember, once he got home, to thank his mother for all her persistence in forcing such a poor student as he to persist.

He walked slowly, enjoying the moment and the warm starlit night when he noticed something strange. Out of the corner of his eye he saw a golden light moving quickly. Intrigued, he raced toward the larger road ahead just in time to see a man disappearing around a corner, heading to the lower parts of Town and the market. The man had been bathed in a golden light the likes of which Angus had never before seen. His Influence allowed him to see the multitude of colours that accompanied his mother's Influence. But only when in action. For Jess, hers had never been used through her time with them, except on that very first night, and it was pure white. But this was different. He would see colours occasionally on his trips around Town. But these were small and fragile in comparison with the man. This man was coated in the glow.

Picking up the pace, Angus raced after the man. He was moving quickly. He rapidly rounded the same corner and saw the man in front. He watched as the figure would slow every so often to look behind. These movements were quick, almost frantic. He would then race forward again. Angus followed at a distance, careful not to be seen to be following. He had no fear of losing him. Tracking the figure was easy. The golden glow gave him away.

***

Pick raced down the cobbled streets into the lower parts of Town. He had best get out before the gate was securely locked for the night. As he descended from the upper reaches into the heart of Town there was still a scattering of people about, most likely completing their business from the day before heading home. He wove his way through them as he continued. He couldn't stay. He wouldn't take the risk that they would follow him to his grandfather's. He couldn't put his grandfather in danger. They were so close. She was of the Black. If she had discerned him, he needed to be far away and … out of the Bowl.

Slowing every so often he glanced behind. It was of no use. Looking for a figure cloaked in black in a lightless street. He wouldn't see them even if they were there. He couldn't help it. His anxiety forced him to look. Heartened each time he saw nothing, he raced on, down the slope and out of Town.

It hadn't taken long. He would be there soon enough. His explosion of Influence would lead those who were looking to the estate. If he was far enough away only someone like his grandfather could track him. That is, if he had not been discerned. He didn't think that she would have had time. He had reacted reflexively. Had he not, she would have had him anyway. But the force of his Influence had taken down the balcony. The freezing suffocation had stopped and … had not restarted. He must have not only broken her concentration but also prevented her from refocusing. She couldn't have been able to discern his Influence while also being hit by it.

But if she had had time. If he had been discerned then … well, then even more haste was needed. The trail of his aura could be followed but … not out of the Bowl. Looking about, he was relieved to see that he was about to reach the main square in front of the gate. If he was lucky the gate would still be open for the last of the stragglers from the market to leave. If not, well then he would have to make his way back to the store. There to hide once more in the room with his grandfather. Once again having to explain what had happened and why. He really hoped that the gate was open.

Pick raced into the square. It was empty. The main gates were closed but that didn't mean the Needle's Eye was as well. This small entry to the side of the main gates often stayed open longer to allow the last few people to exit once the main gates were shut for the night. He was about to run for it when he stopped abruptly.

The air was now dead to sound. It felt heavy. He felt a chill that started to seep into him. Dropping his bag he stared straight ahead. It was there, straight in front. It was from there that the chill was emanating. He stood. There was no point in running. He had been right not to endanger his grandfather. He held his ground: ready, waiting. Vigilant for those that were about to appear. With his senses heightened it seemed an age. They would appear. He knew that. Why were they keeping him waiting? Gradually he observed a deeper darkness that was moving in the shadows. There was one in front. It moved slowly forward. To either side he felt, and then saw, two more. Voids, indistinct, barely visible but he knew they were there. He knew what they had come for.

The chill grew deeper, more profound. All warmth was sucked from him. The sweat on his face crystalised. The dead feeding off the living. He would not make it easy. His mind was clear. Focusing all that he had, he pulled his Influence together. Taking his fear in hand, he fuelled his attack as he unleashed. The Influence, a force akin to that which saved him earlier, was hurled at the approaching central figure. It was this that destroyed a balcony. It would take down a Tower shade.

He felt the Influence as it rushed toward the shade. Its power and strength, potent and volatile. But then, to his horror, as it reached its target, it suddenly dissipated, faded, and was gone. The force that destroyed a building was now less than a whimper.

He looked to the side, the inky voids were approaching … closing in … encircling him. He focused and shot his Influence to the one on the right. Again it evaporated before it hit its mark. Another to the left. Nothing. Panicked, Pick threw his Influence at each of the shades as they approached. Again and again they dissolved into the air without effect. Still they approached, an unwavering progress, both slow and deliberate.

***

Ambrose sat, his head in his hands. His eyes dry, unbelieving, immobile. The shock was extreme. There in the lower Town they had found Pick. Ambrose sat in his chair, unwilling to hear the cacophony of auras but unable to not. The crashing of notes grated against him as it scraped and shredded his raw emotions. There was nothing he could do. His curse was to see, to understand, but to be unable to intervene.

***

Hiding behind a cart left on the side of the square, Angus watched. Horrified, but unable to look away as he saw the desperation of the golden man. The dark voids approached. Shivering in the cold that penetrated every aspect of him, Angus watched as the golden light grew dimmer. The flickering blue lights that emanated from the voids gradually grew closer and encircled their victim.

***

Pick looked from side to side as the shades advanced. He could run. But he no longer had the strength. He had used all he had to fuel his Influence, but to no avail. Their progress never wavered. He imagined he felt their cold dead fingers already probing him, caressing him as they grew closer. They beckoned him. Called to him to release himself. Join them. Be one with them.

Shaking his head to clear his mind from their images, Pick thought back to his father. Of their times working together. Of their small plot. Of his grandfather … of Julia. The images gradually faded as he began to feel light. His terror fell away, only to be replaced by an emptiness. His fatigue vanished. He saw before him a legion of coloured lights, each unique and different but all part of a single whole. They swirled and swarmed, calling to him. They mesmerised him.

202

He looked down at his hands. He watched as they blurred and evaporated. Becoming less substantial, transparent as they washed away. He felt the same, less solid as the world began to pull itself away from him.

He watched, emotionless, as a darkness approached. He felt its hunger, a craving for life, an empty cry that could never be filled. It drew him inwards, longing to engulf him. As it crept closer the colour from the lights faded. They coalesced and shrieked in a discordant cacophony of loss. He shuddered. Before him there was now an image, a memory of his father as he stood defiantly against the figures in black. He saw the sadness and love in his father's eyes the moment before he was Taken. Then there was Felix, as clear as day, as Pick imagined him, standing firm against his Taking, before he suddenly transformed into Silas as he had been the last he had seen him.

Breaking from the trance, Pick remembered himself. Who he was and where he had come from. He was again fully him. They may take him, but he would never be theirs. He would cling to whatever remained of himself and remember. Remember what it was to be alive.

***

It was done. Head bowed and hands clenched tightly, Ambrose wept.

***

Angus remained frozen in place well after the voids had gone and warmth had returned to the air. He now understood Jess' nightmares. It was not something that could be explained.

Having seen and heard nothing for some time, Angus came out from behind the cart. There in the middle of the square was the bag. The one the man had dropped. Angus approached it carefully, looking about as he did. Picking it up he sighed. There might be someone he could return it to. At least he could let them know what had happened. Give them the things that were his. Turning away from the square, Angus walked quickly. This night was no longer something to be enjoyed. He now longed to be home with Jess and Maima. He needed to talk with Maima.

***

Mortella lay on the bed, barely awake. They had given her something. It made her thoughts foggy. It was difficult to focus. But She felt something pressing heavily against her left side. It also had a strange cottony feel to it as if it was both light and airy but solid at the same time. She raised her right arm to feel for it. Her hand found the bandaging that wrapped her arm and chest. She gave it a gentle prod. It felt odd. She knew that she was pressing on her shoulder but was unsure if she felt it there. It must be the bandages.

Thinking back to the balcony, she remembered little. The figure on the wall. Then the balcony shook, and she started to fall. The next thing she remembered was waking up in her chamber.

A figure hovering in the background caught her attention. It saw her acknowledgement of it and came forward.

"Would you like anything Ma'am?" it asked before Mortella recognised her personal maid. She carried a look of concern on the normally placidly blank face. "Should I ask the doctor for more medication?" Mortella looked at the girl, confused.

"Medication? Why would I need medication?" she managed to say through slurring words. Surprised at the difficulty in speaking, Mortella tried again being more particular with her words, achieving greater success and clarity. "Why would I need medication?" she demanded.

"For the pain," stammered the flustered servant as she looked at the bandages that covered Mortella's left arm and chest.

"I have no pain," declared Mortella with a bit more force that she had meant to use. Turning from the maid she tried to sit up but found herself unable to. "Help me sit up," she demanded, feeling both angry and frustrated. "And get me a goblet of wine." Her maid looked at her not knowing what to do. Frozen between helping and running from the room.

"Sorry milady, I had best get Mrs Poole," she blurted forth before turning and racing for the door before Mortella could say another thing.

"Not Mrs Poole again," Mortella groaned as she waited helplessly for someone to come back and aid her.

***

Angus opened the bag with Maima while Jess was in the other room practising her reading. An assortment of items now lay on Maima's bed, but one in particular drew their attention. A parchment that contained a list of ten names and beside each a location within the Bowl. There was also a number next to every name. Angus looked at his mother.

"He was leaving Town when they got him," he said. His mother said nothing. "The Tower Took him," he repeated. Pointing to the list he added, "This one is just outside of Town."

"We have no idea what this list means," Maima said slowly, as she examined her son closely. "You must not go," she said pointedly. "Do not go looking for them. Promise me." Angus just ignored her and turned to leave the room.

"Jess mustn't know any of this," he said as he closed the door, still holding the list. Maima just nodded to herself and gave a small smile. He would go. Of that she was sure. Forbidding him would ensure that he did. They did need to know. To understand what the Tower was doing. Were they at risk? Did they need to leave, as she had once before? She sighed. Risk was part of life. He was sensible. He would be fine. She was confident of that. And she … well she would start getting ready. Just in case.

***

The next morning Angus rose early and made some transparent excuse for heading out before the daily deliveries were ready to be sent. Jess, the sweet little naive thing that she was, believed every word. Waving goodbye she went back to preparing the daily tinctures. Maima just kept her opinion to herself as she continued to prepare for the worst. In all fairness it was inevitable. Three of them in one household with Influence would, at some stage, draw attention. Either now or later, they would have to leave. Better now when things were controlled than if they became urgent.

Jess watched Angus through the window until he was out of sight. She then returned to the kitchen table. It was going to be a lovely day. Preparing medicines and ointments with Maima was both interesting and fun. They could also talk about Angus without fear of him overhearing. Maima gave her a smile of encouragement as they commenced the work. They worked in silence, side by side, each concentrating on measuring and adding each ingredient. Forgetting something would make the medicinal effect less or negate it all together. After working solidly for over an hour Maima looked across at the ever-studious girl.

Jess' long blonde hair was pulled back from her face. She was focusing intently on her work. Her brows were slightly furrowed, and lips lightly separated as she mouthed the memorised instructions. Cocking her head to the side, Maima studied her apprentice. She saw nothing of the Tower in her. But the Tower ran deep, and it didn't let go of its own easily. Yet there was so much to like about the child. She could see why her son was so infatuated.

Looking up and seeing Maima studying her, Jess gave a small, embarrassed smile. Maima smiled back encouragingly.

"Angus won't be long now," she said.

Jess smiled. "He's a very good teacher."

"The reading is going well?"

"He says it is," replied Jess with a broad smile.

Maima nodded. "Shall we break for tea?" she asked, already turning to put on the water.

"Almost finished," Jess replied. "I'll join you soon." Maima washed her hands in the basin and went into the small pantry to gather something nice to have with the tea. On returning to the kitchen she was shocked to see Jess standing rigid, pale and motionless. Her hand hung in mid-air as if about to do something. She stared vacantly at the door that led into the street.

The darkness had grabbed her so suddenly. One moment she was working in the bright, airy kitchen, the next she was bathed in the silver-grey darkness within the smooth black stone that was the Tower. She was alone. Again. There was no-one there. Just the cold, soundless stillness of one of its never-ending corridors. Fear encased her. She then heard voices. They surrounded her. Coming at her from all sides. Small, fragile, and delicate. As she looked about, indistinct, ghostly apparitions gradually emerged, swarming around her as they mouthed the words she heard.

"Come, the Tower calls. We are … we were … we will be the Tower. Come." Together they called her, encircling her as they cried. In terror, Jess covered her ears and ran through the wraiths and down the corridor. Their coldness, emptiness invaded her. Their longing, the desire they had for her screeched in her mind. They wanted her. They needed her to be with them. Crying out, pleading with them, Jess screamed.

Maima watched as Jess began to twitch and then thrash about. This was no seizure. Her face was contorted with fear as she began to plead.

"No, no, no, please, not again," she cried before taking in a great breath. Maima felt the Influence start to engage. The air in the room began to be drawn toward Jess. A barely perceptible breeze at first, but it grew quickly. Maima raced around the table engaging her own Influence as she did. Jess must not use her power. Not here, not now, not ever. The Tower would see. The Tower would come. This must not happen.

Maima reached for the child as wind rushed up behind her. It whipped up her clothes and blew hair over her face. Grabbing Jess' arm she pushed in her Influence as she withdrew some of the emotion that was fuelling the storm. Jess slumped to the ground as Maima absorbed a portion of the unbearable panic that Jess had experienced. She too fell to the floor, clamping down as the emotions threatened to overwhelm her. They were not real, but their potency was intense.

It took some time before Maima was able to rise, still shaken but calm enough to function. She looked down at the sleeping girl. This had never happened before. It must never happen again. It would put them all in danger.

Finally getting Jess into her bed, Maima went to complete the packing. They would need to leave, no matter what Angus found.

Angus returned to a quiet cottage with Maima working at the table as he entered.

"Where's Jess?" was the first thing he asked. Maima looked grim as she explained. Angus nodded. Maima had decided. They would leave. Head to the Western Slopes where she had fled years before. They would be safe there, she promised. He agreed. He thought back to the sadness and terror etched on the man's face he had visited that day. It reinforced her decision. His son had been Taken by the Tower. Just like the golden man. It was clear that none of them were safe this close to the Tower. Not if there was an Influence and … especially him who was not to be tolerated.

Chapter 24

She refused to let it affect her. She had recovered. It would not be any different. They would never know. Mortella sat looking at her reflection. She glared at the mirror. He face stony cold. To those about she had made a miraculous recovery. She had sustained no injury that did not heal completely. She was as young and beautiful as always. Tall and elegant with perfect posture and a slender yet voluptuous figure. But she knew the reality. Her Influence did not work on her. Only on those about. She could see the deformity.

Her eyes remained rigidly fixed examining her face. The emerald, green eyes and luxurious locks were as captivating as ever. Her oval face and porcelain skin, no longer bruised, still entranced her. Her lips were held pressed tightly together. She parted them slightly. They were still full and lush. Teeth bright and straight, but no smile was forthcoming.

How she longed for the Tower. For there she, too, could be fooled by the deception. She continued to stare. It calmed her. Without Influence the creature staring back from the mirror still had a flawless porcelain complexion crowned by luscious fiery brushed-bronze hair. The emerald eyes were clear. The cheeks still had the blush of youth.

She braced herself as her gaze lowered. A knot tightened in her stomach. She needed to look. She had to assess. If she did not assess her weaknesses then how could she prevail? Up to this point she had avoided looking. Still unable to comprehend. But now she must. Must see it for all that it was.

To the maid making the bed, Mortella was perched on the edge of the chair before the dressing table, sitting elegantly upright. In her own eyes, she saw reality.

Involuntarily she let forth a primeval cry as her eyes landed on the horror that was now her body. The maid looked up anxiously.

"Milady, are you all right?" she asked nervously.

"Go," ordered Mortella. When the maid waited, looking as if she was about to ask if anything was needed. Mortella screamed at her, "I said, go." At this the maid frantically turned, knocking over a small table, and ran quickly from the chamber.

Mortella continued to look. Her left shoulder now drooped. It slumped forward, no longer able to carry the weight of a dead, lifeless arm. The balcony's destruction had led to the fall. Debris had then crushed her left shoulder and arm. Irreparable nerve and tissue damage had now rendered it almost entirely numb. Some movement was possible. She concentrated, watching intently as she tried to raise it. She could no longer move her arm more than a few inches. The hand would open, and close, but the numb fingers were next to useless in holding anything.

In the short time since the attack, withering of the muscles had already started. The gentle and fluid curve of her neck that once had flowed into left shoulder was now already sharp and angular as the muscles wasted before her eyes.

Closing her eyes, she stole some Influence from one of the Tormentors stationed in Clara's room. It would not last. She knew that. She just needed a moment to collect herself. Opening her eyes again, the mirror now lied to her as well. Her body was reformed back to its original splendour. She gave a bitter smile. Rising with difficulty from the chair, she tore her gaze from the mirror. It would take practise, but she would do it. She would now have to keep her Influence in place every waking moment.

Going to the table with the wine, she picked up the decanter with her right hand and poured a full goblet. Taking this, again in the right hand, she walked to the window, stopping just short of exiting out onto the balcony. There would have to be some changes. No longer would she enjoy the bloody juices of rare meat at dinner with Charles. She would need to limit herself to things that could be eaten with a fork. When asleep none would be allowed to be near her. When being dressed she would be careful so that none would be suspicious. And her hair … well that was now out of her capacity to do in the manner it deserved. The maid would now do it.

***

In the westernmost spot of the Bowl, a stone's throw from the lower portions of the Western Slopes, the small family began its new life. With the help and support of Jim Albee, Maima's childhood friend, and his family they had cleaned and repaired the old, abandoned plot. The Albees were their closest neighbour, only several hours' walk from their new cottage. From there it was another few hours to the closest hamlet.

Once settled, Angus pleaded to go and search for the other men on the golden man's parchment. To find and talk to them He argued that they needed to know as much as they could. Leaving Jess and his mother in the care of their friends he packed a bag and the little money he had saved and headed back to the passenger cart that headed east.

***

May looked concerned as her grandmother soothed her.

"Trust me. It'll be fine." Placing a reassuring hand on her granddaughter's arm she led her into the sitting room. "I'll be here the whole time." May looked only partially reassured. "It'll make you sleepy ... but afterwards ... things will all be back in the right order. You and Joseph will have a family." May gave a weak smile.

"Noona, you are sure?" she asked. Nara gave a reassuring smile.

"Would I ever put you at risk?"

May shook her head. "No."

"I won't leave you. I promise."

Leading May to the day bed, Nara got her to sit down.

"I'll get the draught." As she went into the kitchen she called over her shoulder, "It'll taste a bit bitter, I'm afraid." May looked nervously around the room. She had been here so many times. Everything was familiar. She sat back in the day bed and waited for Noona to return. She had asked for help. Nothing else had seemed to work. She would try anything.

Her grandmother had been less than clear about things. May knew that Influence ran in the family. Noona's sister had been collected by the Tower many years ago. The family never spoke of it. To them she had never existed. Like so many other families, it was brushed over. Forcefully forgotten. But not Noona. She did speak of her sister ... and not in the past tense. May also suspected that there was more to things than she knew. This was why she had come to her grandmother. She had a way with things. An uncanny ability to get things done when no-one else was able.

Nara returned to the sitting room carrying a mug. Her face was bright and cheerful as she handed it to her granddaughter.

"Now drink it all," she said as she stood and watched. "We want the full effect." May looked at the liquid within the dark cup. It had a bitter smell to it. "Best to drink it fast," Nara advised. Tentatively May raised the mug and gulped down the liquid. It was bitter with a slight sting on the lips. She gave back the mug to her grandmother who put it aside and sat on the edge of the day bed holding May's hand. "You'll feel a little sleepy soon. That's what should happen, so nothing to worry about." Stroking May's hair with the other hand as she added, "And when you wake up, it'll all be done."

As May gradually dozed off, Nara rose and went into the corridor. There waiting for her were two figures cloaked in black. Turning to the taller of the two she asked, "Can you take off that dreadful hood? It's no wonder you give everyone the heebie-jeebies." The figure raised her hands and flicked back the hood.

"Such little respect for those in the Black," laughed Tilly as she hugged her sister.

"Hmm. I'll respect what is done and then the doer. Not a pile of garments," retorted Nara with a frown before smiling back at her sister.

"She is one of ours," said Tilly, turning to the other figure. It gave a slight bow without removing the hood. "Best if she is not known to be involved," Tilly added.

Nara nodded her agreement as she led them into the sitting room "She's asleep. I gave her a draught. She'll sleep for some time."

The cloaked figure approached the sleeping woman, then stood silently hovering over the day bed. It slowly raised both hands and a silence echoed in the room. Nara walked forward as Tilly was about to lead her away.

"I promised I wouldn't leave her," she said as she sat in a chair close by. Tilly followed her and sat beside her.

"It might take some time."

"I've got all the time in the world," quipped Nara, watching her granddaughter intently.

***

Noona was sitting by her side as she awoke. She had slept peacefully. Raising her head she looked questioningly at her grandmother.

"How do you feel?" she asked.

"No different."

"Well, it's all done." Noona smiled. It was nothing to worry about. May just looked confused.

"What happened?"

"Everything is back in order. The way it should be."

"How?"

Noona ignored the question as she stood up. "Cup of tea? I've been waiting for you to wake up before getting one. I'm parched. Apple and ginger?" Without waiting for a reply Nara walked into the kitchen. May stayed where she was, gently pushing on the lower stomach. Seeing if anything felt different.

"Now you must wait a few months," Noona said, re-entering the room carrying a tray. "Let everything settle before giving it a go."

May looked at her.

"That's just the way it has to be," Noona looked serious. "You've waited long enough already. There's no point in rushing things now."

May nodded, understanding that she was not going to get any more explanation from Noona no matter how much she asked.

"Now drink your tea. It'll do you good. And have one of these. I got them from Mrs Perkins at the markets. One of her more inventive and successful innovations, I think," she added as she passed a plate covered with biscuits.

***

Angus returned to the cottage after several weeks to a rapturous welcome. Jess was particularly happy to see him. Of the nine other names on the list, he had only found two. A young boy whose parents had refused to listen. The child himself, however, had. Couching his warnings within the well-accepted stories of the Tower, Angus felt that he had at least given the child a chance. He had left feeling that he had given as much of an understanding as a child of seven could have of the risks of practising his Influence.

The second was a man who appeared well on in years. Angus had arrived in the hamlet in the mid-afternoon. Having had little to eat on the way he made his way into the inn for an early supper. The place was quiet, but the barmaid was bright and talkative. Visitors seldom came to such a place and excited interest. It had not taken long for her to mention a previous traveller. One who had been just recently. For the rarity of two such travellers coming in such a short space of time was notable. He was a friend of their newest resident. An odd man who kept to himself.

As she spoke she was preparing a basket. Placing in some bread, a stoppered tankard of ale, before getting a jar to put in the stew of the day. She grumbled as she did so. Complaining of the extra time it took to deliver the meal to the edge of the settlement when there was always so much other work to do. Angus kindly offered to deliver it for her. He was going to have a stroll about the area after he had finished his supper anyway. Delighted with the offer, she poured him another ale on the house.

Taking the basket and following the directions, he made his way to the last building of the hamlet. There was a basket, similar to the one he carried already sitting by the front door on the porch. Looking into it he saw the residues of the previous day's fare. He would take this one back with him.

Reaching the door he knocked loudly. The elderly were frequently hard of hearing, so he was particularly forceful in his pounding. He heard a grumble from inside.

"It's on the porch … like always."

"I've got your supper here," called out Angus.

"Just leave it by the door," came the voice from inside.

"It's always better when it's hot," called back Angus. When there was no reply he added, "Beef stew tonight. Very good. Just had it myself."

As he spoke the door cracked open a little. "You're not from the inn."

"Yes. Well, no, not really. But I've brought this from the inn," explained Angus. "I told Evie that I'd deliver it."

"Who's Evie?"

"She's the barmaid there."

"Oh, that's her name. Mmm."

The door opened a bit wider and in the dim light inside Angus could see a pale orange halo around the figure. Looking closer he asked, "Are you Silas?" The figure inside gave a start before responding.

"And who are you that you are asking?"

Angus smiled. "Let me in and I'll tell you as you eat." Warily Silas opened the door to allow the young man to enter. Coming inside Angus quickly unpacked the basket on the small table that he found in the front room before encouraging the old man to sit and start eating.

"How is it?" Angus asked.

"Mmm," was all he received in return.

"Pretty good, isn't it. Nothing like a hot, rich stew to lift the spirits." The man looked at him with dead eyes.

"No idea why I even eat," he said. "Better if I wasn't here anymore. Would save a lot of hassle." He took another mouthful before adding under his breath, "But I promised."

Angus took out the parchment to show Silas. Silas dropped his fork when he saw it.

"Where'd you get that?" he demanded. "That's not yours."

Taken aback by the sudden display of anger, Angus sat silent, not knowing what to say next.

"How'd you get that?" the old man asked again, looking directly at Angus with a fervour that counteracted his previous lethargy. Stumbling over his words, Angus started to explain.

"I can see auras. I came to warn you of the Tower. Of what it can do."

"Influence is a curse. The Tower is an abomination. Better never to have an Influence but if so, never use it," spat out Silas. Keeping his eyes locked on Angus he demanded again. "Where did you get that parchment?" Angus then related the story of the golden man as he watched the face of his hearer crumple into the epitome of horror and grief.

The food, left alone to cool. Silas sat slumped forward with head bowed. Angus sat opposite him feeling both grief and guilt at having to deliver the news. Together they sat in silence in shared misery.

"His grandfather would know," said Silas suddenly. "He would have heard it happen." He rubbed his hands over his face. Looking up at the visitor he said, "I think it's time you went. You've delivered your warning. Your conscience is clear. Go back to your family. Pray you will never feel the Tower in your life ever again." Seeing the steely resolve in the old man, Angus stood and left. Taking the basket left on the porch with him, he slowly made his way back to the inn.

Angus looked at his family across the table. He knew that the Tower would always be with them. He would protect them as much as he could. He promised himself that he would. No matter what. Whatever it took he would do it to protect his own. He saw Jess looking at him. Adoring eyes drinking him in. He felt the same. He looked at his mother. She smiled, a knowing smile. She saw and understood. Having received his mother's blessing on their union, they would then live as husband and wife. He placed his hand over Jess' and gave it a squeeze. They would be happy. How could they be otherwise?

Chapter 25

Noona smiled broadly. "How are you feeling," she asked. May looked up at her as Noona carried in the tray from the kitchen.

"Excited," she answered, "and ... nervous. What if I'm not a good mother?" she asked in a small voice as she took the offered mug.

"It's exactly because you asked that you will be," her grandmother replied as she sat down taking her own mug.

"How do you know?" May questioned.

"Oh, I know," Noona nodded, taking a sip. "I remember when I was carrying your mother." Her eyes softened at the memory. "Wasn't the easiest of times." She looked across at May, "But throughout it all I knew, deep within me, that I'd do anything ... anything ... if it was needed for my child." A sad smile crossed her face. "You're the same. You'd do anything. You'll be a good mother," she said adamantly. There was a moment of silence between them as they remembered. "Your mother was a good mother," Noona added, breaking the silence. May nodded silently.

"I wish that she could be here for this," said May.

"So do I. So do I," breathed Noona. May felt the sadness that her grandmother kept hidden so well. Getting up she crossed the room and knelt down beside the old woman and looked at her.

"I'm glad that you're here," she said, leaning forward and hugging her grandmother.

"Oooh, and so am I, dear," said Noona, brightening up. "How exciting. How's Joseph coping with it?" she asked, offering May a biscuit.

"Oh, no, thank you. I am a bit ... well ... a bit off my food at present."

"Now that's normal. The worse it is, the healthier the baby," Noona chortled. "I hardly ate a thing the whole time with your aunt. Look at her ...

never had a sick day in her life." She looked closely at May. "And Joseph, how is he coping with it?"

"Oh, he's so excited. Already half completed the cradle. He said he would have to make it extra sturdy so it would survive through all the children." Noona looked pleased.

"He's a good man, May."

May looked sheepish. "I know."

***

Mortella sat on the terrace watching Clara play. Things had been quiet after the Taking of the intruder. The garden walls were now watched day and night and the Tower had granted her daughter further protection. Mortella's vigilance was less needed. Those of the Tower had learnt how to respect her wishes and provide the security that was required.

Mortella closed her eyes. To the hidden observers she was poised and cheerful. She felt nothing of the sort. Time and again over the last few months Clara had come to her, begging to be picked up. Each time looking up at her mother imploringly. Pleading to be carried. Mortella would then crouch and hold her. But this was not the same for the toddler. Being lifted and carried was what was wanted. Not cajoled at ground level. But it was not possible. Mortella was unable to pick up the solid child with only one good arm. Revealing her failings was equally impossible. So now … Clara no longer asked.

She had also kept to herself. Making excuses to Charles for her lack of presence in his bed chamber. She knew that he had taken one or two of the servants for his pleasure. And a few of the societal wives willing to assist the progress of their husband's political standing. It was the way of men. She did not begrudge him that. Yet she too desired to relive the passion they had shared. She could easily win him back. That was not her worry. But would it be the same? Would things feel the same or was there further damage of which she was unaware?

Things had healed, as much as they were going to. Well, the skin was no longer bruised, and the scars were softening and less tender. Her arm, although gaining a greater range of movement, had withered. Her gowns she had to have adjusted. Care was needed so that they would not slip off the now angular, sloping left shoulder.

Looking up at the cherry blossom she mused. Against the Code's practices she had learnt what a man could do, and she desired it. Her imagination

216

was vivid, but it was not the same as experiencing it. She wanted to feel the desire, the passion again. The ferocity with which he took her was exciting. She needed to feel that again. To feel whole. A full woman. Not just to be the image of perfection but to feel someone really believe that she was.

Shaking her head to clear the daydream, Mortella gestured to the hidden watcher. Coming forth immediately, they waited for instructions.

***

Now dressed, and with her hair ornately done, Mortella sat looking at her reflection. The colour of the gown was perfect. Profound verde, almost black with a deep jade sheen, succulent, yet dangerous. The neckline plunged just a little lower than good taste would allow. Perfect for seduction. Her complexion still needed little help. Her face had not been damaged. Nodding, she borrowed Influence from the resident shades that stood in her daughter's room. She watched as the shoulder and arm were restored. Borrowed Influence also allowed her to perceive that. She too wanted to be transported into the moment.

A formal supper with Charles had been arranged. The menu instructions had been very specific. She would display elegance by eating only with one hand. She planned to make this the norm for all the fashionable, societal women. The wines would be red, robust, and full bodied. The food, rustic, seductive and hearty. An entrée of raw red beef, minced finely, richly seasoned and created to heighten all animalistic tendencies. This would be followed by a rich lamb stew served with fresh asparagus. Then came the peaches with honied walnuts. Luscious, chocolate-dipped strawberries would then seal the dinner. His eye would not waver from her. None could command the room, and his attention, like her.

Standing, she moved toward the door. Tonight she would share in the passion. Her skin tingled with anticipation.

Back in her chamber Mortella prepared to bathe. He had not disappointed, nor had she. Their shared raw, animalistic passion was still there. He had not seemed to notice any difference during their frenzied union. Still aggressively tender, the fervour continued to entice.

Disrobing, she stepped into the free-standing tub with some difficulty. Her balance was not what it used to be, and the sides were high. As always, beside the tub was a bowl of lemons. She looked at them disdainfully. She had left him asleep in his chamber. Unconscious to the routine that she must endure every time they united. Yet was it worth it? She recalled the hunger in his eyes. She had no doubt that hers had mirrored his. Was it worth it?

She could do without. She had for years. But there was something … a craving for the touch that drew her back. She was sure that she could do without it whenever she chose. But why not? Let this pleasure be enjoyed and then cast aside when greater things could take its place.

Washing thoroughly she rose out of the water. It was never easy drying herself with only a single useful arm. Taking a lemon she soaked one of the soft flannel cloths and proceeded to protect herself from yet another insult to her body. Clara was to be the one and only.

***

Everything had been calm and gentle since their arrival at the westernmost plot. A small herd of goats had been found on the lower slopes and corralled in the newly repaired enclosure. Angus milked and cared for them while Jess replanted the kitchen garden. Maima cleaned and cared for them both while preparing tinctures and ointments to take to the general store in the nearest hamlet. Jim, and particularly his son Johnathon, were frequent visitors. Each time bringing a basket of fresh fruit and veggies to make sure there was always enough to carry the small family forward until they were established.

Jess looked to the Western Slopes and smiled. She had become used to the sight. Over the months this had now become home, while the memory of Town was gradually getting more and more hazy. She looked to the east. She could feel it there even if she couldn't see it. Distance from the Tower had helped, but it was not gone. The silver-grey darkness of those endless black corridors still haunted her dreams. She could never forget the Tower's call. Yet she was determined to put it aside. She would enjoy whatever time she had with the people she loved.

Removing the grasses and weeds from the next section of the overgrown vegetable patch, she heard Angus calling the goats. They were so tame. They must have been a domestic flock from those who had once before lived here. Whatever happened to them, she feared to know. To all of them it was proof, yet again, that all within the high slopes was also within grasp of the Tower.

She looked at the already flourishing garden she had created. The weather was perfect for them to grow and be productive. Their first crop would be ready soon enough and they would then not be so dependent on the generosity of their friends.

Standing up she brushed the dirt from her hands. It would be supper time soon enough and she wanted to go pick some fresh wild herbs to flavour the stew. Waving to Angus as he coerced the few lactating females into the milking pen, she walked to the lake where the pickings would be better.

In the darkness of their room Angus watched her as she twitched. He knew those movements so well. He had hoped that they would have stayed gone as they had over the last few months. But recently they had begun again. He felt her tremble. Soon she would become restless and start to thrash about. He had previously tried to wake her when it started. But this would make things worse, even if he was successful. He watched as her pure white aura flicked about her like flames. She was fully in the grip of it now. It would not be long before she woke gasping for air, before clinging to him for comfort. There were times when it was worse. She would wake screaming, inconsolable as he held her tight, trying to break its hold on her. Tonight was not bad. This time she barely woke as the nightmare faded. He soothed her back to sleep as he watched her breathing settle, and the movements soften. Stroking her hair he cradled her in his arms as he too gradually dosed off.

***

It was late. Not that it had been that regular since the balcony. But it was late. Mortella looked at the food in front of her. She wasn't hungry. That too had been erratic over the last few months. She was careful in what she ate. She would not add further insult to the injury. But she normally had an appetite at this time of day.

She knew that her maids reported everything to Mrs Poole. When her time of the month, as erratic as it had been, did arrive, then that woman was sure to know. It was not something that was easily hid in such a populated estate as this. She would not go through it again. As far as she was concerned she had fulfilled her contract with the Tower. The Keeps may want an heir but that was not going to be her doing. He could get another child after she was back in the Black. Many an older man took a young wife and … she was sure that there were a few bastards out there that could lay claim to the name if a legitimate heir was not forthcoming.

Mortella picked at her lunch. She would need an apothecary. One that would not ask too many questions and could keep his mouth shut. She needed to consider how she would be able to get what she needed without being discovered. There was no-one that she could trust. The Abbatissa would not aid her, and the varlet posted at the estate would be bound to inform her superior of any request Mortella made.

She then remembered. It was so easy to forget. She would need to revisit her sisters. There would still be some there that remembered her, and … she would come bearing gifts. They would know, and have access to, what was needed.

"I will be going for a walk," she announced to the air, knowing that she had been heard and that her movements were being noted. Without waiting, she stood and proceeded to make her way toward the main gate. As she arrived a maid appeared, carrying her cloak.

"Milady." She greeted her mistress with a slight curtsy as she laid the cloak across Mortella's shoulders. Mortella immediately adjusted the garment with her good hand.

"I need no escort," Mortella directed. "I would like to walk alone." The maid nodded and faded back into the garden as the gate opened allowing her to exit.

At once turning downslope Mortella headed to the heart of Town, to then veer off toward the alleys less frequented in the daylight hours. Once out of sight of the estate and sure that she had not been followed, Mortella modified the perception of herself into that of a common market stall holder. None would recognise her. None would be able to report back her doings.

It was as she remembered. The red door loudly proclaiming what was offered inside. Any other forms of signage were forbidden. She didn't knock. The door was never locked. Few of the johns were willing to wait outside for an answer. A locked door meant lost income and coinage was always needed. Entering into the dim light of the densely furnished greeting floor, she allowed her appearance to return to its normal state. A girl, questionably over sixteen, but more likely thirteen, looked up at her from one of the threadbare sofas. They would not be expecting clients this early in the day. Those that had stayed the night before would have left. This was now a time for rest and cleaning up, ready for the night to come.

"Where is your mistress?" Mortella asked gently to the obviously new and timid girl. She all too well remembered what it was like to be that young and being placed on the floor. There for anyone to choose and take upstairs.

"She's asleep," was the reply that was then quickly followed by a belated, "ma'am."

"Go wake her. I have a need to talk with her." The child looked scared. Yes, Mortella knew that the mistress of the place was never to be disturbed during the day … not for less than the direst of needs.

"Take this with you," said Mortella, removing a small bag of coins from her gown and taking out three large silver coins. "Say that this is just a token of my appreciation of her getting up so soon out of bed."

The child stood, wide-eyed, and carefully took the coins. Turning them over in her hands, she looked at them with wonder. She would have rarely, if ever, seen one of these silver dollars before, let alone three altogether.

"Give her my apologies but say that this is a matter of some urgency." Looking back up at Mortella the girl nodded as she swiftly climbed the stairs and disappeared from view. Mortella waited below, looking at where she used to wait for her john to arrive. Having been fortunate enough to gain a benefactor, she had had no need to walk the floor. There to be paraded before any potential client. To be inspected and fondled before being removed upstairs by any that was willing to pay.

As she was thinking a figure began to descend the stairs, still busily fixing her dress as she did.

She commenced speaking, "Ma'am, we're at your service ...' before stopping, mouth open, as Mortella turned to face her. "Mortella," she screamed, racing down the last few steps. "We thought you were dead. Or worse ..."

"Issy, really you! You're the mistress now."

"You wouldn't 'ave thought it would you. Yet 'ere I am," replied Issy as she raced over and hugged Mortella. Mortella recoiled slightly before hugging her childhood friend as best she could. The child watched intently, having returned to its place on the sofa.

"Well, you've done well for yourself then 'aven't you" said Issy as she took a step backwards to look more closely. "Always knew that if ever one of us would get out, it'd 'ave been you. Come take the load off. Sit, talk."

"Can we go out the back?" asked Mortella. "Out to our family space. I never liked this room," she added, looking around. Issy nodded and led the way across the floor and behind an old, tattered tapestry.

Once seated in the only room set aside solely for the sisters' use, Mortella looked about. "Not a lot's changed," she commented.

"More so than you might think. There's been a number of us that have gone." She looked down as she continued. "They don't care if one the johns get a bit too physical. They're never going to do nothing. Even when it goes way too far." She looked sad, "And then there's the other working girl's risk."

"That's what I want to talk to you about," interrupted Mortella. "I can't go through it again."

"Again?" responded Isabel. "That little one in there is mine. Not an easy thing bringing up a little one and 'aving to work. I expect yours would've been easier than that."

"Not as much as you might think. I need the infusion." Mortella looked at her sister. "I've got to purge it from me."

"Well we've all done that before," laughed Issy. Mortella put the bag of coins on the table. "I think that this will make things a lot easier for you and the girls. Buy them something nice." Indicating the bag she added, "There's a lot more in there than you think."

Issy nodded as she hid the bag in the folds of her dress. "I'll get it brewed tonight. It'll be ready in the tomorrow." She stopped. "How about a bit of something. You're not got above a bit of gin 'ave ya?"

Mortella smiled. Earthy, but you always knew where you stood with them. It was refreshing. She nodded as the cups were taken down from the shelf and filled to the brim.

***

She returned late the next day. This time she was taken straight through to the family space. Issy greeted her while holding a small bottle. "Pudding grass, sea lavender, oregano and parsley," she said. "Brew it as a tea mixed with chamomile. It needs to be strong. Wait two hours and then start drinking water. Lots of it. It'll need to be flushed right out of you. You don't want it to linger." Seeing that Mortella understood she added, "You can do it a second time if nothing happens within a few days. A third time ... no." Mortella nodded as she turned to leave. "I hope I'll get to see you again. Was good catching up on old times," Issy added as Mortella left the room.

Back in her chamber she held tightly onto the small bottle, keeping it close to her. Her breasts were now sore. She knew what that meant. Sitting down slowly in the easy chair by the balcony door she waited. She had made her excuse for missing supper with the apology that it was that time of the month. Instead she had ordered that a pot of chamomile tea should be sent to her chamber to help her sleep. It arrived and was placed on the table next to her while she gazed outside. She was still yet to go out there, onto the balcony. She needed time. Dismissing the maid with orders that she was not to be disturbed, she waited. It needed to be strong.

Finally taking the cup she poured a thimble's worth of the bottle's liquid into it. It was turbid and green with a powerful odour. Swirling the teapot, she began filling the cup. She had waited until the fluid within was an auburn brown. This then dispersed the green liquid within the tea and together they formed a concoction that invoked memories of a dark, pond-like slime. She would let it cool before drinking it all in one take. It was simply done, and it then would be over. She would have to rethink her interactions with Charles.

Taking the cup Mortella gulped back the fluid, preferring not to think about its taste. In two hours she would start the water. Several carafes were already there ready and waiting. Sitting still and staring into nothing she started to count the minutes.

Gradually she felt something low down in her stomach. A contraction, a cramp, but something was beginning. To her surprise it rapidly got worse. This was not what she remembered happening with the sisters. Their cramps occurred many hours after ingesting the infusion. Only then would the un-wanted parasite be expelled in a patch of blood that gradually leaked out. For her, however, the cramping continued to grow. It now encased the whole of her abdomen. The pain, severe, caused her to drop from her chair onto the floor. There she remained on her knees, bent over, clutching at her stomach with her good hand. She muffled a cry. None must know what she was do-ing. They must not be alerted. Sound travelled far too easily from the open balcony door to downstairs.

Holding herself rigid as she knelt on the floor, Mortella bit her lip to distract from the pain. Her stomach heaved as she started to convulse. Un-able to control it, suddenly all her stomach contents were hurled up through her mouth with such force that they landed a body's length away. Instantly the pain subsided, the spams released. Panting she looked at the dark green stain that was spread upon the carpet.

Without the pain she recovered her composure and climbed up from the floor. Sitting back down she began to prepare a second infusion, but this time placing less of the bottle's liquid within the cup. The tea was already cold when she mixed them together allowing her to swiftly drink the whole cup. Barely had there been time for the fluid to reach her stomach when the contractions began again. This time they hit suddenly, with greater intensity, resulting in the same outcome, but with much greater distress. Panting on the floor, Mortella curled up in a ball as the agony gradually subsided. This was not a coincidence. She had felt something like this before. It was not due to the infusion, this was Influence. Someone was stopping her. Forbidding her to ingest the infusion and the following consequences. With no-one there and none knowing of her intent, she feared to even contemplate its source.

Chapter 26

Jess entered the room looking first at Angus and then at his mother. There was something different about her, looking both coy and pleased with herself at the same time. There was also a calmness projecting from her that they had not seen for a very long time. Walking over to her husband she hugged him, snuggling deep into his shoulder. She gave a contented sigh before looking up into his face. Breaking the embrace she took a step backwards into the centre of the room. Looking quickly from one to the other, she announced, "I think we're going to have a baby."

Stunned, Angus opened and closed his mouth, fishlike, without making a sound. Maima's response was immediate and effusive as she raced over to Jess and squeezed her tightly. "Oh, how marvellous," she exclaimed. Pulling away from her, Jess walked back to Angus.

"You're going to be a father." Still speechless, he grabbed his wife in a bear hug, holding her tightly until suddenly releasing her looking concerned.

"I'm sorry … too tight," he said as he looked down at her stomach. As tears formed in his eyes he held her again, much more gently. "We're going to be a family," he yelled.

*****

Her belly had already begun to swell, and the nausea had not abated. Well aware of what to expect, Mortella had refused to take to her bed. She was not going to be under the control of that woman ever again. Not this time, not ever. This time, no matter how she felt, she was going to remain in control.

She had tried to take the infusion many more times … until the last of the bottle was gone. All with the same result. She was not being permitted to. She was being stopped. Physically controlled to prevent its ingestion. This was not the work of the varlet with the help of the resident shades. Regardless of the time, the day, or even if the varlet was in the estate, the result was the same. The pain was intense.

She did not like it, but there was really only one possibility. There was only one consistency in all the attempts. Only she was there. Alone. Only she and … the thing inside her. No matter how she looked at it, it could only be that thing that was doing it. Protecting its survival, even before it had form or thought. Exerting its primal need for survival. It would not let her do it.

She had thought of starving herself. Or drinking to excess. Doing anything in order to damage, or destroy, the thing. But these would all lead to the same end. She could not actively do anything to harm it. It would be stopped as painfully and effectively as the infusion. Starving herself would not work. The parasite within her would take what it needed before allowing her body the resources it needed. She would suffer long before it did. Then … when too weak to resist … Mrs Poole would force feed her far more effectively than the last time. As had been made abundantly clear, she was merely a vessel for the heir of Keep.

She sat outside on the balcony, out of view of Mrs Poole and her spies. The wind was brisk and cool, but she only wore

a light flimsy nightgown. She might catch something. It was worth the chance. It could end the pregnancy, as unlikely as that was.

***

May stood in the kitchen finishing off supper. Joseph would be home soon. The light was already beginning to fade. Stopping what she was doing she stood still, eyes looking inward. There it was again. Like tadpoles flicking their tails inside of her. They had been active today. Stirring the pot again she smiled. As she was thinking, the door opened and in walked her husband. He greeted her with a wave as he quickly made his way to wash. He always tried to make as little mess as possible. A hard thing when you were a stone mason that always arrived home covered with the dust from the day. They would eat as soon as he was clean. She needed to. She had had little issues so far with the pregnancy … apart from the urgent hunger. When she needed to eat, she really needed to eat.

Joseph returned, hair dripping and a clean shirt on. He came up behind her and wrapped his arms about her waist. He kissed her on the nape of the neck.

"A good day?" he asked. "How's she going?" he added as he looked down at the apron. May smiled.

"Been active today. Swishing and turning. Having a fine old time." He returned the smile. He had always wanted a daughter. A little princess. One that would be just like her mother. Serving out two bowls, May handed them to him. He took them to the table as she went to get the bread. Sitting down opposite each other they both looked at the half-finished highchair that sat at the end of the table.

"Almost done," he said.

"Yes," answered May, patting her stomach. "Almost done."

***

Ambrose sat opposite Silas. Faces mirroring each other. Sadness with a fixed determination was etched in each. There was loss. It was deep but shared. It bound them together with a common purpose.

"Will it make a difference?" Silas asked. Ambrose shrugged.

"You have heard them, not me," was his answer. He was as ambiguous as ever.

"Do Influences remain after we're gone?"

Ambrose shook his head. "They're in the blood. Part of us. Once we're dead, it goes."

"So they are alive," Silas replied slowly. Ambrose's steady gaze was fixed on him.

"Alive? Is that alive?"

"I could find him … them. If given the chance. I would know them," Silas implored. "If they are there … alive … in the Tower … I could find them."

"They will not be the same," Ambrose warned. "The Taken are no longer who they once were." He looked at Silas. "You said it yourself, there are so many voices but no real individuals, just traces of who they once used to be."

"I could make them remember … remember who they once were."

"And what if you did? What then?" Ambrose asked bitterly. "Let them remember who they once were … for what?" He looked down at his hands that were picking furiously at the thread in the chair. "Let them remember what they have lost." He looked back up at Silas. "That is not a kindness."

"Perhaps, perhaps not." Silas looked directly back at Ambrose, demanding his attention as he pointed a finger at him. "If it was you … locked in the Tower. Would you want to claim back some of your humanity?" He paused. "Or just remain a mindless, trace of a person, forever longing but never thinking. Which is better … being you and accepting your loss … or never again being you at all?"

Ambrose looked back, his face like stone. He knew his answer but was afraid to speak it.

***

It was so much harder this time. He felt so much older, and his heart was broken. Yet he needed to do this. He wasn't afraid of being perceived. That would almost be a blessing. They would be together again. Even if he was no longer himself, at least then he would no longer have to feel the loss.

Gradually climbing up the rocky slopes toward the Tower, Silas stopped to catch his breath. Not much further now. This time he had decided to go during the day. He, by himself, was not strong enough to resist the invasion of the Tower into his mind. Not when it was dark. In the day, it was weaker. He was sure that he could do it then.

He would know the mind of Felix. He would be able to find him no matter how little was left of him. That thought made him catch his breath. *How little was left of him*. No, he would not believe that. Felix was there. Locked in the Tower, but he was there. He would just have to help him remember who he was. Reaching the level of the landing before the great door, Silas moved off to the left. Gradually he circled the Tower as he moved away from the door. He would make sure that no-one from there would be able to see him.

Eventually he reached a rocky outcrop. The Tower's walls appeared to grow out of it, rising high above him without a break. No windows, nothing to mar its smooth black surface. Rounding the outcrop with some difficulty, Silas was now shielded from Town. None would be able to see him from the south. To the north-east of him was an uninterrupted view of the mountains.

Making sure that his barriers were up, he placed both hands on the surface of the Tower. It was smooth and cool despite the day being warm. Again, as previously, there was a slight tingling sensation. He felt the presence of the many, just on the periphery of his mind. He listened for the sound of Felix's mind as familiar to him as his own. But all he heard was an echo of his against the barriers that encased his mind.

He would have to delve deeper into the Tower. Carefully he dropped some of the protections between his mind and those within the black walls. This time, instead of clearing his mind, he pushed a part of it in … into the masses he felt surrounding him. They coalesced, before falling back only to unite about him once again. A new mind was floating amongst them, and it both attracted and repelled. Gently he probed, looking for the essence of the one he knew so well. Wary not to let too much of himself be seen. Hiding the vitality of life, he held it well away from the ones that craved it so much.

Again there was that loss, the great depths of sadness … a longing … the despair. He waited. He offered no compassion, acknowledged none of the hurt, but just waited, feeling for his twin. He needed to go undetected by the thing that was the Tower. Without engaging with any of those within, Silas let his mind float deeper into the Tower. He let his consciousness swirl and mingle with those within. He felt feather light touches of the Taken as they flicked past.

As he had done so many times before in his life, he opened his mind to feel for his brother. He had never before thought how he did this, it just happened and then there was Felix in there with him. All barriers now down, without thought, he let his mind float. To let his Influence free to do what it did without direction or control.

Just out of his mind's sight he caught the impression of a resonance that matched his own. Faint, obscure, but present and distinct. Projecting a longing to connect with the match, Silas waited. He portrayed no other emotion. He hid his desires. It came closer. Enticed by the offer. Flittering on the edge of knowing, Silas continued to wait.

The two touched. It was fleeting but Silas caught an image. Two babes in a crib lying facing one another. And then it was gone. A second touch. An image of blue sky. In an instant it was gone. At each touch Silas felt loss … but also a calmness. He felt there was a peace there that stood in stark contrast to all those others that skirted about him. He waited. At the third touch he was ready. As soon as he felt it he threw his mind forward trying to link to it. He drew it close to him. He let it see who he was. It stayed.

***

The reflux was never ending. It burnt in her chest as soon as she ate, if she bent over and every time she lay down. Not that rest was forthcoming. Mortella sat on the sofa in her chamber. She was at least dressed, and for her, it felt like a victory. She looked down at the bulging stomach. Eight months of this. She had eaten what she was given. Not to would have led to it being forced into her. She did not have the strength nor the ability to resist. She had, however, succeeded in refusing the administrations of Monsieur Crab. She had hoped for the mid-wife that delivered Clara, but no-one knew where she had gone. Instead she had settled for the recommendations of Issy. A wholesome, practical woman that had seen to many a birth in the shop.

The creature inside her made her suffer. She planned to return the favour once separated from it. Looking out the window toward the Tower, she sat immobile. There was still a longing but now, more than ever, there was anger at what it had done to her. The Tower had forced this on her. The Presence and the One had conceded to its desires. She would return. Clara and she would rise and none … never again would any take her liberty away. She pledged to herself that she would be the one to control and not the one controlled.

Looking about the room she sneered. How she loathed this finery. Give her the Black. All else was detestable. But she would play the game. Until Clara was of age she would feign compliance. Yet let none dare consider her less than she truly was. The visions of the Tower were true. She had suc-cumbed to the temptations of a man and was suffering the consequences. She was the figure that held the small bundle, forced to against her will. She held within her the hatred and ferocity that the image had shown. He was easy to put away. She would not succumb again. Charles was unimportant. Clara was the child clothed in expensive cloth. Cloth that then was to be covered with the Black.

The subjugation would not be much longer. The child would be expelled, and she would be Mortella.

***

Holding the small, precious bundle, Joseph carried it over to his wife. She was perfect. Her fingers, her toes, all was perfection. Taking the child, May put her to the breast. Latching on, the child suckled a few minutes before falling asleep once again. Only a few days old, Molly was the joy they had always hoped for. May cradled the infant, enjoying its smell as she smiled up at her husband. He never need know about the help they had received. Noona had strongly advised her never to speak of it. But she would always be grateful for the gift they had given her.

***

Jess persisted. She was rounder, but she would not make this an excuse. Getting up from the ground with difficulty she surveyed the garden. It had grown as much as she had. She looked to her favourite walk to the lake. Tonight was special. It had been a year since Angus had returned from his travels and they had been united. They were having roast goat with their own fresh vegetables. Fresh herbs would add just that bit extra.

Heading toward the lake with the now slightly peculiar waddling gait, Jess looked back at the cottage. Home. No matter what the Tower would do, it would all have been worth it to have had this time, however short, with her family. But things had been so much better of late. The Tower had not invaded her dreams for some months, allowing her to sleep throughout the night in a deep and undisturbed slumber. Even Angus was less vigilant. She didn't expect this to last. The Tower would eventually return. She knew that she would never escape it, but until then it was a joy just to be normal.

***

Silas had been back many times. He had spoken with Ambrose about it at length. It was Felix. There had been no doubt. Many of their memories were shared. So often he had seen and felt exactly what his brother had. In many ways they were almost the same person.

Little by little Silas could feel that there was something more of Felix each time he came. He would be waiting for him as soon as he was at the Tower. Once the barriers were down they linked. Slowly, almost frame by frame, Silas would share their life together. Starting as far back as he could remember he would show his brother what they had been though. Every feeling from each experience, every thought he could muster from each event he would share with his twin. It may take forever, but he would do it. Felix would have done the same, or more.

The image that was foremost when they linked was of his Taking. As Felix felt himself dissolving, he had looked over to his brother hiding near the cellar entrance. There he saw his twin, face frozen in terror as his brother evaporated before him. But within Felix he had only felt love and a peace that he would be able to save Silas from the same fate. This was the core that made up the shade he had become. There was loss and sadness but no longing or despair for he had chosen this in order to protect. To protect the one he loved.

Silas looked over at Ambrose who was trying to read. He had been on the same page for over half an hour.

"He is there, you know." Silas paused as Ambrose looked up. "We'll find him. Once Felix is more himself. He'll be able to."

Ambrose nodded slightly.

"It just takes time," added Silas as he stirred the soup. "I won't stop, you know. We'll find him."

Ambrose looked up again as he took off his glasses to wipe his eyes. "Next time I'll go with you." Silas looked surprised. "I might be able to hear him if I was closer," Ambrose added. Silas nodded. It would be very difficult for the old man to make the climb, but Silas understood. How could he not. If there was any chance, of course he would.

Taking some bowls from the counter, Silas filled them with the soup and placed one before Ambrose as he sat down opposite him. "Do you want to go tomorrow?" he asked. "I've at least found the easiest way to get up there."

Taking a mouthful of soup Ambrose nodded. "I'll take both sticks. Mountain goats certainly have an advantage with those four legs." Silas grimaced as he imagined the next day. "It certainly can't hurt," Ambrose concluded grimly. Both knew that it would be very slow and hard going for him. They would need an early night.

Chapter 27

It was with the wet nurse. The thing had been there since day one. She had refused to suckle it and the milk had all dried up several weeks ago. Mortella had then felt a great deal more comfortable. She looked at Clara lying on the floor, eating and rolling around. The other one had already taken all that it ever was going to take from her and that was under duress. It was in the hands of the wet nurse and that was where it would stay. She gave a slight scoff. They had also named it. Charles had supposedly given it its name. She had refused to. One that, ironically, he supposedly considered it to be some sort of tribute to her – Moira.

Mortella sat deep in thought as she watched her daughter. A goblet of her favourite wine was held untouched in the good hand. She looked at the Tower beyond the walls of the estate. She was determined. She would now focus on their destiny … their future. Oh she would continue to play with the minds of all the small-minded people about her. She still needed some fun among these people after all, but her goal was within the Code. Once again she would pass through the Tower and out the other side, but this time with Clara. Together they would rise and, together they would be seen and acknowledged by the Presence. She would continue to practice her craft. Within the Tower she would hone her skills, sharpen her ability. She would be ready for the day the Tower came to claim her daughter.

***

The pregnancy had been easy, and the birth was as anticipated. Maima had educated her well in what to expect. Jess placed little Shan in the rough-hewn crib that Angus had fashioned. She looked down at her little child already fast asleep with a full tummy and dry nappy.

After months of inactivity from the Tower, she had started to feel a niggle on the peripheries of her perception. It had always been there throughout

the pregnancy, silently with her, but up until now had just been letting her
be.

***

They had made the trip up to the Tower together several times now. The rough
ground made it very hard going for the elderly man. The use of two sturdy walking sticks helped but they needed to rest often. Each time at the Tower Silas
would lay his hands on the smooth stone and make himself open to allow his
brother to merge with his mind. Felix would now recognise him but not as once
he had. There was no conversation between them. No back and forth, but at
least the memories that Silas shared were enough to maintain the connection.
Almost like speaking to one in a coma, Silas more hoped than believed that Felix
heard and understood.

Beside him Ambrose would sit on a rock and close his eyes. He would
remain unmoving as he listened. The sounds within the Tower were small
and fragmented. Thousands of tiny snippets of what had once been the
unique tune of each individual's aura were now all that was left. Still unique
and distinguishable, in their way, but discordant and uneven. Hour after hour
he would sit and listen, concentrating as he sought for even a splinter of the
ring that he knew so well.

He had heard nothing of Pick until this day. Sitting as he always did, eyes
closed, and head bowed, he caught the snippets of a recurring phrase that
caught his attention. Could he be sure that this was his grandson? He could
not. But the sound was unique, and the tone was that of Pick. He listened.
Horrified that this was all he could hear of the once vibrant, impulsive young
man. Yet encouraged that it meant that there was hope that he was still him.
He listened as it moved throughout the Tower, wandering erratically within.
He followed it until it faded beyond his ability to hear. He looked up at Silas
as he turned away from the Tower having exhausted his reserves to shield
his mind from all within but one.

"He's there. I'm as sure as I can be. It was him or …" Ambrose paused
as he composed himself, "what is left of him." Silas nodded, saying nothing.
He understood the shock of seeing what had become of the one that was
loved.

He helped Ambrose to stand and handed him his sticks as he said,
"They're there. They are them. They still are, even if they don't remember.
We won't abandon them." Turning his back on the Tower he started slowly
back down the slope. Ambrose took one last look at the smooth black stone

as he too turned from the Tower. He had little hope that there was anything that could be done, but even that little hope was enough for them to keep trying.

***

She was walking within the same stone corridors. As always they were deathly still. The silvery-grey light hung about her, coming from nowhere, but everywhere all at once. She knew that she must be asleep, lying warmly in bed. Angus was still by her side and Shan was safe within the crib by the door. She shivered in her nightie. The air was cold. Was this a memory of her time in the Tower, a dream, or was part of her still really there? She couldn't be sure. It was so real, but it couldn't be. She was not really there. She kept telling herself. She was not there.

The cold seeped into her, draining her of warmth. Looking about nervously Jess wrapped her arms tightly against her chest. Unable to stand still any longer she began to walk down the corridor. Occasionally she looked behind. She felt watched. Nothing was there, but she was sure that she was not alone.

Walking quickly, feeling the cold, hard stone beneath her feet, she turned a corner. The corridor just continued. She turned. Barely audible, like the whisper of a breeze in the still cold air, a hum washed over her. Then there was a second. Then a third. Each combined with the earlier to amplify the sound. Scarcely perceptible she heard a blend of voices gradually grow in force and volume. First as a whisper … she could not distinguish the words. Then as a hiss … some words started to emerge.

"We are … you will."

Frightened, Jess looked rapidly about her. She began to run. Down the corridor she ran away from the sound. The empty, hollow voices, however, continued to swirl as they gradually grew louder and more distinct.

"We will be together … we will be the Tower."

Jess covered her ears as she ran, head down. The voices grew. They craved her. They yearned for her with a cold, dark hunger.

"You are ours … we will be together." The voices cried at her. Their piercing tone grated on her bones.

"Come … you are the Tower," they screeched as Jess slumped to the floor. She cradled her head between her hands, clenching her eyes shut as she tried to block out the screams. The assault on her senses continued. The invocations continued for her to join. To be part of what she was destined to be. To surrender and come. Then … all was quiet. The voices faded, leaving her alone with their sound still ringing within her ears.

In the silent, silver darkness, a soft voice then spoke icily clear. Looking up she saw the outline of a Dark One. A shade of deeper black against the walls around her.

"The Tower has not forgotten you … nor those that are yours."

A panic hit her as she awoke screaming. She violently thrashed about the bed waking Angus. He tried to grab her to calm her down, she pushed him away. Clambering out of bed she raced to Shan's crib. There she snatched up the child, clutching it tightly to her while she turned, looking frantically about the room. Staring into the corner she saw the outline of a figure. Hooded and black, it stood unmoving. She screamed again as she backed against the closed door. Angus reached her a moment later, grabbing her and Shan in his arms and holding them tight. She shook uncontrollably as the vision in the room gradually disappeared.

Her mind raced. It was a threat. It was real and they knew. They knew about Shan. She would have to keep watch. Had to keep Shan safe. Angus and Maima watched in despair as each day Jess became more and more obsessed. She would never let the child out of her sight. Even when Angus, or his mother, was caring for Shan, Jess would hover about nervously. Despite Shan being a happy, easy baby, sleeping well with only two feeds a night, Jess would wake each evening gasping for breath before racing to the crib to stand there for the rest of the night watching. She refused all aid from Maima. Refusing any sleeping draughts as they might affect the milk. Angus was almost as physically drained as his wife. Barely sleeping while attempting to calm Jess every night and continue to care for the goats and plot during the day.

The worry reduced Jess' appetite. She gradually lost weight. This affected her milk supply, causing Shan to become unsettled and irritable. She still tried to care for the kitchen plot, with Shan bundled up next to her. Yet night after night she would sit staring at the crib as the child slept. She was convinced that the Tower would come for Shan and there was nothing that her husband could do to reassure her. Little by little, as time progressed, Jess withdrew further into herself. Sitting for long periods of time, just staring into nothing, as long as Shan was beside her. The garden gradually became unattended. Her milk supply dwindled further, and Shan no longer gained any weight. It was then that Maima would secretly feed Shan boiled goat's milk in the moments that Jess was asleep.

***

After several months Jess suffered her first daytime vision when she was outside near the garden. It called to her across the Bowl. Called for her. In the same dark space, the voices cried. Ghostly figures, wavering spectres of young girls encircled her, reaching out as they attempted to touch her. The emptiness of them chilled her as they tried to pull her to them.

"We are the Tower."

She woke from the trance as she was lifted from the ground. There, as always, was Angus. His face creased in concern as he looked down at her. She clung to him as uncontrollable sobs worked their way out from deep inside. Eventually she was still. She looked up at him and managed a thin smile.

"I didn't escape."

Angus shook his head. Trying to reassure her that the Tower didn't know where they were. There everything was fine. It was only the memories of her time there, nothing more. Jess looked at him with clear blue eyes as she stroked his face and smiled again. Through moist eyes he tried to smile back.

"Yes, of course it is," she reassured him gently. "They're only memories, nothing more. I'll be much better very soon. I know." He looked happier.

"Only bad dreams. We're all fine," he said.

"Yes, they're just bad dreams," she repeated.

Gently taking his hand, she kissed it and placed it over her heart.

"I have never been so happy as I have been with you."

"Neither have I."

"And you will continue to be, I promise," she said. Then she kissed him. Letting go, she made her way back inside the cottage.

She knew what she had to do. She could save Shan and her family. The threats were for her. She was the link to Shan and her family. Break that link and they would be safe. Deciding to do it had freed her from fear. The Tower could still send its visions, but as she had already decided, they no longer held any terror. As it was inevitable, it was not going to be changed. She still dreamed but no longer woke in panic. She could eat and look at those around her. She would enjoy and take in all that was good about her life. All of them had only a limited amount of time to share with each other. Usually none knew how long. Now she would enjoy every ounce of it. Her time was short. It made every second of every day that much more vivid and alive to her.

Walking to the lake, she enjoyed the sunshine. Shan was with Maima. They were both safe. As she approached the water she looked at the glistening flashes of sunlight that reflected off its surface. She was living in the present. She could not count on the future and the past was evaporating. She knew that they had come from Town, but her memory of it was now vague. She didn't even now attempt to make the tinctures that she had known so well. That was now no longer to be found in her memories. Her time was short. She would have to act before she forgot meeting her husband. Of his kind, handsome face as he had looked down at her as she had woken from the cot on that very first morning in Town. Some things were too precious to lose. But they would go if she tarried too much longer.

Reaching the lake shore she gazed at the reeds. The ground here sloped gradually into the water. The lake itself was calm and deep, reflecting the blue of the sky above. Off to the side were the wild herbs she would gather but first she would sit and enjoy the sun's warmth on her skin. It was the perfect antidote to the silver-grey coldness of the Tower. The sun had life and vitality. It energised her. She watched as the water birds fed on the small fish within, occasionally diving under the water before surfacing again with its catch proudly displayed.

Satisfied with her decision, she rose and picked the herbs before strolling back to the cottage to help with supper.

***

It was only a few days later that the Tower inserted itself in her daylight hours once more. Again in the same corridors, Jess looked about the space, unafraid. Fear was only there if there was something to fear. Once accepted then that was nothing. These were just visions. Again the Tower had revealed the transparent residuals of others as they circled and cried out to her. She looked at them, already knowing that she was no longer herself. If a person is the combination of their memories, and if those memories are no longer there, are they still the same person? She thought not. She would want others to remember her as she was, not as she would become. To no longer remember Angus, or her child, was already to be separated from them. She would prefer that they did not have to see it happening.

The vision ended as it had begun with the silent resignation of the one receiving it. It was time.

Kissing Shan on the cheek as she waved goodbye to Maima with a smile, Jess went off to collect some herbs from the lake. Maima always encouraged her to have a walk. To take time away from caring for Shan. She was pleased that Jess had taken her advice. Maima picked up Shan. Jess wouldn't be long. It was almost sunset, and Angus would be home soon and ready for supper.

Jess slowly walked along the familiar path to the lake. She felt that she knew every rock and every blade of grass along the way. Far sooner than she had hoped, she was at the lake shore itself. She looked up at the Western Slopes as the sun gradually slipped behind. Angus was on the lower slopes with the goats. He would be home soon. Looking about the ground she started to collect rocks, putting them together in a pile close to the water. Sitting by the water's edge she watched as the light in the sky turned from gold to orange. It was a beautiful sunset. A fitting send off. Slowly she stood, refusing to let herself look back toward the cottage. Facing the lake she bent over and, one by one, started to place one rock after another in each of the pockets of her dress and the apron that she still wore from making supper.

Face set and determined she looked once again toward the Western Slopes. She had made sure that her husband would be too far away to stop her.

"Angus, my love, my life. Thank you … for everything," she whispered to the slopes. "You and Shan will be safe now. I will now be able to remain me, who I am, right up to the end. The Tower will not win." With that she engaged her Influence one last time as she whispered the words "I love you" into the breeze. Weaving it in the fabric of the air she sent it flying towards her husband, with a kiss to seal her love.

Tears running down her face but with a determined gaze in her eyes, Jess began to walk into the water. The chill did not bother her. It crept up her legs, tingling and awakening her even more to everything about. Thinking only of her small family as she continued to walk, she allowed the water to rise. Taking one last breath, the water closed above her as she looked up at the crimson sky. Farewelling her life she was content to have been able to remain herself, right up to the end.

***

Sybil walked slowly down the slope back to the cottage carrying Shan. What other option was there? What had happened was not hidden. He had to leave.

Angus had found her. In the lake, beneath its waters. She had looked both beautiful and serene. In trying to recover her pale, cold body, he too nearly succumbed to its waters. Saved only in extreme desperation by an Influence he had, to that time, yet to manifest. The water churned by the pressure of sound that exploded forth from him, propelled him to the surface saving his life but identifying him to the Tower. It had seen him, noted him and it would come. Sybil held Shan close to her. To lose his father to the Tower was devastating. To lose her son would destroy her … and then Shan would have no-one. He must leave to be safe. She would now be both mother and father to her grandson as she had been to her son.

Angus had hugged his child, face grim with tears that were yet too raw to be shed. Kissing both Shan and his mother farewell he had turned, forcing himself not to look back as he left his home, his family, and what he thought was the most important part of his future. Leaving to find those he knew must be out there willing, and able, to resist the darkness that came from within the Tower … from the things it spawned.

Chapter 28

Clara raced through the bushes laughing as her little sister chased after her. They weaved through the garden, up and down the terraced steps, along the well-manicured lawns and between the orchard of various fruit trees planted in a little wilderness that was just a bit further from the house. She fell to the ground as Moira landed on top of her. It didn't hurt as the lithe seven-year-old didn't weigh a lot. They felt free when away from the house. Away from the watchful eyes of the servants and those peculiar minders from the Tower that just stood there, barely ever moving.

They rarely saw Father and then only very briefly. They knew that he had so much to do, being the leading figure of Town, that he just didn't have the time for them. They would occasionally be brought down to him before bed. He would look at each of them carefully, telling each that he was assessing their character. Their nursemaids said differently. They said that he was assessing their beauty to see how well they might eventually marry. For to marry well was to bring the family greater wealth and power. And that was what their future would hold.

Then there was Mother. In Moira's opinion, Mother was best to be avoided. Clara felt differently. She would frequently be invited into Mother's chambers to be shown things. Things that Clara said Mother had told her that Moira was too young to know about. Often they would have supper together there. Clara would sometimes be able to smuggle out some of the sweets and lollies that would finish off the meal for Moira to try. Moira was never invited. Clara said that perhaps Mother thought that she was still just too young. That it would happen soon. Then they would both be able to enjoy the sweets together.

Clara rolled over, squashing Moira under her. Moira laughed, her emerald eyes sparkling, as she struggled out from beneath her sister. Standing, she grabbed a ripe apple from the nearest tree. Biting into it she let the juice run down her chin as she munched on it happily. She flicked back her messy, fiery bronze hair from her porcelain complexion. She had inherited her mother's looks and was certain to be able to marry well. Clara grabbed another apple for herself. She was much more her father. Auburn hair, plaited ornately, fell down her back and was complemented by dark eyes. Her complexion was not that of her sister's, more a honey colour. Her face, though comely, did not contain the extravagant beauty of her mother's.

Moira gave her sister a push and then raced away laughing. Clara waited, giving her sister a slight head start before chasing after. She grabbed her as they ran across the beautifully edged lawn, as she tackled her to the ground.

"Got you," she cried triumphantly.

"Took you longer this time," chimed back Moira. "I'm getting faster."

Clara rolled her eyes, "I gave you a head start, you know."

"Doesn't matter. You always do. Still took you longer," Moira responded defiantly.

They stopped as they heard their names called. Sighing, they looked at each other as they got up and began to walk slowly back to the house, making as many detours as they could along the way. Eventually they arrived at the entrance, each content to endure a scolding from their respective nursemaids for taking so long. Sadly they looked back at each other, giving the other a little wave, as they were herded off along their separate ways into the house. Clara was to be washed and dressed for dinner with her mother while Moira was to be segregated away at the back of the building. Securely sealed within her room where supper would be provided to her, there to remain and eat it on her own.

***

Molly swatted the insect away from Elsie while Ava watched. Normally a very timid and unsure child, Molly could be ferocious if one of her sisters was threatened. She would not let either of them be harmed, not if she could prevent it. That mosquito never had a chance while she was there. Elsie didn't even notice, having been fully engrossed in the garishly dressed peg doll she was holding. Ava, however, was totally engaged in the acrobatics that Molly went through to get the mosquito out of the room. She clapped in appreciation after the performance was over.

May lifted up the garment she was sewing and smiled. She then attempted to settle herself more comfortably in the chair. It had been getting harder to lean forward and reach the sewing things of late. She was getting larger. Another few months and, one could never know, but there might be another man in the house. Joseph didn't seem to mind the all-girl contingent that made up his house. His little harem, he would call it. His Amazonian kingdom. But she knew that he would like a son to teach things to.

Satisfied that she had now finished the garment, she looked up. She could always count on Molly to be attentive to her younger sisters. Now seven years of age Molly was processed of a gentle, happy nature that tended to the shy side of things. She hated large gatherings, preferring to lurk at their peripheries, rarely engaging. Within her small family circle she was very different. Ready to take charge and organise her sisters. Vocal and confident, but a homebody.

Calling Molly over, she held up the newly completed smock. Having dyed the material herself, May could now present her daughter a garment of her favourite colour, a pretty pale red, almost pink. Molly beamed at her mother, grabbing her around the neck and kissing her.

"Oh, Mama, it's beautiful. Can I put it on now?" cried Molly.

"Darling, of course. I want to see how pretty you are in it." Molly blushed as Ava came up behind her and hit her with a doll to get her attention. Molly turned and looked at the four-year-old, who smiled at her success.

"Now, Ava, if I've told you once I've told you a thousand times, you mustn't hit," said Molly in an almost perfect imitation of her mother. Ava ignored the gentle scolding and just grabbed Molly's hand to drag her back to play. Molly disengaged herself from the small hand. "I'll be back shortly and I'm sure that Hegarty will be happy to keep you company till then," Molly added as she went and got her own doll to give to the troublesome younger sister. Looking back at her mother she began to race up the stairs as she called back down, "Can I leave it on till Father gets home?"

"Of course, my darling. He would love to see it," yelled back her mother.

***

Shan set the table as Maima put three bowls on it. Dandelion soup with goat's cheese and bread, still warm from the oven.

There was no memory of his father. Nor of his mother. They were both just concepts. Maima had been the one there in place of both parents from as far back as Shan had a memory. Shan couldn't think of anything that could have been better and didn't miss a thing. Maima smiled at her grandchild as

243

she sat down at the table and looked at the empty place setting. One day, she thought to herself, one day.

"I'm off to market tomorrow," she stated as she blew on a spoonful of hot soup. She then looked across the table and asked, "Anything that you particularly need?" before adding with a knowing wink, "or want?" Shan looked up.

"Do you think he will have any more?"

"Well, the last time we spoke he thought that he had found someone who knew where some were hidden, all forgotten and unloved. He was going to have a look." Shan looked excited. "I wouldn't be surprised," Maima concluded.

Shan knew that on the way to the market held in their small hamlet, Maima would pass by the plot of their close friends, the Albees. She and Jim Albee were always searching for old, forgotten books. Reading was a thing not encouraged for those outside the elite of Town. But Maima's thinking had always been an exception to the norm. She always encouraged questioning and learning in Shan, and that from a very young age. Now one of the greatest thrills for both of them was the discovery of some new, though old, book or manuscript that they both would be able to get lost in.

"It won't take me long. The cheese always goes quickly, and Grace Toolly will take as many of the tinctures and ointments as I can provide."

"I'm fine. I always am. Don't worry, I can take them all out to graze and have them back to start the milking before you get back," replied Shan who at seven had a way with the goats that was much better than someone with twice the experience. Maima considered this a gift, but also as something to ponder. Shan's way with the animals was just a little too peculiar not to be something that she needed to watch.

Thinking to herself, with a mother like Jess and a father like Angus, how could there not be something a bit extra? Maima examined her soup. Then looking up she just said, "I know dear."

***

Clara looked down at her sister. "Catch this," she cried as she threw the apple to Moira who made a valiant, but unsuccessful, attempt to catch it. "Almost," came the laughing response from above. Moira looked up. The last of the ripe apples were high up in the tree. Much too high for her, but Clara, well she was older and much better at climbing. Clara also knew how much Moira loved the fruit. She had offered to climb up and was doing her best to get as many of the ones that remained that she could.

"I wasn't ready," Moira complained.

"You never are," laughed Clara. "Never mind," she added kindly, "I'll give you more notice for the next one."

Moira continued watching, jealous that her sister was older and so much better at climbing than she. Clara stopped and turned around to look at the house. There above her was her room. She knew it was hers. It looked slightly awkward as if there was something missing. The proportions didn't feel right, particularly when viewed from this angle. She saw the door that led from her chamber onto the narrow ledge. A ledge that was surmounted by an ornate iron lacework palisade. She always considered it a rather odd, useless thing. Her mother had a balcony, but she had this strange, impractical little ledge. The door was really no better than a window. She didn't understand why the builders had made it like that. Dismissing the thought she looked back at Moira. "There's not a lot left," she called down. "You might just have to do without for a bit. Just until the next crop is in."

Moira nodded. "There's a few more over there," she called back as she pointed to the other side of the tree where a clump of ripe red fruit hung invitingly.

"Where?" called Clara.

"Over there," yelled back Moira as she pointed again, this time with both arms.

"Oh … I see."

Clara climbed back down the branch she was on and rested next to the trunk. The branch holding the fruit was high up and hanging over the southern boundary of the estate wall. A wall that protected those within the wall from the land that sloped sharply away.

Moving around the trunk of the tree Clara chose the branch that led to the fruit. Moira watched in awe. It was so high, but Clara would be able to do it. Straddling the branch with her legs, Clara began to shimmy along it. Getting close to the wall she swung her leg back over the branch and lowered herself carefully onto the top of it. It was firm and broad. She looked back to Moira who waved vigorously. The fruit was now only an arm's length away.

Reaching up, Clara took a hold of a branch that projected out directly above her head. If she leant out just a bit she should be able to grab the closest of the fruit and bring the rest further in. Smiling down at her sister, Clara waved as she started to lean out. The branch above gradually began to take her weight. *Just a little further.* Stretching her arm out, her fingers brushed against the closest apple. *Almost.*

Then as Moira watched, the branch, clasped ever so tightly by her sister, began to peel away from its source. Slipping slightly Clara tried to correct her balance by pulling against the branch she held. This was done to no effect as it broke away leaving her hanging, leaning over at an impossible angle. Still clasping the stem, Moira watched as Clara's face, embedded in her memory like an image moving in slow motion, declared the realisation of the situation. Open mouthed … without a sound … she seemed to drop slowly to the side before disappearing from sight behind the wall. Immediately there was thud followed after by a silence so profound it was deafening.

Glued to the spot, Moira stared at the empty space where her sister had been just moments before. As the realisation, and panic, hit her she screamed … a cry … a shriek … a mix of terror and loss for what she had just witnessed.

Alone, isolated in her room Moira lay on top of her bed … unmoving … curled into a tight ball. As soon as her scream had raised the alarm, she had immediately been dragged to her room by the nurse. Since then she had been neither chastised, or comforted, having not been spared another thought. Lying still, her mind numb, uncomprehending, as to what had occurred, Moira stayed where she was. Unconsciously waiting … for what? She barely knew. But waiting for someone, anyone to come. Heedless of the passage of time, she barely noticed the day fade to night. Alone and forgotten she stayed.

She awoke with the sun filtering through the windows. Her mouth was dry, and she was hungry. Still dressed, Moira clambered out of bed. No-one had been back. Her door was locked. She went to the window and looked out. Opening it she allowed the fresh morning air to enter. She was not fortunate enough to have a balcony or, like Clara, a large door that slid open to allow the outside in. All seemed calm. All was quiet apart from the call of the birds. With nothing else to do, Moira returned to her bed and sat there to wait.

Clara's unconscious and bloodied body had been carried into the house and laid on one of the ornate sofas in the receiving room. Mrs Poole had already sent the junior maid running for the physician as she boiled water and brought bandages to the room. A groundsman had been dispatched to inform the master. The mistress was, as always in the Tower. She would leave the matter of informing her to the Tower's attendants that infested their home. Her duty was to the master and his heir, not to her.

It was only when she entered the gates that she was aware that something was amiss. Their keepers never spoke to her when she passed through, but this time their silence screamed, yelled at her. They just looked. Rattled, she almost forgot herself and asked them why, but she remembered herself just in time.

Walking quickly to the house Mortella was quick to observe the lack of usual activity that went into maintaining the estate. It was quiet. She was not greeted as she entered the building. No servant came to ask her need. More irritated than concerned she continued into the hall. It was only then that she noted that the hallway mirror was covered. A black, sheer organza coated its surface. She sneered. It was a tradition as old as time practiced by the simple minded. Done to protect the living against the recently deceased. Yet she could not recall any of Charles' extensive, and elderly, relatives being on the verge of passing. Still, one less of them was always somewhat of a benefit to her.

She was in the midst of climbing the stairs to her chamber when a pale-faced maid raced past her. In a fluster it stopped briefly to curtsy, "Milady," before continuing on her flight. Reaching the landing, Mortella became sensible of a number of voices coming from down the corridor. The sound caused a chill to shoot up her back. Making quickly for her chamber she entered only to find the Tower varlet seated on the sofa and waiting.

"Mortella," came a dry voice. Mortella stopped and was about to rebuke the affront to her personal apartment when the varlet continued. "I waited … out of courtesy … for your return. I will now return to the Tower." With nothing further the figure rose and made for the door. Lost for words, Mortella watched, stunned. As the figure passed through to the hall, it turned and added in what could only have been described as an attempt at compassion, "My condolences … I know that this was the only way for you to regain the Black." Then she was gone, leaving Mortella feeling suddenly chilled and trembling.

Looking down to her shaking hands and then up at the door, Mortella hastily made her way out of her chamber and down the corridor to Clara's room. There, outside the door was her husband, Mrs Poole, and the physician, deep in conversation. Pushing past them without waiting, Mortella entered. Before her, on the bed, lay Clara, hair brushed back from a pale face. The eyes were closed, and the bed clothes were raised to her shoulders. She looked comfortably asleep, yet her mirror too had been covered.

Racing to the bed, Mortella placed the good hand on her child's forehead. It felt cool to the touch. "Clara," she called, "Clara … Clara," she repeated again and again, now grabbing the child's shoulders and violently shaking them. She frantically looked around for the Tormentors … but they too had gone. Fear, terror filled her as the full realisation crashed in on her. Her mind threw up memories of a sweet, small child looking and smiling at her before flicking back to the reality that was before her … Clara cold and pale. This was true loss. Something she could not control, not reverse. The one being that she had truly loved was gone.

The voice of Mrs Poole sounded behind her. The words barely made sense as she was told what had happened. Of an accident. Something to do with apples. She heard the name Moira.

Fierce, hot tears began to form in her eyes as it dawned on her the extent of the loss she had received. With no child foretold by the Tower, there was no path to the Black. No chance to rise … to claim her place. All the hopes and dreams were nothing without this child. Her fear then turned to anger. The Abbatissa would gloat. The varlets would dismiss her. Her work with the Tower would be forgotten and she would be discarded. And all … all for apples? Apples. Apples for … Moira.

Turning from the one who had embodied her hopes and desires Mortella walked slowly and calmly from the chamber. She still had the ear of the Tower and the Abbatissa could do nothing about that. She would find another way. She would retake the Black. And for Moira, her spite and hatred of that thing was even further entrenched.

Chapter 29

Moira, the only child, and heir, of her father, was to be given the best. He didn't want to be bothered by requests or supplications. She was to be given what she wanted, when she wanted, and he did not want to be bothered by any day-to-day concerns. The servants were at her beck and call all hours of the day and this was the way she had learnt to like it. As she grew, her beauty blossomed with her sleek, glossy auburn hair with emerald green eyes complementing her perfect alabaster complexion. At age thirteen, Moira's figure had started to develop, and her beauty was planned to be used to its full effect to further cement her father's authority within Town. To him, a good marriage was never something to be spurned and soon, very soon, it would be determined. A prize for the highest bidder.

If her father was absent in Moira's upbringing, her mother was even less present. Since the misfortune of the eldest daughter to die in childhood, the mother had firmly embedded herself within her own affairs, incognisant and disinterested in anything to do with the second daughter, appearing only in moments of necessity when her husband demanded it.

Moira remembered little of her sister. At one time she knew they had been close but then Clara had been hurt. At that time Moira was banished to her small room, segregated from all. None were allowed to speak to her. She heard nothing of her sister, who never visited. Locked within the four walls, a captive within her room, she remained lonely and alone, there until her father decreed a change. It was then she had learnt her sister was gone. She felt sad for a while, but then her sister had already deserted her, leaving her with an indifferent father and hostile mother. For that Moira could never forgive her.

The tales of the Tower intrigued the stunning child. She had read of its power and saw the control it held over people's lives. They feared but obeyed the Tower and its edicts. Even her mother gave it reverence. To Moira this was power. She had become well versed in coercion and persuasion as honey often did better than a forceful demand. Yet, at times, she noted some resentment, reluctance, to her desires. These were manageable for the servants, but her father could be more of a challenge. The Tower, however, appeared to do nothing, yet all obeyed it, tithed to it, honoured it.

She had read of the Influences and knew the connection to the Tower of her family's progeny. To her great delight she too discovered that she had Influence. She could affect another person's physical body. Make it stumble or cause cramps, slow the heart or speed it up. She would practise and delight in the control she exerted without the other knowing. She congratulated herself that when she provoked a toothache in an irritating servant that was so painful and realistic the tooth was extracted. How she longed for the Tower to come and share its power with her. Until then she would continue to practise, to prepare herself to ascend the great stairs and enter through the great door into a world she imagined was created solely for her to excel.

***

Molly enjoyed life observing others from the sidelines. For her there was nothing worse than being the centre of attention. Delight was found in the comforts of home, the love of her parents and companionship of her sisters. Having a natural gift of compassion, she sensed the feelings of others. Molly was patient and kind, considerate of their situation. A short, plump, pleasant-faced girl of thirteen, Molly hoped, so very much hoped, that she would one day have a home of her own. She knew that she would never be beautiful but had a "jolly" personality, or so she was always told. She did wish that she was a bit more like her youngest sister, Ester, an exuberant toddler, fearful of nothing and excited by everything. Yet, try as she would, crowds scared her and made her feel small and invisible. Inconsequential was how she felt. People were never unkind, but she often did not seem to exist to them. Already feeling anxious and unimportant, she was frequently overlooked and ignored. More recently it had been getting worse. They would swear that they just didn't see her. Often they would bump into her as she passed them in the street. They seemed neither to notice or even try to avoid her.

She had spoken to Mama about it. When away from home she said that she felt like she faded. At this her mother looked concerned, but quickly hid her discomfort. It was shortly after that when May, her mother, took her aside and spoke, for the first time, about the Dark Ones of the Tower and of Influence. Yes, Molly had heard the stories but had never really believed them. But now her mother spoke of her great aunt, Noona's sister, and how the Tower had selected her. They talked of Influences and the one that Noona's sister processed. One that altered people's perception of things.

Molly had listened and nodded. Horrified that her aunt would have chosen to leave her family to enter the Tower, but happy that she would never make such a choice. Mama had said that only ones with Influence would be asked to the Tower and Molly was content that that would never happen to her.

***

Shan enjoyed the goats. Each one had their own personality and responded in its own way to any request that was made. Reason was not their greatest strength, but emotion – now that was a great way to get them to behave. You just had to tap into what they wanted and tweak it just a bit. Then all would go smoothly. This was a skill that Shan had developed.

Isolated at the edge of the Bowl, Shan and Maima seldom had visitors and they consisted entirely of Jim Albee and his son, Johnathon. Maima had placed them far from the Tower. Influence ran in the blood. With her son as the father and Jess as the mother, Shan had at an early age displayed a minor Influence. One that allowed for the persuasion of goats. Girls, the Tower may take. Boys had a worse possibility. Neither of which were to be desired. Distance and protection was needed against the Tower.

At the time that Maima's health declined, Shan first demonstrated Jess' gift of Influence with force, affecting the air when emotions were high, and control was lacking. With such an explosion of Influence, staying hidden at home was no longer an option. The Tower would have seen. Maima was no longer able to protect them. Shan was vulnerable. It was then decided to leave. To follow in the father's footsteps and find the ones who fought back.

***

Mortella removed the black robe as she sat. She had just returned to the estate. She cared little for her life of servants and the luxury that it offered. Her focus was wholly on perfecting her Influence. Learning to meld the resident auras within the confines of the Tower to realise her will and further embellish her status within that realm. She had worked hard to make herself indispensable to the Tower, and thus to the Code. She must not be ignored.

She did, however, still have some responsibilities to perform within Town. She would not let anyone have cause to charge her with neglecting

251

the commission she had been set by the Presence. There was still one live child within the house of Keep, so, according to the letter of that commission, she had not failed. A child had been provided and could be dealt with as the Tower pleased.

Alone in the windowless compartment she had taken after Clara's death, Mortella allowed the glamour of her Influence to fade. In the Tower, with the use of the Influence of others, she could enjoy its effect. See her beauty in all its fullness, unblemished. But here, when using her Influence alone, it had no effect on her. She would see the wasted left arm and its sloping shoulder. The radiance of her skin had started to fade as she watched the formation of creases that marred the corners of her eyes and edges of her mouth. Grey had already begun to creep into her fiery locks and, as there were none in her compartment to observe her, there was no need to exert herself.

But tonight, she would exert herself. She could not deny that she took pleasure in the demonstrative praises that she received from those who attended such affairs. Tonight was to be a spectacular gala, one to showcase the power and authority of the Keeps. She was Lady of the estate and the first within Town. She would shine and enjoy herself as she baited and insulted those that had, for so many years, been dismissive of her and her sisters that dwelt in the lower reaches of Town.

She would now bathe and then dress. A maid would be required for that … and for her hair. She was tired and it would be best to minimise the amount of Influence she needed to exert during the affair upstairs. Rising, she approached the warm, scented water of her tub. Its warmth would sooth the aches that troubled her back and neck. Then she would dress, preparing for the delight that only the torment of lesser minds could provide.

***

Mortella stood outside the ornate doors that led to the ballroom, ones that were solely for family use. Guests entered through another set of doors, and they had arrived some time ago. She would make an entrance. One that commanded the attention of all. She knew that Charles would have been there to greet his guests as they arrived. He would be working the room, using his charm, and calculating brain, to assess each one and every potential alliance. She had no such obligation. Unlike him, she cared nothing for their power or position. It was this disdain for all those within that helped create the universally held admiration of her authority and mystique.

The affair had already been going on for some time. Wine would have been flowing freely, yet many would abstain, trying to keep a clear head while attempting to reposition themselves for greater gain. For tonight there would be bartering. Who could offer the best price in return for a union with the daughter of the most powerful of families?

She knew that they were awaiting her anxiously. The women would be speculating on her dress, while the men were cautiously hoping to gain a moment of her attention in order to advance their cause. Well, they would have to wait a little longer before she would condescend to appear. Just a bit longer, but well past the time when both decorum and politeness would have demanded her attendance.

Eventually she nodded to the servants. They slowly opened the doors as the music stopped and all gazed upon the image of perfection that was framed within the forming void. A gown of iridescent midnight purple perfectly highlighted her ornately fashioned hair and flawless skin. To them she stood straight and tall, elegant, and graceful. The arc of her neck flowed smoothly into slender shoulders that were shown to spectacular effect by a low-cut, figure-hugging dress. A waist that appeared to be tightly cinched further accentuated the already hourglass figure.

In reality, Mortella's beautiful face was smoothed and perfected by Influence. Her sagging left shoulder and spinal tilt to the left was only exacerbated by the dress design, while her withered left arm hung almost useless by her side. She knew all this but also knew what the others saw. The doors now fully open, she flowed confidently into the room as the hum within the room grew.

It was time. Charles beckoned her to him. Mortella bowed her head as she cut short the tirade of compliments from the supplicant before her. Tonight, Moira would be presented for consideration. A bargaining chip to be used to further cement Charles' position. The subjugation of her daughter for societal gain mattered little to Mortella. It was that or the Tower … if it wanted her. She cared not. Standing by her husband she waited for the music to fade. Within the hall silence fell once again as the family doors opened in fluid silence. All eyes, but Mortella's, were on the figure beyond. With grace and poise, Moira appeared to float toward her father. Despite herself, Mortella looked. Having never spent much time in each other's presence, and not seeing her daughter for months at a time, Mortella was struck with the beauty of the girl that entered. Brushed-bronze hair was intricately woven to highlight a face that mirrored that of her mother from years past. The green gown was appropriately modest for a girl of her age but clearly hinted to the woman that she would become.

Moira reached her father and took his outstretched hand as he turned her to face the room. With pride he announced to the room, "My friends, tonight I have the great pleasure to present my daughter, Moira." Mortella looked on as her daughter took centre stage. Her eyes were hard but she maintained a serene smile that was all but painted on her face. Moira bowed her head to the appreciative applause that followed the statement. Charles then passed Moira's hand to her mother. She was charged to lead their daughter away.

Taking the hand offered, Mortella led the child from the centre of attention and off to the side of the hall. There she left Moira after strictly directing the child to remain still until collected … not to move … not to talk. Returning to the guests, Mortella concentrated on embellishing her Influence a touch further. It was taking a toll on her, but she would not be outshone by that child, not now, not ever.

Working the room, Mortella smiled graciously as she endured the effusive congratulations from clueless sycophants about her daughter. She found the women particularly irritating in their comparisons. Honing her Influence even more, Mortella's breathing became faster as she felt the strain. She would need to retire shortly in order to retain her strength. But for now she must remain and could not allow her Influence to fall.

It was then that she felt it. She may not have the ability of Influences apart from her own, but she knew their feel. Someone was trying to Influence her as her heart rate started to slow, and her head felt light. Blocking its effect, the heart rate increased back to normal. Betraying nothing, she continued to smile at the woman in front. Again she felt the Influence begin to affect her. Once more she counteracted this effect as a light sweat started to form on her face from the effort. Mortella concentrated on slowing her breathing as her heart rate once again normalised. The effort was taking its toll. Not only had she to counteract the assault, she must also not let the Influence fall from her appearance. She felt it again. This time the battle was serious. Her heart rate fell again as her head started to feel light and thinking became clouded.

Looking about, Mortella took in a deep breath. There could only be just one within this hall that would do such a thing. She turned her head towards the corner where her daughter had been deposited. The child was looking directly at her. Indignant at the audacity of the attack, Mortella locked eyes with the girl. Within this look she showed that the source of the affront had been seen, and it had been noted. It would not be forgotten … nor forgiven. Anger rose within her, giving her renewed energy. She would break this hold on her and then she would break the child. With the newly found vitality, Mortella counteracted the Influence directed upon her. Her success was immediate. No longer dampened by the assault, her heart rate jumped dramatically higher causing her blood pressure to explode. She felt her face flush. This was closely followed by a severe pounding in the back of her head causing her to gasp and then … all went black.

***

Mortella awoke. Finding herself lying on a cot in the dark, feeling light and insubstantial. The pain in her head had gone as had the earlier exhaustion that had threatened to consume her. Unsure of where she was, she rose from the bed, and she looked about. As her head cleared it became obvious that she was within the Tower, located in the deep, dark recesses of the great cavern that underlay the structure of the Tower itself. She then became aware of the points of colour that flowed through the space around her, barely giving any light as they meandered. These colours also appeared to surround her, outlining her form with their subtle glow. She then remembered what had happened. The child had used Influence against her. But why was she here?

As she watched in the darkness, the pinpoints of colour began to coalesce. As more and more joined, the slender, willowy waif of the Tower began to form in the air above her. There was a feeling of calm as the figure looked down. Without warning, or invitation, it threw an image into the space between them. It was an image of a young woman not yet fully grown. Mortella instantly recognised it. One of those images given to her all those years ago when she had still been wearing the Black. Beside it there gradually formed a second of those given images. This one was of the figure that stood straight and tall before it started to melt like wax on a hot day. The body shifted as it slumped to the left with the arm withered and hanging uselessly to the side.

Mortella looked down at her own arm seeing the similarity. In the dim light that now bathed her, she also saw that her arm appeared even more shrunken than usual. The skin was discoloured and waxy. She ran her right hand down it. It felt dry and cool. Shocked, she looked back to the image as it started to turn to face her. As it did, she recalled the words spoken by the One just after her fate had been decided.

255

"Your fate is to bare the child foretold.

It will destroy you."

There had also been a promise. If she stayed close. She had stayed close to the Tower. Spending most days within its walls to work on melding the resident auras together. She had held tight to that promise. That if remained close she would be restored to the Black.

The figure had now turned and faced her. It looked at her. A sunken-cheeked, hollowed-eyed face with dusky green skin peeling away from bloodless grey muscle beneath. Fiery red hair cascaded about the head as Mortella finally acknowledged it for who it was. Feeling for a pulse, she felt none. She was also aware that she had not yet taken a single breath. Horrified and confused, she slumped back down onto the cot as the images faded.

Sitting in the dark she waited. For what? She knew not, but still she waited. The waif had gone, and no more images were forthcoming. Eventually she stood, resolved. She was not gone when lesser ones would have. She knew that the Tower was maintaining her. If none were coming for her then she would need to go to them. As a matter of habit, she began to weave the auras about her. As expected, she no longer possessed any of her own. Influence was, of course, within the blood. But the Tower had brought her back. And the Tower had provided her with the Influence of others. With these she transformed herself. Now standing straight, with the appearance of her beauty and vitality restored, Mortella left the cot to make her way back into the Tower structure proper. All those days within these walls had not been wasted. For now she knew what she had to do. Being restored to the Black and to leave the Tower renewed was now just a matter of time and opportunity.

Chapter 30

Ever since that night all those years ago, Mortella felt more herself when inside the Tower than anywhere else. But now she was confined to its walls. Without the use of Influence from those it contained, she would quickly pass beyond the help of any. Never to regain her position within the Black nor within life itself. However, her time was limited. The essence of who she was could be maintained by the power of the Tower, but only for a while. It could animate the cocoon that housed her. Make it beautiful and give it the appearance of life. But it was just in appearance alone. Reality was something different. Her time was limited, for as the body crumbled and decomposed, she would dissipate, there to become simply another of the living souls that flowed through its corridors.

Speed was of critical importance. She must find a suitable vessel to regain the life that had been taken from her. The long days she spent within these walls, over many years, had taught her much. The Tower conceded even more to her. She knew that it would allow her to transfer into the one she chose. One that she must now find. One with Influence and preferably her Influence.

Molly looked at Shan. He had been her lifesaver. Taken by force from her family and thrown into this cold, dark place. Here she had wandered alone though its endless corridors of smooth black stone. But, now having found Shan, she was no longer alone. Shan said that the Tower lied. It showed her things that were not, and could never have been, true. Mother would never have said such things. She could kick herself for even thinking that it could have been true. Shan said that these were a test. Well, just let it try it again, she thought.

She knew that she was not doing well. Each time she had a test, she felt that she lost a little bit of herself. After each event something was taken from her. She was not quite sure what, but she was not as complete as she once had been. Shan was doing better. She knew that. He wasn't losing bits and also because, unlike her, he was given food.

Shan finished the last of their meagre dinner.

"I'm sorry," she said looking at the empty sack.

"What for?" asked Shan.

"For taking your food," she sighed. "They don't seem to give me any."

Shan shrugged. "We'll find more," he said as he looked carefully down the corridor. Of late, it seemed that one Influence upon another had been hitting him. As far back as he could remember he could get the goats to do what he wanted. They listened to him. Maima said that this was a gift. Then, unexpectedly he had caused chaos when he demonstrated his mother's gift. Frustration and panic had caused an outburst that could not have gone unnoticed by the ones they most wanted to avoid.

Major Influences were only for girls. Boys were not allowed even to have the minor ones, but the major ones they never displayed. Never until him. Maima knew that the Tower would not leave him be. It would do dreadful things to him. That was why they had to leave. Maima said that the Tower would come. He had to go. But if he was a she, then he might have a chance, so a she he played. Played so well that now he was here within the Tower, collected by the Tower, just as had Molly. He was to go and find his father. Be safe. Well, safety was not what had found him.

His father's Influence manifested in him only a few days earlier. He now saw colours that floated about him. Lights that meandered haphazard and confused. Every so often, when one of the Watchers came, as Molly called them, he saw a purpose to the movement of a blue light. Now as he looked down the corridor he saw numerous colours coalesce and gradually grow in brightness. They appeared to be making their way towards them.

Mortella knew that the initiates would be scattered about the Tower. Those girls who displayed talent would be collected and tested. Those who succeeded would take the Black. Do well and they would rise higher than the mindless Tormentors … further than the varlets. For them their time within the Bowl would be at an end. The Code required them elsewhere. Fail and then they would serve in another way. Enhance that which was already in the Tower. Never to leave, never to die. There to be of use to ones such as she.

Now she must find them. The Tower was vast, and each was separated from all others by work she had perpetrated during her time here all those years ago. The Influence of Perception hid each from all others, including from her. They could pass close by one another and never have the faintest inkling that another soul even existed. Locked within their own isolated existence they could be tested, and the mettle of their being determined. She needed to find one suitable for her use. One with life and Influence sufficient for her skills and knowledge. Preferably one with her Influence, that of perception.

Mortella passed though the Tower and looked for signs that an initiate was nearby. She would feel if there was a concentration of power. A focus of Influence that surrounded the one being isolated. As she walked, she saw a slight figure start to make its way toward her. Cloaked in the black robe of an initiate it stopped and stood awaiting her in the centre of the corridor.

This gave her pause. It was unusual on several levels. Primarily, an initiate should have been bound by the Perception of Isolation. There, unless they had succeeded to advance. In addition, her experience of meeting an initiate was invariably quite different. This one impressed her. Normally initiates would cower and hide in a corner as she passed. This one stood firm.

She slowed her pace as she considered the figure. To her added surprise a second figure started to approach. Again, cloaked in the initiate's robes, but this one was shorter and, even within the robes, obviously much rounder.

Mortella stopped. The Influence that shrouded one from the other had been broken. She was unaware of this ever having occurred before. Certainly it never had during her tenure within the Tower. The unpicking of this illusion would take time and … significant talent. It was clear, therefore, that one of these two must have her Influence and that at an impressive level.

Smiling, Mortella raised her hands in front of her in a gesture of greeting as she spoke in a voice coated in honey.

"The Tower has never before played host to such as you two. You must be very special to be able to break Influence." The two figures remained silent, looking at her warily as she spoke. She continued, "I should know, my dears, for it was once I who wove that Influence." She gave a little laugh of delight as she asked, "Which of you has the Influence of Perception?" Shan and Molly looked confused at the question. Mortella smiled at one and then the other. "My dears, you can trust me," she said sweetly. "It has been hard, I know. But you are already here. It will become easier, I promise. The Tower selected you. Let me help you. It will not be difficult to discover which of the Influences you have."

As she spoke, Molly stepped forward. "I think I might have that one," she said cautiously. Mortella looked at the uninspiring child that stood trembling in the corridor. *Not a pretty vessel*, she thought.

"You broke the illusion of solitude?" Mortella asked, unable to fully mask her disbelief. To her surprise the girl rose up, defiant.

"Yes, I did."

"Mmm," responded Mortella as she thought, this one has possibility. Unfortunate about its form but that is but an obstacle to overcome. I have used Influence to great effect for years. Turning from her thoughts she asked, "I suppose that you are hungry?" Without listening for the answer, she added, "Then follow me."

Varlets lived within the Tower and, although never that many, they still required sustenance. The Bowl tithed a tenth of everything. What was not required within these walls was moved outside of the Bowl. For Mortella, this had been a blessing as she had still been able to partake in her favourite wine when deployed beyond the borders of the Bowl. Mortella walked quickly down the corridor. Stopping briefly, she broke the cloaking that hid a door before opening it and climbing the stairs. Entering an ornate chamber, she went to the end of the long table which was set for a sumptuous supper. She watched as the two children cautiously entered the room.

Mortella smiled at them as she indicated the side table that was overflowing with fresh fruits, bread, cheeses, and cured meats. The skinny one took a plate and started to load it up. The plump one held back, watching. Mortella waited. She was not one who suffered delay with composure, but the child must accept her. For the transfer to work, the child must allow it. She must trust her. Eventually this one too went to take food before sitting at the long table to eat.

"I hope this will make you feel better, my dears."

"Are you not eating?" asked the plump one.

"Oh no. Not just yet. A bit later perhaps," replied Mortella as she looked longingly at the decanter holding a rich, full-bodied red. The Tower sustained her, but not to that level. She was still void of life and all too aware of the rapid deterioration of the shell that contained her.

"Are you a Watcher?" asked Molly.

"She means one of the Dark Ones," added Shan quickly.

Horrified at the comparison, Mortella tried to compose herself as she laughed. "Oh, darlings, I am not one of the help," she answered a little too forcefully.

"I'm sorry," responded Molly, feeling that she had done something wrong.

"They are the servants of the Tower, my dear." Mortella paused. "Do I look like a servant?" She asked pointedly while looking directly at Molly.

"No, no, not at all," answered Molly quickly. "You're much too beautiful … and so elegant and …" she added as her voice gradually trailed off in embarrassment.

"They're not really human anymore," Mortella continued smoothly.

Molly gave a shudder.

"Where do they come from?" asked Shan.

Mortella smiled a sad smile as she looked up into the air and then back at Molly. "Oh, where you all come from, dear," she said as she walked over to Shan and took his face in her hands. "They didn't do well here," she added dryly as she looked him directly in the eyes. "Well, they did better than some," she added cheerily as she turned to glance at Molly with a knowing look. "Talent is one thing … how to use it is another."

Letting Shan go she lightly brushed her hand against Molly's hair as she turned to face the two of them. "Better know what to do and how to do it." Pausing for effect, Mortella then added, "Now, my darlings, we must go." Leading them down the stairs she recloaked the door before turning away from the pair and walking away. "We shall meet again, my dears. At a more … convenient time."

Mortella considered the situation. Choices were limited, but it was clear that this one contained at least some inherent strength of Influence. She had been able to unpick the barriers, however unknowingly. But she would need to be tested further … and soon. Time was not her friend. And the child must trust her, accept her, willingly allow the transfer to take place. Only then would it succeed.

Calling one of the Tormentors to her, Mortella prepared for the illusion to assess the child's ability further. It appeared that one of the girl's triggers was the Town's marketplace. It would thus be here that she would be brought and examined further.

Mortella looked about. The illusions were always impressive. Such detail. So much beyond what any individual practitioner could achieve. The orchestration of so many, all combined in concert by the Tower. It was magnificent. Such a shame that such power was limited to within the smooth stone structure. Each and every effect was created by searching the memories of the one on trial, delivering such accuracy of detail that it was exquisite.

Mortella glided through the swarming Town square. A path opened effortlessly before her as the images of people and carts readily parted as she moved forward. In the distance she observed a small figure struggling to dodge and weave her way through the crowds. Despite the efforts, figures would bump into her and then leave without acknowledging the collision. *A child who feels insignificant*, thought Mortella. *One with insecurities and craving validation no doubt. Perfect … she will invariably be the epitome of gullibility and easily swayed.* Mortella smiled. *This should be easier than I hoped.*

Mortella waited as Molly eventually made her way to her.

"My darling, wonderful to see you out and about. Isn't it glorious to be outside again?" Mortella said in greeting.

"It's only a trick," Molly responded.

"Indeed, my dear," responded Mortella. "But," she continued as she spread her arms wide as she embraced the scene about them, "The sun still feels warm and the breeze is refreshing."

Molly shrugged, giving a non-committal answer. "But what is the point? What is it for?"

Mortella continued to smile. "The Tower only wants ones who are worthy to rise." Pausing, she added, "It must decide which are unable to rise." Mortella gently stroked Molly's cheek with a soft, feathery touch. She looked into the plump, common face. "Those who do not … the Tower still keeps … they are still of use." Watching intently for a reaction she asked. "I assume that you would prefer to remain … unabsorbed?"

To her satisfaction, Molly gave a jump as she let go a little squeal. "So it is true. The lights?"

Mortella nodded to herself. This display of distress at the possibility demonstrated fear and lack of confidence. She could work with this. She gave a bell-like laugh. "Do not fret, my darling, those lesser ones are happier now." She then looked away from the child as she asked in a stern voice. "Are you one of their superiors?" Molly only answered with an incomprehensible mumble.

"We shall have to see what you can do."

"But I ..." Molly started to object.

Mortella turned back, irritated. The lack of pride was nauseating. She wanted to slap her. "How did you break the illusion of solitude on the other one?" she asked instead.

Molly stopped and thought. "I just really wanted to ... I don't know how."

"Exactly. You *wanted* it." This was better. Desire. Wanting something so much that your body ached for it. This Mortella understood. This was also something that she could use. "More than anything," she added firmly. "You just do it, want it, desire it."

To Molly's surprise an oasis of calm had formed around them. The hustle and bustle continued outside an invisible barrier that seemed to extend about them. The figures appeared oblivious to the anomaly. Molly gradually moved out of the space into the chaos that surrounded it. Immediately the people started pushing past her, bumping her aside. As Mortella watched the child grew in stature. Now much wider and taller, the figures started to flow around instead of into her. It was rough and lacked finesse, but it was effective.

"It's a start, my dear."

"What happened?" asked Molly.

"It's unfortunate that one's Influence does not work on oneself. Suffice to say ... you appeared bigger." It was clear that the girl lacked any understanding of her gift. To test its vitality, the child would need a better understanding. Mortella sighed to herself as she started to explain, in the most simple of terms, how to create the illusions. "You must weave and construct. You *need* to plan."

After providing as much explanation as she could stomach, Mortella turned and strode confidently into the melee that surrounded them. "Let us see what else you can do." Stopping at the edge of the square she stood facing the main access road to it as she waited for the child to arrive.

"Create detail. It must be realistic in order to trick the senses," she advised. "You must want it, desire it. It comes from you," she added. Looking down at the eager face that looked up at her, she commanded, "I want you to stop all movement into the market from this road." Seeing the confusion and indecision in the face, Mortella added curtly, "Be quick. I cannot stand indecision."

Molly faced the crowded road filled with laden carts heading into the market as shoppers wove in and out about them. Mortella waited as the child stood before her, trembling. Hiding her frustration, Mortella looked to the chaos of the street. There was no change. Still, she waited, losing hope that this could be the vessel she required. Finally, giving up she started to turn, making ready to exit the mirage when she noted that figures in the street were looking up. Some dropped their baskets as they cried out and ran for cover down side streets. A horse reared backwards, upending the cart, throwing its driver and contents across the road. She watched as the same driver picked himself off the ground and stared up into the sky behind her. Screams cut the air as others picked up on the panic. Intrigued, Mortella looked behind her. Despite herself she gave a genuine laugh. Hovering in the sky was what could be generously called a dragon. It was green with oversized wings attached to a plump and slightly misshapen body. The snout was more cow-like than a dragon, but there was at least the appearance of smoke coming out of the nostrils. The open mouth was dominated by a pink, oversized, forked tongue that flicked in and out past pointed incisors. In many ways it was comical, but nevertheless it had been effective in ceasing the street traffic.

"Oh, my darling, crude but effective, I'll give you that." Mortella laughed, relieved that at last some talent had been displayed. Placing a gentle hand on the shoulder of the beaming child that looked up at her with both pride and pleasure at the praise, Mortella added, "You will do, my dear. I really think that you will do. I'm so pleased."

Chapter 31

Half buried amidst the dirty laundry, Moira awoke from a troubled sleep. Still locked within a world of illusion, she lay alone and desolate. It all seemed so clear. No-one ever liked her. No-one ever really cared for her. Every interaction in her life was based on what could be gained. Her father saw her as an object to be used. Her mother despised her. The servants of the estate went through the motions of care because they were paid. She had no friends. She never had. Never had until Polly … who probably wasn't real anyway. A creation of the Tower … but she had felt so real. No, Moira thought, Polly was my friend … at least, was my friend. Then … then she, Moira, had deserted her. When Polly needed her most. Wiping a tear from the corner of her eye, she knew. She was her mother. Selfish, thoughtless of anyone but herself. Having so long vowed never be her, Moira had now proven beyond all doubt that she was.

Lying there she looked about the dingy room. The space was confined, but it felt like she wasn't alone. She saw no-one, but fearing that she might be caught and taken back to the kitchen, she hid herself by wiggling further under the dirty linen.

Shan had spotted the light hovering a few feet off the ground. He stopped and he stared at it. Grabbing Molly's sleeve he pulled her over and pointed.

"There's a light," he whispered. "Just like when I saw your one. There," he pointed. "This one's red."

Molly looked concerned. "What should we do?"

"It might be someone like us. We can't just leave them."

Molly nodded, knowing that it would be up to her to tear down the barriers. "Oh, alright, let's give it a go," she sighed.

Moira was certain that she could feel someone, someone close by. Raising her head she again looked about carefully. Off to the right, there … through what should have been a solid stone wall she saw two indistinct figures. One was lying on the ground. The other was bent over it. She watched as the one standing appeared to look directly at her. It raised an arm. It waved. Without thinking, Moira waved back.

Molly slowly opened her eyes. Her head was pounding from the effort. She was so tired. "Was it working?" she asked Shan. Turning her head to the side she saw the blurred outline of what seemed to be a girl with fiery red hair. "Can she hear us?" she asked.

Shan looked at the figure. "We're here to help," he yelled as he raised his arms in welcome. The figure seemed to respond but the words were muffled.

Moira watched in amazement as the image of the others became more solid, more detailed. She could now hear them. They seemed a bit like her. Little by little the distance between them appeared to shrink. The wall dissolved further as their world began to entrench itself in hers.

Exhausted, Molly stripped away the final layer that separated the three and closed her eyes. Moira's world fully dissolved, and she found herself once more within the cool, silver-grey light of the Tower.

***

Mortella could feel it, even if she couldn't see it … the unstoppable decay of the body she had once cherished. The Tower could maintain her but the toll on the flesh was severe. All that Influence was hastening its decline. Rot had set in and the festering would only get faster. She needed to act and act soon. Before the shell she inhabited could no longer contain her and she began to dissipate.

The child had looked up to her. Admired her. But would it trust her enough to submit? It must. She had no time to find another.

***

Moira remained silent. Shan had not seen anyone else. Only her. She sighed deeply, working hard to hold back the tears that wanted to fall. If there was only her in the Tormentor's trial then that meant … no, she was not going to even think it. Polly was real and she was her friend. She looked at Molly lying in an exhausted sleep off to the side.

"But," Moira asked sharply, "how did you find me? How do you know there was no-one else?" She then added in a far gentler tone, "I haven't seen anyone else in the Tower since I got here."

"Neither had we until we found each other," replied Shan as he looked closely at Moira. "Sorry, I'm Shan, and this is Molly," he added quickly when he realised that he had been staring. "I can see peoples' Influences. I see them as coloured lights."

"I've never heard of that one. It's not a major Influence," declared Moira with conviction.

"I can also influence air," added Shan. "Molly has perception."

Moira looked from one to the other and then realised that Shan was waiting for her to speak. "Oh, yes … I'm Moira. Mine … I can influence the physical body." Then turning to Molly she asked, "How did she do that?"

Shan looked at the sleeping figure. "She says that you have to really want it. Imagine it and then wish it to be. It's exhausting. It was very hard for her," explained Shan.

"But you don't even know me."

"So, do you need an introduction before saving someone?" asked Shan.

"I suppose not," Moira replied, aware that this would never have been something that she would have normally done. There were usually other motives. People always wanted something. She had never known anyone to get something for nothing.

They both looked at Molly as she started to stir. Opening her eyes Molly looked at Moira and gave a little squeal of delight. Shan raced over and helped her to sit up before giving her a drink of water.

After taking a drink Molly gave a shy wave. "Hello, I'm Molly. You're very beautiful."

Unexpectedly, Moira began to blush. The compliment felt so genuine without even a hint of jealousy.

"And … I'm Moira," she responded, giving a genuinely stunning smile. As she did, Molly reached out and hugged Moira tightly. "I'm so glad that you're here." Taken aback at the spontaneous show of affection, Moira looked about nervously.

"Are you hungry?" asked Shan. "We don't have much, but you're welcome to share it." Looking at Molly, he grinned at her proudly. "Molly did very well on the last trial." Molly returned an embarrassed smile.

"You are sure?" asked Moira.

"Of course," answered Molly without a moment's thought. "Better that we all get at least something to eat rather than letting anyone go completely without."

Unsure as to whether to believe her or not, Moira joined the other two as Molly unpacked the sack that had appeared next to her after her success in the Town market. Moira was confused. They hadn't yet asked her for anything. She would stay vigilant. Watch for the twist. But as they ate she was welcomed and embraced as a friend. The twist never came. Instead the conversation was light and easy. They all ignored the black walls around them. With all the meagre rations shared equally and far too rapidly devoured, they continued to talk. About the Western Slopes, games played with sisters, and even of a tile terrace shaded by cherry blossoms that was filled by the music of running water. Still only partially sated, but all of them feeling lighter in spirit by newly found friends, they decided to settle and attempt to rest. To prepare for whatever was to come.

***

Mortella moved down the corridor. She followed the Tormentor. She would only have the one chance. Not to succeed would condemn her to an eternal fate within the Tower. She was not going to let that happen. She looked at the figure in front that was leading her to the child. She needed its Influence. That of the Tower. Willingly given by the Tower. Needed to allow the transfer to take place. All those years she had spent within these walls had brought her at least that concession. She had been given that. But only the once.

The Tormentor moved into one of the Tower's open chambers. It stopped and stood unmoving as it loomed over the sleeping form of Molly. Behind it Mortella entered the room only to see Shan and, to her surprise, her daughter Moira there as well. Turning to face the bane that had infected her life fourteen years ago, she smiled an insincere greeting as she glided into the space.

"Oh, what fun, my darling … they found you as well."

"Mother … won't you ever leave?" Moira spat back. Shan turned to look at the woman with surprise. The resemblance was unmistakable. The same fiery red hair, fair complexion and stunning looks.

"My dear," Mortella simpered, "why would I want that? I have everything I need right here."

"Really," replied Moira in a voice as sweet as sugared honey. "Here there is darkness to hide your rotting flesh? No-one to smell the decay you wear as perfume."

Mortella smiled a dazzling smile of pure enjoyment. "Oh, darling … as I said, I have everything I need." Mortella glanced back at the recumbent form of Molly. "I won't be staying much longer."

Moira looked at Shan and then at the sleeping figure of Molly. Rising to her feet she walked towards the image of her mother. Standing directly in front of it she demanded. "Say what you mean, you putrefying corpse."

268

Mortella looked back at the image of her younger self that confronted her. "Innovation, dear. You've used that one before. Try something new. We must always try to use our intellect."

"I stopped you once …"

"Yes," interrupted Mortella with venom, "you did make this rather inconvenient." She stopped and turned to look at Molly again and the figure beside her. "I see that you have met my protégé."

Moira looked at Molly.

"I just need a new body," Mortella continued. "A living one. One with Influence in the blood. One with *my* Influence," she crooned. Waving a hand at Molly she added. "But … one must settle with what one can get."

Moira took a step closer to her mother. "I won't let you."

Looking at the child that stood before her Mortella gave a chilling laugh. "What do you think you can do?" she asked before pausing. "I'm already dead, my dear."

Mortella watched as Moira began to concentrate. She could feel the Influence that was starting to form about her. She watched gleefully as disappointment began to etch itself into her daughter's features. Laughing again, Mortella dismissed the child and turned away, walking over to the Tormentor whilst giving a single command: "Let me enter."

The room gradually filled with the sweet smell of decay as Mortella felt the Influences that sustained her start to separate from the corpse that contained her. Little by little they let the shell revert to its actual form. No longer was she standing straight and tall. Now her left shoulder sank down to an arm that was shrivelled and hanging flaccidly by the side. The alabaster complexion turned a dusky grey-green as cloudy, sunken eyes emerged from a bloated, slack-mouthed face. No longer was she wearing a glamorous emerald gown. The figure that contained her instead was clad in a white shroud stained with the bodily fluids that leaked from the decaying corpse.

Mortella felt the barriers between her and the Tower dissolve. She could see a path that led to the recumbent form of Molly. As the walls crumbled, the way forward became brighter. She could feel the life within the child. Its vitality. It beckoned to her. Calling her to come.

With all obstacles between her and her objective gone, Mortella began to follow the path of life set out before her. Feeling ethereal, vapour-like she floated down. Little by little, bits of who she was reached for the sleeping figure, ready to take up residence and confine its inhabitant. Usurping its control on the life it processed. But first she would need to obtain a willing consent.

Mortella now stood once again shrouded in her former glory. A projection into the mind of Molly, there waiting. The Tormentor had stayed the child, making the transfer possible. This would yet take some time, but the process was underway. But at present Mortella still had no control. In this body she was just an observer. It would now be up to her to convince the child to allow her full possession. Then there could be control. With the transfer proceeding, it was essential for her to gain that approval.

The Tormentor had created a space for them to meet. As Mortella waited, she watched the image of Molly as she was allowed to regain consciousness within this realm. She gradually began to stir and opened her eyes.

"Oh, darling, you're awake. I have been waiting for some time," Mortella chastised the sleepy figure.

"Where's Shan and …" Molly started to ask, confused.

"Shan as you call her and … Moira, yes, my dear, I know, are where they should be," Mortella responded. Walking over to Molly, she stopped and looked down before commanding, "Get up, dear." Molly climbed slowly to her feet as she looked about. The air felt cooler, and everything was even more silent than usual.

Mortella gazed at the child before giving a sad, gentle smile. Her demeanour softened and she spoke gently. "My dear, there is such an important task that I need to ask you to do for me." Mortella lightly brushed the hair away from Molly's face as she made a long sorrowful sigh. "Do you think that you could? Do you think that you could help me?" she asked through half-closed eyes. Mortella watched carefully as the gullible child looked up at her. This was a face that was so open, so trusting, that it made Mortella feel nauseous.

"Of course … if I can," was the response.

Mortella smiled a brilliant smile before raising both hands in front of her and indicating that Molly should take each one in hers. "Oh, my dear, you are sweet," she crooned. "Now," Mortella paused as Molly took each hand, "I need you to relax and let your mind go blank,"

Molly nodded. "Doesn't sound too hard," she said with a smile.

"Good, then shall we begin?"

Molly nodded again.

As Molly relaxed, Mortella gained access to the child's mind, the inner being. All her thoughts, memories, everything that made her who she was.

Now linked to what could be called the child's soul, Mortella was able to share in the memories, the childhood of the girl. A mother that loved and cared for her children. The four younger sisters. Dreams and hopes, fears and longings were now all exposed. She saw Molly's weakness, insecurities, a compassion that compelled her to act. Mortella chuckled silently to herself. A compassion that allowed her access into this feeble-minded child.

The Tower was also there, within the child's thoughts. A dark, foreboding creation that encompassed them. To her surprise Mortella saw Shan as he truly was and not as he appeared to be.

"Oh, sweetie, how fascinating … a boy," Mortella remarked nonchalantly as she looked down on the image of Molly that now stood before her. The child looked back at her, mouth gaping, her eyes wide, scared.

"What's happening, what are you doing here?"

"Oh, didn't I explain? You kindly offered me your body. I unfortunately … lost mine and needed another."

A look of confusion passed across the frightened visage. "No, I didn't!" she shouted.

"It's a little too late now, my dear. Don't worry … you will still be here." Mortella mocked as she looked at the girl with a mixture of condescension and contempt. "Still here … but well out of my way. Safely contained."

Mortella turned and started to walk away as she delivered a sneer over her shoulder, "Oh, and thank you, dear. I really do appreciate it." She casually waved a hand in the air as she went. Throwing a final brief glance backward she nodded to herself as she saw it begin. A wall had begun to build itself about the child. Smooth and black, one row was placed upon another to form a box-like prison about the girl. The look of fear became one of horror as the walls grew. Seeing the space around her contract, Molly screamed out in anger and frustration "I won't let you!"

"But you already have!"

The wall continued closing in on the figure, hiding it away. Mortella was enjoying the process. Eventually the child would be separated completely from what it once had known. Divorced from the control it once had. As the wall rose Mortella felt a twinge. There it was. It was a start. She had begun to feel. Sustained by the Tower, she did not feel. Neither hot nor cold, not pain nor the floor beneath her feet. Within the Tower, she appeared to have life, but this was nothing but a facade. The Tower longed and yearned for it, but it never had, nor could it ever offer … life. Now, however, Mortella was starting to feel, to become more substantial, more solid. The grounding had begun, a binding of her soul back into a physical form. She could feel that there were hands … there were feet. She almost felt that there was a coolness on her skin. She was sure that she could feel the hardness of the stone beneath her. She was gaining control. Just a matter of time and she would control it all. See out of those eyes, feel with those hands. Control everything with her mind while that of its previous owner was safely locked away.

Mortella was enjoying these sensations when there was a change. Unexpectedly she started to feel cold. This was followed by a feeling of light-headedness. A discomfort was beginning to form within what was to be her new self. She could feel the breath getting less, the flow of blood was slowing as she lost the sensation of having hands, of feet. She turned frantically to look at the wall. Not yet complete, its growth had stalled. As she watched she felt thinner, more translucent as her strength began to fade.

Shan turned to look at Moira who was kneeling beside him. The last of the milky mist had finally left the decaying form that had once been the woman that had fed them. As the mist left it caused the body to slump forward onto the stone. Helpless to stop it, he could only watch as the mist passed from the woman to then invade Molly.

Moira's eyes were closed and there was sweat on her brow. Turning back to Molly, Shan saw that her skin was pale, her lips blue. To his horror he watched as her light began to fade. The light that had led him to her was going and then was no more. Molly, his friend, with the light gone, lay cold and lifeless, with the mist still trailing into her.

Moira opened her eyes, breathing heavily. Leaning forward she supported her weight against the floor with her hands. A movement above startled them. They looked up only to see the Watcher silently turn and leave

"I tried," Moira cried exhausted. "It was all I could think of." Looking at Shan she asked, "Did it work?"

"Did what work?" asked Shan as he desperately rubbed Molly's hands, trying to warm them.

Looking at the motionless body of Molly, Moira gave a small cry. "I'm sorry, I thought it might work." She stifled a sob as she wiped her nose on her sleeve.

"What?" demanded Shan.

"Blood. Influence … it's in the blood," Moira tried to explain.

Shan just looked confused.

"It can't happen if you're not alive."

Shan gave a shout. "Look, it's stopped."

"What?"

"The mist, it's stopped," Shan cried again. As he watched, the mist was no longer entering. Instead it started to return to the inanimate corpse from which it had come. There too it was unable to enter. Instead it started to disperse, dissipate into the air, and fade away. Looking desperately at Moira he said, "It's gone. It can't get in. It worked." Grabbing Molly's shoulders he shook them. "She isn't breathing," he cried.

Shocked into action Moira commanded, "Get her onto her back." Forcing both hands down hard on Molly's chest, Moira bent her head and screamed. Focusing all her feelings of pain and frustration, loss and abandonment from her mother, she pushed them into her Influence. Moira willed Molly to live.

Chapter 32

Noona sat quietly cradling her granddaughter's head in her lap. Her experience said that things were never quite as bad as they first appeared. Saying as much, however, would be cold comfort for the grieving mother.

"I never should have," May said again and again. "I should have waited … been patient."

"And never had her?" queried the old woman. "Never had Molly?"

"But if I hadn't got one of them … hadn't asked you to …"

"No, my dear. No. That is not the cause," admonished her grandmother softly. "They did not do this. It's in the blood. We all know that. It can happen to anyone." She lifted May's head off her lap and looked into her eyes. "My Tilly … I also watched as they took her. I thought that she was gone forever." Noona paused and gave a gentle smile "But that was not the way it was meant to be. She came back." Nodding slightly with a determined look in her eyes she added. "And so will Molly."

"How can you be sure?" asked May, desperate for reassurance.

"Because we are not alone. Unlike before, we now have a way to find her. Blood is thicker than Influence … and we are not alone."

***

Silas was tired. It took effort to climb up the slope every day. Effort to shield his mind from those within the Tower. And effort to have to control his emotions every time he connected with what remained of his brother. He wanted to scream, cry out. He wanted to be able to grab hold of Felix and shake him. Shake him until he remembered … remembered who he was. But he couldn't. There was nothing of Felix he could hold. No way he could hug him, see his smile, or hear his voice. Everything was now just a whisper of what it once had been. He felt so alone. Lost in a world where he no longer belonged. He had only ever belonged because Felix had been there.

He looked over at Ambrose, asleep in his chair. The man had aged so quickly. The loss of Pick had drained the life from him. He was now only kept going by his sheer bloody mindedness. He refused to let Pick fade. He would keep going back to the Tower, day after day. Each time he went he found the climb just a little bit more difficult. He was just that much slower. But he would push himself. He would continue to do it … continue until his body gave way beneath him.

Silas let him rest as he rose to make some dinner. Their shared pain had brought them together in a way nothing else could. He would make sure that Ambrose got to the Tower again tomorrow … and the day after … and the day after that. He owed him that much.

***

Mortella stood in a state of shock. Alone in a dark place where she could see nothing. There was no light. Nothing to illuminate where she was. The dark was deep, as impenetrable as the black stone that made up the Tower's walls. There was nothing to allow her to know her surroundings.

It had been going so well and then it all stopped. She had no longer been able to transfer. The Tower would no longer support it … and then the child faded from her. So what had happened? She didn't know. But what she did know was that she was still herself. She had not been absorbed into the Tower. To become one of the many that lit up the corridors for those who could see.

She felt her face, her hair. Her shoulder was now level. Her back was straight. Raising her left hand above her head she drew in a quick breath. Its strength had returned. She was again as she once had been. The Tower must still be maintaining her. Yet she could not see how that could be. She was no longer within the decaying shell. Even with the support of many Influences, without the shell it would no longer have been able to preserve her. But yet here she was … seemingly to be as she would wish to be.

As she looked, a pinpoint of light appeared. It hovered, far off in the distance. A single tempting point of light in the sea of velvety blackness. It illuminated nothing. It just hung there. The only focus within this place. Whether it be wise or not, it was her only option. Moving carefully forward, blind to everything but that point off in the distance, Mortella began to walk. Placing one foot carefully in front of the other she barely felt the ground as she made toward the light.

275

***

Molly awoke, battered and sore, but still herself. Moira greeted her warmly as Shan helped her to sit up.

"That woman was planning to destroy you," Moira said in anticipation of her questions. "That … was my caring, loving … mother," she added with unconcealed loathing. "She needed you …"

"She wanted to take me … be me …" Molly haltingly tried to explain. Shan and Moira both nodded.

"Moira stopped her," added Shan.

"Mother was already dead … she needed someone living to be able to continue." Moira stopped and looked about, "I made sure that that was not possible."

Molly opened her mouth, stunned. "But that means …"

"It worked," interrupted Shan, cutting off further questions.

"I don't expect that we shall ever need to endure her presence again," added Moira in a sombre tone.

Molly looked stunned and was still feeling shaken as she took another mouthful. They had all woken to find that each had a sack of food and water beside them.

"Normally food only comes after a trial … with a Watcher," noted Shan as he ate.

"There was a Watcher," stated Moira.

"You think that that was a trial?" asked Molly, shocked.

"I don't know. How can we know? But we got food, and there was a Watcher … and, well … it was a trial," answered Shan.

"This happened to test us?" exclaimed Molly. "It knows we are together?" She looked worried. "Then it must know everything."

"Well, yes, that would seem to be the case," Shan nodded.

"Then it would know," she whispered to Shan. "The woman found out."

"What?" asked Shan.

Molly paused and then blurted out. "That you're a boy."

Moira looked stunned. "But no boy has ever had a major Influence."

"So?" said Shan.

"If it now knows that … the Tower will …"

"I saw it happen once outside the Tower," Molly said in a small voice. Molly directed her attention back at Shan. "And we were planning to get out anyway. Remember how your mother got out?"

"Your mother?" exclaimed Moira, surprised. "In the Tower?" Shan ignored her as he looked about. Obviously seeing something the others could not. "The lights," he said in a worried voice, "they're changing." Looking back at Molly he asked quickly, "How do we find the stairs to take us up to the window?"

"The woman said that everything about us is an illusion. Perhaps if I can break some of it down," answered Molly.

"I remember the colours that were about the hidden door she took us through. I can find others like it," added Shan.

"We have to find the stairs," added Molly. Shan nodded as his eyes continued to dart about the chamber.

***

She walked, or was she floating, she couldn't tell. Was she even moving? There was nothing that allowed her to tell. Nothing from which to get her bearing. All there was was the pinpoint of light, hanging in the distance, never seeming to get any closer. Some significant amount of time must have passed but she had no way of telling. Yet still she walked, or at least had the impression that she was walking.

***

Molly looked worried as they ran.

"The lights are starting to swirl," cried Shan.

"And?" asked Moira

"It's what they did before. Before they were Taken by the Tower," Shan explained breathlessly as he looked about fearfully. Without another word he lifted the robes higher above his knees and started to run faster, outpacing the other two. "The Tower's getting ready," he called back. "The lights aren't swarming yet ... but they will."

"We can't just keep on running," yelled back Moira. "We have no idea where we're going."

"We mustn't stay in one place," screamed back Shan.

"I can't," howled Molly breathlessly, "... I'm sorry." Exhausted, she stopped running. Leaning forward with both hands resting on her knees, she gasped for air. Shan slowed. He stopped and gradually made his way back to the others.

"We need some sort of plan," complained Moira. "We're too tired to run."

277

Shan looked at Molly and then at Moira. He saw their exhaustion. Sitting on the ground he tried to regain his breath as he thought.

***

Looking up at the Tower that loomed above them they began the climb, yet again. It dominated the eastern sky as the sun rose behind it. A black stain against the golden light of a new day. Silas glanced over at Ambrose and quickly went to help him over a particularly rough patch of ground. Ambrose nodded his thanks as he continued his slow ascent. Back to their usual spot, beyond the rocky outcrop and out of sight of the great stairs to the south. There they would stay for most of the day before returning down the slope once more … only to return again the next day.

Silas sighed. There was little joy in going. Each time he connected with his brother it was like a needle piercing his heart. Sharp and painful, but still he would go. Again he looked at the old man. For him it was even worse. He would sit unmoving for hours, listening for the remnants of his grandson's aura. The ragged notes that once had been so vibrant and alive but now were barely distinguishable from the background noise of the Tower. Yet he also would go. For without hope, what was there?

Eventually they arrived back at the wall. Its smooth surface unbroken except for a single window high above them. Seating themselves down, they prepared for another day. Silas cleared his mind. Shielding it from all within the walls apart from his brother, he opened himself to Felix.

***

She was finally getting closer. It was a window. A window that let light into this realm of night. She could see movement beyond. She saw shadows flickering, images, blurred and indistinct, but definitely there. Standing mesmerised, she looked into the light as the images gradually became clearer. She could make out the outlines of two figures surrounded by haloes of light that pulsated and flashed about them. They shifted silently in and out of her frame of vision, seemingly moving without purpose. As she watched, a blackness began to invade the light. A hollow void of darkness began to grow at the periphery of her vision.

***

They had kept moving. Resting only in short stints before moving on again. Shan looked and looked. Trying to see where Influence had been used to conceal. Eventually they stopped again to rest. Sitting against the wall in the corner of a small chamber that only had two entrances that went off at right angles from one another.

"There it is. That wall. It's not real!" cried Shan suddenly. Gabbing Molly he pulled her to the wall. "What can you feel?" he asked, pointing at the smooth stone. "Can you undo it?" he asked impatiently. Molly stood immobile, transfixed by the wall. Eventually she turned to the others.

She pointed. "There, I got the corner to start to peel back," she announced enthusiastically.

Shan looked anxious. "We don't have time," he grumbled.

"Shan!" snapped Moira. "She's doing the best she can." Shan looked suitably admonished when they began to feel the floor shudder with the all too familiar beat of the Tower. Looking up, Shan gave a gasp as he saw the coloured lights start to coalesce and circle above his head.

"They're coming," he cried as he and Moira watched two dark, hooded figures emerge and stand immobile at the entrances to the chamber. One in the centre of each of the corridors that led out of the room, blocking any escape.

"Molly," Shan whispered as he grabbed her arm to gain her attention. "We're trapped."

***

The day was starting to wane when Silas started to feel agitation. Felix was worried. Something was happening and it was affecting all within the Tower. He was able to glean an image, a feeling that something momentous was about to occur. He looked over at Ambrose who was also feeling the unrest within the notes that made up the Tower. Much of the haphazard nature of the noise was being organised. Ordered. Controlled. Felix was able to share with his brother a desire for freedom. A longing for release from captivity. This was something much stronger and more focused than he had ever felt before from his brother. The clearest feeling he had ever received since the Code had Taken him.

***

As the figures emerged from the haze, Mortella caught the glimpse of fiery red hair. Behind it was a pillar of darkness. The vision then changed. Now it showed a second figure, again silhouetted against a void of darkness. This then was replaced with a view of uniform dull, matted black. She could also now feel something. Something was building. There was a wave of energy that was growing, mounting, getting ready to be released when, just as the crest of the wave

279

was about to break, another unseen force crashed against the matted black image. It then dissolved into a cold silver light that appeared to illuminate a spiral staircase.

***

"Well done, Molly," shrieked Shan as he helped Moira to cross onto the stairs as Molly followed. As soon as they passed the wall reappeared, solid and as impenetrable as before. Moira looked at the wall.

"Can they get through?" she asked.

Molly looked confused. "I didn't do that." She paused. "I was about to try … when it just happened."

"You must have," replied Shan. "It just took time."

Molly looked at him unconvinced, knowing that she had not, but saying nothing.

"Are you really sure that they are wanting you?" asked Moira. Shan nodded. "Then you need to make sure you get out of here." Looking at both Molly and Shan she continued, "I can't climb any more stairs. I'll just slow you down." Shan started to object when Moira looked at him sternly. "Be logical. If they don't want me, then I am in no danger."

"We're stronger together …" Shan said.

"Don't put me in the position that I'm the reason," Moira began. "I've never been of any use to anyone before. Don't let them get you."

Exchanging a look with Molly, Shan nodded.

"I will be back as soon as I can," said Molly.

***

It was like viewing life unfold in a picture book before her. She watched without the ability to intervene. Unable to hear anything, Mortella stared at the red-haired image of her daughter as she mouthed words that were audible to others but not to her. The face was fearful but determined. The field of vision then moved to focus on the dark-haired youth whose worried face looked up the winding stairs that were bathed in silver light. Mortella looked on as he reached to take the arm of the girl that enclosed her.

Turning with frustration from the portal that showed her the world through the eyes of the one she had chosen, Mortella considered the darkness that surrounded her. The transfer had been left incomplete. Her essence was now embedded in the new body, but control had not been relinquished.

280

She would be maintained, securely sustained by the life of the child, but she lacked any authority over the physical form or the aura of the child.

Setting her expression, Mortella knew that she would be able to gain that control. Neither requiring sustenance, nor rest, she would work continuously, all day and night, to gradually infiltrate every corner of the child. Little by little, when the child was at her most vulnerable, Mortella would creep further into her. Without revealing herself, she would subtly wrest control from her host, until it was too late for her to be resisted.

***

They reached the top of the stairs which led to an open door bathed in reddish light. Passing through the door they were greeted by a single great window that looked to the Western Slopes. Walking to the opening, Molly and Shan stood transfixed by the view as they felt a gentle breeze on their skin.

Molly gazed down toward Town before pointing. "My house is down there." Shan nodded. Turning to Shan she said, "You can leave the Tower." Shan looked worried

"It's a long way down. My mother barely survived."

"You have no choice. You have to. Your Influence. You can use the air. Like she did." Placing a hand on his arm she said, "At least one of us got out." Giving him a hug, they felt the Tower suddenly shake. Looking behind they saw a shadow within the doorway. A hooded figure entered the chamber followed by a second and then a third as Molly pushed Shan toward the window, yelling, "Go!"

***

Silas felt Felix. It really was Felix. Not just a shadow of who he once was. He felt Felix embrace him. There was thought and passion and feeling as he heard the words *they are not to be tolerated* shoot through his mind. Involuntarily he looked up to see a figure launch itself from the opening high up in the Tower's wall. He watched in horror as it began to fall, gaining speed as it plummeted to the rocky ground that made up the Eastern Slopes. He watched, riveted to the spot, as he heard Felix's voice cry out to him. A cry overcome with emotion. A cry of joy, release, and freedom.

To Be Continued

About the Author

Ian C Lawrance was born in Wollongong in NSW the youngest of three children. On finishing school he completed a Medical degree at Sydney University and went on to specialise in gastroenterology and complete a PhD in Molecular Medicine at the John Curtin School of Medical Research at the Australian National University. From there he undertook at Post-doctoral fellowship in the USA before returning to Australia and moving to Perth where he continued his basic Science and Clinical research as a Professor at the University of Western Australia. He is currently an Adjunct Professor and continues his research work having published over 130 peer-reviewed research papers and a number of book chapters

He has four children and one gorgeous grandchild. He is involved in the arts as a principal performer in Gilbert and Sullivan productions having learnt vocal technique for several years and plays the Alto Sax.

He was an avid Fantasy and Science fiction reader as a teenager he loved the way new worlds could be created and populated by the imagination. He also loved the classics, particularly Dickens and Jane Austin and the way they wrote in such beautiful melodic waves of prose with comedy. Having enjoyed writing and completing the first book in the Blood Influence series this is the second 'Blood Influence -Apostasy' with the next ready and waiting to be written.